"My name's Marcus Wester."

Rinál's eyes grew wide and he sank back on the cushion.

"You've heard of me," Marcus said. "So you know that the appeal-to-noble-blood strategy may not be your best choice. Your mother was a minor priestess who got drunk with a monarch's exiled uncle. That's your protection. Me? I've killed kings."

"Kings?"

"Well, just the one, but you take the point."

Rinál tried to speak, swallowed to loosen his throat, and then tried again.

"What are you going to do?"

"I'm going to reclaim our property, or as much of it as you have left. I don't expect it'll make up the losses, but it's a beginning."

"What are you going to do with me?"

"You mean if I don't take you to justice? I'm going to come to an understanding with you."

Praise for

The Dragon's Path

"Daniel Abraham's new novel cements his status as the literary successor to George R. R. Martin."

—Grasping for the Wind

"Abraham questions and explores the fantasy-world assumptions that most authors take for granted, telling an enjoyable and genuinely innovative adventure story along the way." —*Publishers Weekly* (starred review)

"A pleasure for Abraham's legion of fans."

—*Kirkus Reviews*

"Comforting yet complex, *The Dragon's Path* is a textbook example of how to do meat-and-potatoes fantasy right."

—The A.V. Club

"An extremely promising first in a series, this is one you will want to pick up and savor before the next piece of the story comes to life." —*RT Reviews*

"Prepare to be startled, shocked, and entertained."

—*Locus*

"*The Dragon's Path* (****½) is a winner. The characters are engaging and well-motivated, the plot intriguing."

—TheWertzone.blogspot.com

"*The Dragon's Path* is an enjoyable read that holds great expectations for the series." —SF Signal

"There's no doubt though that we've got something special here that any fan of well thought out fantasy should be following." —Graeme's Fantasy Book Review

"*The Dragon's Path* is traditional fantasy as best as it gets." —Fantasy Book Critic

"*The Dragon's Path* is a superb achievement, and one that should help Abraham reach the wider audience and acclaim he truly deserves." —Civilian Reader

"*The Dragon's Path* is a tremendous novel and Abraham deftly mixes the classic foundations of the genre with a sophistication expected of him and rarely found in the work of his compatriots." —A Dribble of Ink

Praise for
Daniel Abraham

"Abraham is fiercely talented, disturbingly human, breathtakingly original and even on his bad days kicks all sorts of literary ass." —Junot Díaz

"Daniel Abraham gets better with every book." —George R. R. Martin

"The storytelling is smooth, careful and—best of all—unpredictable." —Patrick Rothfuss

Publications by Daniel Abraham

THE LONG PRICE QUARTET
A Shadow in Summer
A Betrayal in Winter
An Autumn War
The Price of Spring

Leviathan Wept and Other Stories

Hunter's Run (with George R. R. Martin and
Gardner Dozois)

THE BLACK SUN'S DAUGHTER
Unclean Spirits (as MLN Hanover)
Darker Angels (as MLN Hanover)
Vicious Grace (as MLN Hanover)
Killing Rites (as MLN Hanover)

THE DAGGER AND THE COIN
The Dragon's Path
The King's Blood
The Poisoned Sword (forthcoming)

THE EXPANSE
Leviathan Wakes (with Ty Franck as James S. A. Corey)
Caliban's War (with Ty Franck as James S. A. Corey)
Abaddon's Gate (with Ty Franck as James S. A. Corey)
(forthcoming)

THE
KING'S
BLOOD

BOOK TWO OF THE DAGGER AND THE COIN

DANIEL
ABRAHAM

www.orbitbooks.net

Orbit
Hachette Book Group
237 Park Avenue, New York, NY 10017
www.HachetteBookGroup.com

First Edition: May 2012

Orbit is an imprint of Hachette Book Group, Inc. The Orbit name and logo are trademarks of Little, Brown Book Group Limited.

The Hachette Speakers Bureau provides a wide range of authors for speaking events. To find out more, go to www.hachettespeakersbureau.com or call (866) 376-6591.

The publisher is not responsible for websites (or their content) that are not owned by the publisher.

The characters and events in this book are fictitious. Any similarity to real persons, living or dead, is coincidental and not intended by the author.

Library of Congress Cataloging-in-Publication Data

Abraham, Daniel.
   The king's blood / Daniel Abraham. — 1st ed.
      p. cm.
   ISBN 978-0-316-08077-4
   I. Title.
   PS3601.B677K56 2012
   813'.6—dc22
                              2011031647

10   9   8   7   6   5   4   3   2

RRD-IN

Printed in the United States of America

To my brother Xerxes

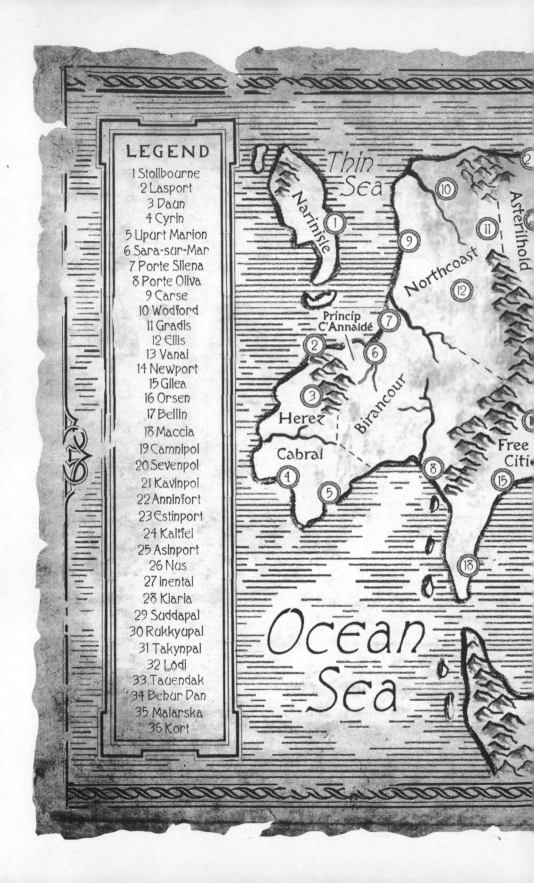

LEGEND

1 Stollbourne
2 Lasport
3 Daun
4 Cyrin
5 Upurt Marion
6 Sara-sur-Mar
7 Porte Silena
8 Porte Oliva
9 Carse
10 Wodford
11 Gradis
12 Ellis
13 Vanai
14 Newport
15 Gilea
16 Orsen
17 Bellin
18 Maccia
19 Camnipol
20 Sevenpol
21 Kavinpol
22 Anninfort
23 Estinport
24 Kaltfel
25 Asinport
26 Nus
27 Inentai
28 Kiaria
29 Suddapal
30 Rukkyupal
31 Takynpal
32 Lôdi
33 Tauendak
34 Behur Dan
35 Malarska
36 Kort

Thin Sea

Narinisle

Astenhold

Northcoast

Princip C'Annaldé

Herez

Birancour

Cabral

Free Citi

Ocean Sea

Introduction

Master Kit

The apostate, called Kitap rol Keshmet among other things, stood in the soft city rain, the taint in his blood pressing at him, goading him, but being ignored. Fear and dread welled up in his throat.

In any of the cities and villages of the Keshet or Borja or Pût, the temple would have been the central fact of the community, a point of pride and honor, and the axis about which all life turned. In the vast glory of Camnipol, it was only another of a thousand such structures, awe-inspiring in its scope, beauty, and grandeur, and rendered unremarkable by its company.

The city was the heart of Imperial Antea as Imperial Antea was the heart of Firstblood power in the world, but Camnipol was older than the kingdom it ruled. Every age had left its mark here, every generation growing on the ruins of the old until the earth below the dark-cobbled streets was not soil, but the wreckage of what had come before. It was a city of black and gold, of wealth and desperate poverty. Its walls rose around it like a boast of invulnerability, and its noble quarters displayed great mansions and towers and temples casually, as if the grandeur was trivial, normal, and mundane. Had Camnipol been a knight, he would have worn black-enameled armor and a cloak of fine-worked wool. Had it been a woman, she would have been too handsome to look away from and too intimidating to speak with. Instead, it was a city, and it was Camnipol.

Soft rain darkened the stone walls and high columns. Wide steps rose from street to landing and then again to the shadowed colonnade. The great spider-silk banner—the red of blood with the eightfold sigil of the goddess at its center—hung beneath the overhanging roof, dark at the bottom from the rain and at the top from the shadows, and the breeze sent ripples across it. The carriages and palanquins of the highest noble families of Antea filled the narrow road, each trying to reach a more prestigious place on the smooth-cobbled street and none willing to retreat a step that might give a rival some opportunity. And it was still hardly past first thaw. When summer and the court season came, the place would be unnavigable. To the north, the great tower of the Kingspire was greyed by mist, its top shrouded so that it appeared to grow up into the spreading cloud: the Severed Throne reaching out in all directions and weighing down the world.

The apostate pulled the hood of his cloak forward to hide his face and conceal his hair. Tiny spheres of rain beaded his beard like web-caught flies. He waited.

At the top of the steps, the hero of Antea stood, smiling and nodding to the few grandees who had come early to the city as they passed into the dimness of the temple. Geder Palliako, newly Baron of Ebbingbaugh and Protector of Prince Aster who was the only son of King Simeon and heir to the Severed Throne. Geder Palliako who had saved the kingdom from the conspiracies of the courts of Asterilhold. Geder wasn't the image of a national hero. His face was round and pale, his hair slicked back. The black leather cloak he wore was cut for a thicker man's frame, pooling around him like an ornate curtain. He stood under the great red banner like a new actor freshly on a stage. The apostate could almost see him repeating lines to himself, straining his ears toward his cue.

This was the man who had brought back the cult of the goddess, long forgotten, and dropped it into the center of the greatest empire outside Far Syramys. In a more pious age, the temple might have struggled to take root, but the priests of Antea had long ago become political spokesmen and champions of the expedient. The voice of the goddess, impossible to resist for long, had found willing ears here, and the nobility streamed in like children before a puppet show, excited by the hint of the exotic, the decadent, and the strange.

They were dead. Their city, their empire, the truths they had learned at their nurses' breasts. Like the first pale mark of leprosy, the rot had touched their city, and none of them could see it for what it was. Nor, in all likelihood would they ever, even as the madness took them. They would die and never understand what they had become.

"Hoy! Old man!"

The apostate turned. The armsman was Jasuru, bronze-scaled and black-tongued. He wore boiled leather and the sigil of a serpent on a field of orange. Behind him, a young woman was stepping down from a gilt carriage with the help of a footman in matching colors. The woman herself wore a black leather cloak, cut too generously. Fashion in all things.

"What's your business here?" the Jasuru demanded, his hand on his sword's pommel.

"Nothing pressing," the apostate said. "Didn't see I was in the way. Quite sorry."

The guard growled low in his throat and looked away. The apostate turned his back and walked. Behind him, the high, rattling sound of the tin gongs began. He hadn't heard the call to prayer since he was a boy and a priest in a mountain temple half a continent away. For a moment, he could smell the dust and sweet wellwater, could hear the scrape of lizards across the stone and taste the curried goat that no one else in the world made the way they had in the village of his youth. A deep voice began the call to prayer, and the power in the apostate's blood thrilled to the half-forgotten syllables. He paused, ignored the wisdom of a thousand children's tales, and looked back.

The bull-huge man wore the green and gold of a high priest preparing the low rites, but he was no one the apostate recognized. The high priest he had known was dead, then. Well, the spider goddess promised many things, but physical immortality wasn't one. Her priests could die. The thought was a comfort. The apostate pulled his cheap wools closer around him and disappeared into the wet labyrinth of broadways and alleys.

The Division split Camnipol down its center like God's knife wound. Half a dozen true bridges spanned the abyss from its rim, standing high above the empty air, massive webworks of stone and iron. Any number of improvised chain-and-rope constructions reached across it lower down where the walls came closer together. If one were sitting near its edge, the history of the city was laid bare, ruin laid upon ruin laid upon ruin until the ancient architecture vanished, indistinguishable from stone apart from the occasional archway or green-bleeding bronzework. Since the age of dragons and before, there had been a city where Camnipol stood, growing upon and out of the ruins of the city before it. Even now, poor men and women of the thirteen races lived deep in the flesh of the city, inhabiting lightless caves that had been the storehouses and ballrooms and palaces of their ancestors.

"You never really think about drainage," Smit said, looking out into the grey air.

"I don't believe I do," the apostate said, shrugging off his cloak. "Was there a reason you felt I should?"

The troupe had taken shelter in a common yard at the Division's edge. The cart's thin doors were open, but they hadn't lowered the stage. Cary sat cross-legged with her back against the wide wheel, sewing beads to the blue gown. They were going to play The Bride's Folly that night, and the role of Lady Partia called for a bit more frippery. Sandr and Hornet were at the back of the high shelter with sticks in their hands, walking the choreography of the final battle where Anson Arranson exposed the treachery of his commander. Charlit Soon, their newest actor, sat with her hands under her thighs, her lips moving as if in prayer. It was her first night playing in The Bride's Folly, and her anxiety was endearing. Mikel was nowhere to be seen, likely off to the market and haggling for meat and river fish. There would be plenty of time for him to return and make ready. It was only the gloomy weather that made everything seem late.

"Well, you think about it," Smit said, nodding at the rain, "the things that really make a city are about controlling nature, aren't they? This here rain may not look like much, but Camnipol's a big city. It all adds up. Right now, just looking at it, it's like God upended a river on the place. All that water's got to go somewhere."

"*The sea, the sea, the endless sea,*" the apostate said, quoting a play they'd done two years before. "*As all water finds the salt waves, so all men end in death.*"

"Well sure," Smit said, rubbing his chin, "but the important thing's how it gets from here to there, isn't it?"

The apostate smiled.

"Smit, my dear, I believe you've just committed metaphor."

The actor blinked a false innocence.

"Did I? And here I thought we were talking about gutters."

The apostate smiled. For fifteen years now, he had traveled the world with his little band of players. They had sung for kings and brutish mobs. He'd taught players from eight of the thirteen human races, and taken lovers from three. Master Kit, he'd been. Kitap rol Keshmet. It was a name he'd given himself even before that, when he had delivered himself into the world out of a womb of desert stone and madness. He'd played a thousand roles. And now, God help him, there was time for one more.

One last.

"Cary?" the apostate said. "A word?"

The long-haired woman nodded, slipped her needle into her sleeve, and laid the handful of beads carefully into a cupping fold of the gown's cloth. It looked casual and unthinking, but not one bead would escape that little nest. The apostate nodded, smiling, and strolled toward the next shelter in the common yard, empty apart from a cold iron brazier and a stone bench. The brick paving was wet where the rain struck, the subtle red and green deepened and enriched until they seemed enameled. He sat on the little bench and Cary sat at his side.

Now that the time had come, he couldn't ignore the sorrow any longer. It had been there for weeks. The fear was an old companion by now; a fire lit in a common house in Porte Oliva months before when he had first heard word that a banner of the goddess flew in Antea. Sorrow had only come later, and he had put it aside as long as he could, telling himself that the thickness in his throat, the weight in his breast, would keep. They would keep no more.

"Master Kit?" Cary said. "Are you crying?"

"Of course not," he said. "Men *weep*. We find crying undignified."

She put her arm around his shoulder. Like a sailor sipping his last freshwater before a voyage, he tried to drink in the feeling of her beside him—the bend of her elbow at the back of his neck, the solid weight of her muscles, the smell of verbena and soap. He took a deep, shuddering breath, and nodded his assent. It took a long moment before he could speak.

"I believe we will need to find another player," he said. "Older man with a certain gravity. Someone who can take the paternal roles and the villains. Lord Fox. Orcus the Demon King. Those."

"Your roles," Cary said.

"Mine."

Raindrops as small as pinpricks tapped the thatching above them, the bricks before. The practiced blows of false swords and the grunts of the boys swinging them. Hornet had been with the company longer than Cary. Smit played more roles. But Cary would guide them. She would hold the little family of the road together after he was gone, if anyone would.

"What's happened?" she asked.

"There's something I feel I have to do," he said.

"We'd help."

"I believe you would try. But..."

"But?"

He shifted to look her in the eyes. Her arm slid away from him. Her eyes were as dark as her hair, and large enough to make her seem younger than she was. He could see her now as she had been that first night, seven years before in the free city of Maccia, dancing in the public square for coin. She'd hardly been a girl then, feral and hungry and distrustful of anything masculine. Talent and ambition had burned off her like heat from a fire. Opal had warned him that the girl would be trouble and agreed that the price would be justified. Now Cary was a woman full-grown. He wondered if this was what it would feel like to have a daughter.

"I am afraid I wouldn't be able to do what was called for if I was also protecting all of you," he said. "You are the family I've made. If I can imagine you safe and content, I think I can sacrifice whatever else is needed."

"You're expecting a high price, it sounds like," she said.

"I am."

Cary sighed, and the wry smile that haunted her lips in times of trouble came to her. *Remember this*, he told himself. *Remember the way her lips twist and her eyebrow rises. Keep it close. Pay attention.*

"Well, piss," she said.

"For what it carries, I am truly sorry to go."

"Do you have anybody in mind to take the roles?" she asked.

He could see the pain in her. He was betraying her, abandoning them all, and she would no more blame him for it than cut off her toes. He wished he could take her hand in his, but she'd chosen the tone for their conversation, and he didn't have the right to overrule her. Not any longer.

"There's a group that makes the northern circuit. Paldrin Leh and Sebast Berrin. Three years ago, they had two fighting for the same roles. Find them, and you might get someone who already knows the lines. Paldrin's a Haaverkin, but that might add a touch of the exotic if you take him south."

"I'll ask around, then," she said. "When are you leaving?"

"Tonight," he said.

"Do you have to go alone?"

The apostate hesitated. It was a question he hadn't decided

yet. The task before him was impossible. As doomed as it was inevitable. His sacrifice was his own, which made it curiously easy. To ask someone else to walk willingly to death beside him was no favor. And yet if it made the difference between success and failure, a world redeemed or lost…

"Perhaps not," he said. "There is one other who might help. But not from the troupe."

"And I suppose it would be entirely too much to ask what this mysterious errand is that's calling you away?" she asked. And then, contradicting herself, "You owe us that much."

The apostate licked his lips, searching for words he hadn't used, even to himself. When he found them, he chuckled.

"This may sound a bit grandiose," he said, scratching at his beard with one long finger.

"Try me."

"I'm off to kill a goddess."

Cithrin bel Sarcour,
Voice and Agent of the
Medean Bank in Porte Oliva

Cithrin bel Sarcour, voice of the Medean bank in Porte Oliva, stepped out of the bank's office with her head high, her features composed, and rage burning in her breast. Around her, Porte Oliva was entering its springtime. The bright cloth banners and glittering paste jewels of the First Thaw celebrations still lay in the streets and alleyways, slowly decaying into grime. Snow haunted the shadows where the midday sun couldn't reach. Cithrin's breath plumed before her as if her heart were a furnace belching pale smoke, and she felt the bite of the air as a distant thing.

Men and women of several races bustled on the cobbles before her. Kurtadam with their slick, beaded pelts; thin-faced, pale Cinnae; brass-and-gold-scaled Jasuru; black-chitined Timzinae; and fleshy, rose-cheeked Firstblood. Some nodded to her, some stepped out of her way, most ignored her. She might represent one of the greatest banks in the world, but as far as the hazy sky over Porte Oliva cared, she was just another half-Cinnae girl in a well-tailored dress.

When she stepped into the taproom, the warm air caressed her. The related, yeasty scents of beer and bread tried to gentle her, and she felt some of the knot in her gut begin to ease. The anger slipped, showing itself only a mask for the despair and frustration beneath. A young Cinnae man came forward to take her shawl, and she managed a tight-lipped smile as she relinquished it.

"The usual table, Magistra?" he asked.

"Thank you, Verril," she said. "That would be kind."

Grinning, he made an exaggerated bow, and gestured her on. Another day, she might have found it charming. The table was at the back, half hidden from the main room by a draped cloth. It cost a few coins more. When she felt capable of civil conversation, she would sometimes sit at the common benches, striking up conversation with whoever was there. There were more sailors and gossip of travelers farther south at the docks, more word of overland trade north where the dragon's road opened to the main square and the cathedral and the governor's palace, but the taproom was nearest to her bank—*her* bank, by God—and not every conversation needed to be a bid for advantage.

The Kurtadam girl who most often served in the daytimes brought a plate of cheese and brown bread with a tiny carved-wood bowl full of black raisins. More to the point, she brought a tankard of good beer. Cithrin nodded sharply and tried to make her smile genuine. If the girl saw anything odd in her, the soft fur of her face covered it. Kurtadam would make good card players, Cithrin thought as she drank. All of them wearing masks all the time.

The front door opened, light spilling into the main room. A shadow moved into it. Without seeing a single detail of face or body, without so much as a cleared throat, Cithrin recognized Yardem Hane. He was the second in command of her guardsmen—*her* guardsmen—and one of two men who had known her since her flight from Vanai. With that city burned and all its residents dead, that made him someone who'd known her longer than anyone alive.

The Tralgu walked gently across the floor. For so large a

race, the Tralgu could be uncannily quiet. He sat down on the bench beside her. His high, doglike ears pointed forward. He smelled like old leather and sword oil. His sigh was long and deep.

"Went poorly, then?" he said.

"Did," Cithrin said, trying to match the laconic banter Yardem and Captain Wester employed. But the words wouldn't stop coming. "She barely even heard me out. I spent all winter negotiating that deal. Yes, there are risks, but they're *good* risks."

"Pyk didn't think so."

"Apparently not," Cithrin said. "God damn, but I hate that woman."

Cithrin had known from the moment the deal was made that answering to her notary would chafe. For months, Cithrin had exercised total control over the wealth of her branch of the Medean bank. Any loan she'd thought worthy, she'd made. Any partnership she'd felt wise, she'd entered. She'd cut thumbs on dozens of agreements and contracts, and she'd made good profits overall. Only, of course, the foundation documents of the bank had been forged and the contracts she'd signed illegal. It was still four months before she reached majority, inherited her parents' holdings in the bank, and became fully adult in the eyes of the law. But even after that, the role she'd taken on of an older woman and only a quarter Firstblood would remain hers. The bank was built on lies and fraud, and her discretion would be needed for years before the suspect agreements could all be purged. She fantasized about throwing it all to the wind just to spite the notary sent from the holding company in Carse. Pyk Usterhall.

You'll sign nothing. All agreements are signed by the notary. And the notary alone. Negotiations don't happen without the notary present. If you're overruled, you accept it. Control rests with the holding company. You're a figure-head. Nothing more.

Those were the terms she'd been offered, and she had agreed to them. At the time she'd been half drunk with relief that she'd kept any hold at all. She'd felt certain that once the notary was in place, it would be a matter of time before she could maneuver herself back into real power. The period in between would be a necessary test of her patience, but nothing worse than that. In the weeks before the notary's arrival, she'd fallen asleep every night imagining herself playing meek before some well-seasoned member of the bank, offering insights that would catch the new man's attention, building up her reputation with him until he trusted her judgment. From there, she told herself, it would be a short leap to making policy for her bank again. Her work was only to win over one man. Even if it was difficult, it was possible.

It had been a pretty story.

Pyk Usterhall arrived in the dead of winter. Cithrin had been in the café across from the Grand Market where she paid Maestro Asanpur a few coins for the use of a private room at the back. Winter's dark came early, even so far south as Porte Oliva, and there was little to do in the dark, cold afternoons besides play tiles and drink down the ancient, half-blind Cinnae's stock of coffee beans. That day, there had been four First-blood queensmen resting after their patrol in the café trading jokes and stories with a Timzinae merchant. The Timzinae had been wintering in Birancour before heading back to Elassae in the spring, and Cithrin had been laughing at his jokes for days, waiting to see if some news of that nation might slip from him. The six of them had pushed two of the tables together and were playing a complex round of tiles when the door had swung open and a cold draught had washed away the warmth of the room, literally and figuratively.

At first, Cithrin thought the woman was an enormously fat Firstblood. She was huge, wide across the hips and shoulders both, fat and strong both. She stepped into the room, her tread heavy on the floorboards, and unwound the black wool scarf from around her head. Her hair was grey where it wasn't black. Heavy jowls and full lips gave her a fishlike expression. When she pursed her lips, the gaps where her tusks had been filed off came clear. A Yemmu.

"You'll be Cithrin bel Sarcour then," the woman had said. "I'm your notary. You have somewhere we can speak?"

Cithrin rose at once, leading Pyk back to the private room. Once the door was closed, Pyk lowered herself to the little table, scowling.

"Playing games with the city guard? That's how you run this place? I'd have thought Komme Medean's voice would be at the Governor's Palace or dining with someone important."

Cithrin still felt the thickness in her throat when she remembered the words and the scorn that soured them.

"There's little going on in the coldest months," Cithrin had said, cursing herself silently for the apology in her tone.

"For you, I'd guess that's truth," Pyk said. "I've got work to do. You want to bring me the books here, or is there someplace you do the real business?"

Every day since had been another minor humiliation, another opportunity for the notary to remind Cithrin that she controlled nothing, another scathing comment. For weeks, Cithrin had swallowed it all with a smile. And for months after that, she'd at least borne it. If there had been even a pause in the assault, a crack in the dismissive façade, she'd have counted it a victory.

There had been nothing.

"Did she say why?" Yardem asked.

"She won't deal with Southlings," Cithrin said. "Apparently

a pod of them killed some part of her family in Pût nine or ten generations ago."

Yardem turned to her, his ears shifted to lie back almost flat against his skull. Cithrin drank deeply from her beer.

"I know," she said. "But what am I supposed to do about it? No negotiations without the notary present. I'm not permitted to sign, even. And if she doesn't cut thumbs on it, it doesn't happen."

As part of her bargain, Cithrin had surrendered all the leverage she had over the bank. If Pyk sent a message back to Carse saying that Cithrin was a liability to the bank, Cithrin had nothing that would keep them from separating her from the business. She broke off a crust of bread, chewing on it absently. It could have been spiced with dirt for all the pleasure she took in it. Yardem pointed at the plate, and she pushed it toward him. He pinched a corner from the cheese and popped it into his mouth. They chewed in silence for a long moment. The fire murmured in its grate. From the alley, a dog yelped.

"I have to go tell him," Cithrin said, then took another long drink.

"Company? I'm stood down for the day."

"He won't get violent," Cithrin said. "He isn't like that."

"Could offer moral support. Encouragement."

Cithrin laughed once, mirthless.

"That's why I'm drinking," she said.

"I know."

She looked over at him. His eyes were deep brown, his head broad. He had a scar just under his left ear she'd never noticed before. Yardem had been a priest once, before he'd been a sellsword. The beer sat in its tankard. One wouldn't do much. Two would leave her feeling looser and less upset. But it would also tempt her to reach for a third, and by the fourth she'd be ready to postpone the unpleasant until tomorrow. Better, she thought, to end it quickly and sleep without dreading it in the morning.

She pushed the tankard back, and Yardem stood to let her up.

The boarding house was in the middle of the salt quarter, not far from the little rooms Cithrin, Yardem, and Marcus Wester had hidden in during their first days in the city. The salt quarter streets were narrow and twisted. In some places, the streets were so narrow that Cithrin's fingertips could have brushed the buildings on both sides. Everything stank of raw sewage and brine. By the time they reached the whitewashed walls and faded blue windows of the house, the hem of her dress was black and her feet cold and aching. She pulled her shawl closer about her shoulders and went up the two low steps to the common door. Yardem leaned against the wall, his expression empty but his ears high. Cithrin knocked.

She had hoped that someone else would answer. One of the other boarders or the man who kept the house. Something that would postpone the actual conversation for another minute or two. Luck wasn't with her. Or, more likely, he'd been perched by the door, waiting for word from her. His ash-grey skin and the oversized black eyes of his race made him seem childlike. His smile was bright and tentative at the same time.

"Magistra Cithrin," he said, as if her appearance were a delightful surprise. Her heart thickened. "Please come in. I was just making tea. Have some, have some. And your Tralgu friend."

Cithrin looked back at Yardem. She thought there was pity in his expression and she wasn't certain who it belonged to.

"I'll be right back," she said.

"I'll be right here," he rumbled.

The common sitting room smelled damp despite the little stove that kept the air almost uncomfortably warm. The high, wailing voice of a colicky child forced its way from somewhere in the back, even when the doors were shut. Cithrin sat on a cushioned bench with lank tassels of red and orange that had probably been beautiful once.

"I'm pleased to see you," the Southling man said. "I've been writing to my son in Lyoneia, and I just got a message back. He said that he could—"

"Before we—"

"—have a full shipment as early as midsummer. Last year's nuts are dried and ready to grind. He said they smell like flowers and smoke. He was always good with words that way. Flowers and smoke. Don't you think?"

He knew then. Or guessed. The words flowed out of him, pushing hers back. As if he could keep the inevitable at bay. Cithrin remembered being at the seashore sometime when she'd been very young. Maybe even before her parents had died. She knew what it was like to try stopping a wave with your hands.

"The bank can't move forward with this plan," Cithrin said. "I'm very sorry."

The man's mouth kept working, trying to bring out new syllables. His brows shifted, rising in the center and falling at the ends until he looked like the caricature of loss and disappointment. Cithrin forced herself to take a breath. Her stomach hurt. When he spoke, his voice was small.

"I don't understand, Magistra."

"I've had some new information arrive, unrelated to our conversations, and I'm afraid at the moment it isn't possible for the bank to move forward with the loan you would need."

"If, if, if I could just read you the letter my son sent me, Magistra. You see, we could—"

The man swallowed, closed his massive eyes and hung his head.

"Can I ask why not?"

Because you've got the wrong eyes, Cithrin thought. *Because my notary won't let me. I'm as sorry about this as you. I think you're right.* She thought all the things she couldn't say, because they would mean admitting that she was ruled by Pyk Usterhall. If that became public knowledge, the last bit of influence she had over her bank would be gone. So instead she hardened her soul and pretended to be a banker who was working her own will, and who had the power to match her responsibilities.

"You know I can't divulge other people's conversations with me," she said. "Any more than I would disclose our discussions to them."

"No. Of course not," he said and opened his eyes. "Is there any chance you might reconsider?"

"I'm afraid not," she said, every word costing her.

"All right. Thank you, then. Did—did you still want some tea?"

I'm not drunk," Cithrin said.

"You aren't," Yardem agreed.

"Then why can't I have another glass?"

"Because that's how you stay not drunk."

They hadn't gone back to the taproom. That was where Cithrin went to have meals and polite company. She didn't want those. She wanted to scream and curse and break things with a stick. Frustration and impotence were like a thin iron cage, and she was a finch beating itself to death against them. Her own rooms were above the bank's office and had been since before there had been a bank. It had been a gambler's stall when she'd first walked up the steps. And she'd shared it with Yardem and Marcus Wester and a cartful of crates loaded with silk and gems, tobacco and jewels, and the wax-sealed account books more precious than all the rest put together. Now it held her bed, her desk, her wardrobe. Where there had been bare boards, she'd put a thick red rug to keep her feet warm in winter. A painting hung on the wall over her bed with the mark of the Medean bank worked together with the sigil of Porte Oliva. It had been a gift from the governor.

Cithrin rose from her table, pacing. Voices rose from below them, reminding her how thin the floor was and how sound could travel. There were always guards in the office, making sure that no one could reach the strongbox set in stone beneath the building. It held the hard reserves of the bank. But the real wealth was in the paper—loan agreements, partnerships, depositors' contracts—that were no longer even in the office. They were a long block to the south in the rooms that Pyk had taken for herself, the secret base of the bank.

"She's *gutted* me," Cithrin said. "She's taken it all."

"That was the agreement," Yardem pointed out.

"I don't care what the agreement was," Cithrin said, fighting to keep her voice—even the tone of it—from leaking to the ears of the guards below her. "It's not just that she disagrees with me. Or that she condescends. She's making bad choices, Yardem. She's walking away with coins still on the table. And she's doing it because she's too proud to take direction from an underage half-Cinnae girl."

Cithrin raised her palms, daring Yardem to disagree. He scratched his knee in a way that made her think it hadn't actually itched.

"Well, I am done with this," Cithrin said. "If she wants war, then she will by God get it."

Dawson Kalliam,
Baron of Osterling Fells

Wars are easier to start than end, and where they take you is rarely where you intended to go," the ambassador said. "It will be better for all of us to avoid it."

Dawson turned back from the window. Sir Darin Ashford, Lord of Harrin and Ambassador of King Lechan to Antea, sat in the old library, his legs crossed at the ankle and a carefully charming smile on his lips. He had come to the Kalliams' holding at Osterling Fells two days before, announced by a letter and bringing a small enough retinue that he posed no obvious threat. They had observed the forms of etiquette since his arrival. This was the first candid conversation they'd had.

The walls of granite and dragon's jade gave the room a sense of terrible age and grandeur that Dawson liked. It lent the room and the holding the sense of permanence that they deserved. The sense of right things in their right order. It was a contrast to the subject of their talk.

"You might have thought of that before you plotted to kill Prince Aster," Dawson said.

The ambassador sat forward, one finger held high. He wore the silver cuffs that Dawson's wife Clara assured him were the fashion in Kaltfel that year and the decorative wrist chain that marked a married man in the courts of Asterilhold.

"Now that's just the kind of rhetoric to be careful of, Baron Osterling."

"As long as you're lecturing me on how to speak, you may as well call me Dawson."

Ashford either missed the sarcasm or chose to ignore it.

"All I mean is that Asterilhold didn't have any ill wishes toward the prince or the Severed Throne."

Dawson walked three steps and gestured to a pelt that hung on the wall. The years had greyed the deep golden fur, but the sheer size of the tanned skin was still impressive.

"Did you see this?" Dawson asked. "Mountain lion killed ten of my serfs. Ten of them. I left court a month after my first boy was born to hunt it. It took me three weeks to track it down, and four of my huntsmen fell before we brought it to ground. You would have been . . . five years old, then? Six?"

"Lord Kalliam, I respect that you are my elder, and I see that—"

"Don't lie to me, boy. We both know there were knives meant for Aster's throat."

"There were," Ashford said. "In both our courts. Asterilhold's not a single thing any more than Antea is. A few people corresponded with Lord Maas about his ambitions. To hold the whole court responsible for the secret actions of a few will drag both our kingdoms into chaos."

Dawson stroked the dead cat's fur as he weighed what to say next. The kingdoms of Asterilhold and Antea were like brothers. In centuries before, they had answered to the same High King. Several generations back, the noble houses had made a fashion of intermarrying in hopes that it would drive their nations toward peace. Instead it had confused the bloodlines and given dukes in Asterilhold a plausible claim to the Antean throne. If only you killed enough of the people in between.

It was the fate of all reforms that they turned against the reformers. History was rotten with men and women who had sought to remake the world in the image they had created of it. Inevitably, they failed. The world resisted change, and the nobleman's role was to protect the right order of things. If only that order were always clear. He caressed the dead animal one last time and let his fingers fall from it.

"What do you propose, then?" Dawson asked.

"You are one of King Simeon's oldest and most trusted friends. You were willing to sacrifice your reputation and accept exile from the court in order to expose the plot against the prince. No one is better placed to speak in favor of negotiation."

"And in addition, I was the Palliako boy's patron."

"Yes," Ashford said placidly. "And that."

"I thought you were a skeptic of the romance of Geder Palliako."

"The sure-sighted viscount who burned the city he'd been set to protect in order that he rush back to Camnipol and save the throne from insurrection. His mysterious self-exile to the east taken at the height of his triumph and his return with secret knowledge of the traitors within the court," Ashford said. "It sounds like something a man would pay good coin to have said about him. Next, he'll be waking dragons to play riddles against them."

"Palliako's an interesting one," Dawson said. "I underestimated him. More than once. He lends himself to that."

"He's the hero of Antea, savior and protector of the prince, and darling of the court," Ashford said. "If that's being underestimated, the truth must be something out of an old epic."

"Palliako's...odd," Dawson said.

"Does he respect you? Does he listen to your advice?"

Dawson didn't know the answer to that. Once, when the boy had just come back from Vanai, Dawson had been fairly certain that he could exercise whatever influence he liked over the younger Palliako. Now Geder had a barony of his own and Prince Aster as his ward. There was an argument that he outranked Dawson, if not formally then in effect.

And there was the temple. Ever since the boy's return from the wilds of the Keshet, it was unclear how much the foreign priests he'd brought back were his pets and how much he was theirs. The high priest, Basrahip, had been central to the raid against Feldin Maas, once Baron of Ebbingbaugh and now bones at the bottom of the Division. From what Dawson understood, without the priest, all might have been lost that night. Geder might not have escaped with the letters of evidence, King Simeon might have gone ahead with his plan to foster Prince Aster with Maas, and the world might be a very different place.

And still, there was an answer to the question that he could honestly give.

"Even if Palliako doesn't bend his neck back to look up at me, he'll listen to my son. Jorey served with him in Vanai. They were friends of a sort even before it became the popular thing to do."

"A word from him would go quite a long way toward throwing oil on these waters. All I'm looking for is a private audience with the king. If I knew what assurances he would need, I could take them home with me. Plots of regicide are no more appealing to King Lechan than King Simeon. If nobles in Asterilhold need be called to justice, Lechan will be the one to do it. There's no need to field armies."

Dawson made a small sound in the back of his throat, neither assent nor refusal.

"King Lechan would be very grateful," Ashford said, "for

any aid you could be in mending the breach with his much-loved cousin."

Dawson laughed now. It was a short, barking sound like one of his dogs.

"Do I seem like a merchant to you, Lord Ashford?" Dawson asked. "I have no interest in turning a profit from serving King Simeon. There is no gift your king could offer me that would bring me to act against my conscience."

"Then I rely upon your conscience," Ashford said, dropping the offer of bribery as if it had never been made. "What does it say, Baron Osterling?"

"If it were mine to choose, I'd want the testicles of every man who wrote to Maas in a pickling jar," Dawson said. "But it isn't mine. Simeon sits on the Severed Throne, so the decision is his. Yes, I'll speak with him."

"And Palliako?"

"I'll have Jorey approach him. Perhaps the two of you can meet when court is called. It's only a few weeks from now, and I assume you were going to Camnipol anyway."

"For the opening of court, as it happens," Ashford said. "But there's much to be done before then. With your permission, my lord, I will take my leave of your holding in the morning."

"What? More Antean nobles to dangle Lechan's generosity before?" Dawson said.

The ambassador's smile thinned, but it did not vanish.

"As you say, Lord Kalliam," Ashford said.

The holding at Osterling Fells had been Dawson's home when he was only a boy, and his memories of it were of snow and cold. The dim patterns he'd divined as a child put autumn's feasts of pumpkin sweets and brandy-soaked cherries in Camnipol, snow and ice in Osterling Fells. Almost into adulthood, he had thought of the seasons as residing in different cities. Summer lived in the dark-cobbled streets and high walls of Camnipol. The ice and snow of winter belonged to the narrow valley with its thin river. Granted, the conceit had become more poetic in nature. He wasn't an innocent to think no snow fell on the bridges that spanned the Division or that the summer heat wouldn't bring hunting dogs to torpor in his father's kennels. But the idea had the deep resonance—the rightness—of a thing known in youth and never entirely disbelieved.

The holding had stood in its place at the base of a sloping hill, unchanged for centuries. Before Antea rose as a kingdom, the walls of Osterling Fells had been there. Dragon's jade, eternal and unyielding, wove through the stone and defied wind and weather. The hard granite had eroded in places, and in some even been replaced, but the jade would never fail.

The room he used for his private study was the same that his father had used, and his grandfather, and so on back and back and back. Before this same window, his father had explained that the walls of the holding were like the fabric of the kingdom, that the noble houses were the jade. Without their constancy, even the most glorious structure would eventually fall into ruin.

When his father died, Dawson had taken the holding as his own, raised his own boys within it, and told the same tale over their winter cribs. *This land, these walls, are ours, and only the king can take them from us. Anyone else who tries, dies in the attempt. But if the king requires it, then it is his for the asking. That is what loyalty means.*

His boys had taken the lesson. Barriath, his eldest, served now under Lord Skestinin in the fleet. Vicarian, second of his sons, and unlikely to inherit, had entered the priesthood.

His only daughter, Elisia, had married Lord Annerin's eldest. Only Jorey still remained with the household, and that only until he was called again to service. He had ridden out once, under Lord Ternigan, fought well, and came back a hero and the friend of a hero, even if it was an unreliable one like Geder Palliako.

Dawson found Jorey in a perch at the top of the South Tower. Dawson had spent time there himself as a boy, sticking his head out the thin window and looking down until the height made him dizzy. From here, the lands of Osterling Fells spread out like a map. Two of the villages were clearly visible, and the lake. The trees were all the pale green of new leaf, the shadows all thick with the last of the snow. The cold, soft breeze ruffled Jorey's hair like the feathers of a crow. Two letters—one still sealed with wax the resonant blue of House Skestinin—were forgotten in the young man's hands.

"Letter from your brother? What news from the north?" Dawson asked, and Jorey started, pushing the letters behind him like a kitchen boy caught with sticky lips and a jar of honey. Jorey's cheeks flushed as red as if he'd been slapped.

"He's fine, Father. He says they didn't lose any ships to the freeze, so they're expecting to be on the water again. They might already be."

"That's as it should be," Dawson said. "I met with that idiot from Asterilhold."

"Yes?"

"I've agreed to speak with Simeon about meeting with him. He was also asking whether you would speak with Palliako. He seems to think that soft words from Geder would keep the wheels of vengeance from rolling too far."

Jorey nodded. When his eyes were cast down, he looked like his mother. Clara had the same shape of jaw, the same quiet. The boy was lucky to have that from her.

"Did you say that I would?"

"I said I'd speak to you about it," Dawson said. "You aren't bound to anything."

"Thank you. I'll think on it."

Dawson leaned against the wall. A sparrow darted in through the window, whirled twice through the narrow space, and vanished again in a panic of wind and dust.

"Are you against the thought of war or of speaking to the new Baron Ebbingbaugh?" Dawson asked.

"I don't want to go off to war unless we have to," Jorey said. The first time he'd faced going on campaign, he'd been equal parts anxiety and joy. The experience of it had pressed both out of him. "But if we have to, we will. It's only that Geder...I don't know."

For a moment, Dawson saw the ghosts of Vanai reflected in his son's face. The city that Geder Palliako had burned. It was easy to forget that Palliako had that potential for slaughter in him. But perhaps it was hard for Jorey.

"I understand," Dawson said. "Do what you think best. I trust your judgment."

For some reason Dawson couldn't fathom, the blush in Jorey's cheeks returned and deepened. His boy coughed and wouldn't meet his eye.

"Barriath sent me a letter," Jorey said. "I mean another letter. Inside his. It's from Lord Skestinin. It's a formal introduction to Sabiha. His daughter."

The pause that followed seemed to have some weight. Jorey's dread was as palpable as it was strange.

"I see," Dawson said. "Introduction to his daughter, you say? Hmm. Well, if you don't care to make the connection, we could say the letter went astray..."

"I had asked, sir. I asked for the letter."

"Ah," Dawson said. "Well. Then good you have it, yes?"

Jorey looked up. His eyes betrayed his surprise.

"Yes," he said. "I suppose it is. Sir."

They stood in awkward silence for a moment, then Dawson nodded, turned, and walked back down the narrow spiral stair, his head almost against the stone of the steps above him, with the uncomfortable sense of having given his blessing to something.

Clara, of course, understood at once.

He'd no sooner mentioned Lord Skestinin's daughter than Clara's eyebrows tried to rise up to meet her hairline.

"Oh good God," she said. "Sabiha Skestinin? Who would have guessed that?"

"You know something about the girl?" Dawson asked.

Clara put down her needlework and drew the clay pipe from between her lips, tapping its stem gently against her knee. The window of their private room was open, and the smell of the lilacs mixed with the smoke of her tobacco.

"She's a clever girl. Very pretty. Sweet-tempered, so far as I can tell, but you know how it is with these girls. They know more ways to lie than a banker. And, more to the point, she's fertile."

Dawson's confusion resolved and he sat on the edge of his bed. Clara sighed.

"She had her boy two years ago by no one in particular," Clara said. "He's being raised by one of the family retainers in Estinport. Everyone's been very good about pretending it doesn't... *he* doesn't exist, but of course it's common knowledge. I imagine Lord Skestinin's quite pleased to write letters of introduction for anyone with a drop of noble blood, and lucky for the chance."

"No," Dawson said. "Absolutely not. I won't have my boy wearing secondhand clothes."

"She isn't a coat, dear."

"You know what I mean," Dawson said, rising to his feet. He should have known. He should have guessed by the shame in Jorey's body that the girl was a slut. And now Dawson had said that getting the letter was a good thing. "I'll find him now and put a stop to this."

"Don't."

Dawson turned back at the doorway. Clara hadn't risen. Her face was soft and round, her eyes on his. Her perfect rosebud lips curled in a tiny smile, and with the light spilling across her, she looked...no, not young again. Better than young again. She looked like herself.

"But, love, if Jorey—"

"There are weeks between now and the first chance he could have to see her. There isn't a rush."

He took a step back into the room before he knew he'd done it. Clara put the pipe stem back in her mouth, drawing gently. Smoke seeped out of her nostrils like she was some ancient dragon hidden in a woman's flesh. When she spoke, her voice was light, conversational, but her eyes were locked on his.

"As I recall, I wasn't the first girl you ever took to bed," she said. "I believe you knew exactly what you were about when my bride's night came."

"She's a woman," he said. "It's not the same."

"I suppose it isn't," Clara said, a note of melancholy stealing into her voice. "Still, we're all round-heeled sometimes. I would have fallen back for you months before you made me honest, and we both remember that."

Dawson's body began to stir without his will.

"You're trying to distract me."

"It's working," Clara said. "Indiscreet and unlucky doesn't make her a bad person. Or a bad wife. Give it time, and let me see what I can learn of her when we're back in Camnipol.

Lord Skestinin might make a very fine ally if Jorey were to lift up his fallen daughter. And really, dear, they may be in love."

She held out her hand, guiding him down to sit beside her. Her skin wasn't as smooth as it had been two decades and four children before, but it was still as soft. The amusement in her eyes called forth a softness in his own heart. He could feel his outrage fading. He plucked the pipe from her mouth, leaned forward, and kissed her gently, his mouth filling with her smoke. When he drew back, she was smiling.

"As long as she's not unfaithful," Dawson said with a sigh. "I won't have someone in the family being unfaithful."

A cloud seemed to pass over Clara's eyes, a moment's darkness but nothing more.

"When the time comes," she said. "We can worry when the time comes."

Captain Marcus Wester

It was a week past his thirty-ninth name day, and Marcus squatted at the alley's mouth, waiting. A soft rain fell on the night-dark streets, beading on the waxed wool of his cloak. Yardem stood in the shadows behind him, unseen but present. In the house across the narrow square, a shape passed in front of the window—a man peering out into the darkness. A less experienced man might have stepped back, but Wester knew how to keep from being seen. The man in the window retreated. The tapping of raindrops against stone was the only sound.

"It's not as if I can tell her what to do," Marcus said.

"No, sir."

"She's a grown woman. Well, she's *almost* a grown woman. She's not a child, certainly."

"It's an awkward age, sir," Yardem agreed.

"She wants control over her life. Autonomy. The problem is that she didn't have any her whole life, and then had all of it at once. She had free rein with this bank for months. Long enough to see that she could do it well. After getting a taste for it, I don't see how she turns her back."

"Yes, sir."

Marcus sighed. His breath barely misted. It was a warm spring. He tapped his fingertips against his sword's pommel. Annoyance and concern gnawed at him like rats in the grain house walls.

"I could talk to her," he said at last. "I could tell her that she's got to be patient. Give the situation time to change on its own. Could she hear that, d'you think?"

For a moment, the rain was the only reply.

"Did you want me to answer that?" the Tralgu asked.

"I asked it, didn't I?"

"Could have been a rhetorical point."

Across the square, a thin line of light marked an opening door. Marcus went still for a few seconds, but the door closed again without opening fully. He eased his grip on his sword.

"No, I really meant it," he said. "She's my employer, but she's also...Cithrin. If you've got a suggestion here, I'm open to hearing it."

"Well, sir, I believe that every soul has its own shape—"

"Ah, God. Not this again."

"You asked, sir. You might let me answer."

"Right, sorry. Go ahead. I'll tell myself it's all a metaphor for something."

Yardem's sigh was eloquent, but he continued.

"Every soul has its own shape, and it determines the person's path through the world. Your soul is a circle standing on its edge. At your lowest point, you will only rise, and your highest is when you are most likely to fall. Someone else's soul might be shaped like a blade or a brick or a branching river. Each of them would live the same life differently."

"Which would make it the same life how?"

"I *can* explain that if you'd like, sir. It's theological."

"No, forget I said anything."

"If the magistra's soul leads her in one way, it will seem the simplest path, whether it is or not. If she's left within herself, she'll turn in that direction just like Old Imbert drifted to the left after he took that hammer to his head. To make another choice would require the action of a different soul—"

Marcus raised his hand, and Yardem fell silent. The door that had opened before shifted. The light behind it was gone, and the movement was only a deeper bit of darkness. Yardem shifted. Marcus squinted into the dim.

"He's going north, sir."

Marcus took to his feet and shrugged back his cloak, the rain dampening his newly freed sword arm. Around them, Porte Oliva slept, or if it didn't sleep, at least huddled close to its fires. If there had been moonlight, the pale walls and blue-painted lintels of the merchant quarter would have glowed. Instead, Marcus navigated by shadows and memory. Here and there, a lantern hung from an iron hook beside a door, spilling thin light, but there was more than enough gloom to cling to for a man who didn't want to be seen. The bricks under his feet were slick with grime and rain. Marcus walked quickly, not quite trotting, and straining his ears for his quarry's footsteps. Yardem could have been his shadow.

The man's mistake was a small one, and inevitable. A small splash of a heel coming down in an unexpected puddle and an involuntary grunt. It was enough. They were close enough. It was time.

"Canin!" Marcus said with a friendliness that might almost have been genuine. "Canin Mise, as I live and breathe. Imagine meeting you out on a night like this."

For a moment, it could have gone either way. The man could have greeted him, pretended some legitimate business, and had their conversation. Instead, there was the soft hiss of steel clearing its sheath. Marcus was disappointed, but he wasn't surprised. He stepped back slowly, putting another foot or two between himself and the man.

"It doesn't have to be like this," Marcus said, easing his own blade free with a finger pressed against it to keep it from singing. "No one has to die here."

"You cheated me," the little merchant said. "You and that half-breed bitch you dance for."

The buzz in his voice wasn't a drunkard's. It was worse than that. It belonged to a man who had taken the humiliation of his own failures and forged a weapon from them. That was hatred, and too much wine would have been easier to recover from.

"You borrowed money," Marcus said, circling slowly to the right. The rain chilled his sword. "You knew the risks. The magistra forgave you three payments already. And now there's a story you're looking to leave the city. Set up shop in Herez. You know I can't let that happen until you clear your debt. Now let's put the sharp things away and talk about how you're going to make this right."

"I'll go where I want and I'll do what I please," the man growled.

"That's not where I'd put my bet," Marcus said.

Canin Mise was decent with a blade. Veteran of two wars, five years as a queensman before the governor's magistrates suggested he look for work elsewhere. His plan for starting a fighting school had been a good one. If he'd followed it, he'd likely have died with a reputation and enough money to set up any children he'd fathered along the way. Instead, his foot scraped against the cobbles and his blade hissed through the rain-thick air. Marcus held his sword in a ready block and stepped back out of his reach.

Probably out of his reach. If there had been even a glimmer of light, it would have been safer than what they were doing now. In the darkness, Canin Mise could no more judge his attacks than Marcus could avoid them. Marcus strained his senses, listening for the small noises that could guide him, trying to judge the pressure of the air. It was less swordplay than gambling. Marcus slid forward and took an exploratory swing. Metal clashed against metal, and Canin Mise yelped in surprise. Marcus pressed in with a shout, blocking the counterstrike by instinct.

Canin Mise shouted, a full-throated roar filled with rage and violence. It cut off suddenly. His blade fell to the cobblestones with a clatter. Soft, wet choking sounds came through the darkness, the splash of heels beating at the puddles. The sounds faded and went still.

"You have him?" Marcus asked.

"Yes, sir," Yardem said. "You'll want to carry his heels."

"So," Marcus said, "you're saying that someone will choose against the shape of their own soul if some other-shaped soul's in the room with them?" Canin Mise's boots were slick and the unconscious man's legs were dead-weight heavy.

"Not that they will, but that by having that, the opportunity arises. The world has no will of its own, so *it* can't. Action that comes from without can change the awareness of other possibilities. Are you ready, sir?"

"Wait." Marcus swung his foot in the darkness until he found the fallen man's sword. He lifted it with one toe until the steel was close enough to grab with his encumbered fingers. He didn't want to be responsible for a horse or a person stepping on a live blade in the darkness. And they might get a few coins for it. Likely more money than he'd paid on the loan. "All right. Let's get him to the magistrate."

"Yes, sir."

"So talking to her may or may not improve things, but keeping silence certainly can't help?"

"Yes, sir," Yardem said as they started off at a slow walk, Canin Mise slung between them like a sack.

"And you couldn't just say that?"

Marcus felt Yardem's shrug translated through their shared burden.

"Didn't see the harm, sir. We weren't doing anything else."

The public gaol of Porte Oliva looked like a statue garden in the first light of dawn. Blue-lipped prisoners huddled under whatever tarps and blankets the queensmen had seen fit to throw over them. The wooden platforms they stood or squatted on were dark with rain. A Kurtadam man, all the beads pulled from his pelt, stood bent double with a carved wooden symbol at his hip that showed he hadn't paid his tax. A Cinnae woman moaned and wept at the end of an iron chain, her pale skin stained by its rust, for abandoning her children. Three Firstblood men hung by their necks in the central gallows, unconcerned by the cold.

To the west, the huge brick-and-glass hill of the Governor's Palace. To the east, the echoing white marble of the high temple. Divine law on one side, human law on the other, and a bunch of poor bastards dying of cold in the middle because they had the misfortune to get caught. It seemed to Marcus like the whole world writ small.

To the north, the wide, soft green of the dragon's road led away, running solid and eternal out to the web of ancient roads that the fallen masters of the world had left behind when madness and war destroyed them. For a moment he stood on the wide steps of the square and watched the queensmen wrestle Canin Mise into a tiny metal box with a small hole on top where his head would be exposed to the air. Canin Mise would be easy enough to find until the magistrate had time to review his situation. By taking the man into custody for breaking a private contract, the governor had tacitly purchased the debt at a tenth of its price. Whatever value the law was able to squeeze out of the man now was no concern of Marcus or Cithrin bel Sarcour or the Medean bank.

Dragons had built this square in millennia past, and the sun had risen on it every day since. Rain and snow and hail had battered or caressed it. Porte Oliva itself was an artifact grown over the remnants of a fallen age. None of these buildings had been where they now stood when the races of humanity had been made. Empires had risen and fallen, and while Porte Oliva itself had never been stormed by an invading host, it had been home to riots and slaughter and death just as any city. It had suffered its fevers and loss. It had become complex, pulling its history around it like a knit shawl. The square hadn't been meant to house the suffering and the guilty, but it served the purpose.

A pigeon took wing, grey in the grey, flying out over the square to alight on the top of the gallows post. Marcus had the sudden and profound sense of living in a ruin. Generations of Firstblood and Kurtadam and Cinnae had risen and fallen, lived and loved and died within the walls of the city. And so had the pigeons and rats, the salt lizards and the feral dogs. He couldn't say that there was a great difference between the walls and roofs and passageways that humanity had built and the birds' nests that huddled in their eaves. Except that birds didn't have thumbs. None of them were dragons.

He considered Canin Mise's lost sword. It was a nice piece, well forged and well cared for. The letters *SRB* were worked into the pommel, but what they meant was anyone's guess. Perhaps the blade had been a gift from a lover or a commander. Or Canin Mise might have taken it from its owner before him. Regardless, the letters had meant something once, and they didn't now.

"All right," Marcus said. "I need food and sleep. I'm getting maudlin."

"Yes, sir."

But when they reached the bank office, Pyk Usterhall was

waiting for them. The grey slate still hung on the wall, an artifact of the building's history as a gambler's stall. Where the day's odds had been posted, the duty roster now stood. The three names for the standing guard—Corisen Mout, Roach, and Enen—were listed in Yardem's block letters, but none of them were present. Marcus had noticed before now that when the Yemmu notary was in the front room, there always seemed to be pressing work in the back.

She sat at a low desk, leaning on one massive elbow. The papers on the doomed Canin Mise loan were spread out before her. Her lips sagged in where her tusks should have been, the gap between front and back teeth giving her face a horsey look. She could almost have been a fantastically ugly, obese Firstblood woman. Almost, but not quite.

"You're back," she said.

"Yes, ma'am," Marcus said.

"She's still sleeping."

"Sorry?"

"I saw you looking around for the girl. She's not here. She's still sleeping. What happened?"

Marcus put the sword on the desk. Pyk looked down at it, then up at him, scowling.

"He was where we thought, and he knew we were looking for him. When I talked to him, he tried to cut me down."

"And?"

"He didn't manage."

Pyk nodded curtly.

"You've handed him to the magistrates?" she asked.

"Saw him in the box before we came back."

Pyk sucked at her teeth, plucked the pen from its inkwell, and wrote a line in the margin of the original contract. For a woman with such huge hands, her writing was tiny and precise. Putting the pen back in place, she sighed prodigiously.

"I need you to fire half your guards," Pyk said. "Whichever ones you like. Use your best judgment."

Marcus laughed before he saw she wasn't smiling. Yardem coughed. Pyk scratched her arm, looking up at him from under her eyebrows.

"We can't do that," Marcus said. "We need the men we've got."

"All right," Pyk said. "Then cut their pay in half. Doesn't matter to me. But I have reports to send back to the holding company, and we need our expenses down. If we see fewer cock-ups like this"—she gestured at Canin Mise's blade—"we can hire some back in the autumn."

"Ma'am, all respect, but the guards will need to eat before autumn. I try to bring them back, they'll have other work. I've run a company. It costs less to pay a few men you don't need than to need a few you haven't got."

"You haven't run a bank," Pyk said. "I'll want the names of the ones you're losing by tonight. Can you handle that, or do you need help?"

Marcus leaned forward, his hand resting on the pommel of his sword. He was tired and hungry and the anger that boiled up in him felt liberating. Like anything that felt good, he distrusted it. He looked over at Yardem, and the Tralgu's face was perfectly bland. Pyk might have asked him whether it was raining outside.

"I can handle it," Marcus said.

"Then do."

He nodded, turned, and stepped back out into the street. In the east, the sun burned at the top of the houses. The rainclouds had broken like a fallen army, and steam was rising from the stone streets. Marcus stretched his arms and his neck, only realizing as he did that they were the same movements he made before a fight.

Marcus took a deep breath.

"I believe that woman is trying to upset me," he said.

"How's she doing with that, sir?"

"Fairly good job of it. So. The day you throw me in a ditch and take control of the company?"

"Still not today. Breakfast and sleep, sir? Or would you rather go about this hungry and tired."

Marcus walked west without answering. A pack of city dogs trotted at his heels partway down the street, then veered off, seeking out some urban prey only they could smell. Porte Oliva was awake now. Sellers on their way to market, queensmen on their morning rounds. A Timzinae boy walked by with a black wooden yoke across his shoulders and two huge buckets of piss swinging at his sides, hauling the pots from taproom alleys to the launderer's yard where he'd sell it for bleach. Marcus stepped aside to let him pass.

Marcus stopped at a small house with a red door where a Firstblood girl, dark skin barely lighter than the Timzinae's scales, sold spiced chicken with barley paste wrapped in wide leaves. He leaned against the wall, Yardem at his side. When he was finished with the meal, he licked his fingers and spoke.

"This fight you worried Cithrin may start with the holding company?"

"Yes, sir."

"I think it's already started. And I don't think she threw the first punch."

"Was coming to that myself, sir," Yardem said. And a moment later, "Are you still going to talk to her?"

"Yes."

"About being patient and mature and waiting for the situation to change of its own accord?"

"No."

Geder Palliako, Baron of Ebbingbaugh and Protector of the Prince

The nature of history itself defies us. To know with certainty what the last Dragon Emperor thought or planned or schemed would require not only an understanding of the draconic mind lost to humanity (if indeed it were ever available), but also a comprehension of the particular form of madness which took him in the violent days that ended his reign. Certain facts are known: that Morade's clutch-mates contested his selection to the throne, that the battle between them raged for three human generations, that their end marked the opening of the ages of humanity. But these are generalities. Vagaries.

As we reach for greater precision, certainty recedes. For centuries it was understood that the Dry Wastes east of the Cenner range had been empty since Seriskat, the first Dragon Emperor, battled his semi-bestial fathers there and founded civilization itself. It was only questioned when the chemist Fulsin Sarranis, made suspicious by the metallic content of certain inks in the ancient Book of Feathers, proved that the documents were forgeries written not by the secretary of Drakkis Stormcrow, but by a scribe of the court of Sammer a thousand years after the death of Morade. Expeditions into the Dry Wastes since that time have confirmed the existence of the Dead Towns, Timzinae agricultural centers that suggest a full and active farm culture. As the Timzinae were not brought into being before the last great war, it must be assumed that these towns were built after the rise of humanity, and that the Dry Wastes result from another more recent calamity.

The documentation of these hoaxes of history has been the work of my life. From the time I first set out for the great universities of Samin and Urgoloth, I knew that my destiny was to chronicle the follies of my fellow historians and define the limits of historical knowledge. I began my quest at the age of seven, when as a follower of the poet Merimis Cassian Clayg, I uncovered a misattribution in the notations of his rival poet, the repulsive half-lizard known only by the name of his philosophy, Amidism.

Geder closed the book, pressing his eyes with finger and thumb. The pages were soft rag, thick and limp. The binding was cracked leather. When the book had been presented to him, a gift for his twenty-third naming day, he'd had high hopes for it. Ever since he'd found the temple of the spider goddess and heard of the age of the goddess that reached back even before the dragons, he'd been looking for some evidence of it. A history of frauds and lies seemed like an excellent prospect for finding some sign of it, even if it was only a suggestion.

Instead, the book was a tissue of increasingly improbable discoveries by the almost supernaturally clever author, leading to the discovery of more and more supposedly earth-shattering revelations, and more than once confessions of sexual misconduct more boastful than repentant. Every ten or twenty pages, the nameless author felt moved to restate his thesis, often using the same phrases. And each time the apparent sincerity of the book began to persuade Geder, some new improbability would come to throw him back out. A half-lizard named Amidism?

With the clarity of disappointment, Geder saw that he'd expected a parallel between the writer of the essay and Basrahip, high priest of the spider goddess. Both, after all, promised to tell of a secret history otherwise unknown to mankind. But where Basrahip had the power of the Sinir Kushku, Righteous Servant, the goddess of spiders, this other person had self-aggrandizing stories. If only Basrahip could judge the truth of written words as clearly as living voices...

"Baron Ebbingbaugh?"

Geder looked up, half annoyed by the interruption and half pleased by it. His house master was a Firstblood man with a long white beard and bushy white eyebrows that reminded Geder of drawings of Uncle Snow from a children's book he'd had as a youth.

"Yes?"

"You have a caller, my lord."

Geder stood up from his desk. His personal study was a disaster of papers, scrolls, notebooks, and wax tablets. He looked around with dismay. He couldn't have anyone see this.

"All right," Geder said. "Put him...put him in the garden?"

"I have put her in the north drawing room."

Geder nodded, more than half to himself.

"North drawing room," he said. "Which one's that?"

"I'll take you there, my lord."

The mansion and grounds of his estate were still new to him. A year before, he'd been the heir to the Viscount of Rivenhalm. Now, after Basrahip had helped him expose the treason of Feldin Maas, he was not only Baron Ebbingbaugh but Protector of Prince Aster. The boy who would one day be king of Antea was his ward. It was an honor he'd never dreamed of in a life now full of things that had once seemed beyond his grasp.

He'd wintered in Ebbingbaugh when he wasn't chasing around after the wandering feast of the King's Hunt. Returning to the mansion in Camnipol had been strange as a dream. Here was the storage room where he'd watched Feldin Maas, the previous Baron Ebbingbaugh, slaughter his own wife. Here were the garden paths he'd fled through in the night, the letters proving Maas's guilt pressed to his chest. Everything about the place screamed danger. But it was his by right now.

The north drawing room was the one he'd mentally labeled "the sitting room by the courtyard." And the guest he'd expected wasn't the one waiting for him.

He'd seen the girl in court the year before, but he'd seen more or less everyone in court. Her skin was the soft brown of coffee and milk, her hair spilling softly around her long, high-cheeked face. She wore a dress of startling green under a black leather cloak cut slightly too large, a fashion Geder himself had unintentionally begun. Her chaperone was a looming Tralgu woman in an almost comically frilly dress who stood in the corner.

"Ah, oh," Geder said.

"Lord Protector Geder Palliako," his house master intoned. "Her Ladyship Sanna Daskellin, third daughter of Lord Canl Daskellin."

"I hope I haven't come at a bad time," the girl said, gliding across the room toward him, her hand out for him to accept. He accepted it.

"No," he said, nodding. "No, this is fine."

Her smile was fast and bright.

"My father is hosting the opening of the season, and I wanted to bring the invitation to you especially. You don't think I'm too forward, do you?"

"No," Geder said. "No, not at all. No. I'm delighted you could stop by."

She squeezed his fingers gently and he realized he was still holding her hand. He let it drop.

"We've only just returned to Camnipol," she said. "How did you find your new holdings?"

Geder crossed his arms, trying to affect an ease he didn't feel.

"With a map and a guide for the most part," he said. "Maas never invited me out. We didn't travel in the same circles. I spent most of the winter just trying to find out where he'd put everything."

She laughed and sat on a red silk divan. It occurred to Geder that she wasn't leaving. The combination of unease and excitement was slightly nauseating. He was talking to a woman in his own house with her chaperone present. There was no transgression against etiquette or propriety, but his blood raced through his veins a little faster all the same. Geder licked his lips nervously.

"So what are his plans for the season's opening. The usual feast, I assume."

"A fireshow," Sanna Daskellin said. "He's found this marvelous cunning man from Borja who can build structures to channel flame and make it burn in all different sorts of colors. I've seen him practicing." She leaned toward him, a small shift of weight that indicated a shared secret. "It's beautiful, but it smells of sulfur."

Geder laughed. Behind the girl, the Tralgu chaperone

remained impassive as a guard at a counting house. Geder moved toward a leather chair, but the girl slid to one side of her divan and tapped gently against the abandoned half, inviting him. Geder hesitated, then sat at her side, careful not to touch her. Her smile was made of sun and shadows, and it left Geder feeling both uncomfortably aroused and subtly mocked.

"Isn't it awkward sharing a courtyard with Curtin Issandrian?" she asked.

"Not particularly," Geder said. "Of course, he hasn't even returned yet. I suppose it could be once he's back. He might be a bit unpleasant to be near. Could be some conflict."

"I wouldn't think so," Sanna said. "Issandrian may be ignorant enough to keep company with traitors, but he knows a lion when it looks at him."

"Well, I wouldn't know about that," Geder said. Sanna's expression invited him to smile along, and he found it very difficult not to. "I mean...I suppose he would." He made a claw of his fingers and scratched at the air. "Grrr," he said.

Sanna's laughter brought her a degree nearer to him. She smelled of rosewater and musk. When her fingers brushed his arm, Geder's throat felt oddly thick.

"Oh, I'm terribly thirsty. Aren't you?" she asked.

"I am," Geder said almost before he understood the question.

"Seribina?"

"Ma'am?" the Tralgu woman asked.

"Could you go fetch us some water?"

"Of course, ma'am."

But she's your chaperone, Geder thought, then bit back before he could say it. He was going to be alone with a woman. A woman of high blood was clearly arranging things so that she could spend a few minutes alone in his house with him. He felt the first insistent stirrings of an erection and ground his lip hard between his teeth to check it. The Tralgu woman moved for the door, as calm and stately as a ship in the ocean. Geder was torn between the impulse to let her leave and the one to call her back.

The issue was taken out of his hands.

"My lord," the master of house said, appearing at the door just before the Tralgu reached it. "I am sorry to interrupt. Sir Darin Ashford has arrived and requests a moment of your time."

"Ashford?" Sanna asked. The surprise in her voice made her sound like a different woman, and a more serious one. She looked at Geder with less coquetry and greater respect. "I didn't know you were entertaining the ambassador."

"Favor," Geder said. Words seemed difficult to come by. "For a friend."

The perfect skin went smooth. Geder had the sense—possibly accurate or possibly imagined—that some complex calculation was happening behind her deep black eyes.

"Well," she said. "I can't keep you from affairs of state. But say again that you'll come to Father's party?"

"I will," Geder said, rising to his feet as she did. "I promise. I'll be there."

"I have witnesses," Sanna said with a laugh and gestured to the servants. She gave her hand to him again, and Geder kissed it gently.

"Let me see you out," he said.

"Why thank you, Baron Ebbingbaugh," she said, offering her arm.

They walked together from the back of the mansion to the wide stone stairs that led down to her carriage, an old-fashioned design drawn by horses instead of slaves. Geder gave her up to the care of the footmen with a bone-deep regret and also relief. Sanna stepped up and let herself be seated behind a cascade of lace. The smell of rose and musk returned to him, but it was only an illusion or a particularly visceral memory. The horses clattered out to the courtyard. He looked past them to Curtin Issandrian's empty mansion and a sense of unease trickled down his spine.

"You play a dangerous game, my lord," an unfamiliar voice behind him said.

The man was a Firstblood with pale brown hair and an open, guileless expression. He wore riding leathers and a wool cloak entirely covered in patterned embroidery that seemed understated until Geder looked at it closely, and then seemed like a boast. Geder didn't need to be told who he was. Sir Darin Ashford was his own introduction.

"My Lord Ambassador," Geder said.

Ashford nodded, but his gaze was set farther out. To the courtyard.

"Lord Daskellin's girl, isn't she? Beautiful woman. I remember when she first entered society. She was all knees and elbows back then. Amazing the difference three years will make."

"She was here to deliver her father's invitation," Geder said, defensive without knowing precisely what he was defending against.

"I'm sure she was, and she won't be the last. A baron without a baroness is a rare and precious thing, and protector of the prince carries as much prestige as a wardenship. Maybe more. You'll have to step clever or you'll find yourself married before you know who you're married to." Ashford's smile was charming. "Is the prince here, by the way?"

"He's not," Geder said. "I thought it was poor form to have him too close to hand when you were here."

Something like chagrin passed over the ambassador's face.

"Well, that doesn't bode well for me. It's hard to ask for your help when you already think I'm an assassin."

"I didn't say that," Geder said.

"No, you acted on it," Ashford said. "And that, Lord Protector, very much matches your reputation. Should we retire inside?"

Geder didn't take him back to the same room. Having the voice and face of Asterilhold in the same room where Sanna Daskellin had been felt like dirtying something Geder didn't want soiled. Instead, they went to the private study where Feldin Maas had killed his wife Phelia and all his elaborate, clandestine plans to join Antea and Asterilhold with her. The significance was lost on Ashford, but Geder knew.

Geder sat on a wide-set chair, leaving an upholstered bench for Ashford. A servant boy brought in a carafe of watered wine and two glasses, poured one into the others, and retreated without speaking or being spoken to. Ashford sipped the wine first.

"Thank you for seeing me, Lord Palliako," he said. "I'd have understood if you'd refused me."

"Jorey Kalliam spoke for you."

"Yes. I'd heard you two were friends. Served in Vanai under Alan Klin, didn't you?"

"We did," Geder said.

"Klin, Issandrian, Maas. The triad, and Feldin Maas the only one who didn't get thrown out of Camnipol that summer. King Simeon sent Dawson Kalliam away instead."

"Your point?"

Ashford looked pained and sat forward, the glass of wine cradled between his fingertips.

"King Simeon is a good man," Ashford said. "No one doubts that. King Lechan is too. But no king can be better than his advisors. If he'd known then what he does now, Dawson Kalliam wouldn't have been exiled and Feldin Maas wouldn't have been let stay. Simeon needs good men to guide him. Men like you and Kalliam."

Geder crossed his arms.

"Go on," he said.

"His son was threatened. Go to any man, peasant or priest or high noble, hold a knife to his child's throat, and he'll kill you to keep his own safe. It's nature. You saved the prince, and Simeon saw justice done when he finished Maas. But it has to stop now. Give Lechan a season—a year—to root out what parts of the conspiracy were in Asterilhold, and there'll be justice done there too. Bring swords to the border, and a few men's follies become a tragedy for thousands. And for no reason."

Geder chewed absently at his thumbnail. Ashford's sincerity was persuasive, but something bothered him. He started to speak, then stopped.

"Both our courts had rot in them," Ashford said. "You've cut it out of yours. All I'm asking is the time to do the same."

"Maas wanted unification," Geder said. "The plan was to unite the kingdoms."

"Maas wanted power, and he made up any story he needed to justify it. If Lechan had gotten word of this, he'd have ended it in the same breath."

Geder frowned.

"Your king didn't know?" he asked, annoyed at his own voice for sounding so querulous. The ambassador looked directly into his eyes, his expression was sober. Solemn.

"He didn't."

Geder nodded, but he didn't mean anything by it. It was only a gesture, a thing to fill the silence. If it was true and the king of Asterilhold would have acted against Maas just as much as King Simeon had, then helping to keep peace would be in everyone's best interests. It would absolutely be the right thing to do. If, on the other hand, the ambassador was only a good actor playing his part on a series of very small stages, taking his side was collaborating against the throne. The good or ill of the kingdom—and more than that, of Aster—rested on Geder's judgment. He frowned seriously, trying to match gravity with gravity.

The fact was, Geder didn't know what to think. He felt he might just as well spin a coin.

"I will think on it," he said carefully.

The long months of winter, Geder's patronage, and a dozen lesser priests from the temple in the mountains past the Keshet had made the temple grander and more polished. Where the grit and grime of centuries had blacked the walls, the tilework glowed now. Most of the traditional religious images and icons had been taken apart and the original material reused to make different images. Most had the eightfold symmetry of the great red silk banner that fluttered over the main entrance. The air was thick with the scent of the nettle oil that burned in the lamps.

In the center of the sacred space, a half dozen priests stood in a circle, laughing and playing a game that seemed to involve pitching hard, uncooked beans into one another's opened mouths. A half dozen priests and one prince of the realm. Aster's pale skin and round features stood out in that company. All the priests shared long faces and wiry hair, like members of the same extended family. Their brown robes looked dusty beside Aster's bright silks and brocade: a songbird among sparrows.

"Geder!" Aster shouted, and Geder waved. It was good to see the prince laughing. Though Aster hadn't complained, the winter had been hard for him. Especially the weeks after the end of the King's Hunt and the return to Camnipol for the opening of the season. This was the first time of any significance that Aster had spent away from his father, and the darkness of the holding at Ebbingbaugh had taken its toll. Geder had done what he could, but he'd never had a brother and few enough friends among his peers. They'd played cards together in the dark nights. It was the nearest thing to comfort he could offer.

Basrahip, the high priest, was in his private room. The huge man sat on a low cushion, his eyes closed in meditation. For a moment it was hard to think why the room seemed bare. It had its bed, its desk, a tall cabinet with carved rosewood and inlays of ivory and jet. The fire grate had unlit logs and tinder ready for the spark. The carpet was a deep red with a pattern of gold that seemed to undulate in the lamp's light. But it wasn't littered with books and scrolls. So that was the difference.

When Geder, in the doorway, cleared his throat the big man smiled.

"Prince Geder," Basrahip said.

"Lord Palliako. I'm Lord Palliako. Or Baron Ebbingbaugh. Prince means something very particular here. It's not like in the east."

"Of course, of course," Basrahip said. "My apologies."

Geder waved the comment away even though the man's eyes were still closed. Geder waited, shifting from foot to foot, until it became clear that Basrahip was neither likely to open them nor send Geder away.

"Thank you for keeping Aster for the day. The ambassador's come and gone."

"We are always pleased to see the young prince," Basrahip said.

"Good. Anyway. Thank you."

"Is there more?"

"What? No, nothing else."

The priest's eyes opened, and his dark eyes locked on Geder.

"Fine," Geder said. He'd tested the arcane powers of the Sinir Kushku often enough. He'd known the lie wouldn't pass. In a way, he'd been counting on it. "May I come in?"

Basrahip gestured toward the little desk with a broad-palmed hand. Geder sat. He felt a bit like a schoolboy answering to his tutor, except that his tutors hadn't ever sat cross-legged on the floor.

"Last year?" Geder began. "When we were in court, and you would tell me if someone was lying? That was very useful to me. When the ambassador came, it was a thing where if you had been there and could have told me what he meant, it would have . . . it would have helped."

"The power of the Righteous Servant burns through the lies of this fallen world," Basrahip said, as if he were agreeing.

"I know that the temple is your work, and I don't want to take you from it . . . I mean I do, but I don't."

"You wish the aid of the goddess," Basrahip said.

"I do. But I'm not comfortable asking. Do you see how that is?"

Basrahip laughed. It was a rich sound, and filled the air like a thunderstorm. The high priest rose from the floor with the strength and grace of a dancer.

"Prince Geder, you ask for what is already yours. You gave this temple to her. You brought her out of the wild and returned her to the world. For all this you are beloved in her sight."

"So it wouldn't be too great a favor to ask?" Geder said, hope blooming in his breast.

"It is already yours. I am your Righteous Servant. I will attend you at any time, or at all times. You need only keep the promise you made to her."

"Ah," Geder said. "And which promise is that?"

"In each city that comes beneath the power of your will, grant her a temple. It need not be so great as this. Do this for her, and I will never leave your side."

The relief was like putting cold water on a burn. Geder smiled.

"I can't tell you how glad I am to hear that," he said. "Really. I'm really not cut out for court life."

The priest laid a huge hand on his shoulder and smiled gently.

"You are, Prince Geder. So long as your Righteous Servant is with you, you are."

Clara Kalliam, Baroness
of Osterling Fells

Winter was a different thing for men. She'd seen it for years. Decades now, and *there* was a thought. Decades. With autumn came the close of court, the ending of all the season's intrigues and duels and political wrestling. The great houses folded up their belongings, put cloths over their furniture to keep the dust away, and returned to the lands that supported them. For a month or two, the lords worked their holdings. The tribute of the farmers and potters and tanners accepted in their name and absence were accounted. The magistrates they'd appointed would consult on whatever issues they'd felt the lord should decide. Justice would be dispensed, tours made of the villages and farms, and a plan drawn up for the management of the holding over the next year. And all of it as quickly as possible so that it could all be finished when the King's Hunt began, and they all rushed off to one holding or another—or, if they were unlucky, prepared their own homes to act as host to king and royal hunters—and ran down boars and deer until first thaw.

There was no time to rest, and Clara didn't know how they managed it. How her husband managed it.

For her, the short days and long nights were the time of year when she could rest. Recuperate. For weeks before and after Longest Night, Clara slept long and deep. She spent her days sitting before a fire, her fingers busy with their embroidering and her mind at rest. The stillness of winter was her refuge, and the thought of a year without it inspired the same dread as contemplating a night without sleep. She was an older woman now, the grey in her hair no longer sparse enough to bother plucking out. Her daughter was married and with a child of her own. But even when she'd been young, Clara had known that winter was her season away from the world.

And spring was her return to it.

"There have always been religious cults," she said. "Lady Ternigan was brought up in the Avish mysteries, and it never seemed to do her any particular harm."

"I'm just concerned that there won't be any silver left for the real priests," Lady Casta Kiriellin, Duchess of Lachloren, said. "Your son's in training for the priesthood, isn't he, Clara?"

"Vicarian," Clara agreed. "But he's always said there are as many ways to worship as there are worshippers. I'm sure if something new comes along, he's quite prepared to learn those rites as well."

Lady Joen Mallian, the youngest of the group, leaned forward. Her skin was pale as daisies and showed every drop of blood in her cheeks. There was a vicious rumor that she had a Cinnae grandmother.

"I've heard," she whispered, "that the Avish mysteries make you drink your own piss."

"The way Lady Ternigan's tea tastes, I shouldn't doubt it," Casta Kiriellin said, and they all laughed. Even Clara. It was uncalled for and cruel, but Issa Ternigan did serve the strangest teas.

The party was seven strong, each of them dressed in new clothes with bright dyes. Clara always thought of these days as a sort of religious rite. The twittering and gossip and bright colors worn as if by mimicking the glory of flowers they might call forth the buds. The gardens belonged to Sara Kop, Dowager Duchess of Anes, who sat at the head of the table in a dress of glowing white lace as pure as the old woman's hair. She'd been deaf as a stone for years and never spoke, but she smiled often and seemed to take pleasure in the company.

"Clara, dear," Lady Kiriellin said, "I've heard the most unlikely rumor. Someone's said your youngest is pitching woo at Sabiha Skestinin. That can't be right, can it?"

Clara took a long sip from her teacup before she answered.

"Jorey has taken a formal introduction," she said. "I'm meeting the girl this afternoon, though of course that's all form and etiquette. I've known her peripherally since she was just walking. I can't fathom why we put ourselves through all the fuss of ritual to pretend to meet someone we already know quite well, especially as Dawson's the one she'll really need to win over. But tradition is tradition, isn't it?"

She smiled and lifted her head, then waited. If anyone was going to bring up the girl's past, this would be the moment. But there were only polite smiles and covert glances. Jorey's unfortunate connection to the girl hadn't passed unnoticed, but neither was it a thing of open derision or false concern. It was good to know, and she tucked the information away in the back of her mind, should she need it later. Joen Mallian suddenly squealed and clapped her hands together.

"Did I tell you I've seen Curtin Issandrian? Last night, I was at a reception that Lady Klin held. Nothing formal, you understand, just a dinner party for a few people, and he is my cousin, so I was utterly obligated to go. And who should be there, sitting by the roses as if nothing was odd, but

Curtin Issandrian? And you'll hardly believe it. He's cut his hair short!"

"No!" one of the other women said. "But that was all he had that made him at all attractive."

"I can't believe he's still being seen with Alan Klin," said another. "You'd think those two would put a bit more air between them after being lumped in with Feldin Maas."

Clara sat back a degree in her chair, listening, laughing, sharing bits of barely sweetened cake and biting lemon tea. For an hour, they spoke of everything and nothing, the words pouring out of them all in a flood. Even Clara with her love of winter also saw the joy of talking in company after so many weeks alone. This was how the court wove itself into a single tapestry—small gossip and news, speculations and enquiries, fashions and traditions. Her husband and sons would have made no more sense of it than of birdsong, but for Clara it was all as legible as a book.

She took her leave early enough that she could walk back to her own mansion. Camnipol in spring could be a shockingly beautiful place. In her memory, the city was all of black and gold, and so the real stone and ivy always surprised her. Yes, the streets were cobbled dark and soot marked many walls. Yes, there were great burnished archways throughout the city, tributes to the victories of great generals, some of them generations dead. But there was also a common with a double line of burgundy-leaved trees, a Cinnae boy, pale and thin and ghostly, dancing on the street corner for coins while his mother sawed away on an ancient violin. Clara paused for a moment in an open square at the edge of the Division to watch a theater company declaim on their small, sad wagon-mounted stage. The actors playing tragic young lovers were decent enough, but the grandeur of the view behind them kept distracting her.

The grandeur of the view, or else some part of her didn't want to dwell on young love and tragedy. Not today, at least.

At her house, Andrash rol Estalan, their Tralgu door slave, stood at the end of his silver chain. His ears were at high alert. His father had been one of her own father's huntsmen, and she had a fond spot for him.

"Your son is with Lord Skestinin's son and daughter, my lady," he said. "They are in the west garden."

"Thank you, Andrash. And is my husband at home?"

"No, my lady. I believe he has gone to the Great Bear with Lord Daskellin."

"Likely that's for the best," she said. She took a deep breath. "All right."

The Tralgu bowed his head. He always could express sympathy gracefully.

The west gardens were mostly rose and lilac, and neither of them yet in bloom. Jorey stood by a low stonework table where a young man and woman sat. The two guests both had hair the color of wheat and round features that looked better on the girl than her brother. In the gentle chill of early spring, all of them wore cloaks, but Jorey's was wool and waxed cotton where the Skestinin siblings wore black, generously cut leather.

"Mother," Jorey said, lifting his chin as she drew near. "Thank you for coming."

"Don't be silly, dear. Next you'll be grateful that I walk myself to the breakfast table," Clara said. "And this must be Sabiha. I haven't seen you in an age. You look lovely. And this cannot be Bynal. Bynal Skestinin is a little boy with a toy sword who took all the roses off Amada Masin's bushes."

"Lady Kalliam," Lord Skestinin's youngest son said as he stood. "My father would want me to thank you for accepting us in your home."

The girl nodded, but didn't look up. Her gaze was cast at the ground, a mask of stoicism and humiliation. In truth, the gratitude offered to Clara was little more than the common form, but that didn't matter. They all knew what none of them would say. Lord Skestinin and his family looked upon this as pity. House Kalliam was graciously lowering itself by bringing Sabiha through its door. In the opinion of most of the court of Antea, it was. Clara might not like it, but denying it was like trying to ignore away the wind.

Clara chose her words carefully.

"My eldest son has served under Lord Skestinin for years," she said. "His children are always welcome in this house."

The boy bowed. He had a dueling scar on the back of his hand. For a moment, Clara was surprised, and then she wasn't. He was old enough for the dueling yards, and had been for years. He was here now as chaperone of his sister's honor. Likely he'd crossed steel over it at some point as well.

"Mother," Jorey said, "I've had formal introduction to Sabiha. I'm going to ask Father's permission tomorrow."

Clara felt her eyebrows bolt toward her hairline and her gaze flickered over the girl. Even sitting and with the covering of the wide-cut cloak, she wouldn't be able to hide a belly. Especially not for a second child, and with the amount of time it would have taken to send for a formal letter, receive it, and return from Osterling Fells to Camnipol, pregnancy simply didn't seem plausible. Sabiha swallowed, her expression utterly empty. Everyone present knew the calculations Clara had just made. Everyone expected them.

"That seems sudden," Clara said. "Engagements can run a season or two these days."

"I don't mind waiting," the girl said.

The pain in Jorey's expression was vivid and fresh and angry. This wasn't the girl's idea, then. It was her son's. He wanted to give her the season. He wanted her to go to the dances and feasts and fireshows as Sabiha Kalliam, and not Lord Skestinin's disgraced daughter. Marrying into House Kalliam—and especially doing it now with the family's star on the rise—would change the story people told about her. And changing *that* changed who she *was*.

It was as profound a gift as a young man could offer the woman he loved.

"Jorey, dear," she said, "weren't you saying that Bynal followed horses? I'm sure he'd be interested in the bay mare that your father brought from the holding."

"I don't... That's to say..." Jorey pressed his lips together until the color was all driven out from them. "Yes, Mother."

When the boys had gone, Clara sat across from the girl. She had a good face, but worn. It wasn't only that she'd borne a child, though God knew that could change a woman's body in ways the midwife never mentioned. It was sorrow. And shame. They'd been ground into the girl's skin like soot. Of course they had.

"Lady Kalliam," the girl said. The pause lasted five heartbeats. Six. Tears were welling in the girl's eyes, and Clara felt them answering in her own. She blinked them back. Empathy was well and good in its time, but that wasn't this.

"Don't ever be grateful to him," Clara said.

Sabiha looked up, confused. A tear escaped, tracing silver down the girl's cheek.

"My lady?"

"Jorey. If you love him and he loves you, then God knows nothing's going to stop the pair of you. But you mustn't be grateful to him. It will poison everything if you are."

Sabiha shook her head, another tear coming free but the last one. Her eyes were drying.

"I don't understand," she said.

Clara shook her head. She couldn't find the words that would explain it. How to explain the difference between a marriage grown from love—more than love, from complicity—and one that was unequal from the start. She had seen too many women married from ambition, and she had seen where they ended. She didn't want her boy married to one of them. But the girl was a girl. Even if she'd suffered hard times, she could no more understand what Clara was saying than a songbird could swim.

"Sabiha, dear," Clara said. "Does he make you laugh?"

Clara couldn't see the memory behind the girl's eyes, but she saw that it was there. The shape of Sabiha's eyes changed and brightened, her lips grew a degree fuller as she forgot to press them thin. Clara knew the answer before the girl nodded.

"All right, then," Clara said. "I'm going to need more time, though. Jorey's father is loyal as a hound, but change bothers him. I'll need…a week. Can you and Jorey wait that long before asking permission?"

"If we have to, we can do anything."

Clara rose, bent, and kissed the girl gently on the top of her head.

"Spoken like a Kalliam," she said. "Go find them, then. Tell Jorey what I said."

"You don't want to talk to him?"

"Not now," Clara said, her heart sinking.

She watched as the girl rose and left. There was happiness and relief in the way the girl walked, in the angle of her shoulders. She radiated. It wouldn't last because nothing ever did, but it was good to see it all the same. Something bright moved at the corner of Clara's vision, calling attention to itself. A sprig of lilac had bloomed, a dozen tiny flowers bright in the sun. It felt like an omen.

How odd, Clara thought, that speaking to this girl would be the thing that clarified the other task she had to do.

There was little call for huntsmen in Camnipol. Guards, yes. Servants, yes. The sort of personal servant who might take on extra duties or serve at the whim of a nobleman or his wife. She found Vincen Coe in the servants' wing among the small corridors and tiny rooms that divided the architecture of the great from that of the low. He was a young man, hardly older than Jorey, with wide eyes and a body well accustomed to hardship and work. She had saved him once when her husband's pique had nearly ended his service. He had saved her once when Feldin Maas would have cut her down. He rose when he caught sight of her, and she pushed away the memory of his lips against hers and the taste of blood. It had been a single stolen kiss, and he'd been bled nearly white when he'd presumed. Since then there had been no talk of it. Not even acknowledgment that it had happened. Nothing.

And there would be nothing.

"My lady," he said, the words crisp as a bark.

"Coe," she said.

There was no call to continue. It was her place to command and his to follow. She didn't need to explain herself to him, except that she did need to.

"Is there a problem, my lady?"

"I love my family dearly," she said. "And I will protect them from whatever dangers I can. And at whatever price is asked."

"Of course," he said. He didn't understand what she was saying any better than Sabiha Skestinin had.

You're a child, she wanted to say. *Go find a girl your own age and make handsome, charming babies with her. You have no business with me.*

"I need you to return to Osterling Fells," she said. "I want you to oversee the construction of my husband's new kennels."

The shock on his face was like a blow. His face paled.

"I don't understand," he said. "Have I given offense? What did I...?"

Clara clasped her hands behind her. The air in the servants' quarters was somehow thinner than in the main house. Harder to breathe.

"We both know what this is," she said. "Are you truly going to make me explain it?"

"I..."

The huntsman bowed his head, and when he lifted it again, his expression wasn't of a servant speaking to his master, and the depth of his voice gave his words an extra meaning that mere grammar didn't carry.

"I will serve my lady as she sees fit," he said. "I have no other task."

"And if she sees fit to send you to the holding to look after the kennels?"

"If she sees fit to send me to hell, my lady."

"Don't be dramatic," she whispered.

For a moment, time stopped between them. A single moment with the duration of a season, because it was the last. Clara turned and walked slowly back to the main house. Her breath was returning to her slowly. She squared her shoulders. She wanted to go to her rooms, to sit with her embroidery and her pipe and recapture, if she could, a few moments of the quiet of winter. She wanted to be calm again. She wanted to be still.

But Dawson's voice carried through the front hall as she entered it. She knew from the tone of it that he was annoyed, but not truly angry. His moods and temper were as familiar to her as her own clothes, and as comforting. Two of his hunting dogs paced nervously in the corridor outside his study, whining under their breath and looking from Clara to the closed door and back again. She paused to scratch them gently behind the ears.

Dawson sat at his desk. A letter spilled out over it. She didn't need to see the royal seal. The quality of the paper and the precision of the handwriting was enough to know it came from King Simeon. She felt a moment's relief. It wasn't likely to be anything to do with Jorey.

"A problem?" she asked.

"Simeon's moved back the audience with that half-wit bastard from Asterilhold," Dawson said.

"The ambassador, you mean?"

"Yes, that," Dawson said. "And the new date's the same as Lord Bannien's feast. And if that's not enough, he's asked for a private audience next week the same time I had a table of cards at the Great Bear with Daskellin and his fat cousin who doesn't know how to play."

"Ah," Clara said. She stepped toward him, her hand on his shoulder. He took her fingers in his, kissing her gently without even being aware that he was doing so. Affection was a habit between them, more genuine for being unconsidered. She felt the rise and fall of his body more than heard his sigh.

"That man," he said, "has no idea the things I sacrifice for him."

"He never will," Clara said.

Dawson

The Kingspire was not the original building that took the name. For as long as there had been a Camnipol, there had been a Kingspire, and so with every remaking of the city, every layer of history and ruin, some new castle had been built. Somewhere deep down, pressed into stone and forgotten, was the first Kingspire and the bones of the first kings.

The building Dawson had known as a boy, the one he walked through now, rose high at the northern end of the city, looking out over the Division. In the lower buildings, King Simeon kept his mansions as his father had before him, and his father before that, back four generations to the Black Waters War. Paths of white gravel wound through gardens kept with a precision that approached mathematics. No leaf seemed out of place, no stone off its center. Only the air was wild here, blowing off the southern plains, up through the city, and making its way along the paths in sudden gusts. It plucked the blossoms from the trees, scattering petals like snow and swirling them high into the air to fall slowly back to earth.

The old temple stood apart, its bronze doors permanently locked by Simeon's grandfather, unopened in Dawson's lifetime. The private temple, with its pearl-white windows and sheets of green-enameled steel like the scales of a great lizard or a dragon. Above it all, the great tower rose, smooth-sided, the height of a hundred men, and within it the high-vaulted ceilings rose like the architecture of dreams. Dawson had been in the great tower only three times, and of those, twice had been in the company of the boy prince when they'd both been young and green. He still dreamed about those spaces on occasion. They had been made to awe those within them, and made well.

The king's chambers themselves were surprisingly understated, given the setting. Elsewhere they might have seemed ostentatious or gaudy, but in the shadow of the great tower, a building encased in gold leaf and strung with roses would still have seemed modest. In fact, it was a wide building of stone and wood, glass lanterns set into the walls themselves so that the candles lit within would glow both inside and out. In the bright afternoon sun, the lanterns were dark and ominous.

A servant man in silks and a bronze chain waited for Dawson at the stone garden that led to Simeon's withdrawing rooms. Dawson acknowledged the man's bow with a nod and allowed himself to be led into the cool shadows within.

King Simeon sat beside a small fountain. He wore a shift of simple white cotton, and his hair was disordered as if from sleep. His gaze was on the falling water, silver and white where it sheeted down a bronze dragon almost lost to verdigris.

"A casual audience, is it, Your Majesty?" Dawson said, and his old friend turned. His smile was melancholy.

"Forgive me if I don't rise," Simeon said over the splashing water.

"You're my king," Dawson said. "However low you sit, it's my duty to kneel deeper."

"You always have loved form," Simeon said. "Oh, stop that. Stand up, or at least come and sit by me."

"Form is what gives the world its shape," Dawson said, rising. "If you don't hold to tradition, what is there? A thousand different people each with his own idea of justice, every man trying to force his ideas on the next? We've seen how that ends."

"Anninfort," Simeon said darkly. "You live in a frightening world, old friend, if the only thing between us and that is etiquette."

"Order has always been precious and fragile. By the time the small things have washed away, the large ones are too powerful to stop. Every man in his place. Those meant to lead, lead. Those meant to follow, follow. Civilization doesn't fall into anarchy. That's how it should be. And it's the world you live in too, Your Majesty."

"So it is," Simeon said. "So it is. And still I wish I could leave Aster a better one."

"Change the nature of all history for one boy?"

"I would. If I could, by God I would do it. A world where not everything rests on his shoulders. Where his own people don't plot to have him killed." Simeon seemed to sink in on himself. His skin was greyer than Dawson remembered it, like a pale shirt gone too many times to the launderer's yard. The king combed his fingers through his hair absently. His reflection in the fountain's waves was only a smear of white. "I am sorry. You were right about Issandrian and Maas. I thought I could keep peace."

"You did. Your only error was thinking you could do it without executing anyone."

"And now..."

"Asterilhold," Dawson said, and let the word hang in the air. It was what he'd been called here for. Simeon didn't speak. The water clinked and muttered. Dawson felt a growing unease at the king's continued silence. What had begun as a thoughtful pause stretched until it seemed almost reproach. Dawson looked up, prepared to defend himself or make apology.

Instead, he cried out in alarm. Simeon's eyes were wide and blank and unseeing. His mouth was slack. The stink of piss cut through the air as rank yellow stained the king's lap. It was like an image pulled from nightmare.

And then Simeon coughed, shook his head, looked down.

"Oh," he said. He sounded exhausted. "Dawson? You're here. How long was it this time?"

"A few breaths," Dawson said. His voice was shaking. "What was it?"

Simeon stood, looking down at the urine stain on his shift, the piss running down his legs.

"A fit," he said. "Just a small fit. I'm sorry you saw this. I thought I was done with them for today. Could you call for my man?"

Dawson trotted across the corridor and shouted for the servant. The man came with a fresh shift already in hand. There was no shock in his expression, no surprise. Dawson and the servant looked away as the king stripped off his soiled clothes and put on the fresh. When they were alone again, Dawson sat at the fountain's edge. Everything was just the same as before, but the act of seeing it was different. He felt as if he were looking at Simeon for the first time, and what he saw—what had been there all along unnoticed and unremarked—shocked him. What had been the weight of a crown was suddenly something more sinister and profound. Simeon smiled at him knowingly.

"It was like this for my father too, near the end. Some days I'm almost fine. Others...my mind wanders. He was younger when he died. I am three years older than my father. How many men can say that?"

Dawson tried to speak, but his throat was thick. When he did manage, it was little more than a whisper.

"How long has this been going on?"

"Two years," Simeon said. "For the most part, I've been able to keep it hidden. But it's getting worse. Once was, I'd have weeks or months between them. It's hours now."

"What do the cunning men say?"

Simeon chuckled, and the sound was deeper than the water's laughter. Gentler too.

"They say that all men are mortal. Even kings." Simeon took a deep breath and leaned forward, his forearms on his knees, his hands clasped. "There is a flower that's supposed to help. I keep drinking the tea, but I can't see any difference. I suppose I might be failing faster without it."

"There will be something. We can send for someone..."

His old friend didn't answer. There was no need to. Dawson heard the impotence in his own words, and was shamed by them. All men died, always had and always would. It was only surprise that hollowed his chest.

"I wish Eleanora and I had had Aster earlier," the king said. "I would have loved to see him as a man. With a child of his own, maybe. I remember when Barriath was born. All the jokes were that the boy had eaten you. No one knew where you were or what you were doing. You were gone from all the old places. I resented you for that. I felt left behind."

"I'm sorry, Your Majesty."

"No reason for you to be sorry. I just didn't understand. Then Aster came, and I did. If we'd had him earlier... But then, I suppose it wouldn't have been him, would it? No more than your Jorey is a younger imitation of Barriath. So I can't even wish that. This is the world as it had to be to have my boy in it, and so I can't hate it. Even if I want to."

"I am so sorry, Your Majesty," Dawson said.

Simeon shook his head.

"Ignore me," he said. "I hate it when I get like this. Whine like a schoolboy. Enough. I wanted to talk to you about other things, like the audience with Ashford. What are your thoughts?"

"That you should have it," Dawson said. "As I said before—"

"I know what you said before. You know more now than you did then. I can't take the audience if I'm going to piss myself in the middle of it. Right now, they're frightened of me. Of what I might do. And they're backing away. If Ashford takes back a report that I'm half mad and dying, that song changes. The last time you brought me advice, I turned you away and came within days of handing my child to a man with plans to kill him. So far as I know you're still in control of your own bladder. It makes you more competent than your king. So tell me. What do I do?"

Dawson stood and tried to gather his windswept mind. He felt like he'd just fought a duel. His body had the sense of expended effort and exhaustion, even though he'd done nothing more than walk across a room and call for a servant. He had the sudden, visceral memory of pelting down a street, Prince Simeon at his side. He didn't remember when or where it had happened, but he knew the street had smelled of rain, that Simeon had worn green and he'd worn brown. He swallowed and wiped the back of his hand across his eyes.

"If the fits can be controlled, have the audience immediately," he said. "Prepare beforehand, and keep it brief. No feasts, no private meals, no second audience. Something formal."

"And say?"

"That you'll give Asterilhold the time to clean its own court, but that you expect a full accounting and the heads of those who supported Maas. It's the only option you have. We can't fight a war. Not with you in this condition."

Simeon nodded slowly. His spine seemed more bent now

than when Dawson had first arrived, but it might only have been that he saw now what habit had hidden before.

"And if they can't be controlled?"

"Appoint someone else. An ambassador or warden. If you want someone particular, name him Warden of the White Tower. There hasn't been one since Odderd Faskellin died. Or else... Ah, God."

Dawson sat again.

"Or else?" the king prompted.

"If you're failing fast enough, postpone it and let the regent address it once you're dead."

Simeon's breath was sharp as a man struck.

"That's where we are, aren't we?" Dawson said.

"We may be," Simeon said. "Thank you, old friend. That was what I needed to hear, and I don't believe anyone else would have said the words aloud. Even if everyone were thinking them. Don't take it amiss if I ask you to retire now. I think I need to rest."

"Of course, Your Majesty," Dawson said.

He paused in the archway and looked back. King Simeon had turned away, and Dawson could not see his face. *This is the last time I will see him*, Dawson thought, and then walked away.

At the gates of the Kingspire, he waved his carriage away. He didn't want to be carried now. He wanted to walk. The path between the Kingspire and his mansion was miles, but he didn't care. He adjusted his sword on his belt and started off. He'd spent nights walking and running through the dark streets of Camnipol, racing horses through the empty market squares, drinking until he was too tipsy to walk a straight line and then hanging over the side of a bridge until the vertigo made his head spin. On a night like that, he'd have walked eight miles. Ten. From his dying king to his own drawing rooms weren't half that.

Despite its name, the Silver Bridge spanned the Division with stone and wood. Its supports dug into the walls of the great canyon, falling away as far below the city as the great tower was high. Dawson paused at the center of the span, looking south. A flock of pigeons wheeled through the shadows below him, whirling above the midden heap hidden by darkness and mist at the bottom. He stood for a long time, his mind scoured and raw. Behind him, the traffic of the city passed over the void, men and women, horses and oxen, nobles and peasants. He wept briefly.

When he walked into the courtyard outside his mansion, an unfamiliar carriage stood by the door. The crest on its side and the colors of its cloth announced House Skestinin. The old Tralgu door servant rose and bowed, his chain rattling as he did.

"My lord," he said. "It is very good to see you again. The lady was concerned when your carriage returned empty. She is with Sabiha Skestinin in her private rooms. My Lord Jorey asked to have a word at your convenience. He is in your study."

Dawson nodded and the door slave bowed. Dawson's hunting dogs greeted him just inside the hall, their wide tails flogging the air and sincere canine grins plucking at their mouths. Dawson couldn't help smiling as he scratched their ears. There was no love so pure as a dog's for its master.

He thought of going to Clara before he saw his son, but her rooms were at the farthest end of the mansion and his hips ached from walking. He knew, anyway, what Jorey wanted to talk about. He'd been expecting the conversation since Clara had told him to. Dawson commanded his dogs with a gesture, and they sat as he went into his study and closed the door behind him.

Jorey stood at the window, the afternoon light spilling across his face. It occurred to Dawson again how much the boy could look like his mother. Not in the shape of the jaw so much as the eyes and the color of his hair. It seemed so recent that Jorey had been a thin-limbed boy climbing trees and playing swords with fallen branches. He was broad across the shoulders now, his face serious. And the swords he wielded cut.

"Father," Jorey said.

"Son," Dawson replied, feeling the just-conquered tears struggling behind his eyes. "You're looking well."

"I'm feeling...I need to ask your permission for something. And it may not be something you like hearing."

Dawson sat with a grunt and then immediately wished he'd thought to call for a drink before he had. Not wine. Not today. But a cup of water would have been welcome.

"You want to marry the Skestinin girl," Dawson said.

"I do."

"Even though she brings no honor to the family."

"She does, though. The world may not see it, but it's there. She did something stupid once, and she carries it with her now. But she is a good woman. She won't embarrass you."

Dawson licked his lips. There were a dozen objections and concerns he'd had when Clara first explained who Sabiha Skestinin was, and more that had grown up and been trimmed back only to grow again since they'd come to Camnipol. Who was the father of the offending child, and was Jorey willing to have that man, whoever he was, hold that bit of scandal over him in court for the rest of his life? Wouldn't Barriath, who served under Skestinin in the fleet, be the better match? How could he trust the girl to keep her sex in harness when she'd already shown she couldn't control it unwed?

"Do you still dream about Vanai? The fire?"

"I do," Jorey said, his expression grim.

"Is that guilt the reason you want a fallen woman for your wife? She's something you can save?"

Jorey didn't answer. He didn't have to.

"It would be wiser if you didn't make this alliance," Dawson said. "The girl's history shows what she is. We already have connections to Skestinin, so the family gains very little by it. Your brothers aren't married yet, and it seems odd to have the youngest marry first. When my father came to me and told me who I'd be wed to, I was grateful to him for his guidance and wisdom. I didn't bring some stray home and beg him to keep it."

"I see," Jorey said.

"Do you?"

"Yes, Father."

"If I tell you now to go to the girl and break things off, will you do it? Out of loyalty to me and to this family?"

"Is that what you're saying, sir?"

Dawson smiled, and then laughed.

"You wouldn't," he said. "You'd go to your mother and arrange some way to force my hand or elope to Borja or some other idiocy. I know you, boy. I've changed your diapers. Don't think you can fool me."

Something shy and tentative plucked at the corners of Jorey's mouth. He stepped forward.

"Go," Dawson said. "Take my permission, and do what you'd have done without it. And take my blessing too. She's a lucky girl, my new daughter, to have a husband like you."

"Thank you, Father."

"Jorey," Dawson said, catching his son at the doorway. "The world's briefer than we think, and less certain. Don't wait to have children."

Cithrin

The *Stormcrow* was one of the first ships Cithrin had accepted an insurance contract against, and it took time to put the story together of how she was lost. She was a three-masted roundboat, deep-bellied and well crewed. The captain, a Dartinae man whose eyes glowed green rather than the usual yellow, had walked Cithrin across the deck when the contract had first been made. She still remembered the pride in his voice. He'd told how many times the ship had made the blue-water trade to Far Syramys before he'd settled into his retirement. No more the long, landless weeks navigating by stars and hoping for the distant coasts. Now he was making the simple, riskless trade between the Free Cities, Pût, Birancour, and Narinisle. The storms of the Inner Sea might swamp the little galleys they ran, but not a real ship like the *Stormcrow*. She'd weathered cyclones in the ocean sea. He'd made light of the pirates that haunted the coast of Cabral. Coast-humpers, he called them. *Anyone makes trouble, just set the sail toward open water and let their own cowardice do the rest.*

Cithrin had found him charming, his record of delivery impressive, and his confidence in himself so high that he was willing to accept very good terms on the contract. He insured the cargo only. *If I lose my ship, I'll be dead anyway, and the money won't matter*, he'd said. It hadn't sounded like prophecy at the time.

The ship had wintered in the great port of Stollbourne, sleeping through the winter in the shadow of the floating towers of the Empty Keep. It left Narinisle as soon as the ice broke, heading south for warmer waters and Porte Oliva despite sleet and storm. The journey south was sure and steady. It had joined a group of ships making for Herez and remained in that company for the better part of a week. Then, when the other ships had turned in toward their home ports, it continued south past Cyrin and around the Embers, the sharp stones that rose from the depths of the sea off the cape of Cabral.

It passed Upurt Marion, hailing and being hailed by the captain of another roundship just coming north from Lyoneia. The *Stormcrow* had come that close to home, but never reached Porte Oliva. The other roundship captain said that half a day after the *Stormcrow* had vanished over the horizon, three small, fast ships bearing the colors of no nation had passed by far to the south, leaning toward the open sea.

After that, more guesswork was involved. Without doubt a storm had blown up three days after that last sighting. It made sense, then, to imagine the *Stormcrow* pulling in its sails and nailing battens over her hatches, preparing to endure the high, white-topped waves and the vicious, cutting rain. The captain might have taken the lookout down from the crow's nest with the very real concern that they might be tossed out by the violence of the weather. If so, the pirate ships could have been almost upon her before she knew they were there; black shapes against dark water.

Against an enemy coming in from the sea, the *Stormcrow*'s defenses had little hope. Pirate ships were smaller and more maneuverable, their rigging unconstrained by the needs of long voyages. Perhaps the *Stormcrow* tried for open water, and was intercepted. Perhaps she turned for shore and was chased down. The wreckage that had been blown ashore stank of linseed oil. Pouring oil on the waters was a well-known trick for boarding ships in rough seas, and it made it seem more likely that the assault had come nearer the land.

When the attackers came aboard, the *Stormcrow* would have had her best and final chance for survival. Hooked chains were the most common tools, but there were also sharp-tined boots and braces that a skilled man could use to scurry up the wooden sides of a ship like an insect. Likely several of the pirates had died on the way up, their bodies fallen into the raging water and swallowed at once. But more would have gained the deck. Cithrin imagined that last struggle as bloody and long, with the crew overwhelmed by inches, the decks black with blood and rain. Thunder roaring over the war of wind and waves, lightning crawling through the storm clouds overhead. But it was just as possible that the captain had tried to surrender and been thrown to his death. Whatever the case, the timbers of the ship and bodies of the crew had found their way to the shore. Of the cargo, nothing.

Pyk held up a thick-fingered fist. Dozens of pages filled it. Bills of lading, letters of intent, requests that the Medean bank do what it had promised and make whole the eleven merchants and traders who had put their faith in the *Stormcrow* and been disappointed.

"And what the fuck am I supposed to do with this?" she asked.

Cithrin sat on her hands. Outside the little room in the back of the café, songbirds were building a nest. The scent of Maestro Asanpur's coffee sneaked in through the closed door, calling to Cithrin like the sound of a friend laughing in the next room. She kept her temper in check.

"Make the payments?" she said.

The Yemmu woman rolled her eyes.

"Yes, thank you. I can read the contract. I mean how am I supposed to justify this to the holding company?"

Pyk began putting the papers into stacks like she was dealing out cards in some deeply complex game. Cithrin wanted to take them from her. Seeing the papers there was like a half-starved man standing in a bakery door but not permitted to enter.

"It was a good risk," Cithrin said.

"Then why am I paying out on it?"

"Even good risks fail sometimes. That's why we call them risks. If we only invested in certainties, we wouldn't turn enough profit to eat."

"You cut thumbs on this contract and took in a hundred standard weights of silver. Now I'm supposed to pay out almost a thousand and call it good? Well, thank God we don't have more good risks, then."

"The branch can absorb the loss," she said as Pyk slapped another page on her piles. It was a yellowed strip with ink the color of rust. Cithrin pointed at it. "Don't pay that one."

"What?"

"That sheet. It's from Mezlin Kumas. He's got a reputation for claiming more cargo than he bought. Just a list like that in his own hand? Not enough. If it doesn't have the captain's thumb, you shouldn't pay out."

"Why don't you go outside and play with a ball of yarn or something," Pyk said with a sigh. "I'll take care of this."

Cithrin's outrage felt like heat rising from her belly to her throat. She felt the flush of blood in her cheeks. The tears in her eyes were made from frustration and rage. Pyk put down another sheet over the top of the suspect list, licked her thumb, and went back to dealing out the pages. She didn't look at Cithrin, and her frown drew a hundred thin lines in the flesh of her cheek.

"Why don't you like me?" Cithrin asked.

"Oh, I can't imagine, pet," Pyk said. "Why wouldn't I like you? Hmm. I'm here to do all your work for you, make all the decisions, take all the responsibility, write the reports, and justify myself to Komme Medean and the holding company. But God forbid that I should actually be the voice of the bank. Because that's you, isn't it? You wander around the city playing at being a great lady when you're not old enough to sign your own contracts."

"I didn't ask them to send you here," Cithrin said.

"What you asked for or didn't ask for is the least interesting thing in my day," Pyk said. "It doesn't change anything. The truth is, no matter what you want or intend, no matter what *I* want or intend, I'm the one who'll be called to answer for the failure, and you'll be the one who dines out on the success."

"You could let me help you," Cithrin said. "You know I'm smart enough to carry some of the weight."

"No."

"Why not?"

Pyk put down the papers and turned to face Cithrin directly. The big woman's expression was steely and cold.

"Because you don't answer for it. You can come in and play at being a banker, but you aren't one. No, be quiet. You asked, you can keep your pretty little mouth shut and hear the answer. You're not a banker. You're an extortionist who got lucky."

"That's not—"

"Now you get the status in the eyes of the city, you get to call yourself the voice of the bank, you get the nice clothes and the food and the shelter, and you get it all on my back. They can't fire you until all the poisoned contracts you signed are purged and replaced with something we could enforce. It'll take years. Me, though? They could send a letter and turn me in the streets tomorrow. They won't, but they could. You get all the carrot and none of the stick, and I do the job. That's not enough? I need to *like* you too? You want to put your hooks in me like you've got 'em in your pet mercenary? Well, tough shit, kid."

The notary went silent. Cithrin rose. She felt like she'd been punched, her body vibrating from the depth of the notary's anger, but her head was clear and cold as meltwater. It was as if her body was the only thing frightened.

"I'll leave you to your work, then," Cithrin said. "If there's anything I can do that would help the branch, please let me know."

Pyk made an impatient click in the back of her throat.

"And, really," Cithrin said, pointing to the pages laid out on the table, "don't pay that list."

Cithrin walked through the streets in the southern end of the city nearest the port. The puppeteers were out in force, sometimes as many as three working different corners when two of the larger ways crossed. Many were variations on old themes: retellings of PennyPenny the Jasuru with his bouts of comic rage and violence or stories of cleverness and crime with Timzinae Roaches—often with the three black-scaled marionettes tied to a single cross, their movements literally made one. Other times, the stories were of greater local interest. A story of a crippled widow forced to sell her babies only to have them each returned as too much trouble to keep

could be just a comic tale with a few bawdy jokes and a
trick baby puppet that grew monstrous teeth, but to the residents of the city it was also an elaborate in-joke about a
famously corrupt governor. Cithrin stopped in an open square
to stand and watch a pair of full-blooded Cinnae girls—
paler and thinner even than her—singing an eerie song and
swaying with marionettes in the shapes of bloodied men.
She noticed the girls had filed their teeth to sharklike points.
She wasn't sure if it was more frightening or pretentious. It
was certainly a large personal investment for an effect that
limited the range of performances they could do.

Cithrin mulled over how much of the performer's craft
relied on excellence in a small range and how much on com-
petence over a wide variety of performances. It was, of course,
a single instance of a more general problem, and it could be
applied to the bank as well. A certain range of contracts—
insurance and loans and partnerships and letters of credit—
required relatively little additional expertise. To widen the
business into renting out guardsmen or guaranteeing mer-
chandise in bank-owned warehouses required more resources
and higher expenses, but it also brought in coin that
wouldn't have come in otherwise.

The Cinnae girls struck a series of high, gliding trills,
matching each other in an uncomforting harmony. The one
on Cithrin's left swirled, her dark skirts rising with the
motion to show blue-stained legs. Cithrin saw it and didn't
see it.

It wasn't only her mutilated tusks that made Pyk like the
sharp-toothed puppeteers. Pyk also wanted to limit what
the bank did, restrict it to the few areas in which she was
comfortable and then increase her profits by reducing cost.
Excellence in a narrow circle. It was safe and it was small
and it was absolutely against Cithrin's instincts.

"Magistra," Marcus said. She hadn't noticed him walking up behind her.

"Captain," she said. "How are the guards?"

"We lost a few," he said. "That Yardem and I took the worst pay cuts pulled the punch a little. Still, I'm keeping either me or Yardem at the main house until people stop being quite so sour about it. I'd hate to be the captain whose guard stole the safebox."

The Cinnae girls scowled, their voices growing a degree harsher at the interruption. Cithrin dug out a few weights of copper and dropped them in the open sack between the performers, then took Marcus's arm and walked west, toward the seawall.

"I'm not going to win her over," Cithrin said. "Not ever. It isn't just that we dislike each other. We *disagree*."

"That's a problem."

Cithrin felt her mind at work. From the time she'd been old enough to know anything, her world had been the bank. Coins and bills and rates of exchange, how to set prices and how to exploit prices that others had set poorly. It was what she'd had growing up instead of love.

"I have a proposal I'm looking at from a man who makes his fortune searching for lost things," Cithrin said. "It isn't the sort of thing Pyk would be comfortable with, do you think?"

Marcus looked sideways at her.

"It doesn't sound like the sort of thing she would," he said. "Do banks even do that?"

"Banks do whatever brings money to banks," Cithrin said. "Still, it's given me an idea, and I'd like you to look into it. If you can."

"You know you can't negotiate anything..."

"I don't think that would be an issue. And really, nothing

may come of this. But if it does, we might be able to bring Pyk enough money to restore the guards."

"That's an interesting thought," Marcus said. "What kind of business are you looking to start?"

"Nothing outside the bank. It isn't really even a new business."

"It's looking for lost things."

"Yes."

"Something we've lost."

"Yes."

The seawall was whitewashed stone, and looked out over the pale water of the bay. The dropoff where the deeper water began was a blue as profound as indigo. Near the docks, it was shallow enough to be almost the color of sand. A guideboat was leading a shallow-bottomed galley through the reefs and sandbars that protected the city's seaward face. In the centuries of its life, Porte Oliva had fallen, but never to force.

Marcus leaned against the wall, looking out over the water. The angle of the sun showed the white hair mixed in among the brown. His eyes were narrowed against the light.

"And what is it we lost that you're thinking to look for?"

"The cargo of the *Stormcrow*," she said. "We're about to pay for it. The pirates have to come to ground somewhere. If we can find where, we might be able to recover some part of what we've lost. Even if it was a tenth of the manifest, it would be enough to put the guards back to full pay."

Seagulls wheeled past the wall, wide wings riding the rising air where the breeze from the sea broke against the walls of the city. Seven young Timzinae men in the canvas of sailors walked past, laughing and talking too loud. One of them shouted something playful and obscene. Marcus turned to watch them pass.

"I can ask around, I suppose," Marcus said. "No harm in that."

"It would have to be done quickly."

"I can talk quickly," he said. "What are we trying to do with it? If we find the cargo and bring it back, what do you think we'll have won?"

"We're keeping money for the branch," Cithrin said.

"Pyk's not going to thank us for that."

"We wouldn't be doing it for her."

"Ah," Marcus said. "So it doesn't help with the real problem."

"Not directly. But if the branch does better because of what we do, it may be of use later. When Pyk's moved on."

"And when are you expecting that to be?"

Annoyance knotted itself between her shoulder blades and she crossed her arms. A seagull swooped past, its shadow darkening her face and then vanishing again.

"I have to do *something*," she said. "I can't just sit here and watch her play the game so safely that we lose it."

"Agreed. And I'm in favor of anything that gets my men paid, not to mention myself. Going behind Pyk's back only makes it sweeter. But if it works, the branch does better, and she's more likely to stay."

"But if we cut down the bank in order to get rid of her, then we've cut down the bank."

Cithrin put her palms to her temples. She and Pyk had the same problem at heart.

"If we could just trade roles," she said. "I don't care if I go to banquets and feasts. I just want control of the books."

"Don't think she's likely to agree to that."

"We could kill her," Cithrin joked.

"I'm not sure that would win the trust and approbation of

the holding company," Marcus said. "But we're going to have to do something."

Cithrin shook her head. His words were like swallowing pebbles, a weight growing in her belly. She thought of the taproom, but pushed the thought aside. Ale wasn't going to help. It wasn't even really going to make her feel better. But it might help her sleep.

"They're never going to trust me, are they?" she said. "Komme Medean. The holding company."

"They might trust you once they know you better."

"Well, maybe I'll write them some pretty letters," she said sourly.

"Can't hurt," Marcus said. "Meantime, though, let's see if we can't find your pirates."

Geder

Aster was smaller than Geder by half a head, and Geder wasn't the tallest of men. The boy's reach was less than Geder's, and they were about equally strong. The advantage the prince had was this: he was fast.

The sword hissed through the air as Geder tried to get his own to block it. The blades chimed against each other, the shock of their meeting stinging Geder's fingers. Aster spun, the blade pulled close to his body, and then reached out. Geder understood the attack too late. Aster's stroke caught his shoulder, skidded off the dueling leathers, and ended on his ear. The pain was sharp and disorienting. Sword forgotten, he clapped his palm over his ear, staggered back, and fell on his ass. There was blood on his fingers. He heard Aster's blade clatter to the ground and looked up. The prince's eyes were round with alarm.

Geder laughed and held up his bloodied hand.

"Look!" he said. "It's my first dueling scar. Thank God there's not an edge on the blade, or you'd have had my earlobe off."

"I'm sorry," Aster said. "I'm so sorry. I didn't mean to..."

"Oh, stop," Geder said. "I know you didn't. I'm fine."

He rolled to his feet. The dueling grounds of his mansion were in the back gardens, away from the streets. Old ash trees lined the packed clay, their roots lifting and cracking the ancient stone wall. White roses were richly leaved, but not yet so much as budding. When they bloomed, the yard would be drowned in white petals. Geder got to his feet. His ear still stung, but not badly. Aster smiled uncertainly, and Geder grinned.

"You are a warrior and a man of infinite virtue, my prince," Geder said, making a florid bow. "I yield to you on this field of honor."

Aster laughed and made a formal bow.

"We should have someone put honey on that ear," the prince said.

"Back to the house, then," Geder said.

"I'll race you."

"What? You'd run against a poor wounded—" Geder began, and then broke off sprinting for the main house. Behind him, he heard Aster's protesting yelp and then the pounding of his footsteps.

Geder's boyhood had been, for the most part, in Rivenhalm. As the son of the viscount, he'd had the privileges of nobility, but very little to do with them. There had been servants and serfs enough, but the gap between the highest-born peasant and the heir to the holding was too great to bridge. His father had no love of court, and so Geder hadn't had the chance to know other boys of his class. He read books from the library and built elaborate structures from twigs and string. In the winters, he walked along the frozen river dressed in black furs. In the springs, he carried books to his mother's grave and sat beside her stone reading until the shadows of evening pulled through the valley.

He hadn't thought of himself as lonesome. He had nothing to compare his life with, and so everything about it seemed perfectly normal. As it had always been. As it would always be.

When he'd come of age and entered the world of the court, it had been overwhelming, exciting, and humiliating. Everyone knew better than he did. He'd felt sometimes that there was a secret language everyone besides himself had been schooled in. Another man might say something that seemed perfectly innocuous to Geder—an observation on the length of a coat sleeve, a simple rhyme, a reference to the dragon's roads that passed by Rivenhalm but never through it—and his friends would chuckle. Geder didn't know what they were laughing at, and so he assumed they were mocking him. Before long they were, whether they'd begun that way or not. It was only after Vanai that he'd gained the respect of the court. And by respect, they meant fear. He liked being feared, because it meant no one laughed at him.

Aster, on the other hand, was a real friend. Yes, the prince was nearly a decade younger than Geder, and had been surrounded all his life by friends and playmates. Yes, he knew the court better now than Geder ever would. But he was a boy, and Geder's ward, and they were safe for each other. Geder could climb trees with him, practice dueling, race and laugh and swim at midnight in the fountains. With a man his own age, Geder would have been too wary of seeming foolish or having the desperation of his friendship mistaken for romantic love. With a woman, he probably wouldn't have had the assurance to speak in sentences. But with the prince, Geder could play and laugh and joke and all anyone would see was a man being kind to a child.

The cut on his ear was small but bloody. One of the servants, a lithe Dartinae man with one blind, unglowing eye, dabbed at it with a salve of honey and nettle, then put a bandage over it. Aster's tutor—a severe man in the employ of King Simeon—found them and led Aster off with an air of proprietary dismay that had Geder and the prince both giggling, the one setting off the other. When he was alone, Geder lay back on a divan and let his eyes close. His ear hurt more than he had let on in front of Aster, but the salve was helping. He was halfway to dozing when a soft sound came from the doorway. He opened an eye. His house master stood just inside the room.

"Mmm?" Geder asked.

"A visitor, my lord."

"Oh," Geder said. And then recalling the last time, "Who exactly?"

"Sir Jorey Kalliam, my lord. I've taken him to—"

"North drawing room," Geder said. "That's fine. I'll see myself there."

The house master bowed at the neck and retreated as Geder stretched, tugged his shirt back down over his belly, and rose.

If Geder had a friend of his own age, it was Jorey Kalliam. They had served together under Sir Alan Klin when they took Vanai and during the long weeks when Klin had been the city's protector. Jorey had been with Geder when Vanai burned, and they had broken the mercenary coup that Maas, Klin, and Issandrian had engineered. Jorey's father had been the one to celebrate Geder when he'd returned to Camnipol expecting censure or worse. Without Jorey and his family, Geder would still be just the son of a small viscount and known for nothing more interesting than a fondness for speculative essays. Geder would have called Dawson Kalliam his patron except that he now outranked him.

The winter had been kind to Jorey. His face was calmer than Geder had seen it in living memory, as if he had stepped out of a long shadow. There was color in his cheeks and his smile seemed effortless.

"Geder," he said, rising. "Thank you for seeing me

unexpected. I'm afraid I've been a little scattered. I hope I haven't interrupted you."

"Nothing to interrupt," Geder said, taking him by the hand. "Now that I'm a baron, I'm living a life of dissipation and sloth. You should try it."

"I have two brothers I'd have to bury before I was baron of anything," Jorey said.

"Well, yes. Don't do that if you can help it."

Jorey rubbed his palm against his sleeve uncomfortably. His smile went a degree less certain.

"I've—" he began, then stopped and shook his head as if in disbelief. "I've come to ask you a favor."

"Of course," Geder said. "What can I do?"

"I'm getting married."

"You're joking," Geder said, and then he saw Jorey's eyes. "You have to be joking. We're the same age. You can't be... To who?"

"Sabiha Skestinin," Jorey said. "That's part of why I want you to be part of the ceremony. Your star is on the rise, and having the darlings of the court involved would go a long way to pull the sting."

"The sting?" Geder asked, sitting on the divan where Sanna Daskellin had been. For a moment, he thought he could smell her perfume again. He liked this divan. Good memories were associated with it.

Jorey lowered himself to the seat opposite, his hands clasped before him.

"Well, you know about her trouble."

"No," Geder said.

"Oh," Jorey said. "It was a few years ago. There was a scandal. People still talk about it, usually behind her back. I want to wash that away for her. I want her to see that she isn't the girl the gossips tell stories about."

"All right," Geder said. "You'll have to tell me where to go and what to say, though. I don't think I've ever been part of a wedding before. Oh! The priest. We could have Basrahip be the priest!"

"I...I suppose we could."

"I'll talk with him about it. He isn't traditional, though. Maybe you could have two priests."

"I think just one is more the custom," Jorey said. "But let me find out. But you don't mind? Being part of this, I mean."

"Of course not," Geder said. "Why would I?"

Jorey shook his head and leaned back. He looked bemused and a bit uncertain, as if Geder were a puzzle he'd only half solved.

"You can be a very generous man," Jorey said.

"Not so much, I hope," Geder said. "I mean, it's just being part of a ritual. It's not as if I have to do anything particular apart from being there, do I?"

"All the same, thank you. This carries weight with me. I owe you for it."

"No you don't," Geder said. "But since you're here, I did have something I wanted to ask about. You remember that ambassador from Asterilhold that your father had me meet with?"

"Lord Ashford. Yes."

"Did anything come of that? Because I spoke with the king, but as far as I can tell, he's never given the man an audience. I was afraid that I'd maybe said something wrong?"

You must be ready," King Simeon said.

"No, Your Majesty," Geder said. "I'm sure this is only a passing thing. You'll be healthy and whole again before the summer's out. There are years still before anything like... anything like... And Aster will...would never..."

Geder's words slowed to a stop. His mind reached, out straining for the next phrase, but nothing was there. He heard himself moan low and breathy, and a light-headedness washed over him. He leaned forward and pressed his forehead to his knees.

I must not vomit, he thought. *Whatever happens, I must not vomit.*

The summons had come with the falling day. The spring sun burned low, stretching out the shadows, drowning the streets and alleys in the rising darkness. Night-blooming ivies were opening petals of blue and white as Geder left his mansion, and subdued lights glowed in the windows of Curtin Issandrian. A year before, it might well have been Issandrian who received the courier bearing the royal seal. Or Maas. Or the hated Alan Klin. When he'd reached the Kingspire, the top of the great tower was still bright with the sun when all around it had fallen into twilight. The wind was coming down from the north, cold but not bitter, and setting the trees to nodding. The man who met him was neither servant nor slave, but a kingsman of noble blood come to lead Geder to Simeon's private chamber.

Even now, with his head low and the world spinning, Geder could remember feeling pleased with himself. Baron of Ebbingbaugh and Protector of the Prince answering the urgent call of the Severed Throne. Put that way, it had seemed like a thing of high romance and dignity, a station above anything but idle daydreams. And then this.

Regent. The word was written in airlessness and printed on vertigo.

"Help him," Simeon said. His voice was a damp growl. Gentle hands took his shoulders and lifted him up. The king's cunning man was a Firstblood with swirling tattoos across his body like a Haaverkin. He murmured softly, fingertips pressing at Geder's throat and the inside of his elbow. A warmth flowed into him, and his breath came more easily.

"Is he all right?" the king asked.

The cunning man closed his eyes and placed a palm on Geder's forehead. Geder heard something like distant bells that no one else acknowledged.

"Only the shock, Your Majesty," the cunning man said. "His health is sound."

"I can't believe this," Geder said. His voice was trembling. "I didn't think when I took Aster. I mean, you looked so healthy. I never imagined... Oh, Your Majesty, I am so, so sorry. I am so sorry."

"Listen to me," Simeon said. "I have more energy at sunset, but the confusion comes on. We don't have long to speak. You must take the audience with Lord Ashford. Do you understand? When the time comes, it will be yours. Protect Aster. Make peace with Asterilhold."

"I will."

"I can do everything in my power to leave affairs in order, but my power isn't what it once was."

In the dim room, Simeon looked already half a ghost. His left eye drooped as if his flesh were ready to fall from the bone beneath. His voice was slurred, and he rested on a mountain of pillows tucked to support his powerless spine. Geder wanted to believe that this could be a terrible illness from which a man might recover, but there was nothing before him to suggest it was true. Simeon began to say something, and then seemed to lose focus for a moment.

"I don't know why he's here," Simeon said.

"You summoned me, Your Majesty."

"Not you. The other one. By the doorway. And what's he wearing?" Simeon sounded annoyed. And then frightened. "Oh, God. Why is he *wearing* that?"

Geder turned to look at the empty doorway, dread plucking at the skin all down his back. The cunning man put a hand on Geder's shoulder.

"His majesty won't be able to help you more tonight," the cunning man said. "If his mind comes back, we will send for you, yes?"

"Yes," Geder said. "Thank you."

The night had only just begun, but the thin moon floated high in the darkness. Geder let a footman help him up into his carriage, and sat with his back against the thin wood. The driver called to the team, and the horses jounced him forward, steel-clad hooves and iron-bound wheels punishing the stone. They were almost to the Silver Bridge when Geder lurched forward and called up through the thin window.

"Not home. Take me to the temple."

"My lord," the driver said, and turned.

The torches were lit in their sconces, burning so clean they didn't leave soot on the columns. The spider-silk banner still hung, but in the darkness the red was as dark as the eightfold sigil. Geder paused on the steps and turned. The city spread out before him, lanterns and candles echoing the stars above them like the reflections on still water. The Kingspire, the Division, the mansions of the highborn and the hovels of the low. All of it would be his to command. To control. He would be protector of the realm, of Antea, of the boy Aster. He would be regent, and so in practice, he would be king, and Antea would answer to his will.

He didn't hear Basrahip come out, not because the big priest was being quiet, but because Geder's mind was only halfway in his body. The other half pulled between euphoria and panic.

"Prince Geder?"

The wide face was concerned. Geder sat on the steps. The

stone still held some of the day's heat. Basrahip gathered up the hem of his robes and sat at Geder's side. For a long moment, the two men sat silently, like children tired at the end of the day looking out into a back alley.

"The king's going to die," Geder said. "And I'm going to take his place."

The priest's smile was serene.

"The goddess favors you," he said. "This is how the world is for those who have her blessing."

Geder turned back. The breeze passed ripples through the dark banner, and a passing dread touched him.

"She's not...I mean, the goddess isn't killing the king for me? Is she?"

Basrahip laughed low and warm.

"This is not her way. The world is made from little lives and little deaths because she wills it this way. No, she does not make the waves, she only puts her chosen in the place where they are borne always up by them. She is subtle and she is sure."

"All right. Good. I just wouldn't want Aster to lose his father in order for things to go well for me." Geder lay back, resting his spine against the steps. "I'm going to have to tell him. I don't know how to do that. How do you tell a boy that his father's dying?"

"Gently," Basrahip said.

"And the ambassador from Asterilhold? The one who wanted me to talk the king into a private audience? Now it looks as if I'm going to be the one taking that audience."

"I will be with you," Basrahip said.

"The king told me what he wants, though, so at least I know what I'm supposed to do. With that one. And there'll be people who help me. The regent has advisors just like the king. It won't be like Vanai where everyone wanted me to fail," Geder said. A fragment of dream slipped up from the back of his mind. The flames of Vanai danced before him again, silhouetting a single, desperate figure. The voice of the fire roared, and Geder felt the guilt and horror freshly for a moment before he locked it away again. He was the hero of Antea. What happened in Vanai was a good thing. When he spoke again, his voice was stronger. "It won't be like Vanai."

"As you say."

Geder chuckled.

"Alan Klin's going to shit himself when he hears," he said with a grin.

"What are you supposed to do?" Basrahip asked.

"Hmm?"

"The ambassador."

"Oh. Simeon wants me to keep Aster safe and make peace with King Lechan. I told him I would."

"Ah," Basrahip said. And a moment later, "And when you cannot do both, which will you choose?"

Marcus

From the fall of dragons to the days still to come, all things human were made and determined by structures made by something greater and crueler. The great monuments were perhaps the least important. The unreachable tower at the center of Lake Esasmadde, the Grave of Dragons in Carse, the Empty Keep. They could inspire fear or awe, they could call forth a sense of mystery, but the greater power lay in the prosaic. The dragon's roads crossed the nations, and where they met, cities grew, fed by the traffic and advantage that good roads brought. The thirteen races were also constrained by the will of the great masters who had first created them. The Cinnae were thin and pale, unsuited for battle, and so confined themselves to the well-defended hills and valleys of Princip C'Annaldé. Tralgu and Jasuru and Yemmu, bred for violence and formed for war, found their homes in the Keshet where the plains gave no natural barrier against invaders and whatever war won in a given season proved impossible to defend in the next. Where the landscape called for war, the races most suited to war prospered. Where it allowed shelter from violence, those in need of shelter came. The mark of the dragons had been on the world from the beginning of history, and would be until the end of all things.

The mark was there, but it was not changeless.

Around every great city fed by paths of dragon's jade, there were others—townships, hamlets, some little more than waystations—where the roads were paved by human hands. Where the great roads met, and the great cities grew, the farmlands were, over the course of centuries, used up. The richer soil farther away grew in value, and new places— peculiarly human places—were born.

And as the landscape changed, so did humanity, straining at the bindings woven into its blood. The races were unmistakable and unmixed only in the minds of the people. True, not all races could interbreed. A Cinnae woman could no more bear to a Yemmu man than a rat terrier could whelp a mastiff, and there were other combinations of blood that gave no offspring, or whose issue were themselves sterile. The difficulty of bearing a mixed-breed child allowed the thirteen races to stand apart from one another, but considered carefully, no race but the Drowned was pure. A Tralgu with wider-set, darker eyes might have Southling blood somewhere generations back. Secret marriages between Haaverkin and Jasuru could take place. Between Firstblood and Cinnae, such pairings were merely distasteful and scandalous. History was also marked by less pleasant pairings, and not all women who suffered rape at the hands of enemy soldiers could bring themselves to slaughter the babes that came of the crime.

The history of the races was a complex tissue of love and revulsion, landscape and design, war and trade, secrets and indiscretions. Cithrin bel Sarcour was only one example in Marcus's broad experience. The man who sat across the low wooden table from him was another. Capsen Gostermak was the child of a Jasuru mother and a Yemmu father. His skin was pocked where the bronze scales of his mother's race never fully formed and his jaw was crowded with pointed, vicious teeth that were as unlike the Yemmu tusks as Jasuru teeth. He looked like a monster from a children's story, neither one thing nor another, but entirely built to fight. No one who didn't know the man would have guessed that he styled himself a poet or that he raised doves.

The house was stone and mortar near the center of Cemmis township. In the falling twilight outside, Capsen's sons played in among the other children of the township, kicking the body of a dead rat around the base of the dovecote, shrieking with the glee that comes of disgust and the heartlessness of boys.

"There is a place," the half-breed said. "It's not nearby, but it's not far either. A cove that people don't go to."

"Can you guide us there?"

"No," Capsen said. "I will tell you where to look, but I have a family. This isn't any business of mine."

Marcus glanced up at the doorway. Yardem Hane leaned against the stone frame, arms crossed and expression unreadable. It was half a day back to Porte Oliva along a road that followed the shore. Marcus didn't like both of them being away from the bank and its safebox, but Yardem had insisted that he not come alone. Outside, a child screamed in what could have been pain or joy.

"All right," Marcus said. "Two weights of silver for a map. Another two if our pirates are there when we get there."

"Paying me to talk and paying me to keep quiet?"

"You win both ways," Marcus said.

Capsen rose and walked to the cupboard. It was made from wood that the tide brought to the beach, and it left the room smelling faintly of tar and salt. As Marcus watched, he reached to the top shelf and brought down a bit of parchment a bit wider than Marcus's hand. Dark ink marked it.

He put it on the table and Marcus picked it up. The curve of the coastline was unmistakable, and four good landmarks were already drawn in and labeled. The man had been prepared. That was either a very good thing or a bad one. If the township was ready to help him against the pirates, it made recovering the cargo more likely. If Capsen thought someone was going to be brought to justice, it would be a little more awkward.

But that was for later. Marcus took a pouch off his belt and pulled out four measures of silver and put them on the table. Then two more. Capsen's eyebrows rose.

"For the name," Marcus said. "I like to know who I'm fighting."

"Why do you think I know his name?"

Marcus shrugged and reached for the extra coins.

"Rinál. Maceo Rinál. He's some sort of noble blood in Cabral."

"All right, then," Marcus said, folding the map and tucking it in his belt. "Good talking with you."

"We'll be seeing you again, I hope?"

Marcus ducked through the door and Yardem fell in behind him. The sea stretched out to the south, the calm grey of lead. The last red and gold of sunset still haunted the western horizon. Part of him wanted to take the horse now, go farther west. The cove wouldn't be farther than the two of them could ride by midnight. In the worst case, they'd be discovered, and then at least there'd be a fight.

But his men were in Porte Oliva. And Cithrin was waiting for word. Going farther was a risk he didn't need to take, not now, but it was a temptation. A restlessness looking for escape.

"Sir?"

Let's just take a look floated at the back of his tongue.

"We head to the city," he said. "We'll get some blades behind us and come back."

Yardem's ears rose.

"What? That's a surprise?"

"Almost expected we'd be going on, sir."

"That'd be stupid."

"I don't disagree, sir. Just thought it might be the mistake we made."

Marcus shrugged and headed back for the horses, troubled by the knowledge that if he'd been alone, he would have done it.

They made camp in a stand of green oaks, their horses tied to an ancient altar tucked away among the trees, ivy-covered, eroded and forgotten. In the morning, Marcus broke the night's fast with a strip of salt-dried goat and a handful of limp springpeas still in the pod. Approaching Porte Oliva from the west was harder terrain than it looked. The hills were green with grass and heather, but it was uneven. Broken stones hid everywhere, ready to turn under a misplaced hoof. There was a story that a king of Old Cabral had launched an invasion of Birancour along this coast, only to have his cavalry lamed before the first battle. Marcus didn't believe it, but he didn't disbelieve it either.

The high, pale walls seemed darker with the sun behind them. The traffic into and out of the city was choked with beggars, but he was well enough known in the city now that they bothered him less. That group of liars and thieves were better attuned to travelers, as if by smelling of Porte Oliva he were already complicit in the wrenching stories of sick babies and the twisted legs that worked better when no one was looking. To be ignored by the beggars was a mark of citizenship, and even though it was invisible, Marcus wore it now. In the midst of the stalls and the houses and the complex web of streets, he passed through the fortification wall and then into the city proper.

Marcus was just leaving the stables when an unexpected voice called his name. By the mouth of a small side street stood a long-faced man with tall, wiry hair and the olive complexion of Pût. He wore a simple brown robe and carried a walking staff that was black from use where he held it. For the first time in weeks, Marcus felt a grin come to his mouth unbidden.

"Kit? What are you doing here?"

"I hoped I would find you, actually," the master actor said. "And Yardem Hane! I am pleased to see you again. I think the city life must be agreeing with you, yes? I don't believe I've ever seen you looking so healthy."

"He means fat," Marcus said.

"Knew what he meant, sir," Yardem said, feigning displeasure. Then he broke into a wide, canine grin. "I didn't expect the company to come back so soon."

Master Kit hesitated.

"They haven't. I've been traveling on my own. I was hoping to talk to you about that, Marcus. If you have time for it. If you have business with Yardem, of course, I wouldn't want to interrupt it."

Marcus glanced over at Yardem. He saw from the angle of the Tralgu's head that he'd heard the same thing. The request for a private meeting, even without his second. Yardem shrugged.

"I'll make the report to the magistra," Yardem said.

"Would you be kind enough not to mention seeing me?" Kit asked.

Yardem's ears were at high alert now. Marcus nodded once.

"If you'd like," Yardem said. "I'll be at the counting house, sir."

"I'll be along shortly," Marcus said. "Soon as I find what Kit's being so mysterious about."

The common house Kit led him to sat at the edge of a narrow square in the salt quarter. A dry fountain no more than a man's height across stood at the center, still seeming too large for the space. Pigeons strutted and cooed and shat. Marcus and Kit shared a bench as a Firstblood woman with brown hair, brown eyes, and a vast birthmark purpling her neck brought them mugs of hard cider. For a time, they talked about the company—Sandr and Smit and Hornet. Mikel and Cary. Charlit Soon, the new actor they'd picked up in Porte Oliva before they'd left for the north. It was the usual gossip and stories, but Marcus thought there was fear behind it.

When Kit paused once a bit too long, Marcus pressed the issue.

"Did something happen with the company?" he asked.

"Nothing more than losing an actor, I hope. I think they are really quite a talented group. Without me, I'd weigh their chances as good as anyone's."

"But you left them."

"I did. Not from want. I've found something I need to do that I didn't want them exposed to. It was hard enough losing Opal, and what happened to her was her own doing."

Marcus sat forward. They weren't too far from the stretch of wall where Opal, leading lady of Kit's actors and Cithrin's betrayer, had ended her life. Marcus felt like he should recall better how she'd died, but for the most part he just remembered that he'd done it and pitched her body through the gap in the seawall.

"Is that why you wanted me?" Marcus asked. "Is this about Opal?"

"No," Kit said. "It isn't."

Marcus nodded.

"What's the issue, then?"

The old man laughed, but there was no joy in the sound. His eyes had dark pouches under them and he held his cup in both hands, as if weary.

"I have come here from Camnipol to talk with you, and now that I'm here I'm finding it hard to choose the words. All right. I am going on an errand. I expect it to be very dangerous. I may not survive it."

"What is this, Kit?"

"I believe something...*evil* has been loosed in the world. I can't think of anyone beside myself who is in the position to oppose it. I feel I must go, and for some rather complicated reasons, I would rather not go alone. In all my travels, I've met very few people who I thought would be well suited to a task like this. You are one. I would like you to come with me."

As if in answer, the pigeons rose up as one: fluttering pearly wings and a rush of dung-scented air. Marcus drank some of his cider to give himself a moment's thought.

"The most likely thing is you've spent too long playing at stories and it's gone to your head," Marcus said.

"I wish I could think that was true." Kit sighed. "If I were mad, it would only be one lost man in a world of people. But I think I'm sane."

"Madmen often do. What's this thing you're supposed to defeat?"

"The details might not make me seem saner," Master Kit said. "And I think they wouldn't be safe to share. Not yet. Not here. But say you'll come with me, and I promise I will give you proof that some at least of what I say is true. I'm going south and then east. Far east. I think it won't be safe, but it would be safer if I had you."

"I can recommend some bodyguards," Marcus said. "I just lost a few that I wish I'd been able to keep, so I even know where there are some swords looking for coin. I can't go anywhere. I have a job."

"You're still happy working for Cithrin and the bank, then?"

"Being happy isn't what makes it a job," Marcus said. "It's what I do."

"How long is your contract?"

"I work for Cithrin."

Kit's eyebrows came together, knotting up like caterpillars. "I see."

"I can find you good men," Marcus said.

"I don't want good men. I want you," Kit said, then laughed. Despite his anxiety, he had a warm laugh. "Oh, I think that didn't come out the way I meant. I wish you would agree to this, Marcus. I don't want to force the issue."

"You couldn't."

"I could," Kit said. "And I am tempted to. But I consider you a friend, and I choose not to. I hope that carries some weight. I have some preparation still to do. I will stay nearby as long as I can, in case you have a change of heart. I would, however, appreciate it if we could keep my presence quiet."

"Is someone hunting for you?"

"Yes," Kit said and took another long bite of his cider.

The birthmarked woman came forward, pointing to their cups. Marcus shook his head. He didn't need more alcohol.

"If you need help, I'll do what I can for you during the quiet days when the bank doesn't need me," Marcus said. "That's the best I've got."

"I appreciate that."

For a moment, Marcus was silent, searching for some other word to say. Instead, he clapped the man on the shoulder and left his half-drunk cup on the bench beside him. It wasn't a long walk to the counting house, but Marcus took it slowly. He hadn't had the opportunity to refuse work since he'd taken up with Cithrin bel Sarcour and her bank. As he stepped around the horse shit in the street and passed the queensmen in their uniforms of green and gold, it occurred to him for the first time that he might have already taken the last contract of his life.

Working for the bank had no clear ending, no keep to be guarded through the summer or taken by autumn. His men weren't soldiers but guards. Not even guards, sometimes, but a private force. Thumb-breakers for a moneylender. That wasn't work that had to end.

For a moment, he imagined himself decades in the future, walking down these same streets. Time would take his hair or turn it white. His joints would thicken and ache. Perhaps he'd find a woman who could put up with his moods and memories. He could work the company until he became so domestic and old and comfortable that he was nothing more than a mascot. The man who'd moved the world once, though you wouldn't know it to look at him now. A future rolled out before him so clearly, he felt he could reach out and touch the old man's shoulder.

He had to stop for a moment and look up at the sky. This was what Canin Mise felt sitting in his debtor's box, buried with his face in the air. This was what death was like. He almost turned back, going to find Master Kit and the cider and whatever madness had taken the old man, only because it wouldn't be the story he'd seen before him.

But it would mean leaving Cithrin. The counting house

was only a couple of streets farther on, and he made himself walk there through simple will. Yardem was waiting for him outside, pacing anxiously.

"Sir?"

"I'm fine."

"Is there anything—"

"No, Yardem, there's *nothing*. Nothing at all, ever, anywhere."

The Tralgu put his ears back. Marcus wanted to see anger in the man's eyes or hurt or something besides concern. Concern looked too much like pity.

"We've been doing very well, sir. The bank's solid. The company's underfunded just now, but they're loyal and well trained. Pyk's an annoyance more than a problem. If you look at where we've come since Ellis—"

"You're not about to feed me some hairwash about how my soul's a circle, and I'm at the top turning down, are you?"

Yardem's hesitation meant yes.

"No, sir," he said.

Clara

Thankfully, Jorey managed to deflect Geder Palliako from using his friends from the Keshet, and so the ceremony was at the high temple, and scheduled for the day after Canl Daskellin's fireshow had opened the season. It allowed very little time, however, to follow all the forms. Clara had arranged two dinners with Lady Skestinin, and one with both families. Lord Skestinin hadn't arrived until the morning of the event, and had all but abandoned the fleet to manage that much. Barriath had come with him, and Vicarian had special dispensation to leave his studies and attend the ceremony as well, so all her boys were there on the day. The chances were fair that they would even behave themselves for the most part. For Sabiha's sake more than Jorey's.

In fact, if Jorey had chosen a lover specifically to make his brothers behave, he could hardly have done better. The hint of scandal and disapproval that hung over the occasion would, Clara thought, bring the boys together where a match with someone above reproach would have begged for teasing. And really, once the teasing started, there were lines the boys would cross before they knew they existed.

Elisia, on the other hand, had sent regrets. As odd as it felt to hope her daughter was ill, Clara preferred to believe she really did have the flux. People recovered from the flux, after all. Shame and disloyalty were harder to overcome. But that was a problem for another day. The work at hand was more than enough to keep her occupied.

The temple itself was perfect.

The great circle of the floor was white marble carved generations ago and worn smooth as water. The altar stood black and green in the center, the great vaulted dome rising above it. The archways were carved as dragon's wings, surrounding and enveloping the wide, white air. Clara had instructed her servants to harvest boughs of the cherry trees from her own gardens. The leaves were few and weak, but the blossoms pulled the white of the stone into their petals. The benches all around the circumference sported silk cushions in the colors of the houses for whom they were reserved, red and gold and brown and black and indigo. And at the front, in the places of honor, chairs of worked copper for the girl's family and bronze for her own. And an extra seat in silver with the grey and blue of House Palliako where Geder and Prince Aster would sit.

Walking through it now, with only hours before the event itself, Clara's footsteps echoed. The silk damask of her gown whispered. She walked to the chair she would take during the ceremony and looked up into the huge, unseeing eyes of the dragon staring back at her. As with her friends in the high circles of court, her piety had always been another kind of etiquette. God was, and because of that it would be rude to sleep during the high chant or scratch during the consecration. Now, staring up, she felt something between sorrow and hope struggling in her, and lifted her hand to the dragon.

"Let them be happy with each other," she said.

"Do you think they won't be?" Dawson said from the columns before her.

He wore black and gold today, the colors of the Undying

City. Against the pale stone, the cloth seemed richer and darker, like a fold cut from the midnight sky. Clara smiled at him.

"I hope they will. That's all. And since I'm powerless, I do what one does when one is powerless."

"Pray?"

She held out her arms as if presenting an example. He walked across the stone, out from under the stone dragon's shadow. He looked tired and pleased and handsome. He put an arm around her waist and turned to look where she was looking. Clara leaned into him. His arms were as solid and strong now as they had been one day, many, many years before.

"Let them be happy with each other," he said, his words echoing against the stone. But of course, his prayer wasn't to the dragon or to God. It was an offering to her, a statement of complicity. "Do you remember when it was our turn to stand there?"

"I do," she said. "Well, parts of it. I'd been drinking wine for courage, and I may have crossed over into tipsy."

"Oh, yes. Yes, you did."

She leaned her head against his.

"Am I needed?" she asked.

"You are. The Palliako boy's entirely over his head, and Jorey needs to start seeing to his own preparations."

Clara took a deep breath and straightened her spine.

"Lead me to the battle lines, my dear," she said.

As with any spring wedding where the wind allowed, the feast was held in the temple grounds. Clara's count was five hundred invited guests, but the press made it seem closer to a thousand. By tradition, Skestinin decorative cloth was tied to the tree branches, and slaves of several races stood in ceremonial cages, singing anthems to Antea and God and the return of spring. Clara found Jorey standing guard over Geder Palliako at one such where a tiny Cinnae girl, so thin and pale she seemed spun from sugar, worked her ribs like a bellows, chanting out a proud, rousing song in a language Clara didn't recognize.

The problem was obvious at a glance. Canl Daskellin's daughter, Sanna, was smiling ice at the eldest of Bannien's girls while Nesin Pyrellin looked on the edge of tears. A flicker of embarrassment pinched Clara's heart, and she wondered if she had ever been so obvious and undignified herself. She truly hoped not.

It wasn't entirely their fault, of course. The life of a woman in court was always bound and defined by marriage, and in a way it was a blessing. She'd taken her turn in the temple before her twentieth name day, and ever since then her place in court had been fixed. She was Lady Kalliam, Baroness of Osterling Fells, but she could as easily have been Baroness of Nurning or merely Lady Mivekilli, wife to the Earl of Lowport. In any case, her place and rank would be determined, and she would have been just as free to make what life she wished within those bounds. Without Dawson at her side, she would still have been Clara. But what that *meant* would have changed. These girls looked at Geder Palliako and saw the opportunity for stability and status and power. They did because they had been taught to, and because they were right.

Still, they couldn't be permitted to ruin the day over it.

"Baron Ebbingbaugh!" Clara said, swooping down and hauling Geder's arm around her own. "I have been looking everywhere for you. You don't mind if I appropriate Lord Palliako, dear?"

"That would be fine, Mother," Jorey said, his eyes offering the thanks he couldn't say aloud.

Clara smiled and angled Geder away, guiding him carefully enough that it wasn't obvious he was being led. There was an alcove at the side of the temple where she might plausibly have a moment's conversation, though for the life of her, she didn't know what it would be about. The odd thing about Geder Palliako—the thing that no one else commented upon—was how much and often he changed. She'd been vaguely aware of him the way you were of people at the periphery of the court before he and Jorey had gone off to the Free Cities. She'd seen him when he returned from there and danced with him at his revel. He'd seemed stunned and lost and amazed, like a child watching a cunning man turn water to sand for the first time. Then he'd disappeared for that long, terrible summer, and returned thinner and harder and confident. And knowing, it seemed, all there was to know about poor Phelia Maas and her husband. And now here he was after a winter in his new holdings with a bit more flesh under his chin and carrying a cloud of anxiety with him so thick it dampened the skin.

"Thank you, Lady Kalliam," Geder said, craning his neck to look back toward the collected young women of the court. She wasn't sure if he was hoping to see them following or fearing the prospect. Both, perhaps. "I'm not at my best at these things."

"It can be awkward, can't it?"

"A baron without a baroness," Geder said with a tight little smile. "None of them liked me before, you know."

"I'm certain that isn't true," she said, though really she was certain it was.

She watched him catch sight of someone or something, eyes narrowing in anticipation and pleasure. Clara turned to see Sir Alan Klin arrive.

The man looked so pale he was almost ghostly. Seeing his

friend and conspirator executed for murder and treason had hit him like an illness, and he hadn't remotely recovered. Geder had been under Klin's command, and Clara knew there was some petty feud between them. The powerful memory came to Clara of Barriath, her eldest boy, just before his seventh name day lighting moths on fire. Innocence and cruelty defined young boys. They were what she saw now in Palliako, and it reminded her of how it had felt to be the mother of three young sons.

"Excuse me," Geder said, extricating his arm from hers. "There's someone here I've been wanting to see."

"Of course," she said.

Geder walked over toward Klin, bouncing slightly on the balls of his feet. Just a little spring in the step. Clara watched him go with a combination of affection and dread. *God help the woman that catches him*, she thought.

A shout came from the other end of the temple, and then a man's voice in a roar. Clara hurried toward it, fearing some new crisis. A group had gathered and was beginning to cheer someone or something, and then Sabiha Skestinin appeared above them all, hoisted onto someone's shoulders. Her gown was the green of new leaves, her hair braided back so that her face was visible. She was laughing and gripping something hard to keep her balance. The roar came again, and the girl's eyes opened wider in alarm as she began to move. The crowd didn't part so much as follow along behind. Barriath and Vicarian ran with their soon-to-be-sister lifted between them, each held one of the girl's ankles to keep her from tipping backward, and she had her fingers wrapped tight in Barriath's thick black hair. Barriath still wore his naval clothes with the emblem of House Skestinin on his shoulder to honor his commander. Vicarian had his white priest's robes, but without the golden braid of final vows. All three laughed and howled as they tore through the gardens in the mock kidnapping of the bride.

Pride and satisfaction rose in Clara's breast. Whether they were aware of it or only divined it by instinct, the message her boys were sending read clear. *The girl is ours now, not only Jorey's. She is a Kalliam, and if you cross her, you cross us.* Clara caught a glimpse of scarlet and gold in the crowd: Prince Aster laughing along with the others, pulled by the gaiety and the young women. The only thing that could have made the day better would have been Simeon walking at Dawson's side.

The ceremony itself began an hour before sunset. Dawson and Clara took their seats. Lord and Lady Skestinin took theirs as well. Then Geder Palliako and Prince Aster, whispering to each other like schoolboys, and slowly, with great pomp and care, the court of Antea filed into the room. Men and women Clara had known since she was a girl, friends and allies. The whole court, or near enough, had come to see her son and Skestinin's daughter remake themselves and become something new.

As the priest led the chant, Clara closed her eyes. Dawson took her hand and she glanced over, wiping away the tears. He, of course, was dry-eyed and proper. To him, the ceremony was calming and reassuring because it was exactly as it was supposed to be. The form that kept the chaos of the world in check. When the time came for them to join the pair at the altar, Clara did it with more grace and certainty than she'd managed at her own.

After the last blessing, they streamed out into the night. There was still a chill in the air, winter reaching back toward them from its grave. Jorey and Sabiha rode away in a carriage, returning to the mansion. In the morning, the girl would be there at the breakfast table along with her sons.

They would all begin the long, tentative dance of conversation and etiquette that would, in time, make her sons' tacit claim true. The girl would become a Kalliam in fact as well as name. There was time.

For tonight, there would be long talks at the Great Bear and the other, lesser fraternities. Dawson and Lord Skestinin would bring celebratory gifts to their friends and allies, drink themselves silly, and sleep too late in the morning. Clara would guard the house and make sure the new couple weren't interrupted or abused by revelry gone too far. She waited at the temple door as the carriages and palanquins clustered in the street and footmen from a hundred different houses shoved and cursed and fought to follow the dictates of their masters. Lady Skestinin came and stood with her for a time, the pair of them talking about nothing very much—the winter just gone by, the dresses worn by the women of the court, the inevitable cough Canl Daskellin's fireshow had inspired in his audience. At no point was gratitude offered to Clara, nor did she make any move to suggest it should be. When Lord Skestinin gathered up his wife, both women felt comfortable that they knew where the other stood. So that was well.

The lanterns were all lit in the courtyard when she arrived home. The full staff of the house, servants and slaves alike, were turned out as if prepared for a massive gathering. On the one hand, the household was her mercenary company, doing her will and watching. No one would come or go from the house tonight except Clara would know of it. And by keeping them in the halls and passages, watching the gardens and windows, they'd be less likely to eavesdrop on Jorey and Sabiha. Her son and her new daughter.

She sat in her withdrawing room eating honeyed bread and drinking tea and thinking about grandchildren. Of course, there already was one, of sorts. Sabiha's scandalous child would be old enough to call for his mother by now. Old enough to crawl. He wouldn't know that his mother had begun a new life today. He might not even know who his mother was. Certainly Lord Skestinin hadn't allowed Sabiha to be with the child, much less care for it.

Clara lit her pipe, picked up her embroidery, and promised herself to look into conditions for the boy in the morning. Now that Sabiha was part of her household, it would fall on Clara to be sure the boy was cared for honorably and otherwise never heard from again.

A gentle knock came at the door, and she called out her permission. The master of house had arranged the gifts and had the accounting ready for her. She held out her hand, and he laid the length of paper in it. Lord Bannien had gifted them with two geldings from his stables and a small carriage in the colors of House Kalliam. Lord Bastin had offered up a silver box with a half ounce of spice worth more than Bannien's horses and carriage together, if it was truly what he claimed. Even Curtin Issandrian had offered up a hand mirror from the glassworks of Elassae, rimmed in silver and stamped with their two names together.

This was what weddings were for, after all. The opportunity for kindness and extravagance. The chance for last year's rivals to become this season's friends or, failing that, at least friendly acquaintances. It was the other side of the battles and intrigues, this creation of bonds and connections. They were weaving the fabric of civilization. What Dawson protected with common rites and tradition, Clara built for herself out of notes of gratitude and imported hand mirrors. Neither strategy was better than the other, and both were necessary.

She went to bed late, Dawson still not returned to the

house, and slept almost at once. She was dreaming of mice and a spinning wheel when the familiar touch brought her partway to wakefulness. The dream receded and her own room swam into focus. Dawson sat at the edge of the bed, still in his festive black and gold. For a moment, she thought he had come to celebrate in his own way, and she smiled lazily at the prospect of their familiar physical intimacy.

The candlelight caught his face, the tear tracks shining on his cheeks, and all vestige of sleep in her died. Clara sat up.

"What's happened?"

Dawson shook his head. He smelled of fortified wine and rich tobacco. Her mind went instantly to Jorey, to Sabiha. Too many tragic songs called forth the calamity of the bridal night. She took her husband by the shoulder and twisted him until his eyes met her.

"Love," she said, keeping her voice steady. "You have to tell me what's wrong."

"I am old and growing older," he said. "My youngest son has a wife and a family of his own, and the companions of my boyhood are leaving me. Pulled away into darkness."

He was drunk, but the sorrow in his voice was unmistakable. He wasn't sad because he'd drunk too much, rather he'd drunk too much from being sad.

"Simeon?" she asked, and he nodded. When he answered, his voice was melancholy.

"The king is dead."

Cithrin

Northeast in Narinisle, the grey stone city of Stollbourne, center of the blue-water trade. Southeast in Herez, Daun the city of lamps and dogs and the great mines of the Dartinae. South in Elassae, the five cities of Suddapal commanding the trade of the Inner Sea. In Northcoast, Carse and the Grave of Dragons and Komme Medean and his holding company. Once, not very long ago in the Free Cities, Vanai, and now in the southern reaches of Birancour, Porte Oliva. The branches of the Medean bank spread across the continent like spokes on a wheel. Cithrin sat at her table and traced her fingertips across the map and dreamed of them.

Her life for as long as she remembered had been in Vanai. When it burned, her past burned with it. The streets and canals she'd played in when she was a child were gone now, as were almost all the people who remembered them. If she couldn't quite recall whether a particular street sat north or south of the market square, the knowledge was simply lost to the world. There was no way to find out, and worse, no reason to.

Porte Oliva was her home because chance brought her there. The branch bank was hers—to the degree it wasn't Pyk's—because she'd gambled and won. And also because Magister Imaniel had taught her his trade. Suddapal was only stories to her. She had never been so far east, had never seen

the great fivefold city standing out on the ocean. Never heard
the cries of the black seagulls or watched the gatherings of the
Drowned under the waves. But she knew quite a bit about
how the gold and spice came up from Lyoneia through it.
How the oxen of Pût would float on great flat barges along
the coast and be sold at the markets on the shore below the
city. Given a week to study the books at the counting house,
she would understand the logic of the Suddapal and the forces
that drove it better than the native-born. Coins had their own
logic, their own structure, and that she knew. So in a sense,
she knew everywhere, even if she'd never been.

She traced the western coastline. There was no branch in
Princip C'Annaldé. But there was family. Her mother's people, full-blooded Cinnae. She knew nothing of them except
that when they'd been offered the half-breed orphan babe,
they'd refused her. The rejection didn't sting. It would be
like a man full-grown missing a toe he'd been born without.
It was a fact like the sky's color and the sea's rhythm. People
of her blood lived here—she tapped the map—and they
might as well have burned in Vanai for all it changed.

And north of them, Northcoast. To its west, the Thin Sea
and Narinisle. To its east, Asterilhold and Imperial Antea. It
was the center of the bank's web, touching all the trade
along the north. Its shadow fell all the way to the warm blue
waters of the Inner Sea.

They might trust you once they know you better. The
captain had said that, only they never would. The way they
might have—they way she'd hoped they would—was through
the reports she sent north. If they could have seen how she
guided the bank, how the profits and losses balanced, how
the contracts grew, they'd know her mind at work. Shackled
by her notary, Cithrin was the servant of her servant, and
there was no way to break free.

She wished she could send Pyk away. If there was some errand of the bank, something important enough that it had to have someone there, but not so much that it constrained the rest of the operating funds, maybe Pyk would have no choice but to leave things in Cithrin's hands.

And while she was dreaming, maybe a dragon would come back to life, carry Pyk out to sea, and feed her to a gigantic crab. Why dream small?

The knock at the street door at the bottom of her stairs broke her reverie. She stood, tugging at her dress to pull it back into order. It was the first job of a banker to be able to appear one thing while doing something else. In her case, she would seem to matter.

The knock came again.

"A moment," she snapped.

She pulled back her hair in the fashion Cary and Master Kit had said would make her seem older and fit pins through the back to hold it in place. She looked at the face paints. She never used much, and what she did was intended to age her. Well, she hadn't bothered, and if Magistra Cithrin happened to have a day where she looked a bit younger than usual, perhaps she was just feeling good about things. Even in the privacy of her own mind, the wit was acid.

The woman waiting for her wore the livery of the governor. Her pelt was a soft brown, and the pattern of beads woven into it were the green and gold of the city. The copper torc fitted around her neck marked her as a courier.

"Magistra Cithrin bel Sarcour?"

"I am," Cithrin said.

The woman bowed and presented an envelope of cream-colored paper sealed with wax and bearing the seal of the governor. The gravity with which she presented it was such that it might have been the head of an enemy king. Cithrin plucked it up between two fingers and popped the seal open with her thumb.

To Magistra Cithrin bel Sarcour, voice and agent of the Medean bank in Porte Oliva, I, Iderrigo Bellind Siden, Prime Governor of Porte Oliva of Her Royal Highness...

Cithrin skipped down the page, not reading so much as skimming meaning off the top of it like the skin off a soup. A formal dinner in a month's time to celebrate the city's formal creation three hundred years before. Of course there had been a city here before that, and before that and before that, back to the time of the dragons. There were ruins in the hills outside the city carved from stone and eroded almost back into it. But three hundred years ago someone had signed a bit of paper, someone had cut her thumb and pressed a bloody mark on the page, and now they were going to slaughter a few pigs, drink some recent wine, and make speeches.

And, of course, she would go. Even though her competitor and once-lover Qahuar Em would be there. Even though the night would bore and chafe. She would go and laugh and talk and behave as if she had power. If she didn't someone might notice, and the illusion of influence once broken was hard to rebuild.

"Thank you," Cithrin said. "That will be all."

The courier bowed and trotted off, her beads clicking against each other. Cithrin considered going back up, maybe putting on the face paint after all, but decided against it. There was the empty form of a meeting at the café she might as well attend. She closed and locked the door.

She could tell a great deal about the state of the city by walking through the streets near the Grand Market. The food sellers on the corners showed what harvests had been good and what disappointing. If crime had been low, there was more horse and ox shit on the street waiting for the guests of Porte Oliva's magistrates to come and clean it. The number of beggars who'd made their way in from the dragon's road leading into the city said whether there were caravans expected or if the traffic to the city was all local. It was like a cunning man smelling someone's breath and knowing the condition of their liver. Cithrin did it automatically, as she had all through her childhood. Only now there would be no Magister Imaniel to go home to and show off her conclusions. It was only a habit.

Pyk wasn't at the café, which on one hand was a blessing because Cithrin could spend a few hours working on the bank's business without her. On the other, anything she did here would have to be discussed with the foul woman later. All the faces around the table were familiar. Maestro Asanpur smiled at her and winked his milky eye.

"One moment," he said, stepping to the back, and she knew he would return in moments with a mug of fresh coffee and a barely sweetened honey roll. She sat at a table in the front looking out over the square and waited. Maestro Asanpur brought her just what she'd known he would, patted her shoulder gently as he did, and made his slow way back inside. Someday, Cithrin thought, he would die and the café would change. It would become something different and unknown. She wondered what it would be like.

She knew the man when he stepped into the square. She had never met him except through the letters of proposal he had left at the bank, but he walked with a sense of purpose. He was thick across the shoulders for a Dartinae and his eyes glowed brighter than most. His tunic was leather and the sigil of a dragon was inked on it. When he came up to her table, she nodded to the chair opposite her own. He sat with the grace of a dancer and leaned forward, his elbow on the table.

"Dar Cinlama, I presume," Cithrin said.

"Magistra bel Sarcour," he said, bowing from the neck.

"I've read over your proposal. I'm afraid our bank doesn't have a history of backing expeditions like the one you propose."

"There is great risk, it's true. There is also great reward. When Seilia Pellasian found the Temple of the Sun, she came home with gold and jewels enough to last a hundred lives. Sarkik Pellasian didn't find gold, but the designs in the old library are what everyone uses in siegecraft now. The list is very long, Magistra."

"And doesn't include the name of anyone now living," she said.

"Not yet," he agreed with a smile. "But who in a generation has taken the chance? The world is sick with history. The dragons were everywhere, you know? It's only us who hold to the roads. We go where it is convenient. Build where it is convenient. But what's convenient for us was nothing to the dragons. Their roads were the open sky. Is there a lost treasure in Porte Oliva? No. People have been building on their own outhouses since forever. But in the Dry Wastes? In the north of Birancour where no dragon's road runs? No one touches these places deeper than a plow will cut. I was a boy in such a place. We would go out to the fields and dig for dragon's teeth. By the time I left, I had a dozen."

The lines were compelling and delivered with the ease of long practice. Cithrin shook her head.

"It's a pretty story," she said, "and there's some sense to it, but—"

He leaned forward and placed something on the table before her. The tooth was as long as her hand and curved. The sharp end was rough. Serrated. The base was a tangle of hooks and broad places meant to root the thing in a massive jaw. Cithrin picked it up, surprised by its weight.

"There are hidden things in this world," he said. "More than you might imagine. And some of them are good for more than decoration."

Cithrin turned the great tooth over in her hand, her mind lit like a fire. It didn't show the bite of a chisel she'd expect on sculpted stone or the flat place that a poured cast would leave. It might still be a forgery, but if so, it was a better one than she could catch out. Even if it was a tooth, there were any number of beasts that might have such a thing. She wondered what Pyk's tusks had looked like before they'd been taken out. For all Cithrin knew, this might have come from nothing more exotic than a particularly large Yemmu.

Or it might be a dragon's tooth.

"All sorts of things were lost in the fall of dragons," the Dartinae said. The glow of his eyes was like twin candle flames. When he blinked she could see the blood vessels tracing through his eyelids. "What could rot's rotted, but there are things that time won't touch. Give me the coin to hire carts and shovels, and I'll bring back treasures that humanity forgot. Things we don't dream of now."

Yes, she wanted to say. *Yes, take it and take me with you. Get me out of this city and let's make enough money to found a whole new bank and drive Komme Medean and Pyk Usterhall into the streets.* Instead, she pushed the tooth back across the table. It was a romance. A dream. Even if Pyk hadn't been sitting on the strongbox, Cithrin knew the right answer to this was no. It was a desperate man's game, and that it attracted her said more about her state of mind than the true risks.

Dar Cinlama pursed his lips.

"No, then?"

"No," she said. "You'll find someone. You're very good at telling the tale, and the logic of it's persuasive if you find someone who wants to be persuaded. I'd try a nobleman with more money than sense. I run a bank. We don't make our coin on grand gestures and glorious adventure."

"More's the pity for you," he said. "You think it's a trick, then? That I'm playing a confidence game?"

"No," she said. "I think you're sincere. But I also wouldn't think less of you if you weren't."

The man nodded and stood.

"Would you like a cup of coffee?" she asked.

"No," he said. "Thank you, Magistra. I'll be off looking for a nobleman with more money than sense. Preferably one you haven't cleaned out already."

There was a little heat in his voice. But there would be. She'd just disappointed him.

"Don't forget your tooth," she said.

"Keep it. Remind you of me when you hear what better I've found."

"Thank you, then," she said and watched him walk away.

She had had her season traveling off the dragon's roads. Moving through snow and freezing mud, desperate to stay ahead of the Antean army and sitting on the wealth of a whole city. It hadn't seemed at all exciting at the time, but the farther away the past drew, the more warmly it glowed. She finished her bun and coffee, licked each finger individually to take the last of the glaze off, put the dragon's tooth in her purse, and started back.

He was right, of course. It wasn't only treasure hunters. Smugglers knew it too. The dragon's roads covered a great deal of the continent, but not all. And where it was not, people were scarce. Dragon's jade ran through forests, but not deep ones. The deep ones were too hard for loggers, because there was no road. Better to find a stand of oaks that had been there for a hundred or two hundred years than go through mud and farmers' paths until you found the ones that had lived for a thousand. And with them, whatever slept in their roots. The desperate and the dreamers and those with something to hide. They left the jade roads.

She remembered slogging through snow with Master Kit and the players. The Timzinae caravan master and his religious sermons over dinner. The way the tin merchant would always try to start arguments. Cary and Mikel and Hornet and Smit. And Sandr, who'd kissed her and almost more. And Opal. If the snows hadn't blocked the pass at Bellin, she would never have known them. Not really. The caravan would have gone to Carse as it was meant to, and never left the—

Cithrin's heart began to beat almost before she knew why. The plan came to her fully formed, as if it had been drawn on the inside of her skull and a curtain pulled back to reveal it already done. Simple and obvious and incontrovertible, the solution to the problem of Pyk Usterhall spread out before her. She stopped in the street to laugh out the relief.

There was no room for the notary in the counting house itself. She'd taken private rooms two streets over between a second-rate bathhouse and a butcher's stall. Her door was heavy oak with a worked iron knocker in the shape of a dog's head. If there was some symbolism there, it was lost on Cithrin. Pyk's voice was muffled and thick, but once it was clear that Cithrin wasn't a taxman or a thief, the bar scraped and the door creaked open on leather hinges.

"May I come in?"

"Of course, Magistra," she said, stepping back. The rooms were smaller than her own, but only just. Her desk was, if anything, larger. The account books were open, and a half-written report waited for pen and ink. Cithrin could see the careful marks and numbers of the bank's private cipher. There was no key. Pyk could read and write directly into the cipher. "To what do I owe the honor?"

"The reports. When will they be ready to go?"

She crossed her arms.

"A week, I think. Not longer than two. Why?"

"I don't suppose you'd be open to carrying them to the holding company yourself? Spending a little time in Northcoast? I could watch things in your absence."

The sneer took up the better part of her face, as Cithrin had known it would.

"I think not, Magistra. My instructions were quite clear."

"Well," she said, holding out a sheet of soft, cream-colored paper, "don't say I didn't try to save you."

Frowning, Pyk took the page and unfolded it. Her eyes scanned it, confusion and distrust growing.

"You're invited to a feast?" she said.

"I am," Cithrin said, "but you will have to attend in my place. I'll be taking the reports to Carse."

Dawson

The funeral ceremony began at the Kingspire. Simeon, King of Imperial Antea, lay on a bed of flowers, red and gold and orange, like a funeral pyre that could not consume its dead. He wore gilt armor that caught the sunlight, and his still features were turned to the sky. All the great families were there: Estinford, Bannien, Faskellan, Broot, Veren, Caot, Palliako, Skestinin, Daskellin, and more and more and dozens more, all those who had sworn their loyalty to Dawson's old friend, those many years ago. They wore mourning cloth and covered their heads in veils. Though the sky was cloudless, the breeze that tugged his sleeves and drowned the chanting of the priest smelled of rain. Dawson bowed his head.

He didn't remember meeting Simeon. It must have happened, some singular first time that led to another, that led to two boys of the noblest blood in Antea running wild together. They had taken to the dueling yards, standing second for each other in matters of honor and jest and the small intrigues that forged long friendships. The happy memories betrayed him now, moving him to tears. Once, they had hunted a deer through the forest, breaking away from the hounds and the huntsmen to tear after the beast alone. The deer had led them through some small farmer's garden, circling the little stone cottage with their horses at its heels

until they'd reduced the rows of peas and eggplant to greenish mud. It had seemed sweet then. Ridiculous and hilarious
and beautiful. Now Dawson was the only one who would
remember that laughter or the comic expression of the farmer
rushing out to find the crown prince covered in mud and
pulped vegetables.

What had been a shared moment was private now, and
always would be. Even if he were to tell the story, it would
be a tale told and not the thing itself. The difference between
those two was the division between life and death: a lived
moment and one entombed.

Simeon had been so young then. So noble and strong. And
still, somehow, he had looked up to Dawson. There is nothing in a young man's world sweeter than being admired by
the boy you admire. And then, inevitably, that love had
ended, and now even the dream of its recapture was gone.
One dead, the other standing with the veil shifting around
his nose while a priest a decade older than the corpse being
consecrated mumbled and lifted hands toward God. The
king's breath was stopped. His blood turned black and solid
in his veins. His heart, once capable of love and fear, was
now a stone.

The priest lit the great lantern, and the bells rang out first
one, and then a dozen, and then thousands. The brass
mouths announced what everyone already knew. *All men
die*, Simeon said in his memory. *Even kings*. Dawson stepped
forward. Etiquette dictated which of the pale-fleshed ash
poles he was to take, who he was to carry before, and who
behind. He was not so near the front as he wished. But he
was close enough to see young Aster walk out to his place at
the column's head.

The boy was pale as cheese. He had accepted coronation
in the ceremony immediately before the burial, as tradition

demanded. Palliako had, to no one's surprise, accepted the regency. The great men of the nation had bent their knees to the boy prince, now king. The worked silver crown perched on Aster's head as if in real danger of sinking to his ears, but his steps were sharp and confident. He knew how to bear himself as if he were a man full-grown, even if the effect was only to more clearly show that he was a child. Geder Palliako, as protector, stood behind him looking considerably less regal than the child prince. The bells stopped together, replaced by the dry report of the funeral drum. With the rest of the hundred bearers, Dawson took his pole and lifted Simeon to his shoulders.

At the royal crypt, they laid Dawson's childhood friend in the darkness and closed the stone doors behind him. The official mourners took their stations at the crypt's entrance. For a month, they would live in the open, keeping a fire lit in memory of Simeon and all kings past. When that was done, the fire would be let die. As the priest read final rites, Dawson's family came around him. Clara stood at his right, and beside her Barriath and Vicarian. Jorey stood to his left with his arm around Sabiha still fresh from her wedding gown. When the last syllable had been spoken and the last bone-dry drum sounded, the nobles of Antea turned back to their carriages.

"For what it carries, I am sorry," a voice said. Lord Ashford wore the dark robes of mourning, his cheek ash-marked like the rest. "I'd heard he was an amazing man."

"He was a man," Dawson said. "He had faults and virtues. He was my king and my friend."

Ashford nodded. "I am sorry."

"Now that Palliako's regent, you have an audience with him," Dawson said.

"I do."

"He's asked me to attend."

"I look forward to it," Ashford said. "This has been hanging over our heads too long. Better to have a clean start now."

There are no clean starts, Dawson thought. *Just as there are no clean endings. Everything is built like Camnipol: one damn thing atop another atop another reaching down into the bones of the world. Even the forgotten things are back there somewhere, shaping who and what we are now.*

"Yes," he said instead.

The walls here were draped with silk tapestry, the air warmed with charcoal and incense. The king's guard stood along the walls, their faces as impassive before Geder as they had been for Simeon. Even Geder Palliako seemed nearly right for his new role. The tailors had outfitted him in a brocade of red velvet and a circlet of gold that had him looking almost dignified. If he wore it like a costume, these were early days yet. With time and experience, he would come to look natural in it.

Lord Ashford stood, his hands clasped behind him, waiting for the Lord Regent of Antea to take his seat, and Dawson wondered whether Geder knew that no one was permitted to sit until he did.

Dawson's displeasure wasn't that other people had been welcomed into what should have been a private audience. It was Geder's first official act as regent. He'd proved an apt tool in Vanai, and whatever magic he'd done to expose Maas had saved at least Aster and likely the kingdom. Lord Ternigan and Lord Skestinin were both present, and rightly so. Lord Caot, Baron of Dannick. Lord Bannien of Estinford. They were more problematic, but at most they signaled an anticipated shift of the powers in the court. No, what irked Dawson was the other person Geder Palliako had chosen to include.

"Lord Kalliam," the priest said, bowing. A season in Camnipol had done little to wipe the desert dust off the man. He still looked like a goat-herder from the depths of the Keshet, likely because it was what he was. Geder's pet cultist looked about as much at home in the chamber as Dawson would have been slogging through a pigsty.

"Minister Basrahip," Dawson said, neither bowing nor allowing any warmth into his voice. "I am surprised to see you here. I had thought we were addressing affairs of state."

"It's all right," Geder said. "I asked him to come."

Dawson held back his reply. There were things he would have said to his equals that he could no longer say to Geder Palliako. Instead he nodded.

"Well, then," Geder said, fidgeting with his sleeve. "Let's get this done. Please. Everyone. Sit down."

Ashford waited, matching his movement to Palliako's so that at no point was he sitting while the Lord Regent stood. Basrahip didn't sit at all, but rather stood back against the wall, his head slightly bowed, like a boy in silent prayer. Dawson sat, slightly mollified. A foreign priest had no reason to be welcome at the meeting, but at least he was acting like a servant. The other lords of Antea ignored the priest magnificently. He might as well not have existed.

"Lord Ashford?" Geder said, leaning forward with his elbows on the table. "You requested this audience, and I think we all know why. Would you like to say anything?"

"Thank you, Lord Regent," Ashford said. He took a moment to gather himself, his gaze meeting each man at the table in turn. "We are all aware of the crimes of Feldin Maas. King Lechan asked that I come to assure you all that he had no knowledge of the plot and would have been utterly opposed to it if he had known. The intentions to kill Prince Aster were and are unconscionable, and on behalf of Asterilhold, I would ask for time to address this conspiracy ourselves."

Ternigan cleared his throat, and Geder nodded toward him. The conversation was open now until such time as Geder closed it. Dawson wondered whether the boy understood that. Surely he had a protocol servant, but what the new regent remembered was an open question.

"There must be a real settling of blame," Ternigan said. "Asterilhold has a long tradition of coddling its own."

"Of course it does," Bannien said. "What kind of king sides with foreigners against his own lords? Lechan hasn't sat that throne so long by inviting strife in his own court."

"If I may," Ashford said, "he hasn't done it by inviting invasion and war either. It's not in the interests of Asterilhold to take the field any more than it is for Antea. This wouldn't be a little gentleman's skirmish on some tradable soil. You want the conspirators. Stay within your borders, and the king will deliver them to justice. But if you violate the sovereignty of Asterilhold, it changes the aspect of things."

"Wait," Lord Skestinin said. "You said deliver to justice. Whose justice are we talking of here?"

Ashford nodded and raised a finger.

"We cannot turn the nobility of Asterilhold over to an outside court for judgment," he said, and the table erupted, voices riding at once, each trying to shout over the other. The only ones who remained silent were Dawson himself and Geder. Palliako's brows were furrowed, his mouth set in an angry scowl. He wasn't listening to the others, which was just as well as the audience was descending rapidly into bedlam.

Tell them to be quiet, Dawson thought at the boy. *Make them see* order.

But instead, Palliako pressed his hands to the table and

rested his chin on them. Dawson, disgust filling his throat, shouted.

"Are we *schoolboys*? Is this what we've come to? Squabbling and barking and calling names? My king isn't cold in the crypt, and we're descending to melee?" His voice sounded like a storm, the force of it rattling his throat. "Ashford, stop trying to sell us something. Say what terms King Lechan wants."

"Don't," Geder said. He hadn't raised his chin from the table, so when he spoke, his head bobbed slightly like a toy sailboat on a pond. "I don't really care what the terms are. Not yet."

"Lord Regent?" Ashford said.

Geder sat up.

"We must know terms," Ternigan began, but Palliako shut him down with a glance.

"Lord Ashford. Was the plot against Aster known to you?"

"No," Ashford said.

Geder's gaze flicked away and then back. As Dawson watched, Palliako went pale and then flushed. Geder's breath was coming faster now, like he'd been running a race. Dawson tried to see what had caused the change in his boy's demeanor, but all he saw was the guards at their attention and the priest at his prayers.

"Was it known to King Lechan?"

"No."

Dawson saw it this time. It was a small thing, almost invisible, but as soon as the word left Lord Ashford's lips, the priest shook his broad head. *No.* Dawson felt the air leave him.

The Lord Regent of Antea was looking to a *foreign priest* for direction.

When Geder spoke again, his voice was ice and outrage, and Dawson barely heard it.

"You've just lied to me twice, Lord Ambassador. If you do it again, I'm sending your hands back to Asterilhold in their own box. Do you understand me?"

For the first time since Dawson had met the man, the ambassador from Asterilhold was dumbfounded. His mouth worked like a puppet's but no words came out. Geder, on the other hand, had found his voice and wasn't about to give it up.

"You've forgotten who you're talking to. I'm the man who knows the truth of this. No one else stopped Maas. I did. Me."

Ashford was licking his lips now, as if his mouth had suddenly gone dry.

"Lord Palliako..."

"Do you think I'm stupid?" Geder said. "Do you think I'll sit here and smile and shake your hand and promise peace while you try and kill my friends?"

"I don't know what you've heard," Ashford said, battling to regain his composure, "or where you've heard it from."

"You see now, *that's* truth," Geder said.

"But I assure you—I swear to you—Asterilhold had no designs on the young prince's life."

Again, the flicker of eyes, and the priest's subtle refusal. Dawson wanted to leap to his feet but he seemed rooted in his chair. Geder seemed to calm, but his heavy-lidded eyes were dark and merciless. When he spoke, his voice was almost conversational.

"You don't get to laugh at me." He turned to the captain of his guards. "Take Lord Ashford into custody. I want the executioner to have his hands off by nightfall and ready to send back to Asterilhold."

The guard's calm façade only broke for a moment, and then he saluted. Ashford was on his feet, all etiquette forgotten.

"Are you out of your mind?" he shouted. "Who in hell do you think you are? This isn't how this works! I'm *ambassador.*"

The guard captain put a hand on Ashford's shoulder.

"You have to come with me now, my lord."

"You cannot do this!" Ashford shouted. Fear fueled the words.

"I can," Geder said.

Ashford fought, but not for long. When the door had closed behind him, the high men of Antea looked at each other. For a long time, no one spoke.

"My lords," Geder Palliako, Lord Regent of Imperial Antea said, "we are at war."

Dawson sat on his couch, the leather creaking under him. Jorey and Barriath were in chairs opposite him, and his favorite hunting dog whined at his knee, forcing her damp nose under his palm.

"He was right before," Barriath said. "About Feldin Maas. He was right. He knows things. Maybe…maybe he isn't wrong. Jorey? You served with him."

"I did," Jorey said, and the dread in the words was enough.

"We can't have done this," Dawson said. "I can't believe we've done this."

"It isn't all us," Barriath said. "If Palliako's right—"

"I don't mean the war. I don't even mean violating the sanctity of the ambassador. The man was a disrespectful, pompous ass. I don't mean any of that."

"Then what, Father?" Jorey asked.

In Dawson's memory, the huge priest's head moved, a finger's width one way, and then the other, as Palliako watched. There was no doubt in his mind. The priest had been telling

Palliako what to do, and Geder had done it. Simeon had died, and they had given the Severed Throne to a religious zealot who wasn't even a subject of the crown. The thought nauseated him. If he'd woken in the morning to find the seas had floated into the air and the fish flying where the birds had been, it wouldn't have been more upsetting than this. Everything was out of joint. The proper order of the king-dom was shattered.

"We have to make this right," he said. "We have to fix this."

A scratch came at the door, and it opened a handspan. A frightened-looking footman leaned in.

"There's a guest, my lords," he said.

"I'm not receiving them," Dawson said.

"It's Lord Regent Palliako, my lord," the footman said.

Dawson tried to catch his breath.

"Show... show him in."

"Should we go?" Barriath asked.

"No," Dawson said, though the proper answer was likely yes. He wanted his family with him.

Geder came in still wearing the same red velvet, though the golden circlet was gone. He looked as he had before, a small man with a tendency toward weight. Uncertain smile, apologetic before he had anything to apologize for.

"Lord Kalliam," he said. "Thank you for seeing me. Jorey. Barriath. Good to see you both too. I hope Sabiha's well?"

"She's fine, Lord Regent," Jorey said, and Palliako waved it away.

"Please. Geder. You can always call me Geder. We're friends."

"All right," Jorey said.

Palliako sat, and Dawson realized he and his boys hadn't risen. They should have.

"I've come to ask a favor," Palliako said. "You see, I served under Ternigan? And of course Alan Klin, and the others, served under him. Everything about Vanai was badly done. My part too, though I don't like to say it, could probably have been done better."

You are a traitor to your crown and the memory of my friend, Dawson thought.

"Anyway, the short of it is, I don't trust him. You and your family have always been kind to me. You've been my patron, so to speak, when I really didn't know my way around court. So now that I'm in need of a Lord Marshal, on the one hand it makes sense to appoint Ternigan, only because he's got the experience most recently. But I would rather it be you."

Dawson sat forward, his head swimming.

Palliako had betrayed his crown and kingdom, had given the reins of power to a goatherd, begun a war with Asterilhold that was doomed to slaughter hundreds or thousands on both sides of the border, and now he had come to deliver control of the army into Dawson's hands. And he was presenting it as asking a favor.

It took Dawson almost a full minute to find the words.

"Lord Regent, I would be honored."

Marcus

Sometime, centuries before, someone had built a low wall along the top of the rise. In the moonlight, the scattered rocks reminded Marcus of knucklebones. He knelt, one hand on the dew-slick grass. In the cove below him, three ships rested at anchor. Shallow-bottomed with paired masts. Faster and more maneuverable than the round-bellied trade ships that they hunted. One showed a mark on the side where she'd been struck not too many weeks before, the new timber of the patch bright and unweathered.

On the sand, a cookfire still burned, its orange glow the only warmth in the spring night. From where they stood, Marcus counted a dozen structures—more than tents, less than huts—scattered just above the tide line. A well-established camp, then. That was good. A half dozen stretched-leather boats rested near the water.

Yardem Hane grunted softly and pointed a wide hand to the east. A tree a hundred feet or so from the water towered up toward the sky. A glimmer, moonlight on metal, less than a third of the way to its tip showed where the sentry perched. Marcus pointed out at the ships. High in the rigging of the one nearest the shore, another dark figure.

Yardem held up two fingers, wide brows rising in question. *Two watchers?*

Marcus shook his head, holding up a third finger. *One more.*

The pair sat still in the shadows made darker by the spray of fallen stone. The moon shifted slowly in its arc. The movement was subtle. A single branch on the distant tree that moved in the breeze more slowly. Marcus pointed. Yardem flicked an ear silently; he wore no earrings when they were scouting. Marcus looked over the cove one last time, cataloging it as best he could. They faded back down the rise, into the shadows. They walked north, and then west. They didn't speak until they'd traveled twice as far as their low voices would carry.

"How many do you make out?" Marcus asked.

Yardem spat thoughtfully.

"Not more than seventy, sir," he said.

"That's my count too."

The path was hardly more than a deer trail. Thin spaces in the trees. It wouldn't be many weeks before the leaves of summer choked the path, but tonight their steps were muffled by well-rotted litter and a spring's soft moss. The moon was no more than a scattering of pale dapples in the darkness under the leaves.

"We could go back to the city," Yardem said. "Raise a hundred men. Maybe a ship."

"You think Pyk would pay out the coin?"

"Could borrow it from someone."

In the brush, a small animal skittered, fleeing before them as if they were a fire.

"The one farthest from shore was riding lower than the others," Marcus said.

"Was."

"We come in with a ship, they'll see us. It'll be empty water by the time we're there."

Yardem was quiet apart from a small grunt when his head bumped against a low branch. Marcus kept his eyes on the darkness, not really seeing. His legs shifted and moved easily. His mind gnawed at the puzzle.

"If they see us coming on land," he said, "they haul out boats and wave to us from the sea. We trap them on land in a fair fight with the men we have now, they have numbers and territory on us. We wait to get more sword-and-bows, and they may have moved on."

"Difficult, sir."

"Ideas?"

"Hire on for an honest war."

Marcus chuckled sourly.

His company was camped dark, but the sound of their voices and the smells of their food traveled in the darkness. He had fifty men of several races—otter pelted Kurtadam, black-chitined Timzinae, Firstblood. Even half a dozen bronze-scaled Jasuru hired on at the last minute when their contract as house guards fell through. It made for more tension in the camp, but the usual racial slurs were absent. They were Kurtadam and Timzinae and Jasuru, not *clickers* and *roaches* and *pennies*. And no one said a bad word about the Firstblood when it was a Firstblood who'd decide who dug the latrines.

And, to the point, the mixture gave Marcus options.

Ahariel Akkabrian had been one of the first guards when the Porte Oliva branch of the Medean bank had been a high-stakes gamble with all odds against. His pelt was going grey, especially around his mouth and back, but the beads woven into it were silver instead of glass. He sat up on his cot as Marcus ducked into the tent. His eyes were bleary with sleep, but his voice was crisp.

"Captain Wester, sir. Yardem."

"Sorry to wake you," Yardem said.

"Ahariel," Marcus said. "How long could you swim in the sea?"

"Me, you mean, sir? Or someone like me?"

"Kurtadam."

"Long as you'd like."

"No boasting. It's not summer. The water's cold. How long?"

Ahariel yawned deeply and shook his head, setting the beads to clicking.

"The dragons built us for water, Captain. The only people who can swim longer and colder than we can are the Drowned, and they can't fight for shit."

Marcus closed his eyes, seeing the moonlit cove again. The ships at anchor, the shelters, the hide boats. The coals of the fire glowing. He had eleven Kurtadam, Ahariel included. If he sent them into the water, that left a bit over thirty. Against twice that number. Marcus bit his lip and looked up at his second in command. In the light of the single candle, Yardem looked placid. Marcus cleared his throat.

"The day you throw me in a ditch and take control of the company?"

"Not today, sir," Yardem said.

"Afraid you'd say that. Only one thing to do then. Ahariel? You're going to need some knives."

Marcus rode to the west, shield slung on his back and sword at his side. The sun rose behind him, pushing his shadow out ahead like a gigantic version of himself. To his left, the sea was as bright as beaten gold. The sentry tree was just in sight. The poor bastard on duty would be squinting into the brightness. The danger, of course, being that he wouldn't look at all. If Marcus managed an actual surprise attack, they were doomed. He had the uncomfortable sense that God's sense of humor went along lines very much like that.

"Spread out," he called back down the line. "Broken file. We want to look bigger than we are."

The call came back, voice after voice repeating the order. Timing was going to matter a great deal. The land looked different in the sunlight. The cove wasn't as distant as it had seemed in the night. Marcus sat high in his saddle.

"Come on," he murmured. "See us. Look over here and see us. We're right *here*."

A shiver along a wide branch. The leaves sent back light brighter than gold. A horn blared.

"That was it," Yardem rumbled.

"Was," Marcus said. He pictured the little shelters, the sailors scuttling for their belongings, for their boats. He counted ten silent breaths, then pulled his shield to the front and drew his sword.

"Sound the charge," he said. "Let's get this done."

When they rounded the bend that led into the cove, a ragged volley of arrows met them. Marcus shouted, and his soldiers picked up the call. From the far end of the strip of sand, ten archers stood ground, loosing arrows and preparing to jump into the last hide boat and take to the safety of the water, the ships, and the sea. The other boats were already away, rowing fast toward the ships and loaded with enough men to defeat Marcus's force.

The first boat was a dozen yards from shore and already sinking.

In the bright water, hidden by the glare of the sun, nearly a dozen Kurtadam with long knives put new holes in the boats.

Marcus pulled up, waving to his own archers to take the

shoreline while the Jasuru charged the enemy and their boat, howling like mad animals. A few figures appeared on the ships, staring out at the spectacle on shore and in the tide-pool. The first boat vanished. The second was staying more nearly afloat as the men in it bailed frantically with helmets and hands. They weren't rowing, though. It wouldn't get them any farther.

Marcus lifted his hand and his archers raised bows.

"Surrender now and you won't be harmed!" he shouted over the surf. "Or flee and be killed. Your choice."

In the surf, one of the sailors started kicking for the ships. Marcus pointed at him with his sword. It took three volleys before he stopped. As if on cue, the black bobbing heads of Ahariel and the other Kurtadam appeared in a rough line between the sinking boats and the ships. As Marcus watched, the swimming Kurtadam lifted their knives above the water, like the ocean growing teeth.

"Leave your weapons in the water," Marcus called. "Let's end this gently."

They emerged from the waves, sullen and bedraggled. Marcus's soldiers took them one by one, bound them, and left them sitting under guard.

"Fifty-eight," Yardem said.

"There's a few still on the ships," Marcus said. "And there's the one we poked full of arrows."

"Fifty-nine, then."

"Still outnumbered. Badly outnumbered," Marcus said. And then, "We can exaggerate when we take it to the taphouse."

A young Firstblood man walked out of the sea. His beard was braided in the style of Cabral. His eyes were bright green, his face thin and sharp. His silk robe clung to his body, making his potbelly impossible to hide. Marcus kicked his horse and trotted up to him. He looked like a kitten that fell in a creek.

"Maceo Rinál?"

The pirate captain looked up at Marcus with contempt that was as good as acknowledgment.

"I've been looking for you," Marcus said.

The man said something obscene.

Marcus had his tent set up at the top of the rise. The stretched leather clung to the frames and kept the wind out, if not the flies. Maceo Rinál sat on a cushion, wrapped in a wool blanket and stinking of brine. Marcus sat at his field desk with a plate of sausage and bread. Below them, as if on a stage, Marcus's forces were involved with the long process of unloading the surrendered ship, hauling the cargo to land, and loading it onto wagons.

"You picked the wrong ship," Marcus said.

"You picked the wrong man," Rinál said. He had a smaller voice than Marcus had expected.

"Five weeks ago, a ship called the *Stormcrow* was coming east from the cape. It didn't make it. Waylaid and sunk, but no sign of the cargo. Is this sounding familiar?"

"I am the cousin of King Sephan of Cabral. You and your magistrates have no power over me," Rinál said, lifting his chin as he spoke. "I invoke the Treaty of Carcedon."

Marcus took a bite of sausage and chewed slowly. When he spoke, he drew the syllables out.

"Captain Rinál? Look at me. Do I seem like a magistrate's blade?"

The chin didn't descend, but a flicker of uncertainty came to the young man's eyes.

"I work for the Medean bank. My employers insured the *Stormcrow*. When you took the crates off that ship, you weren't stealing from the sailors who were carrying them.

You weren't even stealing from the merchants who owned them. You were stealing from us."

The pirate's face went grey. The leather flap opened with a rustle and Yardem came in. His earrings were back in place.

"News?" Marcus said.

"The cargo here matches the manifests," Yardem said. He was scowling, playing to the dangerous reputation of the Tralgu. Marcus assumed it amused him. "We're in the right place, sir."

"Carry on."

Yardem nodded and left. Marcus took another bite of sausage.

"My cousin," Rinál said. "King Sephan—"

"My name's Marcus Wester."

Rinál's eyes grew wide and he sank back on the cushion.

"You've heard of me," Marcus said. "So you know that the appeal-to-noble-blood strategy may not be your best choice. Your mother was a minor priestess who got drunk with a monarch's exiled uncle. That's your protection. Me? I've killed kings."

"Kings?"

"Well, just the one, but you take the point."

Rinál tried to speak, swallowed to loosen his throat, and then tried again.

"What are you going to do?"

"I'm going to reclaim our property, or as much of it as you have left. I don't expect it'll make up the losses, but it's a beginning."

"What are you going to do with me?"

"You mean if I don't take you to justice? I'm going to come to an understanding with you."

A cry rose up from the beach below them. Dozens of voices raised in alarm. Marcus nodded to the captive, and together they walked out into the light. On the bright water below them, the ship farthest from the shore was afire. A plume of white smoke rose from it, and thin red snake-tongues licked at the mast, visible even from here. Rinál cried out, and as if in answer a roll of sudden black smoke bellied out from the flame.

"Don't worry," Marcus said. "We're only burning one of them."

"I'll see you dead," Rinál said, but there was no power in his voice. Marcus put a hand on the man's shoulder and steered him back into the shade of the tent.

"If I kill you or if I burn all your ships," Marcus said, "then by this time next year, there's just going to be another bunch like yours in the cove. The bank's investments are just as much at risk. Nothing changes, and I have to come back here and have this same talk with someone else."

"You've burned her. You burned my ship."

"Try to stay with me," Marcus said, lowering Rinál back to the ground. The pirate put his head in his hands. Marcus took the two steps to his field desk and took out the paper Cithrin had prepared for him. He'd meant to drop it haughtily at the pirate's feet, but the man seemed so shaken, he tucked it into his lap instead.

"That's a list of the ships we insure out of Porte Oliva. If I have to find you again, offering yourself to the magistrate is the best thing that could happen."

The breeze shifted and the smell of burning pitch filled the tent and spoiled the taste of the sausages. The leather walls chuffed like tiny sails. Rinál opened the papers.

"If the ship's not listed here..."

"Then it's no business of mine."

"I'm not the only ships on these waters," he said. "If someone else..."

"You should discourage them."

The color was starting to come back to Rinál's cheeks. The shock had begun to fade and the old righteousness return, but it was tempered now. The voices coming up from the water were brighter now, laughing. Those would be Marcus's soldiers. A wagon creaked. It was time to move on.

"You'll travel with us as far as Cemmis township," Marcus said. "That's not too far to walk back from before your people get sick from thirst."

"You think you're such a big man, no one can take you down," the pirate said. "You think you're better than me. You're no different."

Marcus leaned against the field desk, looking down at the pirate. In truth, Rinál was a young man. For all his bluster and taking on airs, he was the same sort who tripped drunk men in taprooms and groped women in the street. He was a badly behaved child who, instead of growing to manhood, had found a few ships and taken his bullying out in the world where it could turn him a profit.

A dozen replies came to Marcus. *When you've watched your family die, say that again* and *Grow up, boy, while you still have the chance* and *Yes, I'm better than you; my ship isn't burning.*

"We'll leave soon," he said. "I have guards posted. Don't try to go without us."

Outside, the little two-masted ship roared in flame. Black smoke billowed from her, carrying sparks and embers up to wheeling birds. Marcus walked down the rise to where the carts were lining up, prepared to head back home. One of his younger Kurtadam was in the medical wagon, his arm being shaved and bound. Beneath the pelt, his skin looked just like a Firstblood's.

The dead enemy sailor was laid out under tarps. The rest,

bound in ranks with arms bent back, were sullen and angry. Marcus's men were grinning and trading jokes. It was like the aftermath of a battle, only this time there'd hardly been any bloodshed. The wet sand was smooth where the waves washed their footprints away. The mules, ignoring the smell of flames and the banter of soldiers, pulled wagons filled with silks and worked brass back toward the road. The smells of salt and smoke mixed.

Marcus felt the first tug of returning darkness at the back of his mind. The aftermath of any fight—great battle or tap-room dance—always had that touch of bleakness. The bright-ness and immediacy of the fight gave way, and the world and all its history poured back in. It was worse when he lost, but even in victory, the darkness was there. He put it aside. There was real work to be done.

Yardem stood by the head wagon, a Cinnae boy on a lath-ered horse at his side. A messenger. As he approached, the boy dropped down and led his mount away to be cared for.

"Where do we stand?" Marcus asked.

"Ready to start back, sir. But might be best if I led the column. The magistra wants you back at the house as soon as you can get there."

"What's happened?"

Yardem shrugged eloquently.

"An honest war," he said.

Cithrin

The reports were completed and sealed, the pages sewn shut and wax pressed all around with the seal of the Medean bank interspersed with Pyk's personal sign. With all the work that had gone into them, Cithrin had expected something more. Four slim volumes, bound in leather. The notary's report on everything about the Porte Oliva bank would fit into a satchel. The time had come to decide the details of her journey, and Cithrin, for all her preparation, wasn't sure.

The speed at which information traveled was the enemy of certainty. A cunning man's ritual might pass a simple, urgent message from Porte Oliva to Carse in as little as two days. A pigeon could fly there in five and be more reliable. A single courier on a fast horse could cross the wide plains of Birancour, stopping at the posts and wayhouses, and reach Sara-sur-Mar in ten days' time, and then by ship to Carse in another five so long as no bandits caught him and the weather on the coast was favorable. A caravan would be even slower, but safer. If she'd wanted it, Cithrin could have planned half a season on the road there and back again.

She had sat in her room at night with the dragon's tooth and map before her and imagined the different journeys she might take, letting herself debate whether to stop in Sara-sur-Mar for a time and make her introductions to the queen's court, whether to take ship directly from Porte Oliva and see the ports in Cabral and Herez along her way, whether to leave by herself dressed as a courier and ride alone in the wide world. Every new version seemed sweeter, more enchanting, more real than the last. She'd settled on a middle way. Marcus and Yardem Hane and herself, traveling on the dragon's roads all along the way. A small group would move quickly, and the trained blades and little promise of gain would discourage most of the trouble that might come. Rather than pack the dresses and paints and formal attire she'd want in Carse, she would take a letter of credit and purchase them there.

Then came the news of war.

"No," Marcus said. "Not overland. There'll be refugees on all the roads through Northcoast. Thick in the last parts of Birancour too, for that matter."

The counting house was empty apart from the three of them—Marcus, Cithrin, and Pyk. The chalked duty roster showed half a dozen names, but most of them were on the road back from Cemmis township under Yardem's command, and the others Marcus had set to wait in the street. Their voices were audible, but Cithrin couldn't make out any words. Her map was stretched out on the floor, with all of them looking at it as if there was a secret message hidden in its lines. Birancour in the south, with the smaller kingdoms clustered around it. Northcoast above and to the right, looking down at it like a disapproving older brother. And beyond it, the war.

"Sea's a problem too," Pyk said, sucking at her teeth.

"Why?" Cithrin asked.

"We did just burn a pirate's ship down to the waterline," Marcus said. "Might want to give a little time before we offer him a chance at bloody vengeance."

Pyk's expression darkened, but she didn't speak. Cithrin hadn't gone to the woman until Marcus had returned with confirmation that their scheme had worked. She'd left the notary in an uncomfortable place. Cithrin had taken action on the bank's behalf without Pyk's knowledge, but there had been no formal negotiation, no papers to sign. Nothing she'd done violated the terms under which Cithrin was bound. Only the spirit and intention of the thing was compromised, and in the process, the losses of the *Stormcrow*'s insurance contract would be at least partly recovered. Pyk could be unhappy about how it had been done, but the results allowed her as little room for open complaint as for pleasure.

"Overland to Sara-sur-Mar and then by ship," Pyk said. "Cuts out the waters near Cabral and keeps her far enough west she'll miss the worst of it."

"Likely the best route," Marcus said. "It does pass through some rough territory in the center. The farmlands are taxed hard. There's places where the locals see travelers as either predators or prey."

"That's truth," Pyk said, though she sounded less worried about it than pleased. "The reports will want guarding."

"I don't want a full caravan," Cithrin said. "Just Marcus and Yardem will be fine, I think."

"The hell they will," Pyk said.

"That's not a choice you get to make," Marcus said.

The Yemmu woman's thick lips went slack in surprise.

"You're serious?" she said. "And here I was starting to think you weren't an idiot. Or am I the only one who's thought through the implications? Northcoast was on the edge of a fresh war of succession last year. King Tracian's ass has barely warmed up his throne. Now Asterilhold—his neighbor with the longest and least defensible border—is marching into the field against Imperial Antea."

"Your point being?" Cithrin asked archly.

"You want to go there with Marcus Wester in tow? Because the way I remember it, last time he was in Northcoast he killed their king."

"And gave the throne to Lady Tracian," Marcus said.

"So now that it's her nephew wearing the crown, maybe you've come to take it back," Pyk said. "If I were king of Northcoast and you came waltzing back into my kingdom with sword music already singing in my ears, you know what I'd do? Lock your pretty little ass up just to be on the safe side. And I'd start looking pretty damn funny at whoever it was that brought you, and I don't mean the magistra here."

"I'll be fine," Marcus said.

Pyk hoisted her eyebrows but didn't say anything more. A shout came from the street, and then laughter. A single sharp rap on the door announced Yardem Hane. The Tralgu's ears were canted forward, giving him an earnest, attentive look.

"It's all in the warehouse, sir."

"You have a full list?" Pyk snapped

Yardem walked across the room and gave the woman a handful of papers, but Cithrin's attention was still on the map, her mind turning over the journey still ahead. A tightness she hadn't expected was knotting her belly. In the corner of her vision, Pyk ran a scarred thumb down the list. The hiss of paper against paper when she moved the second page was like an impatient sigh.

"This isn't ours," she said, tapping at the page.

"Is now," Marcus said. "It's in our warehouse."

"Oh, really?" Pyk said. "And when some salt quarter merchant files claim with the governor, is that what you're telling the magistrate? Well, we took it from a pirate, so it's ours? If we don't have papers proving our right to have it, get it out of my warehouse."

Cithrin pressed a fingertip against the northern coast, tracing it from Northcoast to Asterilhold to Antea. She had fled Antean swords before now. The Imperial Army had taken Vanai, and some Antean governor had burned it. They would remember that. The border between the combatants was a river flowing up from the marshes in the south and spilling into the northern sea. Only a single dragon's road crossed the water like a gate in a wall. The sea would be, if anything, the wider battleground. When the nobles and merchants of Asterilhold fled west, away from the enemy, Northcoast would be the only place to escape to.

"Yes, they are. Salvage rights are rights," Marcus was saying. Cithrin realized she'd missed part of the conversation.

"When it's your name taking the risk, you can keep anything stolen from anyone and *you* go to the carcer for it. I'm—"

"I'd like to speak with the captain alone now, please," Cithrin said. Three sets of eyes turned to look at her. Pyk and Marcus both smoldered with anger. Yardem was unreadable as always. "Just Marcus. Just for a moment."

Pyk made a spitting sound, but didn't spit. Her rolling gait made her seem like a ship caught on high seas as she strode out. Yardem nodded, flicked one ear, and retreated, pulling the door to behind him.

"That woman is a disaster," Marcus said, pointing two fingers at the door. "I think they sent her just to punish us."

"They probably did," Cithrin said. "That's part of why she's right."

"She's not, though. As soon as Rinál took those crates, he—"

"Not about that. About Carse. I can't take you."

Marcus crossed his arms and leaned against the high table that was the last remnant of the old gambler's desk. His expression was empty.

"I see," he said.

"I'm going to Carse to win over Komme Medean," she said. "If I'm bringing a scandal along with me, it doesn't help. And you're Marcus Wester. You're the man who killed the Mayfly King. I forget that because I know you. And you don't make that who you are. But for the rest of the world, and especially the court in Northcoast, they won't hear your name without thinking of armies and dead kings. I need Komme Medean to like me. Or respect me."

His lips pressed white, sharp lines of anger drawing themselves down the sides of his mouth. For a long moment, Cithrin had the sick feeling that he was about to resign. Quit her and the bank and everything else. Then he looked at her and he softened.

"Well," he said. A dog yelped and a man's voice cursed not far away. Marcus scratched his cheek, the sound like sand falling against paper. "I suppose someone's got to keep an eye on Pyk."

"Thank you."

"You'll still need guards. If it's not me and Yardem, you'll need four at least. We're just that good." Cithrin smiled and Marcus managed to smile back. "Just...just promise me you'll be safe. I have a bad history of losing people in Northcoast."

"I promise," she said.

For all that Cithrin had remade herself as an upstanding and important citizen of Birancour, she had never been inland farther than the coastal mountains and foothills that separated it from the Free Cities, and then in the grip of winter. She had imagined it all to be like that—rolling hills and stones punctuated by forests and meadows. The land between the Free Cities had been like that where it hadn't been mud and snow. It was only when she passed out from the last trailing houses and farms of Porte Oliva that she saw the wide, open sweep of the land and heard the voice of the grass singing for the first time in her life.

The interior of Birancour was flat, without so much as a hill to break the horizon, and the dragon's jade road passed through it. Cithrin found herself imagining that the road was a living thing that folded in on itself behind them and rose up before, a companion sea serpent escorting her across the oceanic grass. If she'd been asked, she would have said that the sound of tall grass shifting in the breeze would be like a scratching, like rubbing handfuls of straw together. It was like walking under a waterfall. Even the lightest breath of wind roared, and after the third day, Cithrin began to hear things inside it—voices and music, flutes and drums and once a vast choir of voices lifted together in song.

Farmhouses and cultivated fields seemed to rise up and fall away like images from a dream. She almost expected the men and women they met on the road to be some new, unknown race, or to speak with the hush of the grasslands in their voices, but instead they were Firstblood and Cinnae, their faces leathery with the sun and palms yellow and callused. The people seemed so familiar and common and prosaic that Cithrin began to tell herself it was only the unfamiliarity and her own anxiety that made the place seem somehow less than real. When a massive creature easily half the size of her own horse but black and wet-looking with dagger teeth and an improbably ornate and flowerlike nose slid across the road before them, it took her guard's yelp of alarm to convince her it was real.

In the end and despite his joke, Marcus had sent only two guards with her. Two Firstbloods named Barth and Corisen Mout. When night came without a wayhouse or caravanserai, one would take his horse out into the grass, walking it in a circle like a dog until a round space had been crushed down. Even though the grass was wet and green, they didn't start fires.

Cithrin lay in her tiny leather sleeping tent, one arm out before her and her head pillowed on the flesh of it. The top of it was only a few inches above her, and it held the heat of her body surprisingly well. She was shakingly tired, her back and legs sore from riding. The knot in her gut was like an old, unwelcome companion, returned when it was least wanted, and it would not let her sleep. So she feigned it, closing her eyes when she remembered to and trying without success or hope not to listen to her guardsmen talking. Gossiping. About Marcus.

"The way I heard it, Springmere knew the captain was the only reason he was winning the war," Barth said. "Got to where he'd scared himself half crazy that he was going to switch sides. So after the battle of Ellis, Springmere got a bunch of the uniforms off Lady Tracian's dead, put his own men in them, and sent 'em after the captain's family. Held the captain down while his wife and baby burned."

"Wasn't a baby," Corisen Mout said. "Girl was six, seven years old."

"His little girl, then."

"Just saying she wasn't a baby. How'd the captain find out it was a trick?"

"Don't know. Wasn't until after Lady Tracian'd been put in the stocks, though."

"I thought he knew before and was just playing along. Spent a year finishing the war and letting Springmere get himself king and feel like he was safe before he brought the bastard down."

"Might have been. There anything left in that skin?"

Cithrin heard the sloshing of wine. The blades of grass at the camp's edge shifted in near-silence, and she realized she'd opened her eyes again. Scowling, she pressed them closed.

"One way or the other, Springmere gets himself made king of Northcoast, starts riding back for Carse, ready to take control of the place. Sitting in his tent, making lists of all the heads he's going to chop off, when the captain comes in and explains how he knows what happened. Next thing anyone knows, Wester's drenched in blood with an axe in his hand. Walks to the stocks, chops Lady Tracian loose, and gives her this crown that's still got bits of Springmere on it, says it's hers now for all he cares. And after that... gone. Steps out of history until there he was in Porte Oliva hiring guards for the magistra."

The round, hissing sound of wine being squirted into someone's mouth.

"You think he's in love with the magistra?"

"Barth! She's—"

"Ah, she's asleep for hours. Seriously, though. Here he is, could build himself a private army, take garrison work at four, five times what we're making now. But he stays there. There's half the girls in the taproom would lay back for him, and he's careful as glass never to let any of them think he means anything."

"No, it's just he's still being faithful to his dead wife. Can't be with a woman except he starts thinking about her."

"Eh, I think he's mad for the magistra."

"I'm telling you it's old grief turned to stone in him," Corisen Mout said. "Besides, the magistra's a sweet face, but she's got no tits."

"Oh, brother mine," Barth said with a chuckle, "you had best pray she's asleep—"

"I'm not," Cithrin said.

The silence seemed to last forever. She pulled herself out of the tent, then stood. The starlight leached the two men of all color. Their expressions were contrite. The wineskin was in Barth's hand. She walked over and took it from him.

"You've had more than enough. Sleep now," she said. "Both of you."

Without another word, the two men curled up in their bedrolls. Cithrin stood over them until she started to feel ridiculous and then went back to her little tent. The conversation had stopped, but Cithrin lay in the darkness awake all the same. The wine wasn't the best she'd had, but it wasn't the worst. After half the skin, it began to loosen the knot in her belly, the way she remembered it doing the first time she'd taken to the road. Her eyes closed more easily now with the alcohol softening her body and making everything seem slightly more benign. When her mind turned to Marcus—he couldn't be in love with her, could he? It would be like Magister Imaniel wanting her as a bride. He was handsome enough, but he was so old—she consciously turned toward the fine work of trade. The losses for the *Stormcrow* were going to be listed in the report, but the gains from its recovery wouldn't. She needed to make sure they knew that at the holding company. And that Pyk hadn't wanted to invoke salvage on the recovered cargo that wasn't part of their insurance contract.

She began to wonder how a contract would be worded to protect recovered goods from then being recovered by someone else. It would be possible, she supposed, but she hadn't seen it done. She'd need to know what the magistrates thought about it. If they were all agreed that Pyk was wrong and the salvage legitimate, the bank could offer very good rates on the contract. Full coverage for ten percent only sounds wise if there's a chance the contract will be enforced...

Slowly, Cithrin felt her mind drifting out from under her, the wine and the distraction of contracts mixing with the hushing grass. She realized that her eyes had been closed for some time now, and without her effort. Half sleeping, she capped the wineskin, rolled over, and let her body sink in toward the trampled grass. Another few days to Sara-sur-Mar. Then the ship. And then Carse, and some way to convince them all to take Pyk Usterhall, drop her down a well, and give the bank back to Cithrin.

Dawson

The army left Camnipol a week after Lord Ashford's hands. With so little time, it was a small force. Twenty knights with their squires. Four hundred sword-and-bows, most of them peasant farmers taken off the land in the middle of the planting. Perhaps two dozen were professional soldiers, though almost a hundred had walked a battlefield sometime in their lives. They wore what armor came to hand and carried the swords and pikes and hunter's bows kept in attics and cellars against this day. They marched even as the word went out to the south and east that the others would gather. It might take a month for the second and larger force to come together, marching up from the southern holdings or west from the border with Sarakal. At an estimate, the empire could field an army six thousand strong, armed and armored, and still have men enough in the fields to avoid starving next spring.

But that would come later. Now the horses of the knights rode along the wide jade path, and carts of food and fodder came along after. Behind the column, Camnipol faded until the Kingspire itself was little more than a smudge against the horizon. And at the head of the army, Lord Marshal Dawson Kalliam rode with his son Jorey at his side, moving fast as if trying to pull the army along behind by example and force of will.

To look at the map, Asterilhold was little more than a

wide strip of land dividing Imperial Antea from Northcoast, caught between the two great northern kingdoms like a squire standing between two knights. The length of Asterilhold's coastline was the least of all three nations. It boasted only two great cities: Kaltfel and Asinport. Its protections were deeper than simple lines of ink on parchment would show. In the south, the river Siyat found its mouth by draining wide marshes fed by runoff from the mountains along its southern border. Invasion from the Dry Wastes would be difficult and time-consuming. From the west, boggy and prone to disease. The river itself—the Siyat—was navigable in the northernmost reaches, but for most of its length was muddy, cold, unreliable, and deep. The only Antean city to declare itself against the Severed Throne in a generation was Anninfort, which sat on the river's edge, breathing the air of Asterilhold and giving home to men loyal to both kingdoms.

Dawson had studied the wars between the minor kings and the separation of Antea before it became an empire of its own, and the difference between a fast conflict, quickly ended and a grinding, bloody war that could stretch out for years was Seref Bridge.

A day's ride south of Kaltfel, a ribbon of dragon's jade spanned the water over a rapids. The story was that the road predated the river, that the dragon's road had once passed through a plain, and thousands of years of erosion had made a bridge of it. Garrison keeps squatted at both sides, glowering at one another across the span. The nation that controlled both keeps controlled the war, and Dawson's best hope was to reach the bridge with a great enough force to overwhelm the farther side before King Lechan had recovered from the shock of Geder Palliako's rage. Any assault across the bridge would take its toll in blood, but to lose five hundred men in an afternoon now would save five thousand from dying in marshes and fords, on ships and beaches, over the course of years.

Dawson's camp tent stood solid as a house. Thick leather stretched across iron frames to make walls and rooms. A brazier stood in the middle of the central chamber, its smoke rising in a pale grey spiral to the chimney hole in the roof. Crickets sang all around him as he ate a dinner of chicken and apples and outrage. His sometime ally Canl Daskellin sat across from him, peeling an apple of his own with a dagger and the strength of his thumb.

"I don't know what you're proposing, old friend," Daskellin said.

"I'm not proposing anything."

"No?" A long green spiral of skin fell to the floor, pale flesh clinging to one side. "Because it sounds as if you were accusing the Lord Regent of treason against the crown."

"I'm not calling for a coup. I don't want anyone's head on a pike. Or at least not anybody important. If we whipped all Palliako's cultists out of the city with chains, I can't say I'd mind."

"Still..."

"I know what I saw, Canl. You'd have seen it too if you'd watched. He goes everywhere with that pet priest. And what do we know about them and their spider goddess? We moved too quickly. We let the panic over Maas and the relief at his failure stampede us."

"First time that's happened in history," Daskellin said dryly. "We've had bad regencies and we've had bad kings. We've had decent kings with bad advisors and kings who ruled half drunk from a whorehouse while their advisors saw to it that the kingdom didn't burn down. Speaking as Special Ambassador to Northcoast, I'm not pleased that we're cutting ambassadors into small bits, but apart from that, I don't see the difference."

"I do," Dawson said. "Those were *our* bad kings. *Our* bad advisors. They were Antean. This time we've given ourselves into the power of foreigners."

Daskellin's silence sounded like agreement. When he spoke, his voice was low and thoughtful.

"Are you thinking that we're in someone else's war?"

"I didn't say that," Dawson said, plucking the flesh off his chicken with his fingers. At home or at a feast, he would never have done so, but this was war, and he was on campaign. "I'm saying that if Palliako does owe his loyalty to these people, we're just as badly off as if Maas had put his cousin from Asterilhold on our throne."

"I have the feeling that you're asking something of me. I'm not sure what it is."

"I want you to sound them out. Not everyone, but the men Palliako brought to respectability. Broot and Veren. Men like that. Find out if they're loyal to Palliako."

"Of course they are," Daskellin said. "We all are. You are. We're here marching and drilling instead of being at court. That's the sign of loyalty."

Dawson shook his head.

"I've come because the Lord Regent commanded it," he said. "Not for Geder Palliako."

Daskellin laughed, and for a moment the crickets stopped their songs. He cut a slice from the apple and popped it into his mouth before pointing the blade at Dawson.

"You're making very fine distinctions. You should watch that or you'll turn into a politician."

"Don't be rude," Dawson said. "There's nothing to be done until the war's finished, one way or the other. But as long as I am Lord Marshal, it's my duty to cultivate the loyalty of the high houses. And when we've finished with Asterilhold, those priests have to be dealt with."

Canl Daskellin sighed.

"You're a difficult man to conspire with, Dawson. The last time we did this, it didn't go well."

Dawson frowned, and then a slow, joyless smile spread across his lips.

"Now I think you're asking something of *me*," he said.

"My youngest. Sanna. She's taken a liking to the Lord Regent. Once we purge these cultist friends of his, I was thinking your boy Jorey might hold a ball. Make some introductions."

The words *You want me as your daughter's procurer?* came to Dawson's tongue, but he took another bite of chicken, and they stayed there.

"Sanna seems a lovely girl," Dawson said. "Whatever happens, I'd be pleased to help her in any way I can."

"Spoken like a diplomat," Daskellin said. Dawson frowned, but didn't reply. He would accept insult. For now, anyway. There was time. If he failed at Seref Bridge, there might be nothing but time. And blood and battles. Daskellin seemed to lose himself in the slow-rising smoke from the brazier. His dark brows were troubled.

"One question for you," he said. "Do you think it's true? Do you think that King Lechan knew. That he approved?"

"I don't know."

"But do you *think*?"

"Yes."

Daskellin nodded.

"I do too," he said. "So for now, at least, your conspiracy of foreign priests is in the right."

The morning smelled of wildflowers. Rain had fallen in the night, wetting the ground, and the morning sun had heated it. Mist hovered no higher than a walking man's knees. The scouts had come to Dawson at first light, and so he was prepared for the sight. The river curved up from the south in a carved canyon of earth and stone. It ran high with the night's rain, white spray rising almost to the pale strip of jade that spanned it. On the far shore, the keep was as round as a drum, as high as three men, and made from grey stone and mortar the color of old blood. On the Antean shore—*his* shore—the building was square and made of chalk-white brick. The arrow slits looked down on the dragon's road as it entered the keep and as it left. The merlons were narrow, with barely enough room for an archer to stand and fire and step back.

The banners of Asterilhold flew over both keeps, but they were few. Three stood on the white keep, limp and dark with dew and damp. Two others claimed the farther side. Behind Dawson, twenty knights from fifteen houses. Bannien and Broot, Corenhall and Osterling Fells, the houses and holdings of Antea. Fifteen banners to their five. Four hundred men to whatever lurked behind those arrow slits.

Jorey rode up beside him. The boy's face was pale and closed. He had a wife at home now. Dawson remembered the first fight he'd ridden into when he knew he'd be leaving a widow behind. It changed things.

"They're split," Jorey said. "Why are they split?"

"In hopes of holding both sides," Dawson said. "If they put all their men on our soil and we beat them back, they come to the far keep in disarray. If they put all their men in the far keep, they lose safe passage over the river."

"They'll pull back now, though," Jorey said. "They're fortified, but we've numbers. They have to know that. If they make a stand together on the farther side, they stand a chance, at least. Splitting their own forces is madness."

"It's bravery," Dawson said. "Those three banners? They're not there to win the battle. They're there to hold us back until reinforcements come."

"We can overrun the far keep," Jorey said. "With the men we have, we will take it."

"Perhaps not with the men we have after the white keep's ours, though. And if their reinforcements come, not at all." Dawson turned in his saddle, his eyes on his squire. "Sound formation. We haven't got time."

They took the field, archers and swordsmen, pikemen and the small siege tower, its ram a log with its head dipped in bronze and long enough for three men to take each side. Dawson had seen midwinter festivals that had put more wood in the grate. But these were not castles, only river keeps, and the small ram was what they had to work with.

His army took formation. There was only one task left before the world turned to steel and blood. He called for Fallon Broot. The man trotted over, his comic mustache flopping up and down with the gait of his mount.

"Lord Broot," Dawson said. "Will you take the honors?"

"Pleased to, Lord Marshal," he said, and to his credit, he sounded as though he actually was. Broot took the caller's horn from Dawson's squire and rode out toward the pale brick keep. When he judged himself just out of arrow's range, Broot stopped and lifted the horn to his mouth. Dawson strained to hear.

"In the name of King Aster, and of Lord Regent Palliako, and in the name of the Severed Throne, do you yield?"

It seemed for a moment the day held its breath. An answer came, but too faint to make out. Then a flight of arrows flashing silver in the morning sun and falling just short of Broot and his mount. The knight lifted the horn to his mouth again.

"Remember that I offered, y'cocksuckers!"

Broot rode back hard, his face ruddy and his weak chin jutting forward. He surrendered the caller's horn.

"I say we split their asses, Lord Marshal."

"Noted, sir. And my thanks," Dawson said. "Call the foot attack."

As Dawson watched, the attack surged forward like water after a dam has given way. Arrows flew from the white keep's slits and archers appeared on the merlons. Over the shouting of the attack, Dawson could make out no individual screaming, but he'd seen enough of war to know it was there. At the distance of command, it looked almost calm, but within that flow of bodies, it was the loudest, most joyful and frightening feeling in the world. They had committed, and now there was no turning back.

Thin ladders rose into the air with barbed hooks at the end to make them more difficult to shove back. The dull thud of the battering ram came, and again, and again. The soldiers of Antea who had shields had them raised over their heads, but there were few. Two of the ladders took hold and men swarmed up them. Dawson watched, his teeth worrying at his lips. There was movement to the north. At the edge of the river. Men, wearing the colors of Asterilhold. A hundred of them at least. They had hidden in the muck and cold by the river's edge, preparing to fall on the enemy from behind.

"Call danger in the north," Dawson said, and his squire lifted the trumpet. Three short blasts for danger, two long for north. The ambush looked to be swordsmen for the greatest part. Only a few pikes seemed to waver in the air. The battering ram's dull thud carried over everything, but the shouting changed. Dawson's men shifted toward the new enemy.

"The charge," Dawson shouted, drawing his blade. "Sound the charge."

Dawson and the knights of Antea flew down toward the river and the waiting foe. There were more pikes than it had seemed, but not enough. A horse screamed and fell somewhere behind Dawson and to the left, but by the time he heard it he was already in the press, hewing at men's heads and shoulders. To his right, Makarian Vey, Baron of Corren-hall, was swinging a battle hammer and shouting out an old taproom song. To his left, Jorey was chasing down an enemy soldier whose nerve had broken. Dawson's fingers ached pleasantly and there was blood on his sword. The steady rhythm of the battering ram changed and a shout rose from the south. The white keep's door, giving way.

"The keep!" he shouted. "Finish them, and to the keep! Push these bastards back! Antea and Simeon!"

A ragged shout answered him, and the knights of Antea turned with him, riding fast to the white keep.

The bodies of Antean soldiers and farmers, men and boys, lay on the soft ground outside the keep, fallen from the ladders or arrow-pierced. Not all were dead. Within, the sounds of combat and murder rang. Dawson didn't dismount, but rode through the keep's yard, leaning hard toward the far gate. His knights rode behind him. The jade bridge reached across the river. Old rails had been built at its sides, worn planks bound to the jade top and bottom and nailed together. The wood was faded and splintering, a broken and decayed human work over the eternal and uncaring artifact of the dragons.

Somewhere between thirty and forty men stood on the bridge. Behind them at the far side of the river the round keep stood. It looked taller from here, its wide wall leaning slightly out to make scaling it more difficult. Its gate was closed, shutting out both enemy and ally.

But when they opened it to bring their men in, there would be a chance.

"To me!" Dawson shouted. "All men to me!"

His squire was long left behind, but the knights and the soldiers took up the call. *To the Lord Marshal* tolled through the keep like a bell. Six men took up the fallen battering ram, trotting up with it to just within the gate. One of them was a mess of blood, his right ear gone. On the bridge, the defeated men wailed and clamored to the round keep for shelter or steeled themselves for the charge.

And then, above them, a new banner rose. And another. A third. A fourth.

The reinforcements had come. Dawson looked over his shoulder at the assembled men. Of his knights, almost all remained with him. Of his foot, less. Much less. But there was a chance.

"Archers fore!" he shouted.

A dozen men, not more, ran to the gate, bows in their hands.

"Don't go all at once, boys," Dawson said over the roar of the river and the laments of the bridge-trapped men. "We're moving the bastards on the far side to pity. So take this slow."

One at a time, Dawson's archers loosed arrows. The men on the bridge had nowhere to flee. They screamed and they wept and they shouted rage. Once, they charged Dawson's line and were pushed back. The crowd of them grew smaller. Twenty men. Eighteen. Fourteen. Ten. The green of the jade and the red of the blood were like a thing from a painter's brush, too beautiful to be wholly real. In despair, one man leaped into the churning water. Nine. Dawson kept his attention on the gate against which the doomed men were beating. It didn't open.

It wouldn't.

"End them all and close the gate," Dawson said at last. "We'll send word to the Lord Regent that the invasion is pushed back and the border secured."

And that we were too late, he didn't say. He raised his sword and pulled it down, making his duelist's salute to the opposing command as the white keep's gate closed before him. The first battle of the war was a standoff, and if his experience told him anything, this was a sign of things to come.

Marcus

I'll kill you," the Kurtadam man shouted. His fists were balled at his sides. His furred cheeks and forehead softened the anguish in his face, leaving him looking less like a man whose hopes of a better life were being crushed and more like a disappointed puppy. "You can't do this, I'll kill you."

"You won't," Marcus said. "Really, just stop."

The queensman was a Firstblood boy hardly older than Cithrin. He nodded toward the weeping Kurtadam but spoke to Marcus.

"That is a threat of death against a citizen," the boy said. "You want, I can take him to the magistrate."

"How would he pay the fine?" Marcus asked. "Leave him be. He's having a bad day."

The house stood on a small, private square. The queensman at Marcus's side was the only representative of the law. The men and women going into the house and hauling out the Kurtadam man's things to the pile on the street were all Marcus's. All Pyk's. All the bank's.

A crowd had gathered. Neighbors and street merchants and whoever happened to be passing by. There was nothing like a crowd for drawing a crowd. Enen, the Kurtadam woman Marcus had hired as a guard when Cithrin first sent him out to build her branch, came out with a complex puppet cradled in her arms like a sleeping child. She laid it gently on the growing mound of things.

"How can you do this?" the Kurtadam man shouted at her. "How can you do this to one of your own kind?"

Enen ignored him and went back in. A Jasuru man—Hart, his name was—came out with a double handful of clothes. Silks and brocades, some of them. It wasn't hard to see where the bank's money had gone, but the collateral on the loan wasn't tunics and hose. Wasn't even the puppet works. It was rights to the house itself, and so now that the terms of default were in play, it was the house Marcus and his guards were taking. Yardem ducked out from under the low doorframe, a sewn mattress under his arm. The Kurtadam man burst into hopeless tears.

From the crowd, a man laughed and started making false crying sounds of his own.

"That's the last of it, sir," Yardem said. "We've started boarding it up. Making it secure."

"Thank you," Marcus said.

"Yes, sir."

The Kurtadam man was sitting on his mattress with his head in his hands. Sobs racked his body. Marcus squatted down beside him.

"All right," Marcus said. "So here's what happens next. You're going to be angry and you're going to want to get back at us. Me, the bank, anyone. It'll take a week, maybe more, to get past the worst of that, but in the meantime, you won't be thinking things through. You're going to tell yourself that burning the house is the right thing. If you can't have it, no one can. Like that. Are you listening?"

"Eat shit," the man said between sobs.

"I'll take that for yes. So I'm going to leave some of my

people here. They'll be in the house and the street just to see to it that nothing interesting happens. If anyone comes into the house, they'll kill them. If anyone tries to damage the house from the outside, they'll hurt them badly. So don't let's dance that, all right?"

Maybe it was the gentleness of the threat, but the Kurtadam man stopped long enough to nod. That was a good sign, at least.

"I'm going to make you an offer now," Marcus said. "I don't mean any offense by it. It's not the bank doing it, it's me. You've got all this and no place for it. Your things are going to rot in the street. Won't do you any good. I'll give you thirty weight in silver for the whole thing, and you can walk away. Start over."

The tears were falling from the man's eyes, beading on his oily, otter-fine fur like dewdrops.

"Worth more," he choked.

"Not lying on the street, it's not," Marcus said.

"I need my puppets. It's how I live."

"You can keep three of the puppets, then. Same price."

Despair washed over the man's expression as he looked at his chests and clothes, a great plaster vase with cut flowers wilting in it. The crowd looked on in amusement or false sympathy.

"I was going to pay," the man said softly.

"You weren't," Marcus said. "And that's all past now. Take your dolls and your silver, and go try again, all right?"

The man nodded. More tears. Marcus pressed a wallet with the silver into the man's hand.

"All right, let's load all this up except whichever three puppets he wants, and take it back to the warehouse."

"Yes, sir," Yardem said. "And after?"

"Bathhouse. I'm feeling a touch soiled."

*   *   *

The summer in Porte Oliva was a bandit. It hid behind the soft sea breeze and the long, comfortable evenings. It spoke in the friendly and reassuring tones of surf and bird-call. If at midday the sun felt like a hand pushing down against his shoulder, Marcus could still call it companionable. The attack would come—blazing days and sweat-filled nights. The Kurtadam would shave themselves back almost to stubble. The Firstblood and the Cinnae would abandon modesty in favor of comfort. The business of the day would stop just after midday, the city falling into fevered dreams until evening when the summer sun lost some of its violence.

The attack wasn't there yet. The spring was still lulling them all into lowering their guard. But it would come.

Cithrin was over two weeks gone, and likely on the water between Sara-sur-Mar and Carse. The days without her had been made from the same cloth as those with—payments to deliver, the strongbox to watch, the payments to retrieve. Now and then, a client or partner would need a few swords to walk with someone or something. Now that Pyk's role was uncontested, she seemed to calm a bit, but she still generated a dozen minor tasks that had to be done and complained at the money it cost to accomplish them. So in a sense, nothing had changed, and in a sense it all had.

"I'm going to go after her," Marcus said.

Yardem sat forward, drinking his beer carefully. His silence was thoughtful and disapproving. Marcus leaned forward over the rough plank table. It wasn't their customary taproom. Three young Jasuru boys, their scales bright as greensnakes, played drums in the yard, the complex rhythms making the air richer. Marcus took his bowl of beef and snow peas, looked at it, and put it down again.

"I was thinking about coming from Vanai when Cithrin was passing herself as a boy," he said.

Yardem nodded.

"You'd be in a dress then, sir?"

"I could go in carter's clothes. Or as a merchant. It isn't as if I'd need to announce myself. Just ride in, stay quiet, and when she's ready to come back I can travel with her then."

"Why?"

"Not much point in staying hidden when I'm heading away, is there?"

"I mean why would you go after her, sir? What's the advantage?"

"I'd think that was obvious. Keep her safe."

Yardem sighed.

"What?" Marcus said. "Go ahead. You know you want to say it. Tell me she's in no danger, and that Corisen Mout and Barth can keep her as safe as anyone. She's heading toward a war. A real one, not one of the little shell games like who runs Maccia. She doesn't understand how that kind of violence can spread. And you know that's true."

"If you think three blades would make her safe where two won't, why not send someone else, sir? Enen's been to Carse."

Yardem's dark eyes met his. Yardem's ironic subservience had become such a habit over the years that Marcus sometimes forgot the hardness that could take the Tralgu's features. In moments like this, it was easy to believe that the Tralgu had been bred for the hunt and the kill as well as a deadly kind of loyalty. Marcus silently hefted a few arguments, but under Yardem's implacable gaze, they all seemed like felling a tree with a toenail knife.

"You want her to be in trouble, sir, but she isn't."

Marcus's impatience shifted. He felt his own gaze cool.

"Meaning what?"

Yardem flicked an ear, the rings jingling, and turned back to his mug. When he started to lift it, Marcus put his palm over its mouth and pressed it back down to the table.

"Asked you a question."

Yardem let go of the beer.

"After Ellis, sir, you looked for revenge."

"I looked for justice."

"If you say so," Yardem said, refusing to be turned. "I was with you for that. Not like we are now, but I was there. I saw it happen. You didn't only kill Springmere. You planned it, you built it. You made sure that he could see his death coming, understood it, and couldn't do anything to stop it. And when he was dead, you thought it would be better. Not fixed. You're not stupid, but you thought that...*justice*... would redeem something. Only it didn't."

"I am just certain you have an argument in this some-where," Marcus said. "Because I just know you aren't haul-ing Alys and Merian out of their graves to score cheap points."

"I'm not, sir," Yardem said. There was nothing like apol-ogy in his voice. "I'm saying you didn't only kill Springmere because he needed to die. You were looking for redemption."

"More of your religious—"

"And you were looking to Cithrin for the same," Yardem said, refusing to be silenced. "She was a girl and she was at the mercy of a merciless world. We helped her. Hatred didn't bring you peace, and somewhere in your soul, you thought that love would. And here we are, Cithrin bel Sarcour saved, only you still don't have the redemption you wanted. So you're trying to tell yourself and everyone else that she still needs saving when she doesn't. She's fine, sir."

"I didn't want to work for her," Marcus said. "I wanted

to walk away. You were the one who argued that we should go back. That was you."

"It was. But that was when she needed us."

"The way she doesn't need us now?"

"Yes, sir. The way she doesn't now," Yardem said, his voice going soft and gentle in a way that was worse than shouting. "We have steady work for fair pay. We have shelter and we have food. Interesting if that's not what we were looking for."

"We spend our days taking people's houses and throwing them out in the street. How's that a way to live?"

"Used to be, we'd kill them, sir," Yardem said. "Not sure this is worse."

Marcus rose to his feet. The drumbeats throbbing out from the yard reached their crisis and collapsed. In the silence, Marcus's voice was louder than he'd meant it to be.

"You can pay for your own damn drinks."

"Yes, sir."

The other men and women in the taproom cleared space as he stalked out, eyes both wide and averted. If any of them had spoken to him, there would have been blows over it, but no one did. In the street, the evening sun was turning the high clouds to red and gold—blood and coins. The sky behind them seemed bluer by comparison. Marcus took himself back north, toward the Grand Market and the café, the barracks and the counting house. The puppeteers haunted the street corners, calling to the crowds for attention and coppers. When his anger had cooled from white to a dull and aching redness, Marcus stopped for a few minutes by one. It was a simple retelling of the usual PennyPenny the Jasuru. The main puppet was nicely made, painted to give the impression of scales, and used convincingly enough that the puppet seemed to have emotions of its own. Not that

PennyPenny required much more than surprise, rage, and remorse. When the hero threw his wife and baby down a well, Marcus tossed a copper into the collecting bag and walked on.

Everything came back to that. Blood and death and the impotence of violence. In the PennyPenny shows, the wife and child would return transformed into agents of retribution, but even then, the answer was only the torture and death of the Jasuru. There was no reconciliation. No chance for time to move backward and the things that were lost to be recovered. That was the story Marcus wanted to see. Except that even if he did, he wouldn't be convinced by it.

From spite as much as anything, he revisited his plan. A good horse and enough coin for fair exchange on the road would get him to Carse. He could take a room or light work in the Firstblood's quarter without anyone particularly taking note of him. Probably. The Medean bank wouldn't be difficult to find, and then he could find a place to sit and play the beggar until Cithrin went in or out, and then...

He paused at the mouth of an alley and spat into the shadows. It had all seemed plausible that morning.

The squat little building across from the gymnasium hadn't been built as a barracks, but now it was. The marks of its other lives were still on it: the patched holes where some great mechanism had been mounted to the walls, then taken out and the walls patched with stone of a different color. The easternmost roof beam blackened by some ancient fire. A series of notches chiseled into stone to mark the growth, year by year, of some long-forgotten child. Perhaps it had been a school or the sort of overcrowded house where ten different families lived all within each other's lives. In winter, the heat came from a brick-maker's stove so old that the ironwork was worn almost as thin as cloth.

The men and women within were his company. The private guard of the Medean bank. In practice, there were few of them there except late at night when they would come in from work or leisure, string hammocks or unfurl bedrolls, and sleep together out of wind and weather. Now there was only Roach, the brown-chitined Timzinae boy whose true name no one used. And less a boy than he'd been when Marcus hired him.

"All well, Captain?"

"Apart from it being a corrupt and fallen world," Marcus said, and the boy laughed as if it were a joke. Marcus shouldered his bedroll and climbed to the roof. A pigeon startled when he pushed open the trap, flailing at the air in panic. Marcus unrolled his bed, and then lay back and watched the clouds grey and the sky darken. Voices came from the street and from the barracks beneath him. His mind kept returning to Alys and Merian. The family he'd had, back when he'd been the kind of man who could have a family. Alys's dark hair with its threadings of grey. Merian's long face, slightly indignant from the moment she'd left her mother's womb. He could still hear his little girl laughing in her crib, could still recall pressing his lips to his wife's neck just where it turned to shoulder. The brilliant young general, champion and Lord Marshal of the rightful heir, Lian Springmere. He'd been going to remake the world, back then.

It was more than a decade now since Alys and Merian stopped feeling all pain. Some days he could barely remember their faces. Some days, he had the physical certainty that they were in the room with him, invisible and sorrowful and accusing. Grief did things to men, but knowing that didn't help.

It was full dark when the trap opened again. Marcus knew without looking that it was Yardem. The tall Tralgu folded his legs beside Marcus's head.

"Pyk was asking for you, sir. Wants to know why things you've bought are in the bank's warehouse."

"Because I'm guard captain for the bank."

"She might find that more convincing from you."

"Unless she wants to go haul it to the street herself, the reason doesn't much matter."

Yardem chuckled.

"What?" Marcus said.

"That was the argument I offered her too. She didn't seem to find the prospect interesting."

"That, old friend," Marcus said, "is a powerfully unpleasant woman."

"Is."

"Still. She's not the worst I've worked for."

"Quite a bit of room in that, sir."

"Fair point."

The pigeon or one like it landed on the edge of the building, considering the pair with one wet, black eye and then the other.

"Well, Yardem. The day you throw me in a ditch and take over the company?"

"Sir?"

"It's not today."

"Good to know, sir."

"Do you think Merian would have made a good banker?"

"Hard to say, sir. I imagine she would have if she'd decided to be."

"I think I'm going to get some rest. Face the Pyk in the morning."

"Yes, sir. Also?" Yardem cleared his throat, a deep and distant rumble. "If I went too far..."

"Going too far's your job. When it's called for, you should always go too far. Everyone else respects me too much," Marcus said. "Well, except for Kit."

"I'll remember that, sir."

Yardem rose and padded away. The moon hid behind dark clouds. The stars came out, first one, and then a handful, and then a host so large as to beggar the imagination. Marcus watched them until his mind began to slide sideways of its own accord, and he pulled his blanket around him. The smell of roasting pork flirted and vanished, borne on the fickle breeze.

When the nightmare came, as he had known it would, it was almost the same as always. The flames, the screaming, the feeling of the small body, dead in his arms. Only this time, there were three figures in the fire. He woke before he could tell if Cithrin was the third or if he was.

Cithrin

In facing her first sea voyage, Cithrin had expected many of the hardships that came with being in a ship: the nausea and the close quarters and the fear of knowing that her life depended on the ship remaining afloat without any particular control over whether it did. All had proven real, though few as unpleasant as she had anticipated they would be. The surprise was how much the enforced inactivity calmed her. At any time of day or night, she would take herself to the deck, lean against the rail, and consider the waves or the distant dark line of the coast as it slipped past. There was nothing she could do, and so there was nothing required of her. If she willed the ship on faster toward Carse or grew homesick for her little rooms above the counting house, it made no difference, and before long she found herself simply inhabiting the moment. She was one of the first to see the Drowned.

At first, it was no more than a slightly lighter tone to the blue. Then it was something under the water—a bark-stripped log or some pale-fleshed fish. Then it was the body of a Firstblood man, naked, staring emptily up toward the air. A sailor called, laughter in the sound, and footsteps pattered behind her as the crew came to the rail with her. The Drowned man wasn't alone. Cithrin saw a woman floating at his side, and then another beyond her. And then hundreds more. Between one moment and the next, the sea was full of them. The slow movements of their limbs could almost have been the water pushing them. As Cithrin watched, one rose up from the depths just under her—a young man almost a boy with the thin, coltish frame of an adolescent or a Cinnae. His dark eyes seemed to find her, and slowly, he smiled.

"Never seen the Drowned before, Magistra?" Barth asked. She hadn't noticed him there.

"Once," she said. "There was one in one of the canals in Vanai. But never like this."

"Usually travel in pods a little smaller'n this. We got lucky, seeing so many at once."

A sailor shouted and leaped, diving out into the water. With his splash, the Drowned sank at once, falling away beneath the water as fast as stones. Cithrin watched the boy beneath her vanish. In the water, the sailor laughed and tried to dive after them.

"What an ass," Barth said with no particular heat in his voice.

"Why do they run?"

"They're slow, they're weak out of water, and they're naked. Sailors and shoremen sometimes have cruel ideas of sport," Barth said. "The Drowned are like anyone else. They see a threat, and they avoid it. Even fish do that."

Cithrin nodded, but she also watched the sailor when his shipmates pulled him up grinning from the water, and she made a point of avoiding him for the rest of the voyage.

Carse. The white chalk cliffs began half a day before the city came into sight, rising from the seashore like a glacier. The sea itself seemed to take on a paleness, and the hazy sky was lighter than blue. The first signs of human life—or rather of the dozen races who built above that water—were the fishing ships. Small and black, they were coming back toward the cliffs now, or else making their way north toward the smaller towns nearer the water.

Despite being on the sea, Carse was not, properly speaking, a port. It sat at the end of the dragon's roads in the north and looked down over the waves. A great network of docks encrusted the base of the cliffs, but few merchants chose to use them. Rather they would travel to where the cliffs ended and haul their goods overland to the great city. Cithrin and the other passengers, having little to carry, got off at the docks and made their way up the switchbacks that rose to Carse proper. She found it somewhat unnerving to see the other, older paths still marking the cliffs, but eroded and crumbling past usefulness. One day the white chalk that paled her shoes and dress as she staggered up the cliff, her balance not yet accustomed to the stillness of earth, would be that same impassable ruin. Only hopefully not today.

At the top of the cliffs, the trail bent east, transforming itself into broad iron stairs that led up to a great courtyard and the city itself. If it had been designed to impress someone walking up to it this way, it could hardly have been better. The council tower rose up, ten stories high, its stone as smooth as skin. The top floor sported a dozen windows on each side with colored glass in each, ready to announce the edicts and decisions of the Council of Eventide whenever it met. Even in the height of war, the tower was sacrosanct. No king or prince would cross the theologians and cunning men who made up the council, and Carse would have been less of a jewel in any crown without it.

Beyond that, a jade dragon larger than the ship she'd sailed there in lay curled with its great snout tucked under a carved wing. Cithrin had read of the Grave of Dragons and the statue of sleeping Morade, last of the Dragon Emperors, at its mouth. Even warned, it took her breath away.

But the city hadn't been built to be seen from the top of the cliff. It had been made to be seen from the air. Buildings had fallen and been rebuilt, what could burn, ancient armies had burned and restored and burned again, but in its heart, Carse was a city of dragons. Its streets and squares were wide to make room for great bodies that had not walked them in more than centuries. The great perches where, according to story, the dragons once met were kept clean and ready, as if someday the masters of humanity might return.

Cithrin had spent her childhood in Vanai with narrow streets and canals, her adulthood in the tight ways and white walls of Porte Oliva. Carse was huge and grey, stately and sober and dignified. The wide streets felt like a boast, the high towers rose like trees. A single man in fine chainmail, a blade at his side, walked through the street, and Cithrin realized with a start that he was part of the city guard. In Porte Oliva, the queensmen traveled in pairs at the minimum and more often groups of five or six. The prince's guard in Vanai had worn ostentatious gilt armor and carried lead-dipped clubs for beating down those who they saw fit. To have a single man with no apparent allies in sight was either high folly or the mark of a city where violence was rare. She wasn't sure if she felt safer or more threatened.

On the street corner, a cunning man conjured flashes of lightning from the air, tiny booms of thunder accompanying him like an aggressive drum. He had no beggar's box. Cithrin wasn't sure if she was meant to watch him or keep moving on.

It took her an hour to find the Medean bank. The front was even more modest than her own counting house; a black door between a fish-seller's shop and a small, disreputable temple. Only the symbol of the bank and a wooden sign in the shape of a coin marked it. She motioned to her guards that they should stay in the street. Anxiety snaked through her belly and exhaustion plucked at the muscles of her legs and back. The calm of watching the Thin Sea was like a dream half recalled.

She stood before the door, breathing deeply. In her memory, Master Kit reminded her to hold her weight low in her hips and walk with her chin higher. She remembered his voice saying, *You can do this.*

She could, but she didn't have to. No one was expecting her. She could have Barth or Corisen Mout take the books in, and they could go back home without ever imposing on Komme Medean or anyone else. If she didn't go in, they couldn't turn her away or belittle her. As long as she didn't try, she wouldn't fail.

She pushed the door open and walked through.

Within, the counting house was less gloomy than she'd expected, lit by clerestory windows and filled with potted ivies and violets on the edge of bloom. A man about Marcus Wester's age—beginning to thicken and grey, but not yet old—with skin the color of polished mahogany leaned out of a door she hadn't seen.

"Help you?" he asked.

Cithrin held up the books as if they were a ward against evil.

"I've brought the reports from Porte Oliva," she said. Her voice was tight and high. She gave thanks she hadn't squeaked.

"Ah, you'll want the holding company. It's three streets north and one west. Use the gate on the west side."

"Thank you," she said, and then, "Are you Magister Nison, then?"

A degree of interest came into the man's expression.

"I am."

"Magister Imaniel used to talk about you," she said, forcing herself to smile.

It wasn't truth. She'd taken his name from the papers and books that had come with her from Vanai. But Magister Imaniel was dead. Cam was dead. All the people who could say otherwise were gone from the world, and so the truth could be whatever she wanted it to be. And right now, she wanted it to be that she and this stranger shared a connection, however slight.

In less than a heartbeat confusion gave way to surprise, and surprise to amusement.

"You're bel Sarcour, then," Nison said. "Wait just a moment."

He vanished again, and she heard his voice calling for someone, and another man's voice calling back. The accent of Carse was fast and clipped, and the only words she could make out were *old man* and *tomorrow*. Not the most informative.

He stepped back into sight wearing a cloak of undyed wool and a smile that didn't seem entirely benign.

"Let me escort you, Magistra," he said.

"Thank you," she said.

If the counting house had been modest, the holding company more than made up for it. Five stories high, it looked less like a building within a city than a fortified keep of its own. The unglazed windows were thin as arrow-slits and the roof had decorative stonework that could easily act as ramparts. Nison guided her through an iron gate and into a courtyard like a palace's. A fountain chuckled and burbled, and incense wafted from windows covered by intricate carved shutters. Servants or slaves had washed the paving stones until there seemed to be neither dirt nor dust anywhere in the yard. He led her into a wide, airy chamber of brick and tapestry and from there up a stairway that curved with the wall to a doorway of oak inlaid with ivory and jet.

It made sense that the holding company would have greater wealth than any of the branches. It was, after all, the reason to have a holding company rather than simply a central branch of the bank. The profits and losses from any individual branch—her own, Magister Nison's, or any of the others—were specific to that branch. They rose or fell on their merits, and all of them paid into a separate business that was the holding company, which gave out no loans and accepted no deposits, but rather mediated the flow of gold between the branches. No one outside the bank held a contract with the holding company or Komme Medean. If Cithrin gave out too many insurance contracts before a war or a bad storm season, she could bankrupt her branch, but her debt ended with her. No one could make claim from this building or from any other branch. In fact, depending on the situation, the holding company might be among the creditors she would suffer to repay.

It seemed little more than a told story, but it was a fiction that made this house a port of safety for wealth and her own an engine of risk. She knew all this and understood it as she knew her numbers and letters. Only she had never before seen it in practice. Silently, she began to recalculate her branch and its worth in terms of the doors and fountains, tapestry and incense. Her head swam a little.

The woman who opened the door to Magister Nison's rapping was dressed in a dark robe of fine cotton and had her sleeves rolled up to the elbow. Cithrin smiled and nodded, totally unsure whether she was seeing a woman of the highest status or a well-dressed servant and trying to land somewhere that would offend neither one. At her side, Magister Nison nodded his head in her direction.

"Magistra bel Sarcour just in from Porte Oliva. She's brought the reports. I thought Komme might like to meet the girl with the biggest balls in Birancour."

"Actually, I'm from the Free Cities," Cithrin said. "Originally."

It was idiotic, but the words spilled out of her mouth as if she'd planned them. The dark-robed woman lifted an eyebrow.

"He's a bit under the weather," the woman said. "It's a bad day."

"I can come back another time," Cithrin said, already half turned away.

"Who's come?" a man's voice called. "Who is it?"

The woman put a hand on Cithrin's wrist like holding a dog's ear to keep it from straying, then leaned back and spoke loudly,

"Magister Nison and Magistra bel Sarcour."

"And you're going to keep 'em standing there?"

The woman and Nison exchanged a shrug, and she stepped back, motioning them into the private rooms. The floors were golden-brown wood of a kind Cithrin had never seen before lacquered until it shone like wet stone. Sconces of gold and silver hung from the walls, the polished metal throwing back the light of small, delicate candles. A tapestry hung on the wall unmistakably showing the building that they were presently in, but in colors so bright and vibrant that Cithrin couldn't begin to imagine what dyes could have done it; it was like looking at the iridescent wing of a butterfly. She wished that she'd stopped to buy some grander dress before she came. Or at least cleaner sandals.

The room they entered was open on one side to a balcony

that looked down into the courtyard. The branches of a tree shifted in their spring green, the new leaves catching the sun and glittering like water or coins. Komme Medean lay in the center of the room, reclining on a seat woven from leather straps. Apart from a loincloth, he was naked, his brown skin powdered almost white. His belly was the solid fat of middle age, and a fringe of white hair clung to his scalp. He reminded Cithrin of a lump of bread dough coated with flour and left to rise.

His right leg was bent and of normal human proportion, but his left stood straight out, held in its own sling. The knee and ankle were massive, misshapen, and angry. A young Timzinae in the robes of a cunning man was crouched beside the diseased limb, chanting under his breath. Cithrin had never seen a man with gout before, and while she'd known it was an unpleasant ailment, she hadn't understood the degree. She forced herself not to stare. Something in the cunning man's fingers clicked, and he grunted as if in pain. Komme Medean ignored him. Pale brown eyes swept up and down her, evaluating her not the way a man would a woman, but as a carpenter might a plank of lumber.

"I've brought the reports from Porte Oliva," Cithrin said.

"All right. What do you want?" Komme Medean said. And when she didn't answer immediately, "You carried your reports yourself instead of sending a courier. You came here yourself. You want something. What is it?"

The moment balanced on the edge of a blade. It was true, she'd come all this way, and for this. To speak to the man at the center of the great labyrinth of power and gold and win him over to her. She'd imagined the delicate conversation of a courtier, the half-playful and half-serious questions that Magister Imaniel had raised her with. She'd imagined herself impressing the man slowly over the course of hours or days. And now, instead, she stood before a mostly naked, sick man, as the central question lay out on the floor between them like a broken toy.

The moment stretched, and Cithrin felt her opportunity slipping just beyond her reach. She was embarrassing herself in front of the very man she'd meant to impress. And then, from the back of her mind, an old voice whispered. Cary, the actress who'd helped Cithrin play the part of a banker, of a woman full-grown and at the height of her power. *The woman you're pretending at*, her imagined Cary whispered, *what would she say?*

Cithrin raised her courage and her chin.

"I've come to tell you your notary has the soul of a field mouse and the tact of a landslide. And after that, I want to charm you into giving me more of your money and greater freedom to use it," Cithrin said. Her voice a little hard and buzzing at the edges. "How'm I doing so far?"

The room was silent. Even the cunning man stopped his chanting. And then Komme Medean, soul and spirit of the Medean bank, barked out a laugh, and Cithrin let herself breathe again.

"Bring her a chair, and pass me those reports," he said. She put the sealed books into his hand. He was a bigger man than he'd seemed at first. He broke the seals and opened the ledgers, reading the ciphered text as easily as if it had been simple letters. "All right, Magistra. Let's see how you're doing. So far."

Geder

As a boy, even a young man, Geder had imagined what it would be like to be king. His daydreams had seemed perfectly benign at the time. If he were king, men like Sir Alan Klin would be called to heel. If he were king, he would see that the libraries of Camnipol—of all Antea and its holdings—were well stocked and maintained. If he were king he would command any woman he wanted to his bed, and no one would laugh at him or reject him or comment on the size of his belly. They had been the sort of fantasies a young man could have safely, without any threat that they might one day come true.

Except, of course, that they had.

Now he woke in the mornings with a dozen servants already standing around his bed. There was the ritual humiliation of being bathed and dressed. He understood that it was all meant as a show of dignity. The Lord Regent of Antea was not a man who put on his own clothing, who shaved his own chin, who laced his own boots. He submitted to being helped up from his bed, to having his night clothes taken from him and standing naked for that terrible moment until other men's hands pulled fresh undergarments over his body. He could not bathe without his body servants attending him. Or perhaps he could, but it would have meant ordering them away, and ordering them away would have been admitting that it bothered him to have them see him undressed. And once he admitted that it bothered him, then every time it had happened up until now became shameful in retrospect.

He should have refused the very first time, but he hadn't known then, and now it was too late. He was trapped by what had come before into enduring what was inevitably going to come next.

As to the idea of asking a woman to bed with him, he'd have died first. There was no doubt—*none*—that at least one servant would be discreetly in earshot the whole time. Even if he'd known how to bring up the subject to a woman, the idea that he would be putting on a display for the help was intolerable.

Once he'd gotten through the worst of it, though, the breakfast was always brilliant, and the mornings until midday he spent in the personal library reading ancient books and working on his translations. Or else he would visit Aster and they'd mock his tutors together. Usually his awareness of the great cloud of servants would diminish over time until they almost seemed to be there for their own reasons, and Geder stopped feeling quite so much onstage.

The Kingspire itself seemed constantly implausible. During his time in court, Geder had been to a few of its great halls, but living in it he began to see the place less as a building and more like a great insects' mound like something out of Southling fairy tales. The walls were only apparently solid. Most were crisscrossed with servants' passages and hidden ways. A thin, dingy hallway might loop through the basements only to open into a vast private bathhouse with indigo tiles and heated water steaming down in a waterfall. There were listener's holes everywhere—under benches, hidden inside archways—where an eavesdropper might be placed.

There was even an entire chamber that was built as a massive dumbwaiter and ready to haul the king and his guests up to the greatest heights of the spire without the trouble of being carried up stairs to get there. All the air was perfumed. All the conservatories stood ready with musicians to play at the king's command, or in Geder's case, the regent's. He constantly felt as though he was living inside someone else's idea of who he should be, and it left him feeling a bit tentative. Unless, of course, Basrahip was with him. The priest was a steadying presence.

"Little change, Lord Regent," Lord Daskellin said as he stepped across the war chamber.

Wider than a dueling field, the floor of the room had been covered in soil and sod all formed and shaped to match the geography of Asterilhold and western Antea. Geder's working desk stood near the wall where Camnipol would have been. The promontory on which the city stood was a little step down. The mountains dividing Asterilhold from the Dry Wastes came up almost to his knees. The northern coast was bordered by tiny blue beads poured out until the false sea met the walls like running into the edge of the world.

Canl Daskellin stepped across the fields of Asterilhold, over the great knot of armies playing stop-me-stop-you in the marshes of the south, then the Siyat and the arrayed army crouched around the Seref Bridge. The only changes since the day before were the positions of the ships on the sea of beads, and really only four of those were significant.

"Good morning, my lord," Basrahip said.

"Minister," Daskellin replied, and both men seemed pleased to leave the conversation there.

"I haven't had word from Lord Kalliam," Geder said. "Something could have happened in the south, still."

"Could," Daskellin said, and his tone finished the sentence. *Something could have happened, but it hadn't.*

Geder hated the vague apology in his own voice, but Canl Daskellin had been King Simeon's Protector of Northport, among other things. Growing up, men like Daskellin and Bannien, Issandrian and Maas had been the great lights of the court. Now that Geder was Lord Regent, Daskellin paid court, and still Geder always had the feeling of being the junior when the man was in the room. That he had recalled Daskellin from the field and was prepared to command him again now only made the awkwardness more profound.

"I was thinking," Geder said, rising from his desk, walking gently to avoid crushing his own forces camped near the Seref, "that we could build a second bridge. I read an essay about Koort Mahbi, the third Regos of Borja? He had a moving bridge designed with little boats on the supports. The way he did it, his army could push the bridge out over a river, and then move across it, and pull it up on the other side. There and then gone again. If we made one like that we could go to the river over here." He touched the ground where the Siyat curved. "We wouldn't be near a good road, but even overland, I don't think we'd be more than three days from Kaltfel."

"It's a thought," Daskellin said. "There's still the problem of getting enough men onto the far side. If Kalliam had managed to get us both sides of the Seref, there would have been a protected place for the troops to gather. A movable bridge like that? If it's not wide enough to bring a large number of men across at once, a couple of dozen bowmen could kill our full army a few men at a time."

"But Kalliam says they can't move in the marshlands," Geder said.

"And he's right. The reason Asterilhold and Antea split

when the High Kings died was that river, the runoff from the mountains, and the mud between the two."

Geder cleared his throat.

"That's why I want you to go to Northcoast." Daskellin looked up at him now. Geder wasn't sure, but he thought there was a hint of pleasure in the man's expression. "The gap between the mountain ranges there and there is hilly and it's got about a thousand little holdfasts and garrisons, but if King Tracian were to move a force to his border, Asterilhold would have to draw men back from the south to keep them from invading, yes?"

Daskellin paced the room to the fields of Ellis and looked back. He stroked his chin.

"It's possible, yes," he said.

Geder glanced over to Basrahip, who nodded. A small, relieved smile drew Geder's lips wider.

"He doesn't actually have to invade, even," Geder said. "If he's just there looking as if he might..."

"Have you told the Lord Marshal about this idea?"

"Ah. No. Why? Should I?"

Daskellin shrugged.

"Dawson doesn't like involving other kingdoms in Antean affairs. I think he finds having allies undignified. But yes, I have friends and contacts in Northcoast. Not all of them are in the court. I'm not sure what the situation is there, but I can find out. Where's Bannien?"

"Lord Bannien's holding Anninfort," Geder said. "Kalliam thought there was too much chance of a fresh rebellion. His sons are with the larger army. When can you be on your way?"

"As soon as you'd like."

"Tomorrow, then," Geder said. "I've sent to Lord Skestinin. He'll have a ship ready to take you, provided Asinport hasn't broken the blockade. But Skestinin doesn't think it will have."

"I will do my best," Daskellin said, with a small, crisp bow. He hesitated. "I don't mean to be rude. But may I ask something about the southern front?"

"Yes?"

"I'd heard that Alan Klin was in the field. At the front, in fact. Quite far in the front."

Geder shrugged.

"We're hoping to lure the enemy out of position," he said. "And I thought giving Klin the opportunity to regain some part of his honor seemed kind. Don't you think?"

"Of course, Lord Regent," Daskellin said with another bow. "I understand."

After the door had closed behind him, Geder turned to the priest.

"Well?"

Basrahip cocked his head.

"My prince?"

"Was it true?"

"Yes, he understood," the priest said calmly.

"What did he understand?"

"He didn't say, my prince."

"Does he approve?"

"He didn't say," Basrahip repeated and showed Geder his palms as if offering him the empty air cupped there. "The living voice carries what it carries. If you wish to know these things, ask him. And then we will know."

Geder paced over to the small model of Kaltfel and squatted down. It was such a short distance. He could step to Kalliam's command from there. He had the deep urge to step on the model, flatten the offending walls and street and towers. Grind them into the dirt. If only he could do the same to the real city. He became aware of a deep sound. Basrahip, laughing.

"What?" Geder said.

"Lord Prince—"

"I'm regent," Geder said, peevishly. "Regent's better than prince."

"Lord Regent," Basrahip said. "My friend. Your people are strange. They want to do something out there in the world, and so they lock you up in here, with little toys."

The priest rose from the table and walked across to the Seref Bridge, sitting cross-legged before it. He picked up the figure of the horseman that represented Dannick and pretended to address himself to it.

"Why do you fight, little soldier? Mm? What do you hope to win? What does your heart tell you?" He pretended to listen. Or maybe he did, and pretended to hear. He looked up at Geder with merry eyes. "He doesn't say."

"Well, it isn't as if I could go out and be in the middle of it myself," Geder said. "I have to see it all, somehow. This is how I can keep track of everything. I mean, all I need to do to see that the supply lines are getting too long in the south is look there. I can see it."

"No, you cannot. Nothing here is real. You see that this toy is so far from that toy, and not closer. And from that you think there is something to be learned. Here, look."

Basrahip reached over and pushed one of the southern armies forward.

"Now your supplies come quick when they're needed, yes?"

"No!" Geder said. "You can't just move something and make it happen."

"No, you can't," Basrahip said. "It is empty. It is a sign without a soul. And the orders and reports they send you.

Words on paper. Empty. How do you hope to win battles between men using paper and toys?"

"Do you have a better idea?" Geder asked. He meant it as a sarcasm, as *of course you don't*, but part of him wanted—wanted badly—for the huge man to say yes.

"Yes," Basrahip said. "Wait. This bridge—not this little toy, but the bridge you all speak of. This bridge to end your war. May I give it to you? Will you accept it from me?"

"I don't...I don't know what you mean."

Basrahip rose to his knees and then his feet. The soil of the false battlefield stained his knees, and he brushed at it with a wide palm. His voice was calm.

"Let me send three of my priests to this place, and allow me twenty days. Then bring your armies and we will open this way and end your war. Let me do this for you, yes?"

"Yes," Geder said. "If you can do that, then yes."

The first time—the only time before—that Geder had been given command over something, it had been Vanai and it had been as a cruel joke. He still didn't know what machinations had left some faction of the court hoping to lose control of Vanai by putting the idiotic, unprepared Geder Palliako in charge of it. Now that he had the kingdom, he had the allegiance and support of everyone. The intrigue politics of the court would never end, but the great minds answered to him now, and his cause was the victory of the kingdom over its enemies. No one could want him to fail without also being a traitor.

It changed everything. Even the men who had laughed at him, who had looked upon him as a sad joke, feared him now. Even they helped him when he demanded it.

He sat that night at a feast held by Sir Gospey Allintot.

There had been a time not very long ago when Allintot had been if not his enemy then certainly not his friend. And now his full household was bent double for Geder's honor.

Basrahip sat at his side as the hall filled with Allintot's guests. Lady Oesteroth, wearing her husband's dagger to show that he was in the field for the crown. Jorey Kalliam and his new bride. Sir Emund Serrinian, Earl of Whiteford. And coming in late and last to the high table, the Viscount of Rivenhalm, Lehrer Palliako. Geder's father.

Geder went to him, tugging him toward the front. His father looked out over the crowd, squinting.

"I don't believe I've ever been at the high table," his father said. "Traveling above my circles these days, m'boy. Above mine."

"I think if your son's regent, that makes you part of the high circles," Geder said, laughing a little nervously.

His father clapped him on the shoulder and nodded, but didn't say anything more. The meal was lavish—candied pork with onions, winter-bred pheasant basted with its own fat, lark's tongue and blackberries—and all of it served on plates of silver and gold. A cunning man came out as entertainment, calling the names of angels and spirits until a ghostly light filled his eyes and his palms became bright as candles. Geder watched it all, his delight cooled by his father's quiet eyes and unfinished food. When the cunning man's show was finished, his used and prostrate form hauled off by servants amid laughter and delight, Geder leaned close to his father.

"Is something wrong?" he asked.

"No," Lehrer said. "No, my boy. Everything's fine."

He didn't need Basrahip's gift to know it wasn't true.

"Come walk with me," Geder said.

They were alone, except that of course they weren't. The regent's guards and body servants followed along at a distance as Geder and his father walked down the long, black-paved path to Allintot's courtyard. The carriages and palanquins waited in the fading sunlight, ready to whisk away whatever noble blood wanted to go elsewhere. None of them would move so much as an inch while Geder remained at the feast. If he stayed until the dawn, each of them would too. The thought was strange and hilarious, and it made Geder want to try it, just to see the great men and ladies of the court trying to stay awake and pretending to enjoy themselves as the night grew longer beneath them.

His father found a bench and sat on it. Geder sat at his side.

"It's quite a lot in not much time, isn't it?" his father said. "My son, the Lord Regent. Who would have thought it, eh? It's an honor. It's . . . yes."

"I wish Mother'd lived to see it."

"Oh, oh yes. Yes, she'd have had something to say about it all, wouldn't she? She was a firebrand, your mother. Hell of a woman."

A cricket sang. The first one that Geder remembered hearing all season. A sudden powerful sadness rushed up in his chest, and with it a sense of grievance. He had done everything he could. He'd come as near to kingship as any man could who wasn't chosen by blood. He'd saved Aster and protected Camnipol. He'd won, and still his father seemed distant. Disappointed.

"What's the matter?" Geder said, more harshly than he'd meant to.

"Nothing. Nothing, it's just the war. You know. All that fighting last year. All that unease. And now this, and . . . I don't know. I was never meant for court life. All these people used to ignore me, and suddenly they pretend to care what I make of it all."

Geder snorted.

"I recognize that," he said.

"Do you ever wish it would all just go back to the way it had been? You back at Rivenhalm with me?"

Geder leaned forward, his hands knotted together.

"Sometimes, but it wouldn't have happened that way, would it? If I hadn't been in Vanai and then come back when I did, Maas and Issandrian's showfighters would have taken the city. Aster would have died. We couldn't be who we were anyway." Geder shrugged. "The nature of history defies us."

"I suppose that's true. And still, I look at the future, and I dread it. Where does it all end, after all?"

"I don't think the war will go on much longer," Geder said. "And when it's over, this mess will all be ended."

Dawson

Dawson didn't like it, but the war now was in the south. His men couldn't cross the river, and barring a fresh rebellion in Anninfort, Asterilhold had nowhere to land on the eastern side. The blockade in the northern sea blocked trade and kept Antean ships from being harassed, but as long as the border with Northcoast remained open, food and supplies could pour into Asterilhold from the back.

The late spring was thick with mosquitoes, but cold. The high grasses rose to a walking man's elbow, hiding bogs and cutting the horses' flanks until they bled. The roads weren't paved, only thin paths of stable land laced between creeks. The chill water had been fresh when it left the high glaciers topping the mountains to the south and was now undrinkable. Trees blocked their path where pools didn't. The men's clothes were starting to fall apart from mildew, and he had lost more soldiers to fever than to the enemy's swords. His only comfort was that the forces of Asterilhold were suffering the same. There were no garrisons to take shelter in, no holdfasts. The nearest thing to real battle that anyone had seen was the poor idiot Alan Klin whom Geder Palliako had insisted be at the vanguard, and he'd only had a single real skirmish in a high meadow and been driven back from that.

And then the orders had come, written in Palliako's own hand and under his seal. Withdraw his army to Seref Bridge to meet a group of priests who would somehow overcome the round keep and open the fast way to Kaltfel. Dawson had sent back for clarification. Not that he'd misunderstood, but if he accepted the order and drew his men to the north, it would only mean hauling them back down and beginning the whole painful campaign again when Palliako's cultists failed. Clarification came, and Dawson had been left nothing except to obey.

Marching north on the cusp of summer, he had at least imagined that he would find a company of warrior priests, drunk on theology and righteousness and ready to throw themselves across the narrow bridge. Even that was a disappointment.

The three men wore robes the grey-brown of sparrows. Their wiry, coarse hair was pulled back from their faces, and they wore expressions of serene benignity that Dawson associated with men drunk past reason or else simple from birth. They stood at the end of the little parade ground outside the keep and bowed to Dawson as he passed.

Dawson leaned in toward Rabbr Bannien, eldest son of Lord Bannien of Estinford and now garrison commander, meeting the boy's expression with something between despair and rage.

"Tell me this is a joke," Dawson said.

"I thought the same when they arrived, Lord Marshal," the young Bannien said. "But now I've been watching them for a time . . . I'm not sure anymore."

Dawson turned back to consider the garrison force. He hadn't left a full company at the bridge. There was no point, when a few dozen could defend the keep and a few hundred couldn't win across to the other side. They looked sharp, smart, and well rested. Unlike his own men. An uneasy thought stirred in his mind.

"Are they cunning men?"

"I don't think so, my lord. Not like any I've ever seen. They don't...they don't do anything exactly. It's just... You'd have to see it, sir."

"Right, then," Dawson said. He strode to the tallest of the three priests, nodding at him rather than saluting. "Show me why I should trust my men to your plan."

Half an hour later, the priest walked out onto the wide span of the bridge alone with only a caller's horn. The span of the bridge and the rushing water below and the blood-and-stone of the round keep made the priest look like a painter's image of faith: a sparrow overwhelmed but unbending. Dawson stood at the white keep's open gate, watching with his arms crossed and tired to the bone from the march and the long, muddy slog of a war before that. Contempt swam at the back of his throat, tasting of bile.

The priest lifted the horn to his mouth and began to shout over the rush of the water below him.

"You have already lost! No force can stand against the army of Antea! You have no power here! You have already *lost*! Everything you fight for is gone already. Everything you hope for is lost. You cannot win."

Dawson glanced over at the boy. Young Bannien looked out across the bridge, rapt. His eyes were on the priest, and the ghost of a smile played about the boy's lips. Dawson felt laughter boiling up in his own throat; it felt like horror.

"This?" Dawson said. "This is how we take the far shore? We nag them out of it?"

"I know," the garrison commander said. "I had the same reaction at first. But they do this every day and into the night. And the more they do this the more it seems like...it might be true."

Dawson said something obscene.

"Get that idiot off the bridge before someone puts an arrow in him and bring him to me," Dawson said. "We're ending this before we waste any more time."

"Yes, Lord Marshal," the boy said, looking abashed. Dawson stalked off through the courtyard and up a flight of stone stairs. The commander's private rooms were close, dark, and poorly lit. The choice was between light and air, but Dawson would by God see the face of the men he was speaking to. Meantime, he sat in the dim and he seethed.

Palliako's cultists came together, all three. They bowed at the door and sat on the cushions at Dawson's feet. They looked up at him with a profound calm, their dark eyes glittering in the candlelight. The garrison commander took his place behind Dawson, standing.

"Tell me the rest of the plan," Dawson said. "Once you've finished your little theater piece, then what?"

The priests looked at one another. They seemed uncomfortable, so that at least was good. They had enough brains between them to notice when they were being dressed down. Dawson sat forward in the camp chair, wood and leather creaking under him.

"When they have understood, you will take what is yours from them," the middle one said. He had a rounder face than the others, with thin nostrils and lips. He had an accent that reminded Dawson of reading ancient poems as a boy. The cadences of the words seemed like they'd been dug out of a ruin. Or a barrow. "There need be nothing more."

Dawson ran the tip of his tongue across the inside of his teeth and nodded. It was a gesture he'd picked up as a boy by watching his father when the man was enraged to the edge of violence.

"The hell we will," he said. "I don't care if you talk until your tongues cramp. We don't have the men or the position to take that bridge, and I won't see a single Antean life lost by this folly."

"The goddess is with you. You will not fail," the round-faced priest said.

"Enough! Garrison commander Bannien, I will take full responsibility for ending this, and I will send my written judgment and corrected plans to Camnipol tonight. Please make a courier and horse ready as—"

"Listen to my voice," the priest said. "You will not fail. We are servants of the truth and the goddess. What we tell you is true. Their men cannot stand against you. They will fail."

Dawson leaned back. The heat of the room and the smoke of the candle were doing something unpleasant.

"How can you think that is possible?" he said. "Do they have fewer men than they did?"

"It does not matter how many they are."

"Are they all sick? Is there plague?"

"It does not matter whether they are sick or well. You are the men of Antea, strong at heart and blessed of the goddess. They are weak, and their fear is justified."

"Be that as it may," Dawson said, "they are in a fortified position with our only line of attack clear, open, and insecure. All I need to do is look at a map and the numbers, and I can tell you as surely as I can tell you my own name that that keep can't be taken any more than this one can."

"Listen to my—"

"I don't care to listen to your voice, boy," Dawson said. "I don't care how often you tell me that a pig is really a kitten. That doesn't make it true."

"Yes, my lord," the middle priest said. "It *does*."

Dawson couldn't do anything but laugh. The candle flames danced and flickered.

"What is a word except what you mean by it, Lord?" the priest said. "This is a dog and that may be a dog, and yet they look nothing like each other. One is half the size of a horse, the other would fit in a woman's lap. And yet we call them dogs."

"You can breed them."

"Timzinae and Haaverkin can't breed. Which one is the human? A finch and a hawk are birds, can they share an egg? Words are empty until you fill them, and how you fill them shapes the world. Words are the armor and the swords of souls, and the soldiers on the other side of that bridge have no defense against them."

"Nothing you just said," Dawson said, stressing each word individually, "makes any damn sense. A war isn't a word game."

The priest lifted a finger. "When you became Lord Marshal, nothing about you changed. Your fingers were the same. Your nose. Your backbone. All of your body was as it had been, and yet you were transformed. The words were said, and by being said, they became true. A pig can be another kind of kitten if I say it and you understand its truth. If we say the Timzinae are not human, then they are not. We are the righteous servants of the goddess, and all the world is this way for us. Lies have no power over us, and the words we speak are true."

"The words you speak won't turn a blade," Dawson said.

"Blades turn because hands turn. Hands turn because of hearts. Listen to my voice, Lord, and know what the men who have listened to us already know. What you want is already yours. The blades of Antea are of steel, and your enemies are grass before you."

"Yes, well, you haven't seen the grass I've just come from," Dawson said, but his mind was already elsewhere.

The room was close and hot, and the air was thick. It felt like the war. Trapping, confining. They would be years in those marshes, fighting their way to the north mile by mile. Already they'd missed too much of the planting. Food would be scarce in the autumn, and next spring men would starve. And that was as it stood now. Today.

If only what the priests said were true, hundreds—maybe thousands—would live who now were slated to die. Many of them were the men he commanded now. The dead waited in ranks outside the keep, only waiting for their turn to die. Perhaps it didn't matter if they died here on this bridge or a year and a half from now, starving in the mud of Asterilhold.

"Listen to my voice," the priest said again. He seemed overly fond of the phrase. "The war is yours if you will accept it from us."

Dawson took a deep breath. He knew it was doomed. All sense and experience told him that it would fail. And yet, against that knowledge, there was some new force, some waking part of him that he could neither embrace nor deny. It felt like trying to wake from a dream, and being uncertain which was the dream and which the waking world. His skull filled with uncombed wool.

"This is madness," he said.

"Then you can take joy in madness," the priest said. "And then in victory."

They armed.

The priests had wanted to talk to all the men, to assure them all that what was about to happen wouldn't be Lord Marshal Kalliam marching three hundred men into a slaughter chute. Dawson didn't allow it. Bad enough that Palliako was taking orders from foreigners and priests. That he was taking them from Palliako.

As soon as he'd left the close little room, the regrets and misgivings had begun to crawl back. But by then the order was given, and there was still that small, almost-silent voice in his mind that said maybe it could all end well.

All night, the priests had stood on the bridge, shouting themselves hoarse in the darkness. The river seemed to shout with them. The rhetoric was much as Dawson had heard before, but there were occasional flourishes. The spirits of the dead marched beside the soldiers of Antea and protected them from harm. The arrow shot at Antean soldiers would turn aside. The river itself was allied with the Severed Throne. It was all about as subtle as schoolyard taunts, but taken over the long, black hours, it built a story in which being loyal to Asterilhold was an unfortunate thing.

Dawson tried to sleep, but only managed a few hours. And then his squire came and told him it was time.

The charge would come at dawn when the sun would be in the enemy's eyes. They had a better battering ram now— a wider log, and a bronze wedge fixed on the end. A thin roof of slats and thatching would slow the arrows down. Any number of other things could be rained down on it. Hot oil or boiling water. Open flame. It might take half an hour to shatter the opposing gates. How many men could he lose in half an hour? All of them, near enough.

Mist rose from the ground as the first pale light of dawn appeared, blue and rose stretching fingers across the sky. The shouting priests were harsh as crows.

"Men," Dawson said, addressing his knights. "We are the lords of Antea and the Severed Throne. Nothing more need be said."

Their swords rang as they cleared their scabbards, his knights making their salute. Dawson turned his mount, and they took their places.

As the first sunlight struck the round keep, Dawson sounded the charge. His farmers and peasants and landless soldiery surged forward across the bridge, their voices blending into a single roar that shouted down the water. For a moment, Dawson let himself believe that the enemy had been stunned into inactivity, paralyzed by the sight of them. Then arrows began to rain down. He watched a man struck in the shoulder stumble and fall into the river and be swept away. More arrows. More screams.

And then the thud of the battering ram began. His mount danced beneath him, frightened by the chaos or feeling his own anxiety or both. The three priests stood by the open mouth of the white keep, huddled in their brown robes looking sleepy and worn.

If we fail, I will send Palliako their heads, he thought.

The press of bodies on the far side of the bridge seemed to breathe, a great, half-formed giant. The ram was its elephantine heart. They weren't scattered. The arrows weren't breaking the formation, and while there had been a few torches dropped from the merlons above, the ram hadn't taken fire. They were doing well. Even if they died, they died bravely.

Something changed. The thud and thud and thud became a crack. And then a splintering. And then a shout went up and the men before him were pushing into the round keep through broken doors.

"Take them!" Dawson shouted. "Knights of Antea, to me! To *me*!"

Leaning close to his horse's back, he flew across the bridge, his lips pulled back in a grimace of rage and joy and the lust of battle. The clot of bodies he struck on the other side was as much his own side as the others, but they scattered all the same. And then all of them were there, inside the keep's round courtyard, breaking over the enemy like a wave and washing them away. Something was burning, the smoke acrid and dense and invigorating. The screams of the soldiers was music.

By midday, even the last of it was over. Sixty soldiers of Asterilhold dead. Twice that captured. He could only guess the number scattered to the winds and the waters. Most of all, the dragon's jade road was his, cleared and opened into the heart of the enemy's kingdom.

He stood on the ramparts of this, his new keep, the first soil west of the Siyat that an Antean had unquestionably held for a generation. The courier that he'd meant to take his refusal to Palliako stood by, waiting. Dawson handed the boy seven letters, folded and sewn and marked with his seal. The orders to all his commanders in the field, telling each of them the same thing. *The war is won. Leave the swamps and come to me.*

It should have been glorious. It should have been the finest moment in a life rich with them.

Below him, in the courtyard of the keep, the men were laughing and dancing. Two of the farmers were kicking the head of an Asterilhold soldier between them like a ball until the garrison commander saw them and put a stop to it. Wine flowed, and things stronger than wine. The banners of Asterilhold were put to the flame, and the banners of Antea lifted.

The banners of Antea, and also one other. Red, with an eightfold sigil. And in the courtyard, the three sparrows laughed and shook hands and received the gratitude of the men. Palliako's pet cultists. This wasn't his victory. It wasn't the Severed Throne's or even Palliako's. It was the foreign priests', and even if none of the others knew it, he did. He knew it, and more than that, he knew what it meant.

He had let himself be perverted.

Clara

News of the victory spread through Camnipol like a soft wind; very little changed, and everything did. Clara saw it in a hundred small things. The baker put a wider strip of honey across the top of her buns. The fashion for dark leather cloaks of too generous a cut had been on the verge of fading, and now surged again. The conversations at the gatherings of the wives of the great nobles began to shift from dreading their husbands' being away to dreading their return. It was, Clara thought, very much like watching a winter tree take the first rush of sap into its bark, greening slightly even before the first leaf came out.

Word kept coming day by day, as much of it rumor as truth. The armies had taken Kaltfel or they had been driven back. One of the soldiers had seen Simeon's ghost in the midst of the melee or striding across the battlefield or standing beside the Lord Marshal. Clara had lived through other times of strife and battle, and the fascination with the spirits of the dead was new. She wondered whether there were fashions in wartime rumor just as in anything else. Put that way, she couldn't imagine why there ought not be.

The letters from Dawson, however, were worrying.

They came almost twice a week. Often, but not with the regularity that left her worried if one was late. He related few solid facts to her—she might be his wife, but she wasn't on the war council—relying more on general statements and impressions. With every new victory, he seemed a bit more angry. Often he would meditate upon the political and filial connections Antea had with Asterilhold; like two fighting brothers, he said. Also, his opinion of foreigners, which God knew had never tended toward charity, was darker than ever. She felt, reading his words, as if he were writing the messages more to himself than to her. Perhaps the ghost of Simeon was riding with him, even if it was only as a metaphor.

The other notable shift in the life of the court was the growing popularity of Geder Palliako's private priesthood. After he'd celebrated his victory over Maas by founding a temple, there had been a certain morbid curiosity among the court. Then, after he'd become regent, the courtiers had descended on the place, looking for new ways to curry favor. But even beyond that, there seemed to be a growing interest for the temple in its own right. She wasn't sure yet what she thought of that, but she was hesitant to go without talking to Dawson about it. Better to judge his mood first and then decide whether broadening her piety was worth the effort.

With the road to Kaltfel open and the armies of Asterilhold struggling up from the southern marshlands, she expected Dawson home by midsummer. Sooner than that if the inevitable peace talks were held in Camnipol. And before that happened, she had an armistice of her own to negotiate.

Marriage had been good for Elisia. Clara would never have said it aloud, but her daughter had always seemed too thin growing up, sharp-featured and narrow-hipped. In truth, Elisia Kalliam had been a cruel girl. As with anyone living in the royal court—man or woman, boy or girl—Elisia had had her clique, and as an adolescent, she'd ruled it ruthlessly. Now she was Elisia Annerin, wife of Gorman Annerin. Her face and bust had a softness in them that made her look more her mother's daughter. And she had hips, and thank God she had or birthing her son would have been even worse. There was confidence in her body, and an ease.

Sabiha, by contrast, seemed almost more tentative than she had during the courtship.

The three of them sat in the summer garden under the shade of a great catalpa. Clara, Elisia, Sabiha. The daughter she'd lost and the daughter she'd gained. The two girls—well, women now, really—looked at each other across the table with a brittle politeness that told Clara exactly how large the chasm was between them. From the little pond just beyond the rose bushes, little Corl Annerin, not yet five years old, shrieked with delight and was hushed by his nurse.

"I had the flux just before my thirteenth name day," Sabiha said. "I still remember it. I thought I was going to die."

"It is terrible," Clara agreed. "But you seem to have recovered nicely, dear. I'm only sorry that you missed the wedding and of course the funeral so close after that. Odd how the world seems to pair things that way. Something pleasant right up against something awful."

"God's sense of humor, I suppose," Elisia said. Her voice had changed a bit. Taken on the slightly clipped vowels of the eastern reaches where Antea shared its borders with Sarakal. "I'm glad Corl didn't get it. When he was younger, he'd catch everything, and there is simply nothing worse than being ill with an ill child."

Sabiha's smile came from past the horizon.

"I wouldn't know," she said.

"Of course not," Elisia said, "but I imagine you will soon. New brides and all that. It was hardly a year after I was married before I had Corl."

"I think it may take a bit longer for me," Sabiha said. "Jorey's gone so much with the war."

Elisia made a sympathetic clucking, then shrugged.

"Still better too long than not long enough."

Sabiha laughed and nodded as if the insult hadn't struck home. There was hardly even a flicker in her eyes. Clara thought Jorey's wife really was an impressive girl in her fashion.

"Oh!" Clara said. "I've forgotten my pipe. Honestly, I think my memory's starting to fail. It did for my mother, you know. Spent her last years wandering about the house trying to recall what she was looking for. Perfectly amused by the whole situation, even when she was quite out of her mind. Did I have my pipe in your sitting room, Sabiha dear?"

"I don't think so. Perhaps your withdrawing room. Would you like me to go look for it?"

"Would you, dear? I don't want the servants to think I've gone mindless on them. They start taking liberties."

Sabiha rose, nodding to mother and daughter as if they weren't all of them perfectly aware that Clara had asked for a moment's privacy. As the girl stepped into the house, Clara let the mask of geniality fall. Elisia rolled her eyes.

"She isn't my sister," Elisia said even before Clara spoke. "I can't believe you've let Jorey marry her. Really, Mother, what were you thinking?"

"Whatever I thought, her name is Kalliam now. Prodding her about dead scandals isn't going to do any of us well. And you could at least pretend you were actually ill."

"I have spent weeks defending you and Father to my husband and his family. Do you know what they call us? Kalliam's shelter for lost girls. How do you think that makes me feel?"

"Ashamed of your husband, I should think."

Elisia's mouth closed with an audible click. A loud splash came, and the nurse's scolding voice. A breeze almost too gentle to feel set the rosebuds nodding. A few had already bloomed, white and orange. Clara had always preferred simple roses with two or three rows of petals to the grand and gaudy balls that others seemed to favor. She took a deep breath, gathering her composure before she turned back to Elisia.

"Family is what we have, dear," Clara said. "There will always be others, people on the outside, who will try to tear us down. It's not even their fault. Dogs bark, and people gossip. But we don't do that in the family."

"She is—"

"She is going to be mother to my grandchildren, as much as you, my dear. She has an unfortunate past which you and your husband are bringing to my table. She isn't. You are. And I have never heard her say a word against either of you."

Elisia's mouth pressed thin and two bright spots of color appeared on her cheeks. Clara raised her eyebrows and leaned forward, inviting comment or reproof. It was the same pose she'd taken before Elisia since her daughter had been a child in diapers, and long training had its power.

"Excuse me a moment," Elisia said. "I think Corl called for me."

"I'm sure he did, dear," Clara said. "I'll wait here."

Clara took up her cup. The tea had grown cold, but she drank it anyway. Children were difficult because they became their own people. There had been a time when Elisia had run to Clara with every scrape and hurt feeling, but that girl was gone, and this young woman had taken her place, and Clara would never say aloud that she wasn't sure of the exchange.

Clara watched the footman trot out from the house. He was a new boy. Messin or Mertin or something along that line. She would have to find out discreetly. He wore his uniform well, though, and his voice was gentle.

"My lady, there's a gentleman here to see you. Sir Curtin Issandrian."

"Really?" Clara said. "How very brave of him."

"Shall I show him out, my lady?"

"Out to the garden or out to the street, do you mean?" Clara said, then waved the question away. "Take him to my husband's library. I'll speak with him there. God knows what he'd hear if we brought him out among these women."

"Yes, my lady," the boy—Meanan, that was it—said. Clara sat a minute longer to give the servants time to guide Issandrian to the right place, then stood, straightened her dress, and sailed into the house. Elisia wouldn't be speaking to her again until she'd calmed down, and Sabiha was likely off crying somewhere private. Clara guessed a half hour's audience wouldn't leave too much opportunity for more unpleasantness.

Curtin Issandrian looked older with his hair cut short. Or perhaps it was that the last years bore down on him more heavily. There were lines around his mouth and eyes that hadn't been there the last time he'd come to her house. A different world, that had been.

"Lord Issandrian," she said, stepping into the room.

"Baroness Osterling," he said, making a formal bow.

"I hope you weren't coming to meet with my husband," Clara said. "He's off leading the army at the moment."

"I think everyone's aware of your good husband's successes in the field," Issandrian said. "No, I came to speak with you. To ask you to intercede."

Clara sat on her divan, and Issandrian sat across from her, his hands clasped in front of him. He looked desperately tired.

"I know your husband and I have been at odds on several occasions," he said. "But I have never doubted that he was an honorable man, and loyal to crown and kingdom."

"Very much so," Clara said.

"And your sons are some of the most promising young men at court. Vicarian is a model student and well spoken of. Barriath and Jorey now are both allied with Lord Skestinin. And, of course, Jorey is considered by many to be the regent's most trusted friend."

Issandrian swallowed. Clara folded her hands together.

"Is this about what happened to Feldin Maas?" she asked. "No one has accused you of treason, my lord. You aren't accused as he was, and really, the court isn't such a large place. We are all connected to one another somehow. Poor Phelia was my own cousin, and certainly no one thinks that we were involved in Maas's treachery."

"All respect," Issandrian said. "You and Phelia Maas were instrumental in stopping Maas. And Lord Regent Palliako. I didn't have the good fortune to be part of those events."

"I'm not entirely sure that watching one's cousin cut down by her husband qualifies as good fortune," Clara said coolly.

"I apologize. That came out poorly. I only meant that your loyalty to the crown was demonstrated. Unquestionable. I didn't know of the depths of Maas's plot until after the fact. And a loyalist and traitor say all the same words at that point."

It was a fair analysis, but not one that asked Clara to do or say anything in particular, so she kept silent and waited. The moment stretched.

"Sir Alan Klin was another of my compatriots at that time," Issandrian said. "He serves under your lord husband now. I haven't been asked to serve. I was wondering...I was wondering if you might enquire on my behalf why that is."

"This is a very convenient time to be asking why you are not on the field," Clara said. "It would have spoken better of you to ask when victory was less certain."

"I have written to the Lord Regent several times," Issandrian said. "I haven't yet received the courtesy of a reply."

"I see."

"We have disagreed profoundly on some issues, but your husband and I have always been loyal to the Severed Throne," Issandrian said. "I didn't want to bring Asterilhold into the conflict any more than he courted Northcoast. But like him, I wasn't working alone. And I . . ."

"And you see Sir Klin being given the chance to redeem his name while you are kept in Camnipol," Clara said.

"Yes."

"I don't know anything about it," she said. "I don't take part in those decisions or discuss them with Dawson."

"If you could ask . . . Just ask—"

"Sound out my husband on your behalf?" she asked with a smile. "Gather information and report it back to you? You can't think that."

Issandrian paled, and then chuckled ruefully.

"You make it sound more than it is," he said.

"No, I only see the same thing from another angle," she said. "I will tell my husband you came, and what we said. I will tell him you seemed sincere because you do. And if he wishes to converse with you about this, I won't argue against it."

"Baroness Osterling, I could ask nothing more."

"You could ask," she said. "But you couldn't have it. And now I must ask that you go. I have family here."

Issandrian practically sprang to his feet, his face and voice rich with apology.

"I hadn't known that, my lady, or I wouldn't have intruded. I owe you even greater thanks, it seems. If I can ever be of service to you, only let me know."

"Lord Issandrian?" she said. He paused. "My husband hates you, but he respects you as well. It isn't so bad a position to be in."

Issandrian nodded soberly and made his exit. Clara walked

back out toward the garden slowly. Her impression from
Dawson's letters was that Sir Klin wasn't at all enjoying his
time winning back his honor. And, in fact, that Palliako had
gone out of his way to make the poor man's time in the field
as hellish as possible. She wondered whether she should
write to Dawson about this or wait for his return.

In the garden, Elisia and the nurse were still by the pond,
splashing and playing. Sabiha sat alone at the table. Clara's
pipe was in the girl's hand.

"Where did you find it?" Clara asked, taking the little
clay bowl and stem from the girl's hand. There was already
a hard wad of tobacco stuffed into it, ready for the fire.

"In your withdrawing room," Sabiha said. "Just as you
thought. I've been listening to your grandson. He's a beautiful child."

"He is. Takes after his mother that way. She was always a
pretty child, even when she was growing half a hand a year
and looked like a blade of grass come to life, she wore it well
And he doesn't sleep any more than she did. I'll tell you a
secret. Watching your children struggle with the same things
you did when they were babes is a grandmother's revenge."

Sabiha smiled. It wasn't obvious that she'd been weeping.
Only a little redness about the eyes and a tiny, fading blotch-
iness at the throat. The girl was lucky that way. Being able
to hide tears was a gift. But now a fresh shining came to her.
Clara pursed her lips.

"Sometimes," Sabiha said, "and it isn't often, but sometimes I think of how the world could have been if I hadn't
been Lord Skestinin's daughter."

"Ah, but you always were," Clara said, trying to keep the
girl from going down the path she was headed. The girl
wouldn't be turned.

"I know. It's just there are freedoms women have when

they aren't what we are. There are struggles too, I understand that. But there are ways to shape a life even within
those, and then maybe—"

"No," Clara said.

Sabiha's tears welled, but did not fall. Not yet.

"No," Clara said again, more gently. "You can't think of
that child. You can't even wish for him back. It isn't fair to
ask everyone else to forget and only you remember. It doesn't
work like that."

"I miss him, though," Sabiha whispered. "I can't just stop
missing him."

"You can stop showing that you do. Jorey has risked a
great deal to give you another life. Another beginning. If
you didn't want it, you should have refused him. Accepting
him and also keeping hold of the past isn't fair. And it isn't
wise."

"I'm sorry," Sabiha said, her voice thick. "He was my
boy. I thought you would understand."

"I do. And that's why I'm saying this. Look up. Look at
me. No, *at* me. Look *at* me. Yes."

Sabiha swallowed, and Clara felt the beginnings of tears
in her own eyes. There was a boy out there—a child—whose
mother loved him enough to break her heart, and he would
never know it. Perhaps it was fair to the girl. She'd at least
made a decision, even if the punishment seemed too much
for the lapse. But the child was blameless. He was blameless,
and he would suffer, and Clara would do what she could to
see that the estrangement between mother and son was permanent, and that Sabiha's old scandals were all kept in the
past where they belonged. A tear tracked down Sabiha's
cheek, and Clara's matched it.

"Good," Clara said. "Now smile."

Cithrin

The last Dragon Emperor slept before her. Each jade scale was as wide as her open palm. The eyelids were slit open enough to show a thin sliver of bronze eye. The folded wings were as long as the spars of a roundship. Longer. Cithrin tried to imagine the statue coming to life. Moving. Speaking in the languages that had made the world.

On one hand, the bulk and beauty and implicit physical power of the thing was humbling. The claws could have ripped a building apart. The mouth, had it opened, would have fit a steer. But size alone didn't define it. The sculptor had also managed to capture a sense of the intellect and rage and despair in the shape of the dragon's eyes and the angle of its flanks. Morade, the mad emperor against whom his clutch-mates had rebelled. Morade, whom Drakkis Storm-crow schemed against. Morade, whose death was the emancipation of all the races of humanity.

At her side, Lauro Medean scratched his arm.

"They say that the dragons could sleep as long as stone when they wanted to," he said. "It was part of the war. The dragons would bury themselves or put themselves in deep caves. Hidden. And then when the armies had their back or flank, the dragons would spring back to life. Come boiling up out of the ground. Slaughter everybody."

Komme Medean's son was a year older than her, but he

acted much younger. He shared his father's brown skin and
dark hair, and when she looked carefully, she could see
where the young man's face would broaden, his jowls sink,
and he would look even more like Komme. She wondered
how old a man had to be before gout took him. He smiled
at her.

"You want to go inside?"

"I've come a long way not to," she said.

Coming to Carse, the thing she'd worried about least was
the journey. Bandits, pirates, illness, wildcats. She knew of
them all, and understood the risks of them better than most.
Her work from childhood had been to understand risk. In a
journey of a thousand miles taken by a hundred ships, about
how many would be lost. In summer. In winter. Along the
coast. Crossing the blue water to Far Syramys. How often
caravans were killed or simply vanished. The actuarial tables
were in her mind, and more than that the tools with which
the tables were built. She could estimate chance better than
a gambler, and so the journey held no terror.

The handing over of the reports had been worse. She
knew that the branch was doing well, but not what would
be well enough, or what the other branches were doing, or
how her improvised branch in Porte Oliva affected the greater
strategies of the holding company. It wasn't risk that frightened her, but the inability to figure it, to place a number
against it. To be unknown was worse than to be dangerous.

And of all the things that had kept her from sleep in the
long weeks since she'd left Porte Oliva, the worst was this:
how would she manage to stay long enough to win over the
holding company? She had come to do a job, and she didn't
know how she would insinuate herself into the day-to-day
life of the business well enough to keep them from sending
her back.

When the occasion came, it hadn't been a problem at all. She was a figurehead in Porte Oliva, a curiosity in Carse, and Komme Medean was more than happy to have her where she wasn't even a social presence in the company. Oddly, she didn't resent it. She had the feeling—true or not—that Komme Medean was willing to play this game with her. Willing to see if she could charm and impress him. And that along the way, he would throw obstacles in her path.

His son, for example.

As they walked past the great jade statue, the Grave of Dragons opened out before them. Cut down into the living earth, the tiers of the grave were wider than streets, curving and turning like the drawing of a riverbed, but too perfect to have been cut by any real water. The stone flowed out for over a mile, ten tiers deep, and at each level, the tombs.

The bodies, if they had ever really been there, were gone centuries ago. But the dragon's jade altars still showed the clawmarks of the dead. Most had three great toes at the front and one in the rear, but some had only two in the front. Some two in front, and two in back. In the deepest tomb, a single massive dragon's footprint sank into the ground almost as deep as Cithrin's waist. Mineralized lines on the sides showed where rain had collected in it as if in a pond, and dried away. It was clean and empty now.

"Go ahead if you want," Lauro Medean said. "It's all right. Everyone does."

Cithrin smiled, looked around, and then lowered herself into the footprint and lay down, stretching her arms above her. Her feet and fingertips couldn't quite touch the edges at the same time. She imagined the dragon floating through the sky above her, blotting out the sun. Once, it had. Once, they had flown in this air, above these cliffs. The thought took her breath away.

When she stood, she saw Lauro's grin.

"Funny?" she asked, putting up her hand. He took it—he had a strong grip—and helped her back out. They began walking back.

"It's just I've grown up here. I never get impressed because it's always been here. I like seeing people see it for the first time. It means something to them that it never does to me."

"All this," she said, gesturing at the empty tombs and the death prints, "has been here, right here, since before the beginning. People have been cleaning and neglecting and cleaning these graves almost since before there were people. And that doesn't move you?"

"Maybe it should," Lauro said, shrugging. "But no. It's just the Grave. It's this amazing thing to people who don't know it, but it's no more impressive to me than the sea or the sky or the cliffs, and I see all of them every day."

"Hmm," Cithrin said.

"What?"

"I work with Marcus Wester," she said. "I think that knowing him is a bit like that too."

The two great surprises of the holding company were first that Paerin Clark, the auditor she had extorted into letting her keep a place in Porte Oliva, was also living at the holding company's unofficial holdfast inside the city. The second was that he was pleased to see her.

Coming back through the bronze gates now, Lauro called out to the pale man sitting on a bench. Paerin Clark waved to them, paused, and then waved them over. As they drew near him, Lauro tried to take Cithrin's hand and made do with putting his arm around her shoulder.

"Brother," Paerin Clark said. Technically it was true, as Paerin was married to Lauro's sister, but Cithrin couldn't really imagine the two being part of the same family. "What have you two been doing?"

"I took Cithrin to the Grave of Dragons," Lauro said. "She'd never seen it."

"And did you enjoy it, Magistra?"

"I did, and thank you," Cithrin said. She could feel a small discomfort in the way Lauro held himself beside her, thrown off by the easy formality of her talk with Paerin. And there was the smallest spark of amusement in the older man's eyes. If Lauro wanted to play at familiarity with her, she would play at being an adult with Paerin and throw the young boy off his stride. Comfort was never the fate of an obstacle.

"I was wondering if I might borrow the magistra's company for a few minutes. Something's come up I wanted to discuss with her. Bank business."

"Of course," Lauro said, a little coolly. He took his arm from around Cithrin's shoulder and bowed to her. "Thank you for the pleasure of your company."

"No, thank you, Lauro," she said.

She sat on the bench at Paerin Clark's side and watched as the son of Komme Medean walked away through the courtyard. Clark, she noted, shifted over slightly to be sure that the two of them were not touching.

"May I ask you a question?" he said.

"Of course."

"What are you hoping to win here?"

Cithrin glanced at him sharply, but his face was as blank and pleasant as always. In all her life, Cithrin had never known anyone better at not giving information away. As good, but not better.

"I thought I'd made that clear," she said, trying for the brash half-humor she used with Komme Medean.

"No," Paerin said, and there was no lightness in his voice. "What you've said is what you want. What I'm asking is why you want it. What are your ambitions?"

"I'm sorry," she said. "I don't understand the question. I want to run my bank."

"Yes, but why is that what you want?"

"Because it's mine," she said.

Paerin took a deep breath and shifted on the bench so that he was half facing her. The tree above him cast shadows across his face, and for a moment he reminded her of children's pictures of forest ghosts.

"Do you want to be rich?" he asked.

"I suppose," she said.

"Then that isn't the answer. Do you want power?"

"I want the power that belongs to me," she said. "I want what I've earned."

"Even if you've earned it through forgery and fraud?"

"I haven't harmed anyone," Cithrin said, crossing her arms. "What I've done was good business. I kept my contracts. They're only not legal because I'm too young."

"Not for much longer, though," Paerin said, more than half to himself. He tapped his fingers against his knee, frowning. "Are you aware that Komme's been shoving Lauro at you to find out if you're fishing for a husband?"

"He could have asked. I'm not. I don't want someone to run my bank for me. If I did, I'd marry Pyk Usterhall and be done."

Paerin laughed.

"There's an image. All right. There's something I'd like you to do tonight," he said. "Not a feast, just a meal. But the man who's coming is important."

"All right," she said. "Why do you want me there?"

On the street, a horse neighed and a carter shouted. The

breeze shifted the shadows across the pale man's face. She waited while he weighed his answer.

"I recall being your age," he said, portioning out each word, "and I remember what it was like to look for something without knowing what it was. You have one of the best minds for coin and the powers of coin that I've ever seen, but you lack experience. That's not a criticism, it's only true. And there's a negotiation happening tonight. I would like you to be there. See how the game is played."

Cithrin turned this over in her mind. Her heart was beating a little faster, and she felt the flush in her cheeks. This might be the opportunity she'd come all this way to find.

"May I ask you a question?" she said.

"That seems fair."

"Why is that what you want?"

He nodded. Almost a minute passed.

"You're young. You're still making yourself into the woman you're going to be, looking for the project that your life will become. People sometimes need help to find that. I am older, and in a position of some power, and I think you may become the sort of person I would like to owe me favors later on."

The smile forced its way to Cithrin's lips. It felt like victory.

"And here I thought it was altruism," she said.

"Oh, Magistra." Paerin Clark smiled. "We don't do that here."

The meal began just before sundown around a table of wooden planks no grander than a laborer might sit at. Platters filled the space between: clams in garlic sauce, pasta and cream, bottles of wine, loaves of fresh-baked bread. Komme Medean sat at one end, the swelling in his ankle and knee gone down enough that they looked almost normal.

Cithrin and Lauro sat along one side across from Paerin Clark and his wife, Chana, who looked even more like her father than Lauro did. At the other end of the table, the Antean nobleman with skin as dark as coffee. Canl Daskellin, Baron of Watermarch and Protector of Northport and the Regent's Special Ambassador to Northcoast, grinned and broke bread with his hands.

"Think how I feel," Daskellin said. "I'm sent on a fast boat with desperate pleas for King Tracian to help us in the war, and by the time I get here, we've all but won. It doesn't make me look smarter, let's say."

Komme Medean chortled and nodded.

"I know just how you feel," he said. "I was trying to win a concession in a sugar plantation on an island off Elassae. Year and a half of negotiation, and I was just sending back the final contracts to their council when the whole damn thing burned flat. Wound up with a concession on a salt cinder in the Inner Sea. Thank God I hadn't paid for it yet."

"I remember that," Cithrin said.

"Do you now?" Komme said.

Canl Daskellin's gaze turned to her, and she realized how thin the ice was she'd just put herself on. If it came out she'd been living at the Vanai branch, it might come out why. If anyone looked into her age, there could be a great deal at stake.

"Heard about it from Magister Imaniel," she said without missing a beat. "It was done out of the Vanai branch, wasn't it?"

Komme Medean pursed his lips as if in thought.

"I suppose it was, now you mention it," he said. And another danger was stepped past.

"This new regent of yours," Paerin Clark said. "Geder Palliako. It's not a name I've heard often. I'm surprised we didn't see a more familiar man."

"I hope you aren't looking at me," Daskellin said. "No, Palliako's father is a viscount. Unremarkable man. His son's something different, though. He stopped the showfighters' coup. He exposed Feldin Maas. There's a strong case that this war is his private project from the start."

"What sort of man is he?" Chana asked, then winked broadly at Cithrin and said, "I hear he isn't married."

They all laughed because it was expected.

"He's a strong man," Daskellin said. "He comes almost from outside the court, and it makes him very independent. His own thoughts. His own plans."

"Ambitious?" Komme asked, cracking open a clam and pulling out the flesh.

"He'd have to be," Canl said. "People underestimated him at first. That's happening less now. His unofficial patron is Dawson Kalliam, and I think he's got the feeling of riding a tiger."

"Bad enemy to have," Paerin said.

"That," Daskellin said, "is the regent in a phrase. Would someone pass me that wine? I seem to have finished mine."

"No," Komme Medean said, feigning horror. "Never that."

The meal went on until well after dark. The conversation ranged over art and politics and the indignities of travel. Everyone was very casual, and traded jokes and stories. The wine was very good, and left Cithrin feeling a little above herself, warm and happy and more relaxed than was strictly wise. Before he left, Daskellin shook all the men's hands and embraced Komme Medean like a brother. He also kissed Cithrin on the lips, so he might have been more than a bit tipsy himself.

After he left, servants came in and cleared the table, bringing a stool for Komme's bad leg. It had gotten visibly worse during the evening, but it was only now that he showed that it bothered him. The others took their seats, and so Cithrin did too.

"Well?" Komme said, his voice perfectly sober and crisp. "What do we have?"

"The regent's unpredictable," Chana said. "And Daskellin doesn't like him."

"Fears him, though," Paerin Clark said.

"Do you think so?" Lauro said. "He seemed to speak well of him to me."

"No," Cithrin said. "Fears him is right. And there was something else, I couldn't make out. He's uneasy about the war. Even though they're winning it. Why is that?"

It was eerie. All her childhood had been spent around a different table with Magister Imaniel and Cam and Besel having conversations much like this. Analysis, debate, discussion. Dissection. And now here she was in a strange place with different people and utterly at home.

"Either he doesn't think it's going to end with Asterilhold or he expects the balance of power in court to shift because of it," Chana said. "Did you see how nervous he looked when I joked about the regent not having a wife?"

"You're thinking there might be a political marriage with Asterilhold?" Komme said. "Unification?"

"I think it's on his mind and he doesn't want it," Chana said. "Does he have a daughter?"

"Yes," Paerin said. "And of the right age."

"Well then," Chana said as if the matter were settled.

"I'm not sure," Komme said. "I think there was something more to it than that. How much do we know about Palliako's allies?"

"Very little," Paerin said. "His reputation is as a scholar. And newly pious."

"Pious, eh? That may be an issue. King Tracian should

send a group," Komme said. "Sound out the court. This new war went awfully well for Antea. It'd be good to know if this Palliako's gotten a taste for blood. If this doesn't end with Asterilhold, that will change quite a few calculations."

"I'll speak with his majesty," Paerin Clark said. "I'm fairly sure he's of a similar mind. Not anything official, I think. Not an embassy. A dozen important people from court. A few powerful merchants."

"Meaning you," Lauro said. He sounded peevish.

"Meaning me," Paerin Clark said. "I have some other contacts in Antea it might be wise to visit. See what we can find."

Cithrin found herself nodding, but her mind was elsewhere. The wine fumes confused her, but only a bit. In her memory, Paerin Clark was saying, *You lack experience. It's not a criticism, it's only true.* As if the truth couldn't be critical. Something in the back of her mind shifted. This wasn't the moment for more brashness. This was when to show some range. She could do that. She cleared her throat and lifted her hand like a schoolgirl asking to be recognized. Komme Medean nodded.

"With your permission, sir," she said, "when the group goes to Camnipol, I'd like to go too."

Geder

The Kingspire was as busy as an anthill. Servants and workers and merchants moved through the sacred places of Antea with faster steps and louder voices. It felt like at any moment they all might break into song or else battle. And it wasn't only the Kingspire. When Geder appeared at a feast or a ball, the sense was the same. The whole court was vibrating with a wild, barely constrained energy. The whole of Camnipol. They were preparing for the celebrations that would come when King Lechan of Asterilhold surrendered to Lord Marshal Kalliam and the short, decisive war—hardly a half a season long—ended with the Severed Throne triumphant.

It all made Geder very nervous. It wasn't that he didn't expect the victory to come. Every day brought more couriers and reports, and the news was consistent: Kalliam and the armies were advancing steadily toward Kaltfel. The enemy was demoralized and falling back. The priests of the spider goddess seemed to be a very real help. Morale in the ranks was high, and three enemy commanders had already offered private surrender and been taken prisoner. Geder had the impression from Dawson Kalliam's letter that there might be some friction between him and the priests, but it didn't seem to be affecting anything. And the man could be a little prickly sometimes, so likely that wasn't a problem.

No, the thing that bothered Geder most was catching glimpses of bright costumes and servants cutting bright paper into bits small enough to throw. He understood that there would be celebrations when the war ended and that people would have to prepare. The city was like the taut bud of some lavish flower, only waiting for the right moment. And still, to assume a victory that hadn't actually happened seemed like courting bad luck. And as much as the half-hidden costumes and half-made gaudy bothered him, the sober discussions of how to proceed once Asterilhold was crushed bothered him more.

"Once Lechan sues for peace," Emmer Faskellan said, lacing his fingers across his wide belly, "I believe we have established that the Seref Bridge must be permanently under our control. That's the absolute very least."

"And reparations," Gospey Allintot said, "We've lost most of the planting season, and it's not fair that our women and children should go hungry. And we've lost good men whose widows and children will need to be supported."

It was a discussion that had clearly been going on in the rooms of the Great Bear, now translated into Geder's meeting chambers, a grander venue for the old conversation. The walls here were draped with silk and tapestries from Far Syramys and fine golden chains from Pût, the floor covered with Southling-woven carpets from one of the small nations in the interior of Lyoneia. The table around which they all sat was a single piece of carved basalt from Borja; representations of the thirteen races of humanity made up the legs, all supporting the tabletop-wide stylized crown. Furniture as political sculpture. The air was perfumed with a musky Hallskari incense that made Geder think of rich food and ripe fruit.

Geder's personal guard stood in the corners of the room,

armed and impassive, and Basrahip sat at a small table by the doorway where Geder could see him. The priest was only apparently meditating, his not quite closed eyes glittering under their lids.

It wasn't the most formal of councils, as many of the most important and powerful men in Antea were presently in the field. This was a gathering of sons and grandfathers and secretaries. Men who'd fought the war from their chairs, and were happy now to congratulate each other on how well they'd done. The only ones present who'd been in the field at all were Gospey Allintot, still recovering from an arrow in the meat of his arm, and Jorey Kalliam, just come with the reports from his father. The army had reached Kaltfel. The final siege was under way.

"If I may?" Jorey said slowly. "What are we trying to achieve? I mean if we want to cripple Asterilhold for a generation, it's easy enough to do that. But is that what we want?"

"Well, they have to be punished," Emmer Faskellan said. "My cousin died from their scheming. Died in the streets of Camnipol!"

"That's what I mean," Jorey said. "Are we trying to punish them and then go back to the way things were before? Are we trying to take control of Asterilhold? They wanted to unify the nations. Do we?"

"I see what you're thinking," Allintot said.

"I don't," said Geder. It wasn't something he would have admitted usually, but this was Jorey.

"Taking the bridge, for example," Jorey said. "That helps us win the next war if there is one. Maybe it makes one less likely because they'd be afraid of losing. But they didn't want a war in the first place. Asterilhold was acting with people in our own court. There aren't any reparations we can demand that will keep that from happening again."

The group was quiet for a moment.

"Hostages?" Geder said. "We could take hostages. Raise their children. If there was ever any sign of conspiracy, we'd have someone here at hand."

"I was thinking something more permanent," Jorey said. "Lechan has two sons and a daughter. If the sons abdicate their rights to the throne and the daughter weds Prince Aster, he'll become heir to Asterilhold's throne."

"This *did* all start as a drive for unification," Emmer Faskellan said thoughtfully. "Perhaps it's inevitable. If that's true, it would be best if we were the ones to set the terms. They'll want something done at once, of course. Waiting until Aster's of age and Lechan dies is too long."

"You've all given me things to think about," Geder said quickly. He had a sense of where the conversation was heading. "But if you'll excuse me, I'm called elsewhere."

A small chorus of *Yes, of course* and *Thank you, Lord Regent* rolled through the air as Geder rose and made his private exit. The guards followed him through the narrow passages reserved for the men who sat on thrones and the blades that guarded them. Even Basrahip would have to leave by the normal door and rejoin him elsewhere.

It was just the sort of thing that Geder had imagined he would enjoy, one of the unnumbered small privileges of power that he'd gained with the regency. In practice, it felt oppressive. Being the most powerful man in Imperial Antea meant being busy all the time, being constrained by form and etiquette, and carrying the world on his shoulders. He would never again be able to ride out through the streets whenever he saw fit. And never, ever alone. He had traded poking through the old scriptorums for this small corridor that only he and his guards could use, and the exchange seemed less attractive than it had before he'd made it.

The private corridor widened into the royal apartments. High windows looked out over the Division and the spreading land beyond, filling the vaulted ceilings and tall air with light and just a hint of the woodsmoke of the city. These were the rooms where King Simeon had lived. The queen had died in one of the wood-paneled bedrooms. Aster had taken some of his first steps in the candlelit hallway Geder walked through. It was where Aster had grown up. When the boy had become Geder's ward, Aster had expected to be leaving these walls for years, not months, and now he was back. It was and would always be more Aster's home than his own.

Geder knew from experience that it might be some time before the meeting he'd left spiraled to its true, if unofficial, close. Basrahip would stay there, and if the others picked and chose their words carefully, knowing that Geder's right hand was still with them, they didn't know how much the priest could still divine from the mixture of truth and lies. And a few minutes—an hour or two—entirely his own was welcome in a way that made his joints ache a little.

He heard Aster's voice reciting lines, and then the tutor— an ancient Cinnae man so frail-looking that he seemed always on the edge of collapse. Geder followed their voices to the study and hung in the shadows of the doorway for a moment.

Aster sat at a small table, looking up at the tutor's podium. The old Cinnae smiled encouragingly, and Aster began the lines again.

"*Information without practice can never grow to knowledge. Knowledge without silence can never grow to wisdom. And so practice and silence, doing and not doing, are at the heart of the right man's path.*"

"Marras Toca," Geder said. "I didn't know you were learning military philosophy."

The tutor's watery smile greeted him as he stepped into the room.

"You know the text, my Lord Regent?" he asked.

"I read an essay mentioning him that was very important to me. Afterward, I made a point of finding some of his work. I made a translation of it over the winter. I didn't use *silence* in mine. I thought *stillness* was closer to the original meaning."

"I think it's dull," Aster said.

"Some of it's dry," Geder said. The room was small, but sun-warmed. "Some of it was pretty interesting, though. Did you read the section about the spiritual exercises?"

"Like a cunning man's tricks?" Aster said, brightening a little.

"No, they were more like ways to practice thinking. When he's talking about silence or stillness, it's not just about not moving around. He's got a particular technical meaning."

"Have you done the exercises, my Lord Regent?" the tutor asked.

"No, not really, but I read about them a lot, and I think it's very interesting. Wise, even," Geder said, and leaned close to Aster with a rueful little grin. "I'm better at reading about those kinds of things than doing them. Can I see the translation you're using?"

The tutor leaned over his podium and held out the book. Geder took it carefully. It was very old, and the binding was leather and string. The pages were cloth, and thicker than usual, which gave the thing a feeling of solidity and weight. Geder turned the pages reverently.

"It's *beautiful*," he said. "Where did you get it?"

"A teacher of mine gave it to me when I was hardly older than Prince Aster," the tutor said, smiling. "I've kept it with me ever since. I have heard that you have quite the sizable library yourself, my Lord Regent?"

"Well, I wouldn't go that far. I used to have more time to read. And translate. I was working on an essay that tracked the royal houses of Elassae by the dates of their births, and it argued that Timzinae have two annual mating seasons. The actual dates were a little sketchy, but the argument was brilliant."

Aster sighed and leaned his elbows against his desk, but the old tutor's eyes were alight.

"It sounds fascinating, my lord. Do you recall the name of the author?"

"It was speculative essay, and only about three hundred years ago, so it had an attribution, but..."

"Yes, not much use to it. Not in those days," the tutor agreed.

Geder turned the pages, the cloth softer than skin under his fingertips. Toca's section on battle maps looked different in this than the one Geder had. There were at least three more diagrams, and a table of comparison that must have been added in by a later scribe. He traced the ancient ink with his fingertips.

"Could I borrow this?" Geder asked. "I'd like to compare it to mine."

The tutor's expression froze, and his hands made small spider's fists.

"Of course, my lord," he said. "I would be honored."

"Thank you," Geder said. "I will bring it back. I'm just going to go put it in with my books, if you don't mind."

"Of course not," the tutor said.

"Does that mean we can do something else?" Aster asked as Geder walked out of the room. The boy's voice sounded hopeful.

Geder walked with the pages open before him, his finger tracing the words. A little glow of excitement warmed him.

This wasn't a translation he'd ever seen before, and the original text seemed more complete than the one he'd worked with.

> The goal of war is peace. The small general leads his army into battle to achieve victory, and so his own nature will force him to return to it. The deep general leads his army into battle to confirm victory, and so the world's nature will force him to return to it. The wise general leads his army into battle to reshape the world, and so he creates a place which does not need him.

It wasn't at all like the copy Geder had. His copy hadn't, he was almost sure, included the verse about the deep general. Deep wasn't a form Toca used often, and when he did it was usually in reference to the priesthood. Geder wondered if a discussion of warrior priests had been taken out by a later translator.

"Ah," Basrahip said. "Listening to empty voices again, Prince Geder?"

The high priest was in the main room, sitting on a cushioned bench with his hands on his knees.

"I like books," Geder said.

"Some are pretty, but they are toys. They mean nothing."

"Well," Geder said, closing the book and setting it aside, "it's something we're just going to disagree about."

"For now," Basrahip agreed.

Geder sat beside the window. The afternoon sun pressed on the back of his hand.

"What did you find out?"

It was little that Geder hadn't expected. The court was certain that victory was imminent, and the credit for that rested with Geder and his ally and onetime patron Dawson

Kalliam. Opinion about how to deal with their conquered neighbor was mixed, but the disagreements were between gentlemen. Of course, there were particulars. One man advocated waiting for Baron Watermarch's return from Northcoast. Another thought that a marriage between Aster and Asterilhold's Princess Lisbet should be arranged as soon as the suit of peace arrived. Geder might draw the war out long enough to destroy the farmlands and mills and shipyards of the enemy, or he might preserve them for the use of the combined kingdoms in later years.

They talked for hours as the sun slid westward, pulling Camnipol slowly into the red light of sunset, the grey of dusk, and then darkness. The moon had not risen, and the stars shone in the high summer sky. At last, Geder, his head overfull, made his apologies and took himself to bed where men he didn't know undressed him, powdered his body, and laid him under thin spring blankets. Half awake, he was annoyed to discover that he'd forgotten the tutor's book. It would have been pleasant to read for a little while before sleep. He had so little time to read anymore...

Morning came clear and cold. He lay in bed for a while, watching the sunlight stream through the windows. Then the ritual humiliation, and he stepped out into the royal family dining hall. Basrahip was already there, as was Aster. The two were talking about something, Basrahip smiling and Aster laughing aloud. Geder sat, and a young servant brought him a length of baked duck and stewed pears, a small loaf of sweet black bread, and honeyed coffee with the grounds thick as mud at the bottom.

"Did I miss something funny?" Geder asked.

"Minister Basrahip's been doing impressions of the men in court," Aster said.

"Are they good?"

"No," Aster said, hooting. "They're *terrible.*"

Basrahip smiled.

"I am no man to play pretend," he said. "It is not what I am."

"And thank God for that," Geder said, plucking a bit of the duck free and popping it in his mouth. It was salty and rich and entirely the perfect way to begin a morning. "I've been thinking about the terms of peace with Asterilhold. I think I know what we have to do."

Priest and boy both sobered, turning their attention to him. Geder sipped the coffee, enjoying the moment of suspense more than he probably should have.

"I don't think we'd be wise to accept tribute and reparations and still leave them in control of the kingdom. If anything, we'll have made their court less likely to treat us as friends."

"And you must build temples to the goddess in the cities you conquer," Basrahip said.

"Yes, and that," Geder agreed. He'd forgotten that he needed to do that, but it was certainly true he'd agreed to. "Which means I think we have to move toward uniting the kingdoms."

Aster's face went still. "I see," the prince said.

Geder shook his head and waved a heel of bread.

"No no no. Marrying in won't work. Being married to a woman doesn't mean that all of Asterilhold is suddenly going to be placated. This is what got us here at the first, isn't it? Mixing bloodlines so that there were plausible claims to the Severed Throne in Asterilhold's court. If we hadn't tried making peace through marriage generations ago, there wouldn't have been the opportunity to even appear legitimate now. It didn't work then, and it won't work now."

"What, then?" Aster asked.

"*We* take the land. The cities. Asterilhold comes back to being part of Imperial Antea, just the way it was under the High Kings. There are any number of men in the court who deserve reward for the work they've done. And with loyal Anteans controlling the place, we'll have less to worry about. It's simple, really. I don't know why it wasn't obvious earlier."

"And the present ruling caste?" Basrahip asked.

"Well, they can't be trusted, can they? We've exposed them, humiliated them, and taken their positions and holdings," Geder said. "I'm sure they'd do anything in their power to undermine us. And these are the people, some of them, who were plotting to kill Aster. Losing a war doesn't change who they are, you know."

"I see," Basrahip said.

Geder took half of a stewed pear, sucking it into his mouth and pressing the juice out against his palate. Sweetness flooded him.

"No," he said, around the food. "I wish I saw another way. I do. But to keep Aster safe, I don't think we can leave our enemies with power. If they can't be friends and allies, they've made their choice. They have to die."

Dawson

Kaltfel stood on a wide plain rising up from the long strips of farmland like a strange dream. Its spires and towers were built from red stone, its walls stood as high as four men one atop the other. In gentler days, it was the home of the greatest breeders of messenger birds. It had been said that a bird bred in Kaltfel was fashioned with the secrets of the dragons, and for all Dawson knew, it might have been truth. Dawson had been there before as a young man. He still remembered the pale streets and the hot peppers and chocolate they seasoned their coffee with. He had fought a duel in the odd triangular yard that Asterilhold courts employed, and had won. He'd gotten drunk afterwards, and woken in another man's room, Prince Simeon beside him.

The day his army arrived at the royal city of Asterilhold, Dawson had begun by burning every structure that stood outside the city walls—farmhouses, storehouses, stables, tanners' yards, dyers' yards. What still stood when the smoke cleared, they had razed, with the exception of the necropolis to the east of the city. The tombs, he respected. Antea had no quarrel with the dead. After that, his engineers began constructing the siege engines. Trebuchet and catapult rained stones against the great red walls and the sealed gates. They worked in teams, eroding the tops of the walls day and night for seven days. At dawn and dusk, he would send runners through his camps to collect the shit and offal of the day, reset one of the trebuchets, and rain it down into the city itself. Soon his men were including other bits of refuse— dead cats and bloody bandages, spoiled meat alive with maggots. The gates did not open. The enemy did not appear. He hadn't expected them to. On the ninth day of the siege, a scout had discovered where a buried network of pipes had been emptying the waste of the city into a hidden gully. Dawson's engineers had destroyed them.

When they ran out of stones, they switched to tar-soaked wood set alight. For three more days, Kaltfel withstood the rain of fire. Twice, smoke began to take hold of the city, and twice the beseiged beat back the flames. On the tenth day, Dawson saw his first sign of real hope. The birds were all set free. The great flocks whirled around the towers, confused and looking for a way to come home. At dusk, they went north. Dawson considered sending huntsmen after them and flinging the corpses of pigeons and rooks back over the walls. He chose not to. The birds and the dead, then. They could escape.

Simeon had loved Kaltfel. The court manners there had just a hint of the exotic about them. Familiar and unfamiliar both. The men and women there spoke with a slight accent, stressing their long vowels in a way that made even the First-blood among them seem more foreign than the Jasuru or Timzinae back in Camnipol. The King's Palace stood before a wide, open square where a thousand girls had danced for them. More stones arrived from a quarry his soldiers had taken to the north, and the attack against the walls began again. One night, a desperate handful of soldiers slipped out of the city and came under cover of darkness to set fire to the catapults. They managed to destroy two before they were caught, and Dawson returned them using a third. He did not kill them first.

And every morning, the three priests came to him.

Dawson sat in his leather camp chair, his legs bared, while his squire plucked ticks out of his skin. The bright, damp summer morning reminded him of swimming in a lake. The priests, creatures of the desert, seemed to hate it.

"My lord, we will win this battle for you if you will allow it."

"But I won't," Dawson said, as he did every morning. "Antea is strong enough to break Kaltfel without your help, and that's what I intend to do."

"Listen to me, my lord—"

"We're done. Go now," Dawson said, as he did every day. They were silver-tongued. If he let them make their arguments, he might weaken again here as he had at the Seref and the paired keeps. He watched them walk away, and he smiled to himself as they went.

The camps ate through their supplies, and then turned to the landscape. No tree stood, and the smoke of green wood left the air hazy and white. Carts came in from Antea, and raiding parties pushed farther and farther south toward the marshlands, killing cattle and razing farms. It was a war of endurance, the slow, grudging end to a war that had gone too quickly at the beginning. Dawson's best estimate was that the landscape would bear the scars for a generation.

Twenty days into the siege, one of his own men died of a fever he'd caught in the southern marshes. Dawson stood rites over him in lieu of a real priest, then he'd ordered the fallen soldier dismembered and his body flung into the city.

On the twenty-first day, a banner of parley rose over the southern gate, and three unarmed men on horseback rode out. Dawson took Fallon Broot and Dacid Bannien for his. The three priests he left pointedly behind. They sat at a table in the empty space between tiring army and eroding city.

The men of Asterilhold held themselves proudly, but they rode thin horses and their cheeks were sharp. Dawson's squire had brought a ham and a basket of summer apples, a wheel of cheese and a tun of beer. Dawson saw his enemies looking at it, but he made them no offers.

"Lord Kalliam, I take it," the eldest of the three riders said as he took his seat. "Your reputation precedes you."

"I am sorry not to say the same," Dawson said, sitting.

"Mysin Hawl, Count of Evenford."

Dawson nodded. The ground was uneven, and the table rocked slightly as Count Hawl leaned against it.

"You know," the Count of Evenford said, "that we have the resources to withstand your siege."

"No, you don't," Dawson said. "We came faster than you anticipated and with more men. You were caught napping. And even if you had the food and water to squat behind your walls for a year, it wouldn't change the end."

The man sucked his teeth and shrugged.

"I have come to ask what terms you would require to end this."

"Are you empowered to offer surrender?"

"I am not," the count said. "Only the king has that authority."

"Then perhaps I should speak to the king."

Behind him, Fallon Broot chuckled, and Dawson felt a pang of annoyance. Perhaps he should have brought someone else.

"I am authorized to bring whatever message you care directly to his majesty."

Dawson nodded.

"He will open the gates of Kaltfel and surrender himself and every man involved in the plot against Prince Aster to me. We will sack for twelve hours. Not more. After that, all the holdings and territories of Asterilhold are under my pro-

tection until such time as your king and Lord Regent Palliako come to a final agreement."

"Then perhaps I should speak to the Lord Regent," the
count said.

"You wouldn't enjoy the experience," Dawson said.

"I will carry this to King Lechan," the count said. "May
we meet again in the morning?"

"If we remain under parley, then yes."

"We will make no attempt to attack or escape," the count
said.

"Then I will wait for your king's reply," Dawson said, and
nodded to Broot and Bannien. The pair brought the food-
stuffs and placed them on the table. "A token of our esteem.
They're not poisoned."

He rode back to the camp smiling. It was almost over.

My lord."

Dawson shifted in his cot, fighting toward consciousness.
The tent was dark except for the squire's candle. Dawson sat
up on his cot and shook his head.

"'S happened?" he asked. "Is it a fire? Are the bastards
coming? What?"

"A courier, my lord. From the Lord Regent."

Dawson was on his feet. The night was cool but not cold.
He shrugged on his cloak and stepped out. The cookfires
had for the most part burned out, and the night around him
was dark. The thin sliver of moon and the scattering of stars
couldn't outshine his candle. The courier stood beside his
horse, satchel in hand. Dawson took the letter, checked the
seal and the knotting to be sure it was authentic, and then
ripped out the threads. The contents were ciphered.

"Wait here," Dawson said to the courier, and then to his
squire. "Bring more light. Do it now."

It took an hour to decipher the text, and Dawson's belly grew thicker and heavier with every word he uncovered. The matter was clear. It was the considered decision of the Lord Regent that the crimes against Antea were too grave and threatened the safety and sovereignty of Imperial Antea as a whole. For this reason, Lord Regent Geder Palliako, in the name of Aster, King of Antea, claimed rights to Asterilhold and all the lands and holdings owing fealty to it. The Lord Marshal was instructed to gather together every man, woman, and child of noble birth in Asterilhold, seize and confiscate all lands and holdings, and put them all to death in as painless and humane a manner as was convenient.

Dawson sat in the darkness, bloodless. He read the words over again. Every man, woman, and child of noble blood in Asterilhold. Palliako's bloody thumb smeared the bottom of the page. His seal was on the wax. It was an order, given by the regent to whom he had sworn loyalty. True, the regent was Geder Palliako. True, the order was bloody-minded and cruel. But honor that was conditional was not honor; loyalty offered when he agreed and rescinded when he did not was not loyalty. Dawson sat by himself in the darkened tent, the flames of his candles the only light. He ran his hand across the pages, his throat thick. His hands were trembling.

Honor demanded. It *required*.

And then, as if coming before him in a dream, he saw Palliako look to his pet cultist, and the cultist nod.

My Lord Regent,

I am pleased to bring you happy news. This afternoon, I have accepted the surrender of Asterilhold and all holdings owing fealty to it. King Lechan is under my immediate control, and through his body, all those who swear loyalty to him.

As part of the terms of surrender and in accordance with tradition, I have accepted King Lechan, and through him all the noble persons and houses of Asterilhold, into my protection. I am devastated that your most recent instructions as to the terms of surrender reached me when the agreement had already been made. I feel certain that the respect and reverence we both have for the honor of the empire will compel you as it does me to respect the word as I have given it in your name, and Prince Aster's.

Dawson took a small silver blade, pressing it to his thumb until a drop of blood appeared, and then pressed it into the thirsty paper. He sewed the letter closed himself, melted the wax, and pressed his seal into it. He felt the hours of the night slipping by him, and he trotted out to the sounds of the first birds. There was no light in the east, no sign of the dawn apart from the bright and cheerful birdsong. He pressed the letter into the courier's hand.

"Take this back. Give it to no one but the Lord Regent. No one else, you understand? Even if his priest swears he will deliver it at once, you put this in the regent's hands, yes?"

"Yes, Lord Marshal," the boy said, and was gone.

Dawson stood for a moment, listening to the hoofbeats, soft against the mud and patchy grass, grow softer. And then the distant tapping when they reached the eternally solid jade. There was still time. He could send a fresh rider after the boy on a fast horse. Dawson had set this thing in motion, but he could still take it back. He closed his eyes and breathed deeply, the cool air filling him and then seeping away. He waited for his heart to feel some misgiving.

He found his squire dozing and shook him awake.

"Listen to me," Dawson said. "Wake up and listen to me,

you little bastard. You go and find the flag of parley. Take it out to the city. And take someone with you to carry it if someone gets excited and puts an arrow through you by mistake. Tell the count that I need to speak with him immediately. The situation has changed, he and I have very little time. Can you do that?"

"Y-yes, Lord Marshal."

"Then stop looking at me and *go*!"

When the sun came up, Dawson and Mysin Hawl, Count of Evenford, were at their little table in the no-man's-land. At midmorning, the count rode back to the city, shaken and weeping, the deciphered letter tucked in his belt. All day, Dawson sat at the parley table. His chair was as uncomfortable as a saddle, but in a different way. His back ached afresh, and he was hungry and thirsty, and desperately tired, but he remained at the table, the parley still not officially concluded.

The sun had started its long, weary arc toward the horizon when a sound came. A great, dry mourning drum. Far away before him, the gates of Kaltfel cracked and slowly swung open. The soldiers who came out carried the banner of Lechan, hung in reverse, and the yellow pennant of surrender. From behind him, Dawson heard the swelling, roaring shouts of victory. The sound washed over him like surf against the shore. All he felt himself was relief. King Lechan was a small man with poor teeth, but he held himself with dignity as Dawson accepted his surrender and took him into protection. In exchange, Dawson swore to do all he could to maintain that protection. All of the things he'd written to Palliako became true, except for a small matter of timing.

A small matter of timing that was the difference between loyalty to the man sitting on the throne and loyalty to the honor of the throne itself.

He gave command of the sack to Fallon Broot. For twelve hours, Kaltfel would feel the price of its loss as the soldiers of Antea ran riot over it, stripping its gold and gems and silver, its spices and silks. All the soldiers of Antea except two. If Dawson had looked for a better way to be assured privacy, he couldn't have invented one.

Alan Klin was paler than Dawson remembered him. A fever had taken him during the southern campaign, and he had not entirely recovered. The cunning men said he might never. He sat on the ground, his expression closed and sullen. Dawson considered his onetime enemy with a bitter amusement. The world made for strange partners.

"Curtin Issandrian met with my wife," Dawson said. "He was jealous of you. He hoped to have his own chance in the field. A way to regain his honor and good name."

"He's always been a bit of an idiot," Klin said. "Sincere, but..."

"You do have a chance to regain your honor," Dawson said quietly.

"I'm not here to get back my good name. I'm not here because of what Maas did. Back before Vanai, I pulled a prank on Geder Palliako. And now he's killing me without even the favor of doing it quickly."

"I think that's true," Dawson said and handed Klin a cup of honeyed water.

"I mean less than a book to him. My life is worth less than a book."

"How many of your friends do you still have in the court?" Dawson asked.

"A few, but none that'll speak to me anyway. Everyone knows that Palliako bronzes a grudge. I'm going to be trapped under his idea of revenge for the rest of my life." He sipped the water.

"Sir Klin," Dawson said. "I need your help. Your kingdom needs your help."

Klin chuckled and shook his head.

"What is it this time? Does the greater glory of the empire require me to climb a mountain naked with bear bait strapped to my neck?"

Dawson leaned forward. He had a sudden and powerful apprehension that the three priests would be nearby, that they would hear him.

"There's a difference between being loyal to a man and loyal to a nation," Dawson said. "I thought once that Palliako was nothing more than an apt tool."

"I think you called that poorly, Lord Marshal," Klin said, but his eyes were more focused than they had been. He scented smoke in what Dawson was saying. He wasn't a stupid man.

"No, I was right. My mistake was that I thought he was *my* tool. He isn't. He belongs to those priests he pulled back out of the world's asshole. They are uncanny, and I suspect they are more powerful than we understand. He's dancing to whatever song they call. He is letting them choose our way, and he will do so until Aster's of age. He is a monstrosity and we, in our folly, have given him the throne. As long as he has it, Antea will suffer. And you, my dear old friend, will be marked for an unpleasant death."

Klin drank his water again, but his gaze was solidly on Dawson now. He handed the cup back and licked his lips.

"I think you're telling me something," Klin said. "But I'm very tired and I've been very ill, so I think you should say exactly what you mean in very simple terms, yes?"

"Fair enough. I am offering you freedom from Palliako's wrath and the return of your good name and reputation. And more than that, I am calling you to the defense of Antea and the Severed Throne. We have been betrayed from within, and we allowed it to happen. Now we have to make it right. Antea needs a different regent. Anyone other than Geder Palliako."

"And how am I to manage that?" Klin asked, but Dawson could see that he already knew the answer.

"You help me kill him."

Marcus

The trade ships from Narinisle arrived in Porte Oliva, and the city was a madness of activity. Merchants flooded the inns and pubs near the port, digging for information, pouring beer into the sailors and coin into the purses of keeps and brewers. Which ships had left first, which last, which traders had met with each other on the distant island kingdom. No detail was too small to be wrung of all significance. It was the high season of Porte Oliva, and even in the exhausting heat of the day, trade and barter and negotiations filled every corner. The Medean bank had placed no direct stake the previous year, and so the absence of Cithrin bel Sarcour could be excused. It could not, however, go unnoticed.

A light rain fell from a low, white sky, leaving the air steamy and thick. The interior of the taproom was punishingly hot. Given the choice between the damp and the heat, rain won out, and the courtyard that overlooked the sea was thick with benches and chairs. The keep had taken away the tables to make more room. Marcus sat with Yardem, Ahariel Akkabrian, and the Jasuru named Hart. Four men of four different races all sitting together. They were, Marcus noted, the only such group in the yard.

"You need a cunning man who can turn the beer cold," Ahariel said.

"You need a desert," Hart said.

"How'd a desert help?" the Kurtadam asked. He'd had his pelt shaved almost to the skin for the summer. Seeing his pink skin dotted with thick black stubble and improbably pink nipples exposed to the air felt slightly obscene. Without his beads, he looked more like a Firstblood, but also eerily less like a human—neither one race nor another. Some other of his race left a decorative V of fur to keep the beads in place, but Ahariel had opted for the extreme.

"You take a great pot," Hart said, making his arms round. "Put a small one within, and sand between them. Damp the sand, and it will keep meat or beer cool. Only it won't work here. Too wet." His teeth clicked on the last word like it was threatening it. "What about you, Yardem? What do the Tralgu do?"

"Drink warm beer," Yardem said with a wide, canine grin.

The others laughed, but not Marcus. He'd come drinking because he didn't want to stay another day in the barracks or at the counting house, and a taproom by the port seemed to offer the chance of something interesting. Once he'd gotten there, the press of bodies and the roar of the voices left him anxious. There were too many people in not enough space. There was no way to see a threat coming. The tension was building across his shoulders and in the pit of his stomach.

He scanned the crowd, looking for something without quite knowing what it was. A familiar face, perhaps. Cithrin or Pyk. Or Master Kit. Yes, that was it. He was looking for Kit. Not—he told himself—because of the mad scheme the man had talked of. Only to pass an evening in conversation with someone who'd seen the world outside Porte Oliva recently. Someone whom the world hadn't yet nailed in place.

He wondered where Kit had gone. What he was doing just then. It was hard to imagine him away from the other players. Kit had built a life and a family and then had walked away from it because he felt he had to. It didn't matter that the reason was nonsense, it was still the mark of a brave man in a world of cowards. Marcus wasn't going to leave his work here to run off on some mad and doomed adventure. Unless, perhaps...

Someone put a hand on his shoulder and he looked up into the face of Qahuar Em. The half-breed had the coloring and features of a Firstblood, but with a rough skin where the Jasuru scales hadn't quite formed. Once, he had been Cithrin's rival and lover, and that he couldn't father children had been the only thing Marcus liked about him.

"Buy you men a round?" Qahuar Em asked, and then waited for an answer.

"Why not?" Marcus said, shifting on the bench.

Qahuar shouted to a harried serving boy and gestured toward the little knot of guards before he sat. His smile was both practiced and sincere. He was a difficult man to dislike. That was his job.

"The magistra seems to be missing the season," Qahuar said.

"Pressing work in Carse," Marcus said. "Don't know much about it. Just poor soldiers, us." Qahuar Em laughed, because they both knew better. "I heard your escort fleet hasn't gone as well as planned."

"We knew it would take a few years before we saw profit," Qahuar Em said, with a shrug. "*I* heard that I might have some gratitude to offer you, though."

"Always sorry for that," Marcus said, his smile pulling the sting of the words, but only a little.

The serving boy came, a tray held above his head as he

threaded his way through the crowd, and delivered mugs of last year's cider to the five men. It was sweet and crisp and the fumes from his first mouthful went to Marcus's head so that he only sipped it after that.

"The story goes that half the pirates between Cabral and here have moved elsewhere because the famed General Wester has been attacking them in their sleep and burning all their boats."

"Exaggeration," Marcus said. "Burned one boat once. But you know how these stories go. By next year, I'll have lit the ocean on fire and anyone who loses a cargo someplace besides here will say it's my fault for pushing the pirates in their way."

"Likely true," Qahuar said, and someone at the far end of the yard called his name. He looked up and waved at a First-blood woman in a blue cotton gown, but he muttered something under his breath as he did it.

"Friend of yours?" Marcus asked.

"Client," Qahuar said. "I'm afraid I'll have to—"

"We'll drink your cider without you," Ahariel said with a broad smile. "Think of you while we do it."

"Good man," Qahuar Em said, rising to his feet. He clapped Marcus on the shoulder. "Give the magistra my regards when you see her. The game's less interesting without her."

"She'll be pleased to hear it," Marcus said, and watched the man walk away. He knew his animosity wasn't entirely fair. Porte Oliva thought Cithrin to be older than she was. Marcus knew Qahuar Em had been sleeping with a girl barely more than a child, but even the half-Jasuru didn't.

"Hm," Hart said. "I'd say the captain's got an admirer."

The woman in the blue gown was speaking with Qahuar. She glanced back toward Marcus as Qahuar nodded, then she looked away perhaps a bit too quickly. She was too old to be pretty, but so was he. And she was handsome. Younger than Alys would have been, Marcus guessed, and older than Merian. Marcus sighed and handed his mug across to Yardem. The rain plastered her dress to her body, much as it did with everyone.

"You boys behave," Marcus said, standing.

"You're going for an introduction?" Hart asked with a leer.

"I'm going for a walk."

The streets were less crowded than the courtyard had been, but they were just as hot, just as damp. Horses and oxen pulled carts across filthy pavement, their heads hung low and heat spume on their lips. Men with hands on sword pommel walked beside loads of silk and spice, gold and tobacco leaf come from Far Syramys. The air smelled of horse shit and rotting vegetables and curry. All familiar, Marcus thought, but he wouldn't go so far as to say it smelled like home. Having no place in mind he cared to be, he found himself falling into a lonely patrol. The bank warehouse was open, bills of lading being compared with a cartful of crates. Enen and Roach waved to him as he passed. The barracks was nearly empty, the heat of the day making the interior unpleasant, but several of his guards sat in the shade of the building playing music and telling one another unlikely stories of battle or sexual misadventure. The counting house was open, the planter of tulips that Cithrin had put out when they had first purchased the building was a splash of celebratory red and pink.

Inside, Pyk was squatting on a stool, her legs splayed. Sweat ran down her face and stained her robe under her arms and breasts. She lifted her chin in greeting.

"You look like a drowned cat. Was about to send for you," she said.

"What's the matter?" Marcus asked.

The Yemmu woman heaved a tectonic shrug. "Depends on how you look at it. Maybe nothing. Letter came. On the table there. I'd get up and hand it to you if it wasn't so fucking hot."

The pages were coarse, and the ripped edges where they'd been sewn had tiny tears going into the page. The cheap paper the bank used for things that didn't need keeping. The signature at the bottom was Cithrin's, but it didn't bear her thumb. Not a legal document. He started from the top, reading slowly, and his heart went stiller.

"Camnipol," he said. "Thought they had a war going there."

"They do," Pyk said. "All but over, from what I hear. My money'd be on old Komme keeping his eye on the next war. Antea's a big place, and may be about to get bigger. Good to know who the players are."

"Didn't know it was a game."

"It's all a game," Pyk said. He wanted to find a sneer in her voice, but she only sounded tired. "The girl's a good choice. Pretty. Young. Smart. People say things in front of her and think she won't understand. What's this do to you?"

Marcus put the letter back on the table. It lay limp and broke-winged.

"Nothing," he said. "Just means I'll be watching the store a little longer before she gets back."

Pyk smacked her lips.

"And if she doesn't come back?"

Marcus leaned against the wall, his arms crossed. He took a deep breath, and felt hollow. "Why wouldn't she come back?"

"Because she's young and finding her place in the world. It may not be here. Maybe she gets out there and finds there's something she'd rather do than be my mask."

"Tell me that this wasn't your plan," Marcus said. "Tell me you weren't trying to get her to go out there so that she'd find something else to do. Leave you with the bank."

"I don't make her decisions. And I don't know that she'll stay away. Only I can see that she might."

"All right," Marcus said. "That could happen."

"If it does, do you still work here?"

Marcus smiled. The hollowness had a touch of anger now. He didn't want Cithrin to leave the bank and Porte Oliva, and he didn't like thinking what it meant that he didn't.

"Why do I get the feeling there's a particular answer you're looking for?"

"There is," Pyk said. "I want you to say you will. Having Marcus Wester collecting the debts gives the bank a certain weight. And you're good at it. But if you're only here for the girl, then you're only here for the girl."

"Well, I'm here until the girl comes back," he said. "If she doesn't, we can talk about it then."

Pyk's wide, yellowed eyes took him in and she sucked at her teeth.

"That's good enough," she said. "And you can hire back the men I had you take down and put the other back at full rates."

"Now that she's gone, you mean?" Marcus said, pushing himself off the wall. "Cithrin's here, you'll make it hard and mean and small, but when everyone knows it's your hand on the purse, it's all open? That how this is?"

Pyk's smile was so wide, he saw the holes where her tusks had been gaping dark in her gums. Her laughter wasn't a sound but a motion in her shoulders and her belly. She shook her head.

"The girl's letter didn't come alone," she said. "The holding company saw the reports. It approved my request to budget more for the guards. So now I put in more money for guards. It's not a mystery. I'm not the villain here. You can stop treating me like one."

Marcus stood, anger and confusion and embarrassment growing in him.

"Sorry," he said. "Didn't know you had to have your budget approved."

"Don't, strictly speaking," Pyk said. "But the Porte Oliva branch has a reputation as unpredictable. I'm tacking into that wind. Can't think where it came from."

"Anything else?" Marcus said.

"Is. Keep an ear to the ground for anything about a captain name of Uus rol Osterhaal. He'll have been coming up from Lyoneia, but he might not be announcing the fact."

"Anything I'm trying to find out?"

"Whatever you can. Bring me what you find, and I'll know whether it's useful or not. You can go now. I'm going to sit here and sweat a while more."

Marcus walked back out. He felt like he'd been in the gymnasium, down in the fighting pits getting a fist sunk just under his ribs. The world was unchanged, but it was also different. Porte Oliva seemed smaller. Thin. As if the only thing that had given the city any sense of reality was that Cithrin lived here. And if this wasn't her city, then it was an encrustation of buildings stuck on a rock overlooking the sea. Wasn't much charm in that.

He walked slowly, retracing his steps. The rain was still falling, though if anything less now than it had been. The streets were wet and slick, and they stank. In an hour, maybe two, the heat would loosen its grasp a little. He'd still be sweating through his shirts until morning. It would be like that until the days got short again. But he would be here when it happened. He'd be working for Pyk Usterhall and the Medean bank and waiting for Cithrin to come home until it was clear that she wouldn't.

He held the thought in his mind like pressing his tongue to a sore tooth.

"She's not my daughter," he said to himself. A small voice in the far, dark reaches of his mind answered, *She's Cithrin.*

He wasn't sure what he'd thought. What he'd expected. That they would stay there, he supposed. That he and Yardem would keep her and her bank safe, if not forever, then for years at the least. It wasn't something Cithrin had promised him or that he'd asked from her. If she found a better path, a better plan, taking it wasn't any betrayal of him.

A beggar came up to him with her hand out, then met his eyes, started, and backed away. He was almost back at the taproom before he knew he was going there. The sound of the voices in the courtyard was just as loud. Maybe louder. He made his way in. He saw Yardem see him. The Tralgu's ears went up and forward, straining at him, but Marcus only lifted a hand, more acknowledgment than greeting.

Qahuar Em and his client were sitting at a small table in the shade of a wide white wall. Seagulls were screeching and wheeling out beyond them, grey against the white sky. Marcus hesitated. He'd taken enough lovers in the years after Ellis that he knew what sex would ease and what it wouldn't. Right now, his body wasn't hungry. He didn't need release for its own sake. The thing that would soothe him now, he wasn't going to find in a woman's bed.

Or anywhere else.

We have steady work for fair pay. We have shelter and we have food. Interesting if that's not what we were looking for.

And more than that? What did he want that was more than that? What had Cithrin taken with her that left him angry with no one to be angry at?

The woman with Qahuar Em looked over, saw him, smiled. Marcus smiled back. This was a mistake, but it was his to make. He found the serving boy, made his order, and gave him a silver coin that would have paid twice over. When he approached the table, Qahuar Em smiled and lifted his eyebrows.

"Evening," Marcus said. "I hoped I could return your kindness. Stand you to a round?"

"Of course," Qahuar Em said. "This is Arinn Costallin, a dear friend of mine from Herez."

"Marcus Wester," he said, taking her hand.

"So I've heard," she said.

Yardem found him by the seawall just before dawn. Marcus wasn't drunk anymore. The rain had stopped sometime after midnight, and the clouds had scattered. Yardem had a sack of roasted nuts in his hand. When he squatted down next to Marcus, he held its open mouth toward him. Marcus took a handful. They tasted sweet and meaty.

"Didn't see you at the barracks," Yardem said.

"I am an ass."

Yardem nodded and bit down on a nut. They chewed together quietly for a time. A seagull called, lofting up into the darkness, then, as if confused, swung back and landed on the cliff face below them.

"Moved too fast with her, sir?"

"Did."

"Should we be expecting children?"

"No. I was careful about that, at least. But then after, I started talking about..."

Marcus leaned forward, his head in his hands.

"Might have been a little early to talk about them, sir."

"Might have."

"Scared her off of you."

"Did," Marcus said. Below them, fishing boats had put out to sea for the day. Tiny black dots on a nearly black sea.

"Was this about Alys and Merian?" Yardem asked. "Or was it about the magistra?"

"Cithrin."

"You think she isn't coming back, then."

"I think she may not. I wouldn't blame her if she didn't. And someday I'll need to find what it's going to take to get a family I can keep."

Yardem nodded and flicked one jingling ear. They were silent for a moment.

"I have an answer for that," Yardem said.

"Is it theological?"

"Is."

"Best we save it, then," Marcus said, clapping his hands on his thighs and standing up. His back was a single long ache, and his mouth felt as dry as cotton. When he stretched his arms, something between his shoulders cracked like a dry stick. "I take it Pyk has a list of work for us?"

"Does, sir. But if you'd like to sleep, I can take a group through it all. It's not so much we can't manage without."

"No. There's a job needs doing," Marcus said. "Show me what we've got."

Dawson

Camnipol opened its gates to Dawson and his men as if to a hero from legends. The sober black and gold of the city was covered over in bright, celebratory array. Pennants as long as five men standing fluttered from the windows of the Kingspire, and the great bridges were hung with flowers produced by both nature and artifice. As he marched through the great streets, honor guard surrounding him, choirs of children sang the ancient songs of heroes and wars with Dawson's name included among the great generals of the past. He was hailed as a great man and a patriot. The irony was rich. All of it was true, and not a word of it had been earned.

Not yet.

His army, of course, waited in camp outside the walls. No armed force was allowed within Camnipol. That had always been true, and after the showfighters' riot, the old tradition had been reinforced. And even if Dawson had ordered the attack, it would have done no good. He was praised and honored today only as far as he was the tool of Geder Palliako and his cult. To turn against the man too soon was to invite failure. Dawson raised his chin, smiled, waved, accepted the garlands of white and red flowers offered to him, and reminded himself that all of it was not earned by what he had done, but borrowed against what he was about to achieve.

Behind him, King Lechan walked with as much dignity as the old man could muster. The chains around his neck and wrists were made of silver and thin enough that they might almost have passed for adornments, but they were still chains.

At the Kingspire, the Lord Regent waited in his grand audience chamber. Prince Aster sat at the man's side, and the bull-massive priest stood behind the throne. Palliako wore the small, golden crown of the regency and his own signature black leather cloak, despite the heat of the day. The priest wore a dust-brown robe, much as the other priests did. A sparrow whispering to a crow.

The crowd around them was quiet. Not silent. Dawson could hear mutterings and complaint, but near enough that when he spoke, the callers could make out his words clearly.

"Lord Regent," he said. "You have tasked me with the submission of Asterilhold. I have come to report that duty is done."

And on the word *done*, the crowd erupted in cheers. Dawson kept himself from smiling and watched Palliako's face. No one knew that he had refused the regent's order, and no reply had come to Dawson's report that the nobility of Asterilhold was under his personal protection. It was possible that Palliako would have him named traitor for what he'd done, but with the adulation of the crowd ringing the city like a bell, it seemed unlikely. Nearly impossible.

And, in fact, the regent was smiling. He looked about with a wide grin, as if the cheers were for him. Palliako stood, motioning for silence, but the cacophony went on, trailing off only slowly.

"Lord Marshal Kalliam. You have shown yourself again to be an invaluable friend to the Severed Throne. It is my duty and pleasure to add to your titles and holdings. From this day forward, you are Dawson Kalliam, Baron of Osterling Fells and also of the Barony of Kaltfel."

Dawson felt a sudden tightness in his breast. The renewed cheers were wild as a windstorm. He had guessed that there would be no suit of peace, no treaty. The war now behind them had not been a conflict between civilized kingdoms. It had been raw conquest, and now as its spoils, Palliako had granted Dawson a city almost as great as Camnipol itself. He had made Dawson effectively the second most powerful man in Antea, behind only the regent himself.

Dawson gave salute, but his mind was possessed by the implications. He imagined the wealth of Kaltfel pouring into his hands, his house, and the fortunes of his sons. Even Lord Bannien would look a beggar by comparison.

All he would have to do was accept Geder's rule and the rule of his priests. All it would cost was his honor. Dawson took a garland of flowers from around his neck and placed it on the ground before him, as if offering them up to Palliako.

I will earn these, he thought, but even if he had shouted it, no one would have heard.

After the official audience, Dawson suffered through hours more of his official duties. The surrender of the prisoners, which took some extra time as he needed to impress on the gaolers that King Lechan especially was being surrendered only for holding, and that he remained under Dawson's personal protection. Then he ordered the disband, freeing his men to return to their homes and families and ending his tenure as Lord Marshal.

He tried to avoid being in a room with Palliako and the priest, but form required at least a private glass of wine. The private audience was in a small garden near the dueling grounds. Prince Aster greeted him formally, and then excused himself to go play with a handful of other boys born of noble houses. Palliako and Minister Basrahip sat at a table of lacquered rosewood, servants rushing to them with cooled wine and fruit. Dawson bowed to the regent and took his seat, but his gaze was on the personal guard. Ten of them. Ten blades set to protect Palliako at all times. They would be difficult to overcome, but not by any means impossible...

"I hope your journey back wasn't too arduous," Geder said. "I hear you left Fallon Broot as Protector of Asterilhold?"

"I did, Lord Regent."

"Now there's a man whose fortunes have changed in the last years," Geder burbled. "You know I met him on the Vanai campaign?"

Dawson drank from his glass. The wine was excellent. Simeon had always cared about his drink. Now Palliako was getting the benefit of that.

"I believe I had heard that, my lord," Dawson said.

"Well, it's bad fortune for him that he'll be missing your revel. I still remember what you did for me. After Vanai. I've been looking forward to returning the favor. It will be amazing. Honestly, I think people will be talking about this for a generation."

Dawson permitted himself a smile.

"I hope that you are right," he said.

"I was sorry to hear that you didn't have Basrahip's priests help with the battle at Kaltfel. They were useful taking the bridge, weren't they?"

"I didn't believe their help was required at Kaltfel," Dawson said. "And I thought it would be better for morale if the victory were unquestionably Antea's."

"Oh, that's silly," Geder said with a wave of his hand. "Everyone knows they're on our side. I mean, they weren't out driving down the enemy's confidence over some private feud they had with them."

"I suppose not," Dawson said, fighting not to stare his anger at the priest. "But for the sake of form, if nothing else."

"And once all this is over, I'd like to talk with you about how to manage the transition with Asterilhold. I've been reading the histories, and I don't find any single good model for this. I mean, I know it helps that we both used to answer to the High Kings." Geder sighed. "I wish my orders had gotten to you a day earlier. This would all be so much easier. I mean, when you're at war, death's to be expected. Now that they've surrendered, things will be more difficult."

"They can't be slaughtered wholesale," Dawson said.

"But we can't just leave them," Geder said. "It doesn't make sense to have half a victory. If you don't destroy your enemies utterly, aren't you just asking for another fight later when they've regained their strength? If you want peace—real peace—I think you have to conquer, don't you?"

"We need justice, not petty revenge." There was more bite in the words than he'd intended. "Forgive my saying so, my lord."

"Oh, no. Please. Speak your mind. You're one of the only men in this city I trust."

Dawson leaned forward in his seat.

"We are noblemen, my lord," Dawson said, choosing his words. "Our role in the world is to protect and preserve order. The houses of Asterilhold have Antean blood, many of them, but even if they did not, we share a history with them. What they have done against us must be answered, and answered between equals."

"Oh, I absolutely agree," Geder said with a rattling nod that meant he hadn't understood at all. The priest had his eyes half closed, but seemed to be listening to him carefully all the same. A twist of anger floated up from Dawson's heart.

"The world has an order," Dawson said. "My men are loyal to me, and I am loyal to the throne, and the throne is loyal to the system of the world. We are who we are, Palliako, because we have been born better. When a low man crosses me, I execute him. When a highborn man, a man of *quality*, crosses me, then there is the dueling field. If I were to wantonly spill noble blood on behalf of a pig keeper, even if the nobleman were of a different kingdom and the pig keeper my own vassal, it would be an abomination."

"Let me think about that. Of course, we are more or less equals, aren't we?" Geder said. "We're nobles, they're nobles. And we've done all this because they were scheming against Aster, who's the highest blood in the land. We did it for him."

We've done it for your foreign zealots, Dawson thought.

"I suppose so," he said, and the priest made a small sound in his throat, like a boy who'd caught sight of a curious animal.

"You seem troubled, Lord," the priest said, sitting forward. His gaze was on Dawson. "Is something else bothering you?"

You are a goatherd, and you have no right to question me.

"Nothing," Dawson said, and the priest smiled.

Seeing Clara again was like putting a burned hand in cool water. Everyone else, from the footmen to Jorey, were made of smiles and pleasure and congratulation. Dawson felt as though he were living in a dream where he was in a burning ballroom and no one else could see the flames. Clara looked at him once and put her arms around him like a mother comforting her child.

Most of the evening they lay together in her bed, his head in her lap when she sat or sharing her pillow when she lay down. The world with its idiotic gaudiness and mindless cheers—face paint on a tainted woman—faded for a time while she told him of all the small domestic crises he had missed during the brief, decisive war. One of the maids had married and left the house. A cistern had sprung a leak and had to be drained before it could be repaired. Sabiha was settling into the household, but Elisia was being difficult. She'd had a letter from the holding at Osterling Fells that the new kennels were going nicely, and would be complete before winter.

The scent of her bed and the sound of finches at the window mixed with her familiar touch, and he found himself relaxing in a way he hadn't in weeks.

"Canl Daskellin's due back soon," she said.

"Where's he been?"

"Northcoast," Clara said. "Apparently he went out to get allies against Asterilhold, and he's bringing them back just in time for the victory. I don't believe anyone expected it all to be over so quickly."

"It isn't over," Dawson said. "Not really."

"Well, of course things will be a bit thin at the harvest," Clara said. "But next year..."

Dawson took her hand and rolled back, looking at the ceiling.

"Next year will be a different place, love," he said.

Clara sat up, frowning. He ran his fingertips along the curve of her arm.

"Is there something I should know?" she asked.

"No. Only perhaps it would be best if you and Jorey and Sabiha went back to the holding for a bit. Now that we've got two baronies to look over, the boys will need to know better how to run the place. And there's no one better to show them than you."

Her face closed.

"There's something more coming," she said. "What's happened? What are you going to do?"

"You can't ask me that, love," Dawson said. "I'll be too tempted to tell you. And it's better for now if I carry this one alone."

"Dawson—"

"I didn't win this war. And Palliako is a monster, but he didn't order it. There's rot at the heart of the empire, and I am doing what honor demands. There's risk to it, but there's not an alternative."

Clara looked at him for what seemed an hour, her eyes shifting back and forth, searching for something in his expression.

"You're moving against Palliako's priests," she said.

"I am doing what honor and duty demand," Dawson said. "Don't ask me more than that."

She stood, her hands clasped before her.

"If Jorey and I leave, it will be remarked," she said. "It's a very odd time for the wife of a war hero to leave. If I stay, what will I need to be prepared for? Will this come to violence?"

"It will."

Clara let out her breath and closed her eyes. It was something she had done as long as he'd known her. He could remember her as a girl barely come to womanhood lowering her eyelids just so, making her exhalation that was not quite a sigh. Perhaps all those previous moments had been rehearsal for this one. He rose from the bed and took her hand.

"I have no choice, dear. I've seen what is stalking our kingdom. If it isn't stopped, it won't be Antea anymore. It may keep the same forms, it may even be made up by the same people, but the kingdom will be gone, and there will be something debased where it was. I will do anything I have to in order to see the nation safe."

"All right," Clara said. "You do that. And I will see to the family."

He kissed her gently on the forehead. And then on the lips. And then she pressed him back to the bed, and they forgot the world together for a time.

The last time Dawson had walked into the darkness of the ruins under Camnipol—the abandoned archways and hallways darker than midnight—the huntsman Vincen Coe had been at his side. Going alone now, he found himself missing the young man's company. He'd been a quiet man, but loyal and fierce. He didn't understand why Clara had taken her sudden dislike to him. Perhaps in the winter when he returned to Osterling Fells the two would have the chance to mend whatever breach had separated them.

Rats scurried ahead of his lantern's light, sharp claws stirring up ancient dust. Once, all this had been the city. These stones had seen daylight and known the voices of street vendors. The rubble Dawson picked his way around had stood as a tall column celebrating some victory now long forgotten. The deeper he went, the more collapse had taken the ruins, and the fewer paths there were to follow. Still, he was fairly sure he knew the way.

The first glimmer of light, far ahead, filled him with hope and dread both. Hope, because he had found the meeting place he'd sought. Dread for the same reason.

Four men sat round a fallen slab of granite. Sir Alan Klin, but also Estin Cersillian, Odderd Mastellin, and Mirkus Shoat. A knight, a count, and two earls, pressed down in the darkness. He wondered whether Shoat, Cersillian, and Mastellin had been part of Klin's conspiracy from the start. Maas might have had other allies Dawson had never uncovered. He sat down on a lump of stone, considering the men who had turned to Asterilhold and against Simeon. A year ago, they had been on opposite sides. Now fortune had united them.

"I'm pleased to see you were able to gather so many like-minded friends," Dawson said.

"This helped, my lord," Klin said, pushing the execution order across the slab to him. "Some people in court are still close with their families across the border."

Dawson picked up the page and folded it into his wallet.

"What are we going to do?" Shoat asked, his voice high and tight.

"What needs doing," a voice said from the shadows. Dawson rose as Lord Bannien, Duke of Estinford, stepped into the light. His face was calm and steady, sandy hair over black eyes. "I took your letters, Kalliam. And I spoke to my son. I have been forced to the same conclusions. Antea has been taken over by foreign sorcerers."

"Your son told you, then," Dawson said. "About what happened at the bridge."

"He did," Lord Bannien said. "And I am with you. But we must move quickly. If word of this comes out, it's worth all of our lives."

"How many men can you bring?" Dawson asked.

"Twenty that I trust utterly for the event itself. A hundred once the die is cast."

Shoat promised seven, Cersillian and Mastellin ten each, and then the full resources of their houses, for another seventy men.

"I can give twelve for the first attack," Klin said. "Including myself. But only if we're agreed that Palliako dies."

Dawson looked around the ruined space and nodded.

"In three days, Palliako will be staging a revel in my name," Dawson said. "Celebrating the capture of Asterilhold. I don't know this, but I suspect that he means to execute King Lechan at that time. The men can gather at my house. If they arrive in my livery and announce themselves as my honor guard, they can come into the grand hall during the feast. We end Palliako where he sits."

"I don't want to start a civil war," Mastellin said.

"We won't," Dawson said. "Once the deed's done we will all surrender ourselves to Prince Aster. We must not allow any question that we have done this in service to the crown."

"That relies a great deal on a very young boy's judgment," Shoat said. "If he decides to call retribution, we'll all find ourselves in a small place."

"If you were planning to avoid risk, you've come to the wrong table," Dawson said. "And if we all die in the effort, it will be a small price against the reclamation of the throne. We kill the traitor and support the king. There is no other path."

"Agreed," Bannien said, slapping his palm against the stone. "But killing Palliako's only striking the sword arm. There is another issue."

"Of course," Dawson said. "The priests. They must be rounded up and killed. And the temple will burn."

Cithrin

Cithrin had never been so far north in her life. Many of the small details, she knew from the stories and descriptions that Magister Imaniel had given her, but the images she'd built from the words didn't often match the reality. She knew that the northern coasts were dotted with stone fishermen's huts, but in her mind they had been square, solid buildings, like the ones in Vanai only grown small. The mossy, earthen lumps strewn over the grey-green shores looked less like buildings than something that had grown up out of the land itself. She knew to expect the great, soaring lizards that lived on the stone islands and ate fish, but she had imagined them as small dragons instead of the awkward, batlike things they were. And then there were other things, unexpected and strangely wonderful. The days were even longer here, the sun hardly seeming to give over to night before the dawn began to threaten. The winters would reverse that, with the darkness and the cold swelling up to take back their due. And once the sea voyage was done, and their boat safely in its dock at Estinport, Cithrin stepped onto the earth of Imperial Antea.

She had rarely thought of land having its own personality, but as they made their way to great Camnipol, she saw the differences in the world. All her life had been spent near the shores of the Inner Sea. She had traveled through mountains

and across the hills to the east of Porte Oliva. She had seen
the forests north of the Free Cities. But for most part, those
lands had been one thing or else another. Here, everything
mixed, hard stone beside rich green meadow beside thick
trees. Rich farmland lined the roads, the long, thin fields
marked by fences built of rough black stone. The mountains
here curved softly toward the sky, like a hill that had been
left to rise too long before it was baked. Compared to the
Free Cities or even Birancour, Antea seemed sure of itself.
Old and staid and eternal. It was the most beautiful landscape she had ever seen, and she wanted to love it. But she
didn't.

Camnipol rose on the southern horizon, still three days
away. Coming from the north, it looked like a shallow hill,
spiked and gnarled with bare trees and brush. Smoke rose
from it like the fires of a massive army. She knew that the
city was reputed to be beautiful, and perhaps as she grew
closer it would become so. From here, it was not.

"You notice the way the group splits?" Paerin Clark asked
her, breaking her chain of thought.

They were sitting near the cookfire. It was too warm to
need the flames for warmth, but the cheerfulness of the light
and the routines of long habit brought them there. She followed his gaze to another fire on the far side of the road. A
bright silk tent glowed from within. Of the two dozen men
and women put together by King Tracian and Komme
Medean to take the pulses of Imperial Antea, only five were
noblemen, and they kept to themselves. Canl Daskellin, who
had broken bread with his fingers at Komme Medean's
table, was among them.

"Highborn on one side, merchant class on the other,"
Cithrin said.

"It always goes like that," the man said. He handed her a

bowl. Black beans shining bright as insects and covered with a grey sauce that looked terrible and tasted like the finest cook in Birancour had made it fresh. "Do you ever wonder why that is?"

"No, I don't," Cithrin said. "It's because we all know that the idea of noble blood is a sham."

Across the fire from them, one of the other merchants chuckled. Cithrin felt a blush rising in her cheeks, but Paerin took a mouthful of his own meal and nodded her on.

"You only have to enforce boundaries where they're being imposed," she said. "Think about the races. It's been hundreds, maybe thousands of generations since the dragons made the last of us. In all that time, you would think all of the thirteen races would have blended into one, but they haven't. We're all more or less what we would have been if the Dragon Emperor were still in the sky. There are real barriers between Jasuru and Yemmu and Cinnae. They don't need to be enforced. They just are."

"To clarify, though. You're between races."

"And has that made Cinnae and Firstblood one thing? No. But nobility? People have become knights and earls and counts through force of arms or by buying their way in. And even the highest families have a few unwelcome members living among the poor and despised. The dirty secret of nobility is that it's another way of saying power. We may tell other stories, but when we do, it's because we're building fences where there aren't any."

"And why would that make them sit there and us here?" Paerin said.

"Because otherwise we couldn't tell who had the greater value. Say I have ten coins that all look the same, only some will buy five bolts of cloth, but the others are worth just one. Can you picture that?"

"But all the coins look the same," Paerin said.

The other conversations around the fire had stopped. They were listening to her. She reached for the skin of watered wine and drank a mouthful before she went on.

"Yes. So it's in your interest not to confuse them, isn't it? You put one set in a tent over there, and the rest by a fire over here. Because if you put them all in the same purse, you wouldn't know if you'd drawn a coin worth five bolts or only one. We are those coins. You and I and Komme and everyone here. We're worth one. They over there are worth five. But if you mixed us all together, you wouldn't see a difference. That's why everyone hates bankers so much."

"I think we respect noble blood," Paerin said.

"We don't because we lend at interest. A wise loan can make a poor man rich. A unwise one can unmake the powerful. We're the ones who can move the coins from one side to the other, and we take our living from doing it. We're agents of change, and the people with the most to lose are right to fear us."

Paerin Clark looked across the fire at the man sitting there. The other man nodded, and Cithrin felt a pang of self-consciousness.

"You, Magistra, have a fascinating way of seeing things," Paerin said, leaning back.

"I'm sorry," she said.

"No. Be proud of it. It's why Komme sent you."

The walls of Camnipol were so thick that the tunnel from one side to the other needed lanterns in the middle. The streets within were packed as tightly with bodies and carts as the narrowest alleys of Porte Oliva. Cithrin stayed close to Paerin Clark and kept one hand on her purse. She hadn't come all this way to let a roadside pickpocket embarrass her now. The knot in her gut had been for the most part absent during her travels. It came back now as hard as a cramp. It was like stepping into the city had stripped all her certainty from her. As if the city itself disliked her and they both knew it.

This was the heart of the empire that had changed her. An army had marched from this city. Some commander wearing Antean colors had given the order to burn Vanai, and those flames sent her skirling off on the wind like a dry leaf, every imagined life left behind. The men who had closed Vanai's gates and set it afire lived here. They walked the streets and drank at the taprooms and might for all she knew be beside her at any moment. Magister Imaniel and Cam were dead, and their deaths began here.

She set her jaw and her resolve.

The thing she noticed first and most about Camnipol was how many Firstbloods there were. Yes, here and there she might catch a glimpse of a Tralgu wearing a slave's collar and carrying someone else's packages, or Jasuru litter-bearers. But of every twenty faces she saw on the streets, nineteen were Firstblood. The thing she noticed second was that many of them were drunk.

"Is it always like this?" she shouted to Paerin, two feet ahead of her.

"No," he called back. "It's never been like this before when I've been. Never seen it this happy either. Stay close. The inn's not far."

Cithrin clenched her teeth and pressed on. If it had been Porte Oliva, the heat of bodies and the jostling wouldn't have been nearly as bad, only because it would have been familiar. Here, the sky was a different shade of blue and the air was thinner and everything was different.

The inn was thankfully fronting its own courtyard. No

carts were trying to press their way through, no one came there who didn't have business. Cithrin felt as if she were stumbling into it.

"Wait here," Paerin Clark told her. He ducked into the shadows of the inn. The stone walls were like a fortification's. Bright cloth hung from the windows and doorframes like a fine veil on an ugly girl. Someone shouted from the street, an angry buzz in the voice, and Cithrin wished that Marcus and Yardem had come with her. The journey to Carse had been one thing. It had been a move against Pyk Usterhall and the encroaching control over her bank. Coming to Camnipol had been a whim, a moment's madness played out over weeks. She held her elbows, trying to be small.

She closed her eyes, but it didn't help. The noise of the street was the roar of a river. Voices and iron-wheeled carts. Dogs barked, chasing rats into the shadows and then back out again. One voice was calling out an offer of apple tarts and two coppers each. Another promised a play at dusk. Another merely shouted invective and abuse.

Cithrin's heart began to race before she knew why. The voice announcing the play. She knew it.

"Smit!" she yelled, straining to be heard. "Smit! Is that you?"

And a moment later, from very close and terribly far away, "Cithrin?"

"Smit! Over here," she called. "I'm by the inn."

He stepped out of the crowd like he was walking onto a stage, nowhere and then suddenly there. His eyes were wide with surprise and delight, and Cithrin ran over to him, throwing her arms about him. He whooped and lifted her in the air.

"What are you doing here?" he asked as her feet touched ground again. "I had you playing the magistra for a long run."

"Still am," she said, not taking her arms from around him. Of Master Kit's players, she'd never been as close to Smit as she was to Cary or Sandr. Or Opal, though that didn't bear thinking of. But having Smit here in the middle of the strangeness and far, far from home made her reluctant to let him go, and he didn't object. "The holding company sent me with a few others to get the lay of the land with the new regent."

"And the end of the war," Smit said. "It was bad trade there for a time, but we're swimming in coin now. You have to come see us. We've put together a version of the Lark's Lament with all local references. Took us a long time to get all the names right, but now all the people we're making fun of come every other show just to hear their names said. S'brilliant."

"How is everyone? What's Master Kit doing?"

Smit's face darkened.

"Master Kit's gone," he said. "Gave over everything to Cary and headed out. Said something gnomic about killing gods and went like dandelion fluff in a high wind. Miss the hell out of that man."

"I'm sorry," Cithrin said. She couldn't entirely imagine the acting company without Master Kit.

"We'll do. Cary's a damn bit harder on us, but she's got a good eye. And the new one, Charlit Soon—d'ya know her?"

"Met her a few times," Cithrin said, and someone bumped Smit forward into her.

"You two get some privacy!" a man's voice shouted. "Don't care to see you rubbing on each other!"

"Lick my ass!" Smit yelled over his shoulder. "Anyway, she's gotten better. Really growing into the roles."

"And Sandr?"

"Sandr's Sandr."

"Well. Pity, that."

"I'll tell him you said so," Smit said with a grin.

"You won't," Cithrin said, taking her arms away for the first time and hitting him lightly on the shoulder.

"You'll come see us, though? We're at a taproom called Yellow House. Not the cleverest name, but it's hard to mistake since the whole place looks like it's painted in yolk. It's just at the edge of the Division by the one bridge. Autumn. Autumn Bridge."

"What's the Division?"

"Big crack down the middle of the place. Yellow House, by Autumn Bridge. Say that?"

"Yellow House by Autumn Bridge," she said, and he patted her on the head like a puppy.

"Know your lines already. I'd best go. Lots of players in this town. We'll want our share of audience."

"Tell the others I said hello," Cithrin said. "Tell them I miss them."

"Shall," Smit said, and then the flow of the street took him again. She heard his voice calling the play. Faint, fainter, and gone.

When she turned, Paerin Clark was in the doorway of the inn. His expression hovered in the no-man's-land between scandalized and amused. Cithrin walked to him the way Cary had taught her, low in the hips and steady. The walk of an older woman. When Paerin spoke, his voice betrayed nothing.

"Did I just see the voice of the Medean bank in Porte Oliva embracing an actor in the street?"

"The voice of the Medean bank in Porte Oliva is a many-faceted woman," Cithrin said. "Do we have rooms?"

"We do. I thought I would tour you through the city, if you'd care to."

"I would be delighted," she said, offering him her elbow. He took it with a bow.

Camnipol, now that she wasn't quite as overwhelmed by it, was a city of grim and terrible beauty that was at present dressed in its holiday ribbons. The dark stone and grandeur of the buildings showed through once she knew to look for it.

The great chasm of the Division stood in the center of the city, the great architectural wound exposing the bones beneath the foundations of the buildings. The Silver Bridge they crossed to reach the Kingspire had no particular silver about it, but great timbers that creaked and swayed over the abyss. At the bridge's edge, she stopped a girl and asked which was the Autumn Bridge, for later. The girl pointed south with a pitying expression as if Cithrin had asked if the sky was up or down.

The Kingspire itself was astounding. It was easily the largest tower Cithrin had ever seen, and she was willing to believe it was the largest in the world. And all around it, the mansions and estates of the high families, the tombs of the dead, the temples. She stopped before one with a massive red pennant with an eightfold sigil at its center. Paerin Clark looked up at it and then down at her, but she only shook her head—some wisp of memory come and gone without leaving its name—and they walked on.

When, near dark, they came back to the inn, Cithrin's feet ached, but the knot in her gut was less than it had been. Not gone, but a half a skin of wine with a bit of meat would let her sleep, she thought, even in an unfamiliar bed. Paerin Clark sat with her in the cramped common room.

"It's a lovely city," she said. "But I can't think you came here just to walk me around."

"No, we only had an evening, and it seemed pleasant," he

said. "Tomorrow, the work begins. I have two merchants not far from here that we've had dealings with. I'll want to speak with them. And then another one, less reputable, who works down the side of the Division."

"*Down* the side?" she said.

"Not the highest-rent part of the city," Paerin Clark said ruefully. "Picturesque, but the foot traffic's terrible."

"That can't be someone very important."

"Not very rich," Paerin said. "That's not the same thing. Knowing the taste of a city's cream isn't the same as drinking the dregs. We want both. And you'll be with me when I go."

She nodded and took a mouthful of wine. It wasn't very good, but it was strong. That was better than being good. The warmth was resting comfortably in her belly, and starting to spread out toward her shoulders and face.

"So am I with you because I'm being kept on a leash, or because I'm being trained for something?"

"Trained," he said without a space between the words. "I spoke with Komme about this before we came. I spoke with him about you when I first got back from Porte Oliva, for that matter. We agreed that you were an investment worth making despite the risks. You have a good mind for what we do. More experience than anyone your age has a right to. And you understand how *we* work."

"Which makes me your best ally or your worst enemy," she said.

"Yes. Or possibly something else, but regardless of interest."

Cithrin smiled.

"I will do it, you know. All this? I *will* do what's called for to get it."

"I think you will," Paerin Clark said. "But I have been

wrong before, and I won't do a thing to keep you from falling. You'll stand on your own strength or you'll leave. But
I'd rather you stood."

"We understand each other," she said.

"Good. Once we've done with my acquaintance on the
Division, we're both for the tailors. We'll need better clothes
than we've packed. Our very good friend Canl Daskellin is
holding a private meal at his estate tomorrow. Several people will be there who would be very interesting to speak
with."

"You'll tell me what to listen for before we go?"

"Of course."

"And after the meal?"

"After the meal, we will go to the Kingspire. Lord Marshal Kalliam is having his revel, and the regent and the
prince will both be there. And then, Magistra, we'll see
what's worth seeing."

Geder

Geder rose to his ritual humiliation. His servants powdered him, dressed him, and prepared him for the grand and glorious world. He told himself, as he did every morning, that the servants barely noticed what he looked like naked. And even if they did, he was the Lord Regent, and their opinions of him ought not matter. But always in the back of his mind, he imagined them giggling when he was safely away. And his personal guard. Those men followed him almost everywhere, but never spoke to him. Never asked anything of him or laughed at his jokes. That wasn't the same as having no opinion of him. It was beneath the dignity of the regent to ask them, of course, but how could he keep from wondering?

The revel itself began at dawn, well before Dawson, Geder, or Aster officially arrived. The pavilion set aside for it had been draped in pale silk, and jugglers and showfighters and tables of sweets had been brought in for the children's revel at dawn. There would be games and competitions through the morning, with prizes given to the winners wrapped in cloth the colors of House Kalliam and engraved with Dawson Kalliam's name. Geder planned to join in at midday when the first meal came. Dawson would be there, and Lady Kalliam. And with luck Jorey and his new wife, Sabiha.

He walked through the wide halls of the Kingspire,

scattering the servants and slaves by the simple fact of his presence, and he wondered what it was like for Jorey. He couldn't
really imagine him wed, even though he'd been there at the
joining. To wake up every morning not to a crowd of near-
strangers, but to a woman. One particular woman. To be naked
before someone whom etiquette didn't require to look away.
The thought alone was enough to make his chest ache, just a bit.

And now, how would he ever know if a woman wanted
him, or just the position he'd fallen into? He'd read enough
about sex to understand it. There had even been diagrams in
some of the books. That wasn't the problem. It was the fear
a thousand times worse than his unease with the morning's
servants that she—that unformed, universal *she*—would be
putting up with him because he was Lord Regent. That she
would pretend love or lust as carefully as the others pretended indifference. He couldn't stand the idea.

He could order the death of kings and the destruction of
kingdoms, and what he mostly felt was lonesome. Lonesome
and envious that his friend had something that he couldn't.
The only one who could really understand was Aster, and
Geder couldn't talk about that kind of thing to a child. A
boy he was supposed to protect and raise up to the crown.
No. Impossible.

"My Lord Geder," Basrahip said. His rockslide of a voice
echoed a little.

"Morning," Geder said. "I was just...I was just doing
nothing very useful or important. Is everything all right?"

"My fellows and I have heard things that trouble me,
Prince Geder."

"Lord Regent."

"Lord Regent. I am worried that there may be some
unrest. Those who love deceit too much and fear the justice
of the goddess feel her presence, and they do not repent."

Basrahip leaned closer, and his voice fell to a whisper. "You must be aware. The world looks bright and blameless, but there is danger in it."

A cold dread tightened his shoulders. He hunched in toward the priest.

"What should we do?" Geder asked.

Basrahip smiled.

"Come with me," he said. "And let us bring your guardsmen."

The room was an old ballroom, not used in living memory. The light was bad, and the floor was worn to splinters and blocks. Tiers of benches rose steeply up on three sides like a theater, the last bench so high it almost touched the vaulted roof. Standing along that top row were the priests of the goddess. Twenty of them at least. They had blades at their sides and crossbows in their hands. Geder heard one of his personal guard gasp. Basrahip motioned for Geder to stop, then walked to the center of the first tier of benches. He motioned Geder to come stand by his side. The personal guard arrayed themselves unobtrusively against the wall, but Geder could see their eyes shifting around the room.

Basrahip pointed to the man farthest to the left.

"You, my friend. Step forward, please."

The guard didn't move.

"It's all right," Geder said. "Do what he asks."

The man came out to stand in the center of the room. In the gloom, he looked like a player about to deliver a speech. Geder had never really considered the guards as people before. This man looked to be in his fourth decade, with a pale scar that ran along his jaw on the left. Geder wondered what his name was.

"Have you conspired to harm Lord Geder?" Basrahip asked.

"No," the guardsman said in a sharp voice.

Basrahip nodded. "Please step back, my friend. You beside him, step forward."

One by one, the priest called each of the guards forward and asked the same question. At the end, he clapped Geder on the shoulder and grinned.

"These men can be trusted," the priest said. "Keep them close. And I will do all I can to be close by at all times. Until we find the extent of the threat against you, you must be wary and clever."

"I'm sure it's going to be fine," Geder said, but he wasn't.

"It will," Basrahip said. "But there will be some times of danger also. Your Righteous Servant will protect you."

It was less comforting than it should have been. He went to the revel as he had planned, but with a growing sense of threat. Aster was there, sitting at the high table in regal array, but with his eyes traveling to the dueling yard where the boys of the great houses were battling with chalked practice swords; caught between the man he wasn't yet and the boy he could never entirely be. Geder sat at his side and gestured toward the playing boys.

"You should," he said. "It's in Kalliam's honor."

"It's just playing," Aster said, feigning contempt.

"I think it isn't," Geder said. "Those boys are going to be the men you lead one day. You'd be wise to get to know them now. I mean . . ."

Basrahip, sitting behind him, nodded. It would be safe. Safe enough. Aster licked his lips and glanced at the boys. One of the oldest was showing the smaller ones how to twist the practice sword across his wrist and catch it overhand.

"You're right," Aster said with a little nod. "Thank you, Geder."

"But Aster? Be . . . be careful."

"I will," the boy said.

Geder sat back in his chair, his hands worrying at the tablecloth. The entertainers went through their common paces. The servants brought him a dozen different platters of food. The singers extemporized praises of Dawson Kalliam. Geder found himself enjoying none of it. When Kalliam arrived—unfortunately alone, as both Clara Kalliam and Sabiha were feeling unwell, and Dawson had left Jorey to watch their conditions—Geder let himself relax a degree, but the memory of Basrahip questioning his guards stood at the back of his mind like an unwelcome guest. He could no more turn his unease aside than he could will himself to fly.

After the meal, the revel moved on, the hours between midday and the feast proper filled with games of sport and chance. It was like watching a small tourney. The great houses all came, sat in their boxes, and gossiped. They were like a flock of peacocks, strutting for one another's benefit, and Kalliam's thinly veiled contempt mirrored Geder's frame of mind.

The jousting came and went, then the melee, then a series of show duels more fanciful than any real combat could be. Kalliam acted as judge, and his awards held the sharp wit he was known for. Sir Minin Laat was awarded a special prize in the melee for the most artful falling down. The joust between Lord Ternigan and his nephew Oster was declared a draw "to avoid dividing the family's loyalties any further." The jests were sharp, the laughter they called forth had an edge of cruelty, and Geder began to feel calmer. Whatever dangers Basrahip might have feared, they failed to appear.

The feast itself was held an hour before sundown in the largest hall of the Kingspire. Chandeliers of oil lamps and cut crystal filled the air with a soft, almost shadowless light and the heat of a smith's forge. The room was built in the

shape of an X with the high table in the center on a massive
turntable that revolved twice an hour. Dawson, Aster, and
Basrahip sat nearest him, his personal guard kneeling at the
ready behind. Lord Ternigan and his son sat to Basrahip's
right looking pleased and amiable. Canl Daskellin and his
daughter Sanna sat to Kalliam's right, farther from Geder.
The woman kept catching his eye, and he didn't know
whether to smile at her or look away. In the heat of the summer, all court fashion tended toward lighter clothing, and
the sheath of silk Sanna Daskellin wore made him wish she
was sitting closer and that she hadn't come at all both at the
same time.

"I've some people I'd like you to meet, Lord Regent,"
Daskellin said as the table made its slow revolution. "I came
too late to help with the war, but my conversations in Northcoast were very interesting. I'd go so far as to say that the
whole world's interest is on you these days."

"I don't see why," Geder said. "I mean, the war wasn't my
choosing. That lies at Lechan's feet. And winning so handily
was all Dawson and Basrahip."

"Minister Basrahip?" Daskellin said, shooting a glance at
Dawson. The elder Kalliam's face was ice and stone. Chagrin flashed through Geder's heart as he saw the insult he'd
unintentionally delivered.

"As spiritual guide and comfort," Geder said, the words
coming too quickly, bumping into one another on his lips.
"The victory was Kalliam's."

The urge to go on, to complain about his failed orders of
execution, pressed at him, but he held back. There was time
for that conversation later. He'd need to call a larger council
for that, and no doubt Daskellin and Kalliam would have
more than enough time to talk over how best to go about
assuring Antea's permanent safety from its enemies then.

"I see you brought your banker," Kalliam said. Geder was confused for a moment, then realized that the comment had been meant for Daskellin. "I'm surprised that you'd include him in a revel in my name."

"Really?" Daskellin replied. His voice was as warm as before, but there was something underneath it. It was like watching the afternoon's duels all over again, except with words and subtle meanings in place of blades. "And here I thought the two of you had parted on good terms. He certainly gave the impression that his time at Osterling Fells was pleasant enough."

"I didn't cut his hands off," Dawson said.

"He didn't lie to you," Daskellin said.

Basrahip's calm, enigmatic smile and deceptively sleepy eyes gave no reaction to anything the men said. Geder wondered what it would be like to hear the truth and deceptions in what the men said, and whether it would make the conversation clearer or more obscure.

"Who are we talking about?" Geder asked.

"Paerin Clark," Daskellin said. "He's the son-in-law of Komme Medean of the Medean bank. He's very powerful, though not from noble blood."

"That is what they will write on your tomb, old friend," Dawson said. "*His friends were powerful, though not from noble blood.*"

"Have I done something to offend you, Kalliam?" Daskellin asked.

Geder shot a glance at Aster and Basrahip. The boy seemed frightened by the animosity between the two men, but the priest was quiescent. Dawson's face was dark with blood, but then he pressed his lips thin and shook his head.

"No," he said. "I'm feeling a bit anxious this evening. Nothing to do with you. All apologies."

"At least we didn't need to break your revel for a formal duel."

"No," Dawson said. "Not for that."

"Perhaps I could meet this banker?" Geder asked, grasping for something to turn the subject of the conversation. "Which one is he?"

Daskellin pointed out a pale man in green velvet sitting between an enormously fat man in the formal clothing of a Borjan knight and a remarkably thin woman so fair-haired as to be almost white. Cinnae, but also not. Daskellin's gaze followed his.

"She's Cithrin bel Sarcour. Magistra of their branch in Porte Oliva," he said. "Very new to the bank, and apparently something of a wild talent."

"Why are they here?" Geder asked, and then when he heard how the words sounded, "I mean, they're welcome of course, but are they on some business in Antea?"

"They're come to meet you," Daskellin said. "As have the Duchess of Longhearth, and the Dukes of Whitestone and Wodford. I think you should consider—"

But what he thought Geder should consider was lost in a sudden shouting from behind them. Geder craned around in his chair. At the end of the vast room's southern leg, something was happening. Men in boiled leather were marching into the hall. They had swords drawn. As Geder watched, one of the palace guards marched up to demand explanation. When they cut him down, the screaming began.

"Prince Geder!" Basrahip shouted. Geder didn't remember rising to his feet, and when the great priest shoved him hard enough to drop him to his knees, the only thing he felt at first was confusion. He turned, tried to stand, and the image confused him. A dark, spreading stain marked Basrahip's left arm just above the elbow. The priest's face was twisted in pain, and on the other side of him Dawson Kalliam stood, a bloody dagger in his hand. A woman was screaming, but Geder didn't know where. Dawson flinched as if stung, dropping his blade, and Geder's personal guard swarmed toward him.

"To me!" Dawson shouted as he leaped over the high table. "He's over here! To me!"

"No, wait," Geder said. "Stop. Something's wrong."

Basrahip's hand took him by the arm, four wide fingers almost filling the full distance between shoulder and elbow.

"We must go, Lord Geder. We must go now. Come."

Something crawled across Geder's skin. A tiny black spider drenched in the priest's blood, tiny feet leaving a trail of red as it scrambled. Geder pulled his hand back with a shout, but Basrahip was already pushing toward the east, bullying him along like a child. The revelers were on their feet, the mass of bodies surging forward and back. The crash of a table overturning came from behind him, and shattering glass, and the clash of steel against steel.

They reached the far door and Basrahip forced his way through, bellowing like an animal in pain. The tiny spider or another one like it bit Geder at the soft flesh inside his elbow. He cried out, slapping at it, and Basrahip lost his grip.

"Come, Prince Geder! Come quickly!" the priest shouted, and Geder was about to follow when a terrible thought came to him like icewater running through his heart.

"Aster!" he shouted. "Where's Aster?"

"Come to me, Prince Geder!"

"I have to... Wait for me. I'll be right back."

Geder ran back into the chaos of the bloody revel. The violence had spread. To his left, a wide arc of blood spattered the wall. To his right three of his guardsmen were surrounding two of the attackers, but two more enemy were pelting toward them, bloodied blades at the ready. Geder jumped over the body of a middle-aged man, unsure whether he was alive or dead. His focus was set on the high table, and Aster cowering under it. Geder ran as he hadn't in months. When he regained the high table, he barely had the breath left to speak. He pulled Aster from his crouch, yanking the prince by the arm as Basrahip had to him not a minute before.

"What's happening?" Aster cried.

"You'll be fine," Geder said, asserting it as if certainty of tone could make it true. "But you can't stay here. You have to come with me."

Only when he rose, the path east was blocked. A dozen attackers were overwhelming what was left of his personal guard. And in the center of the attackers, Dawson Kalliam hewed alongside the enemy with a sword in his awkward left hand. As Geder gaped, Kalliam caught sight of him.

"There! He's at the high table."

Geder turned north and bolted. The hall was less than half full now, men and women fleeing into the Kingspire shrieking. Geder's heart was going so fast that he thought it might begin a beat before the last one was finished, seize up, and kill him on the spot. An old man in servant's dress saw him running with the prince. For a terrible moment, Geder saw the fear in the man's face, and then determination. The servant scooped up a soup ladle, brandishing it like a mace.

"For Aster and Antea!" the old man screamed as he charged the swordsmen pursuing them. Geder didn't pause to watch the man die.

The corridors outside the feast hall were a stampede inside a slaughterhouse. People were running in all directions, dodging each other, turning, fleeing without any sign of knowing where they could flee to. And Geder was as lost as any of them. Basrahip could be anywhere by now.

"You're the Lord Regent," a voice beside him said. The pale woman. The banker. Her gown was ripped at the sleeve and something dark but not blood spattered her snowy skin. Soup, maybe. "What in hell are you doing? It's a coup. You have to get away."

"I don't know where to go," he said. "They could be anyplace. I don't know where's safe."

The woman stared at him, and he thought there was a moment of bright madness in her eyes. She grinned, perfect pearl teeth in pale gums.

"I do," she said.

Cithrin

Following the Lord Regent when the knives came out had been more a matter of instinct than judgment. She certainly hadn't meant to save him or the boy prince. She'd only wanted to see what happened. But when at last she'd caught up with him, the man standing in the corridor outside the hall with the boy on one hand and eyes as round as coins, he'd said he didn't know where would be safe.

Her first thought was *It's your damned city. Think of something.*

Her second thought was *Yellow House by Autumn Bridge.*

Escaping the Kingspire itself was easy. She had the prince, and the prince had all the knowledge that young boys acquire of shorter routes and secret ways. The Kingspire had always been his home, and once she had tasked him with finding the way out to darkness and night, the hardest part was keeping pace.

Outside, men were shouting and torches flared all through the gardens and along the gates. They made their way, careful but swift. Around a long hedge and then over a wall and into the street beyond. As she helped the Lord Regent crawl over the rough stone, Cithrin wondered how many times Prince Aster had used this route to escape his tutors.

In the gloom of the night street, Cithrin paused. The shouting was both louder and more distant, the riot of swords and voices still rising. The prince wore a robe of white sewn with threads of gold and a ceremonial crown. His sleeves were sewn with pearls, and gems studded his cuffs. He'd stand out in the darkness like a candleflame. The Lord Regent was somewhat better. His garnet-colored tunic wouldn't grab the torchlight. He was a round-faced man, not much older than her true age. His build said he'd been strong not long ago, but was well on his way back to soft.

"We'll get to the Division," Cithrin said. "And then move south to the Autumn Bridge. I think the house we're looking for is on the far side, but I'm not sure of that."

"What if they're holding the bridge?" the Lord Regent asked in a high, tight voice.

"We have enough trouble right now," Cithrin said. "Let's not borrow more."

They set out, trotting through the dim streets. Once, when a half dozen horsemen pelted down the road, Cithrin had to haul them all into the shadows of a great marble statue of a Firstblood man putting the sword to a particularly bestial-looking Yemmu woman. Another time, the square she'd hoped to cross was filled with men shouting at each other and brandishing swords. They hadn't come to blows yet, but she heard the violence in the timbre of their voices. Cithrin pulled the prince by the hand, and the Lord Regent followed them both down into the darkness, searching for another path.

Cithrin felt the fear, breathed it, but it seemed almost to be happening to some other woman. Her footsteps didn't falter, her decisions were swift and unhesitating. The men and women who saw them only looked confused, not alarmed. They were running ahead of the violence like a seabird outpacing a wave. Even if they were seen now, the citizens of Camnipol didn't know what it meant, a man, a woman, and a child all dressed in the clothing of wealth and running through the night. They tacked through the dark and treacherous sea of alleyways and courtyards, aiming—she hoped—for the bridge she'd been pointed to once, and in daylight.

It stood at the edge of the cliff face, arching slightly upward as it leaped the wide air. Ancient trees had given their bodies to the making of the bridge. It was wide enough that two carts could pass each other and a man still walk between them. The upward curve meant she couldn't see the other side, hiding it like the arch of a hill. There could have been a dozen men charging at them, swords bared, and she wouldn't have known it until they met in the center.

Beside her, Lord Geder Palliako was panting. She turned slowly, looking for something that might have been a taproom or a wayhouse. All she saw was a thick flicker of smoke to the north.

"All right," she said. "We have to cross."

"We can't do that," Palliako said. "We'll be seen. We'll be recognized."

"We can stay here and see who finds us," she said. As if to punctuate her words, the sound of shouting floated across the broad, empty air and echoed against the Division's walls.

"It'll be all right," the prince said.

"Wait," Cithrin said. She plucked the thin crown off the boy's head. From the weight, it was silver throughout. She heaved it over the edge, sailing it out through the wide air. "Lie down. Help me rub muck over this. Do it quickly."

It was a long, breathless minute, but the white formal robes of the Prince of Antea was reduced to rags. The pearls and gems were sewn on too tightly to pull free, but their glitter was at least dimmed. It would have to do.

Cithrin led the way, and at the top of the bridge she paused. In the north, the Kingspire was alive with hundreds of torches, and also larger flames. A building was burning, the column of rising smoke lit by the fire at its foot. Cithrin didn't know the city well enough to guess what it might be. There were lights along the Silver Bridge too—the torches and lanterns of riders spreading fast from the battle. The news would be all through the city soon. She didn't know what that would mean except that the time left to find shelter was fading. Lights were also spreading along the edge of the Division, flowing along the top of its eastern face. Coming closer to her. On the west, visible now, was the steady glow of glass lanterns and even, in a courtyard with its back to the precipice, something that might be a theatrical troupe's cart silhouetted by the lights of the stage.

Palliako's voice was unsteady.

"I don't...um..."

She turned to look at him only to find him staring at her. Without thinking about it, she'd hoisted herself on top of the curved body of the trees that made the bridge. She was suddenly aware of the abyss beneath her, and only a few feet of sloping, oiled wood between her and the air. A wave of light-headedness swept over her, and she stepped back, heart racing.

"I'm all right," she said. "I'm fine. Keep going."

Yellow House was unmistakable once she saw it. Three floors high, each one narrower than the one below, so that every level had its own small courtyard looking out over the Division. The walls were the improbable color at the heart of a daisy, and the yard was half filled with men, women, and children looking up at the lowered stage and the people standing on it. The yard wasn't more than a hundred feet from the massive stone sockets where the Autumn Bridge ended. But with so many eyes needing no more than a flicker to see them make the crossing to the back of the cart, it could as well have been a mile. On the other side of the Division, torches were drawing closer to the Autumn Bridge. She drew her two charges into the shadows beside the bridge.

"Stay here," she said. "When you see the people in that yard turn away, run to the back of the cart and tell whoever's there that Cithrin sent you and that you need to be hidden. You understand?"

The prince nodded.

"But," Palliako said. "But what if..."

"Listen to my voice," Cithrin said. "You can do this."

She made her way to Yellow House's yard, her eyes flickering over the crowd. Familiar voices came to her. Hornet and Sandr, declaiming to one another the way she'd heard them do a thousand times before. There would be someone in the crowd to lead it. There, in the rear, Cary sat in the middle of a group of five. As she watched, Sandr delivered one of the punch lines, leaning on the words too hard. Master Kit would have chided him for it. Cary was the first to laugh, and the crowd followed with her. Almost trotting, she made her way around the edge of the crowd. Cithrin saw Cary's recognition by the change in the angle of her shoulders and the faintest nod known to humanity.

When she came to her side, Cary's eyes narrowed. Cithrin leaned close, whispering in her ear.

"I need you to make the whole crowd look away from the stage for a few seconds. I know Sandr will kill us, but it needs to be done and done now. Can you?"

Cary's smile was wicked.

"You should know by now, sweet sister, I can do anything. Good to see you again, by the way. You've been missed."

Before Cithrin could say, *I've missed you too*, Cary lifted the hem of her dress up over her head and pulled it back.

The woman's breasts were larger than Cithrin remembered, with dark nipples made hard by the cool night air.

"My God!" Cary said, her voice carrying even over the players on the stage. "Is that mule on *fire*?"

Cithrin felt her eyes go wide and a violent blush rose up her neck through her cheeks and out to the tips of her ears. There was a flicker of movement from the bridge, and then Palliako and Prince Aster running as if dogs were at their heels. Cary pointed toward the street at the far side of the yard. On the stage, Sandr and Hornet were rooted as trees.

"Right over there," Cary said, gesturing in a way that made her breasts bounce. "Honestly. On fire."

Man and boy reached the rear of the cart. The stage shifted as they climbed in the back door. Cithrin imagined she heard whispering voices, but it might only have been her mind playing tricks.

"Oh, no," Cary said and pulled her dress back on. "Sorry. My mistake. Please go on."

There was a moment of utter quiet.

"And I...ah...I say no, Lord Ternigan," Hornet managed. "There will be no wedding this day."

"There shall!" Sandr shouted, stamping his foot. Voice and action commanded the attention of the yard with mixed result. "I'll not be refused by the likes of you. So draw your sword and blades be true!"

The men pulled out wooden blades and began the fight sequence that ended the second act as Cary put her arm around Cithrin and angled her back toward the street away from the play.

"You didn't have to do *that*," Cithrin said.

"It's only a body," Cary said. "And there are just a few reliable ways to command attention with no preparation. So will you tell me now why I've just destroyed everyone's concentration and halved my night's take?"

"Look north," Cithrin said. "What do you see?"

Cary frowned and peered into the darkness.

"They've got God's own bonfire at the Lord Marshal's revel," Cary said. "And there's more traffic than I'd have thought on the bridges." She smoothed back her hair. There were a few strands of white at her temples that hadn't been there last year. "That's not what it is, though, is it?"

"Dawson Kalliam tried to kill Palliako. Armed men came into the revel. I don't know whose they were, but what's going on there isn't a celebration. It's a civil war."

Cary's face went cool. In a conversational voice, she said something profoundly obscene.

"And the two men hiding in my cart?" she said.

"The Lord Regent and the prince," Cithrin said.

"Well of course they are."

The clatter of hooves came from the great span of the Autumn Bridge, growing louder and louder until they threatened to drown out the voices of the players. Torches appeared at the crest, and moments later a dozen men in the colors of House Kalliam and House Bannien pelted into the street.

"Treachery!" one of the men shouted. "Fire and treachery!"

The audience was on its feet. Cithrin could almost see the fear moving through them, a ripple on a pond. The riders went on, driving their horses deeper into the city. Someone shouted, catching sight of the billowing smoke to the north. The crowd scattered like startled birds, leaving Hornet and Sandr standing forgotten on the stage.

"Pack it in, boys," Cary shouted, striding back into the yard. "We've storm weather coming, and we're staying small until it passes."

A round-faced girl peeked out from the back of the stage. Charlit Soon. She was pretty in a full-cheeked way, and her eyes were wide with the first echoes of panic. Sandr and Hornet looked at each other, and Sandr shrugged.

"Some nights it's a good show, some nights it's a good story," he said.

"What's the plan, Cary?" Smit called from the back.

"Pull up the stage, get the cart into the stable, and let's not have any political opinions for a while," Cary said.

"And our guests?" Charlit Soon asked, her voice fluting up to a bird's chirp at the end.

"We haven't got any," Cary said. "Now move."

Sandr hopped off the stage and started hauling the chain. Hornet disappeared in the back. Mikel appeared in an oversized black cloak and a false stomach that left him looking pregnant.

"Cithrin," Mikel said. "Welcome back."

In the back of the stable, by the light of a hooded lantern, Geder Palliako and Price Aster became different men. They tried Palliako in four different costumes before settling on Father Hope from The Midwinter Princess, the brown robes and crooked stick making him look older than he was. Aster only took a pair of old breeches tied tight around his waist, a stained shirt, and dirt ground into his hair and skin. Cithrin changed into a peasant dress made for a Firstblood woman and too wide for her hips and bust, but Charlit Soon threw stitches on to bring it closer.

"Can't do anything with the hands," Cary said, surveying the work. "Anyone looks at their palms and you're caught."

More fires were dotting the city, towers of smoke rising higher even than the Kingspire and windblown so that they seemed always falling.

"I have to thank you," Palliako said. "All of you. The danger you're putting yourselves in for me..."

"Feh," Mikel said with a grin. "Sometime we'll tell you about the first time we worked with Cithrin. Made a play about it."

"Let's get our heads out of this noose first, shall we?" Cary said smartly.

"If we stay here, they'll find us," Cithrin said. "One side or else the other."

"If there's only two sides," Smit said. "Lot of times these things wind up more complex than when they start."

Sandr rolled his eyes.

"Oh, worked a lot of insurrections, have you?"

The city was in the grip of riot, the two most powerful and important men in Imperial Antea huddling in fear of their lives before him, and Sandr was peevish at having been upstaged by Cary.

"Didn't I tell you about being in Borja when the plague winds came?" Smit asked. "That was when I'd only just met Master Kit. I must have been twenty, twenty-two. Right in there, and—"

"Gentlemen?" Cary said.

"Sorry," Smit said and lapsed into silence.

The stable reeked of piss and horse shit, and beneath that a growing scent of smoke. Camnipol, burning. Cithrin's gut was a solid knot. She knew that if she ate now—or even if she drank—she'd vomit it all back up. And also, she was exhilarated. She wondered where Paerin Clark was right now. She had faith he'd survived the initial attack and that, barring the mischance that came with the violence, he would be able to find a place of relative safety. But she wouldn't go looking for him, and she was certain he wouldn't come looking for her. He'd be too busy making his soundings of the tactics and politics.

But he didn't have regent and prince to talk with. And she did.

"We can go under the city," the prince said. "It's all ruins. If we can find someplace where it won't collapse, we could stay there."

"Food," Palliako said. "Water. And how do we know when it's safe to come back out?"

"We'll take care of that," Cary said. "Cithrin can come up for supplies. And we can be your eyes and ears. Otherwise, we're just what we are. A half dozen actors trying to keep out of trouble, no?"

"Not much food for an actor no one's watching," Sandr said.

"If we take the stones off that rag the prince was wearing, we could sit in this yard playing to rats and dogs for a year and still have enough for food and beer," Cary said, shrugging. "As far as I see, we've just been hired."

Palliako sat forward, hugging his legs. For the regent of a great empire, he looked a bit lost. It was more than the desperate situation. More than the violence. Dawson Kalliam had been this man's Lord Marshal, leader of his armies. Palliako had called the man's revel, and in return he'd nearly taken a knife. She tried to imagine what it would feel like to have the person you trust most revealed as an enemy.

Easy enough. It had happened to her.

Cithrin walked the two steps to him and sat at Palliako's side. There were no tears in his eyes, but something worse. Something lost and emptied. Cithrin took his hand in her own. He had wide palms and short fingers, the angry welt of an insect sting on his arm.

"Listen to me," she said. "We've only just met and you have no reason to trust me, but do it anyway. These people are my friends, and they're no part of your court or anybody else's. If they say they'll keep us safe, then they will."

"How do you know that?" Palliako said, his voice tight. "You can't be sure they won't turn on you. I need to find Basrahip. I need to see if he's all right."

"We'll find out for you," Smit said. "I mean, not tonight. But when the dust's settled a bit, we can find that out for you. Unless they really burn the full city down."

Palliako's gaze focused on her for what seemed like the first time.

"I don't know you," he said.

"I'm Cithrin bel Sarcour," she said, nodding as she said it. Encouraging him to do the same. And by doing it, begin to mean it. "There. Now you know me."

Clara

The letter from Osterling Fells was written in a poor hand, the letters awkward as kittens and the spelling approximate at best. There were scribes at the holding, and at least one in the township nearest it. Vincen Coe could have easily had some more practiced hand aid him, but he had not. The text itself was innocuous—the progress of the kennels, the watering tanks to provide for the hunting pack, the number of pups whelped in the spring—and she couldn't precisely object to his having made the report. It was like a light, unnecessary touch on the hand. Like the other letters from him, Clara wouldn't respond. Sooner or later, the boy would recover from whatever madness had fixed his mind upon her. He would find some more appropriate infatuation, and the letters would stop. She put this one down again for the hundredth time, it seemed, and resumed her uneasy pacing.

The night hadn't let her sit still, not even for handwork. The revel had begun in the morning and was set to travel through until the middle part of the night. And with it, something darker. She let herself hope that whatever her husband had in mind, it would fall apart at the last moment. That he would come home annoyed and disappointed, but without anything dramatic having taken place. She told herself it could be like that. That the world tomorrow could look very much like it had yesterday.

She plucked at her sleeves and chewed on the stem of her pipe, teeth tapping against the hard clay. Dawson had lived all his life with the politics of court and the tactics of war. He would be fine. Whatever needed doing, he would do, and they would survive it and the family would, and it would all end well. She fought to believe it. She struggled and she failed.

The first sound to herald the chaos was a single horse running hard into the courtyard. The second was the yelp of the footmen. Dread pulled her toward the main doors almost against her will. When they burst open, Dawson stumbled through on the arm of the door slave. Her husband's sword was in his hand, and blood soaked his right arm and side. His hunting dogs circled the pair, their ears back and faces rich with concern. She must have made a sound, because he looked up at her sharply.

"Arm the house," he said between gasps.

The fear that had been welling up in her broke, flooding her with ice. She didn't know yet what the worst was, but she had no doubt it had happened. She grew calm. She walked to her husband, pushing the dogs aside, and put a supporting shoulder under his arm.

"You heard my lord's order," she said to the door slave. "Spread the word. All doors and gates are to be locked immediately. Shutter the windows. Gather the servants and be ready to defend the house. When that's done, find Jorey and send him to the kitchens."

"My lady," the door slave said, and gave Dawson over to her.

With every step Dawson winced, but he didn't slow. The dogs followed them anxiously. When they reached the kitchens, Dawson lay on the wide oak preparation table and squeezed his eyes closed. As Clara went to the pantry, her head cook came into the room and stopped.

"You aren't armed," Clara noted as she took cooking wine and honey from the pantry shelves.

"No, ma'am," the old cook said.

"You should be. I'll take care of this. You get your people and see that they're ready to fight if the need comes."

"It will," Dawson said. "The need is coming."

The cook scurried away, possibly to find a weapon or possibly to flee the mansion. Clara put the odds about even. At the table, she used a carving knife to slit his shirt, pulling it away from the skin with a wet sound that horrified her. A rag hung from a peg at the table's end, and she wiped away the worst of the gore with it. There were two cuts, one along his ribs just under his left breast, the other above his collarbone. Neither were deep, but both bled freely. She opened the wine bottle, pulling the cork with her teeth.

"They knew," Dawson said. "Not the details, but they knew something was planned. They were ready for us."

"Stop talking," she said. "This will hurt."

She poured the wine into the cut on his side, and Dawson arched back, sucking in his breath. He did not scream. She did the same again with the other cut. His breath grew ragged. With his shirt gone and some, at least, of the blood washed away, she could see a dozen angry red welts all down his right side and out along his arm. They didn't bleed, but the skin around them was hot to the touch and tight as a drum.

"What happened here?" she asked as she prepared to honey the wounds.

"Spiders," Dawson said. "That mad bastard cultist must have been carrying a sack of them under his robes. And soon as I cut him, they came boiling out."

"You cut him," she said. It was neither a question nor a statement, but something between.

"If I'd meant to, he'd be dead," Dawson said as she slathered the honey over the lower of his cuts and pressed her cloth to it. "I was trying for Palliako."

With her free hand, Clara pressed palm to mouth, only realizing after that she'd bloodied her own face. Dawson drew her hand away from the cut and pressed down on it himself. It was still bleeding, though not quite as badly.

"You," she began, then tried again. "You tried to slaughter the Lord Regent? That's what this was all about?"

"Of course it was. Palliako didn't give me an option. I did and Lord Bannien and Alan Klin and a few others besides. This wasn't done alone or for glory. We're fighting to save the throne from those foreign bastards Palliako's wedded himself to. Only somehow they knew we were coming. The guards were on alert. It should never have been me holding the blade to start with, but they couldn't reach the high table. Not in time."

Clara's heart darkened. If there was a way to save this, to make it right again, she didn't know it. She could only hope that they would win, and even that was thin comfort.

"What happened to him? Does Palliako still live?"

"I don't know. When I tried to take him, the bastard priest got in my way, and then the personal guard was at my heels. One of the others may have caught him, but I didn't. Stop. Enough."

He sat up. The cuts still bled, though less freely. Wine stained his skin more deeply than the film of drying blood, and the honey shined on him. He was old. The hair on his chest was more grey than black now, and his forehead was high where the hairline had begun to retreat. His sword was still in his hand. She wondered if she had anything to salve a spider's bite, and what sort of spiders a priest carried with him into an ambush.

"What are we going to do?" she asked, proud of herself that the question came out sounding like matter of planning and not a cry of despair.

"We do what we have to," Dawson said. "We win. There are forces on our side. Allies. We have to gather them and defend ourselves. We have to find Aster."

"Find him? He's lost?"

"He is. Once it was done, we were going to throw down our blades right there and surrender to him, but..."

"But now the palaces are thick with violence, and the prince, who was in the middle of it all, is missing," Clara said. "God. Dawson, how could you have done this?"

"It's my duty. And however badly it's played out, the risk was worth taking," he said, his expression closing. He shifted to the edge of the table and let himself down. "I'll want something to wrap this with. And a fresh shirt."

"Stay here," Clara said. "I'll bring them."

She walked through her own house like it was an unknown country. The papered walls, the glowing oil lamps, the rich tapestries that hung from the walls. All of it had taken on the too-sharp sense of something from dreams. The servants were gone, and with no one to help her, she chose two shirts from Dawson's wardrobe. One was pale yellow to shred and use as bandages. The other was a dark blue that neared black so that when the wounds wept, the blood wouldn't show so clearly. Outside the bedroom window, she saw three men she knew—the cook's boy, the footman with the unfortunate ears, and the farrier's assistant. They stood clumped together like birds in the cold despite the warm night air. They held blades and hammers, pretending with their postures to know the use of them. Clara closed the shutter before she walked away.

Jorey was in the kitchen when she returned to it. His hair

was in disarray, the leathers he'd worn to war hung half-laced from his shoulders. He'd started to affect a beard, but it was still only stubble; a shadow across his cheeks no light dispelled. As she stepped in, her son looked up at her. The distance in his eyes was terrible to see.

"Help me bind him up," Clara said, forcing a smile into the words. "Your father's a dear man and always has been, but I won't have him leaking on the floors."

Dawson chuckled if Jorey didn't. They stood at the wide table and tore the pale shirt into strips, the cloth parting under her fingers, threads ripping apart.

"Bannien's got the most men," Dawson said, carrying on a conversation they'd already begun, "but his estate's not defensible. Too open, too many low hedges a man could vault. Klin's isn't as good as Mastellin's, but until we know how word of this leaked, we can't trust the men I've trusted."

"But you can trust Klin?"

"He wouldn't take Palliako's side if he was on fire and Geder had the only water in the world. Strange as it is, Klin's the only man I feel certain I can rely on now."

She prodded at Dawson's elbow to make him lift it, then laid the strips of pale cloth against his injured skin. Her fingers seemed to know what to do without her direction. Just as well, since her mind was a whirlwind and no two thoughts within it connecting to each other. When she needed to get around back to tie the bandaging down, Jorey held the cloth for her, and she had the sudden, powerful memory of helping her sister wash their father's body for burial. The thickness in her throat was as unwelcome as undeniable.

"I'll go to him," Jorey said. "If you think it's best."

"No," Dawson said. "Send a runner. You take Sabiha and your mother. Get them to safety."

"And what makes you think I would consent to go

anywhere?" Clara asked tartly. "Last I saw, this was still my home."

The last of the bandages in place, she reached for the darker shirt. Dawson caught her hand. She couldn't say which of them was trembling.

"If you stay, Jorey will," Dawson said, "and if he does, the girl will too. I'm not defeated, but I can't both fight this battle and keep eyes on all of you. If you're all here, I will keep eyes on you. Won't be able to stop."

"You would have to," Clara began, and the words choked her. She swallowed. "You would have to believe that there's someplace safer than here."

"Jorey will take you out of the city. And when this is done, he will bring you back."

"Are you telling me the truth?" she asked, but they both knew it wasn't a question he could answer. She kissed him sharply on the forehead: love and anger. "Let me gather a few things. Jorey, get your wife."

Horses and carriages would have been fastest, but they would also have called the most attention to them. Instead Clara and Sabiha wore dark cloaks with the hoods drawn up. Jorey walked in front wearing his leather and a sword at his side. Uncharitably, she wished now that she hadn't sent Vincen Coe away. An additional sword either here with her or at the mansion guarding Dawson's back would have been welcome. In the north, fires were burning.

The city was transformed. The wide streets seemed dangerous, too open and leaving someone too easily seen. The shadows called to Clara, promising protection in their obscuring darkness. From the way that Sabiha walked close to her, she guessed the girl felt the same. These dark buildings and black-cobbled streets weren't the city they'd lived in, but someplace unknown, unsafe, and malign wearing a mask of their home.

They reached the square where in daylight farmers would sell their goods to the servants of the great houses on the western side of the Division. The smell of rotting leaves in the gutters marked where the last day's fallen greens had been bruised into muck. Across the way, a crowd of men strode into the square, torches held high above their head. Without so much as a word, Clara and Jorey stepped into the alcove of a little shop, pulling Sabiha along after them. The torchlight seemed too bright; it hurt to look at too closely. The men were shouting to each other, rough voices drunk with violence and wine. They were going back the way Clara had just come. Toward the mansion and Dawson. Clara squinted, trying to make out the colors the men wore, trying to guess whether these were allies come to reinforce the position or enemies ready to kill and loot and burn. She couldn't tell, and she didn't dare go closer.

When the last of them had passed, Jorey snuck out and Clara and Sabiha followed. Sabiha took Clara's hand and wouldn't let it go. Clara pulled the girl close. Somewhere to their right, a woman was screaming. If the city guard was in the street tonight, Clara saw no sign of them. The woman stopped suddenly, and Clara could only tell herself that someone had come to her aid; she couldn't bring herself to believe it.

Halfway to the western gate, they came to a barricade in the street. Tables, chairs, crates, and a wide overturned cart. There were men on both sides of the obstruction. She couldn't tell if it was meant to stop people like her trying to escape to the countryside or to block soldiers and thugs coming into the city. The men wore no uniforms. The pennants of no houses flew. If war was a violence conducted with rules and traditions on a field of honor, then this was not war, but something worse.

"What do we do?" Clara asked in a whisper.

"Come with me," Jorey said.

The back alley was filthy, but Clara couldn't bring herself to care. If the hem of her cloak dragged through the gore of a slaughterhouse, it would only be what the night called for. Etiquette and delicate sensibilities had their place, but it was not here. Jorey was craning his neck, looking up it seemed at the night sky as if the stars might sweep down to carry them away. His small grunt of pleasure caught her attention.

"What?" she asked.

"That roof," he said, pointing at a single-storied taphouse with its lights doused and its shutters locked. "If I lift you up, can you get onto it?"

Clara looked at the structure. It had been decades since she'd been a little girl climbing where she wasn't wanted. And even then it had for the most part been trees.

"I can try," she said.

"Good," Jorey said.

They lifted Sabiha up first, and then Jorey lifted Clara into Sabiha's waiting hands. He scrambled up last. Gesturing in silence, he led them along the rooftop to an alcove where a rough wooden ladder hid in the darkness.

"If you go up here," Jorey whispered, "there's a place where we can lay the ladder across the alleyway and get past that barricade. Providing they don't look up."

"I am beginning to think I raised you poorly," Clara said, but she took herself up the ladder. From the top of the second story, the street looked very far away. The men at the barricade laughed with each other, joking in a way that made the fear and tension in them clearer than sunlight.

Sabiha clambered up at Clara's side while Jorey knelt and began lifting the ladder one rung at a time.

Clara looked out over the city. Her city. There were more columns of smoke, but the one nearest the Kingspire was beginning to fade. Either someone had organized a fire team or the building set alight was exhausted of everything but stone. Far away, the walls of the city were dotted with torches and the low half moon seemed about to rest its head on the western gate.

The western gate.

"Stop," Clara said. "You can put the ladder back down."

"No, it will work," Jorey said. "I know it doesn't seem sturdy, but I've done this before. It was a bet we used to make when I was—"

"The gates are shut," Clara said. "Someone's sealed the city."

Jorey appeared at her side. The wall of the city wasn't so far from them. In daylight and sanity, she could have walked from the street below them to the huge gates in only a few minutes. Even in the darkness, there was no question that the wide bronze doors had been closed. Closed and likely dropped from their hinges, as they would be in time of war.

"We're trapped," Sabiha whispered.

"We are," Clara agreed.

Marcus

It was raining in Porte Oliva when the reports came, the kind of flooding summer storm that began in the morning as a scent on the wind under a perfect blue sky and by midday was squalling against the streets and walls. It turned the streets into ankle-deep rivers and washed the trash and shit and dead animals from their hidden corners and out to the sea. Marcus struggled against the wind, but he didn't run. Roach had brought word that Pyk needed him at the counting house. Within a minute of stepping outside, he'd been soaked as wet as it was possible to be. Running now seemed pointless.

The tulips in their bowl were vivid red. Several of the petals were lost, and as he came close, a gust of screaming wind whipped another free. Marcus watched it spin away on the surface of the flood: a tiny scarlet boat on a vast river. He pushed his way through the door.

Pyk was pacing the room. Sweat beaded on her wide forehead, but rain had cooled the room to the point that she could at least move. Yardem sat on a tall stool smelling like wet dog and looking at least as drenched as Marcus. No one else was present.

"Bird came this morning," Pyk said without preamble. "Sent from the holding company."

"Good it didn't wait for afternoon," Marcus said, wringing out his cuffs. "Did they decide to send a fresh auditor?"

"Other people are going to start getting word of this in the next day or two, so we're going to have to move quickly. There's trouble in Antea. According to our man in Camnipol, someone tried to stick the Lord Regent full of knife-sized holes. They've closed the gates, and there's been fighting in the streets ever since. Odds-on bet is civil war."

The words took a moment to resolve. Yardem's wide brown eyes were on him, watching him understand.

"I have a list of the contracts I want placed," Pyk said, "but it has to be done today. Once the word goes out, the prices on grain and metalwork are going to head toward the sky. We may only have hours to do this, and so of course, this is the day we can wash all the ink off a piece of paper just by walking it down to the corner. God hates me, but we'll do what we can."

"What about Cithrin?" Marcus said.

Pyk scowled. She wouldn't meet his eyes.

"The note doesn't say. The chop is Paerin Clark's, so he's the one making report. She's not mentioned."

"But she's in Camnipol," Marcus said, his voice growing hard. "She's with him."

"She went there, but I don't know how she stands. Safe, dead, or missing, he wouldn't have spent space on the page for word of her. This isn't gossip. It's what will make us coin. He sent us what we need to help the bank, and now it's ours to follow his lead."

"I'm going for her," Marcus said. "You can work the contracts yourself."

"God's sake, Wester," Pyk said, "it's Camnipol. It's weeks from here on a fast boat and more over land. By the time you got there, it would all be done. Even the bird's not going to tell us what's happening there now. Maybe it's resolved. Maybe the whole place is burned flat. Either way, our work's here."

"I don't accept that," Marcus said.

"I don't accept being the only good-looking woman in a city full of bendy little twig men," Pyk said, "but it doesn't change the situation. The magistra's in Camnipol and we're here. If you want to take care of her, take care of the things that matter to her. And while you're at it, do what you're paid for."

Pyk lifted a handful of papers. Contracts. Letters of enquiry and agreement. Yardem cleared his throat and Marcus forced himself to take his hand off the pommel of his sword. For a moment, the only sounds were the rush of water and the howl of wind. Pyk walked across the room and held out the papers. Slowly, half against his will, Marcus took them.

"This is dangerous work," Pyk said. "No one sees these except you and Ears."

"Ears?"

"She means me, sir."

"Ah."

"Nothing else you're doing matters compared to this," Pyk said. "Manage it well, and we'll have enough profit to keep this place afloat the rest of the year. All of the contracts have the names of the people I want them going to. Don't put them in anyone else's hands. And get it done now."

Marcus paged through the contracts. He nodded.

"We have something dry to carry them in?" he asked.

Yardem stood. He held a leather satchel in one hand and a broad oilskin envelope in the other. Marcus took them, folding contracts into envelope and envelope into satchel. Pyk folded her arms, her eyes black and narrow and satisfied.

"Don't cock this up," she said.

"We'll do what needs doing," Marcus said. "Yardem?"

"Coming, sir."

Marcus stepped into the storm. The raindrops cut at his face and stung his eyes. Yardem padded along beside him.

"Ears?"

"I think she's taking a liking to me, sir."

"Well, you're a charming man. I have to stop by the barracks. Come with me."

"Yes, sir."

The city was blurred, as if the water could wash away not only objects but lines and color themselves. As if the idea of Porte Oliva was dissolving. In the barracks, a dozen guardsmen were sitting in a rough circle playing at dice. Marcus considered them. He'd hired every person in his company except Yardem. They were good people. Solid men and women, loyal to the bank and to him personally.

Part of him would miss them.

"Ahariel."

"Yes, Captain."

Marcus tossed the satchel across the room. The Kurtadam caught it out of the air.

"There's some contracts in there need delivering. Do what you can, eh?"

"Yes, Captain," the guardsman said, undoing the satchel's buckles.

Marcus turned back toward the door. Yardem stood there, his face blank but his ears standing tall and forward.

"Waiting for something?" Marcus asked.

"No, sir."

"Let's go, then."

The inns and taprooms by the port were thick with bodies huddling out of the weather. Gossip and news and uncon-

firmed speculations came as cheap as a bowl of barley soup
or a bottle of cider. Marcus hadn't considered that one virtue of living in a single place for more than a year was that it
gave a sense of which faces and voices didn't belong. Those
were the ones he followed, because those were the ones who
had come from places where the petty wars were being
started or fought or guarded against.

Merrisen Koke and his men were in Lyoneia, fighting for a
local lordling against a pod of tribal Southlings. Karol Dan-
nien, on the other hand, had taken garrison work on the border between Elassae and the Keshet. Tiyatra Egencil, smaller
and more recently formed than Koke's company or Dan-
nien's, was in Maccia enforcing the law for a prince whose
guard had turned. Another company Marcus hadn't heard
of calling themselves Black Hounds was supposed to be
doing something in Herez, but the details on that were vague.

The storm blew itself out to sea. When the sunset came
late in the day, it turned the high clouds in the south gaudy
red and gold. The grey veil beneath them looked almost gentle at this distance. The streets were wet and clean, even the
mud washed away. The puppeteers and musicians came out,
plying their trades at the street corners and taproom yards.
Marcus bought a waxpaper cone of cooked beef for himself
and another of eggs and fish for Yardem, and they walked
down the wide streets.

"I like Koke best, but I don't see going to Lyoncia. Maccia's close, but Egencil's new at this, and I don't know that I
trust her yet."

"And she's working for a prince," Yardem said.

Marcus shrugged and popped a chip of beef into his
mouth. "Why's that a problem?" he asked around the food.

"I thought we didn't work for kings, and that princes
were just little kings," Yardem said.

"I'm not looking for someone to work for. I have someone to work for. I need someone to hire."

Yardem flicked a jingling ear.

"For what, sir?"

"I'm going to get Cithrin," Marcus said. "Thought that was clear enough."

"That's a large favor to ask," Yardem said. "Even if it was someone from the old days."

"I don't know what you mean."

"We don't have anything like the gold to hire a company."

"I know where there's a bank's strongbox."

Yardem bowed his head and grunted. Marcus went on a half dozen steps before he realized that Yardem had stopped. The Tralgu's face was perfectly empty. Impassive. Marcus walked back and stood before him.

"You've something to say?"

"Do I understand, sir, that your plan is to steal from the bank, hire a mercenary company, and march it into the middle of an imperial civil war?"

"My plan," Marcus said, his voice conversational but with a buzz of anger, "is to get Cithrin back safe. Whatever I have to do in order to see that happen, I'm doing. If it meant sinking this city in the sea, I'd do it."

"This is a mistake, sir."

"Are you saying she isn't worth it?"

"I'm saying that taking an outside force into a civil war is marching barrels of oil into a fire. Crossing the bank to do it means nothing to come back to, even if you did find her."

"What else am I supposed to do? Sit by and wait?"

"The magistra's smart. Capable. You could have faith in her."

"She's a girl in the middle of a war," Marcus said, "and we both know what can happen to girls in the middle of wars. I'm going to find her, and I'm going to keep her safe. I've never asked you to come with me. If this isn't something you can do, then it isn't."

Yardem's scowl seemed to change the shape of his bones.

"I'm going to ask you to reconsider this," he said, his voice low. "The strongbox—"

"Tell me it's worth more than she is," Marcus said. "Tell me the bank is worth more than Cithrin."

They stood in the street. On the horizon, the clouds flicked with lightning, but they were too far away for thunder. Marcus took another bite of his food, and Yardem sighed.

"How do you plan getting to the strongbox, sir?"

"I set who's on the watch," Marcus said. "A hammer. A chisel. A cart with a decent team. We know the low roads between here and the Free Cities, or else we can charter a little coast-hugger. Hell, buy a fishing boat and just don't come back. Could be in Elassae in twenty days. Maccia in considerably less."

"Still an awfully long way to Camnipol."

"That's an argument for starting tonight," Marcus said.

Buying a handcart took Marcus almost no time. A potter with a small yard near the counting house was willing to part with one, and Marcus was willing to overpay. Finding a hammer and chisel meant finding the smith in his home and explaining what he needed. Decades of hammer blows had made the man nearly deaf.

The plan's simplicity was its strength.

The street was empty and dark, the righteous men and women of Porte Oliva asleep in their beds and the unrighteous tending to stay nearer the salt quarter. Fewer queensmen patrolled here in the night, and if they did, what could they object to? Marcus and Yardem were known to be part of the bank. If someone came across them on the way to the counting house, they were only on their way to a turn at the watch. And once they left, Marcus assumed they were gone forever. It wasn't likely that Porte Oliva or anywhere that the Medean bank was a force would be open to him again.

Small price.

In the gloom, Yardem pulled the handcart into the house, locked and barred the door. Marcus went below to the sunken strongbox. The lock was stronger than it looked, and opening it took the best part of an hour. When the lid finally did swing back, silent on well-oiled hinges, Marcus brought his lantern close. Only the most sensitive and valued contracts were kept here. Papers were only paper, and the number of people who could use them was small. Gems, though. Sacks of gold coin, weights of silver. Jewelry and sealed tubes of rare spice. Those were things that anyone could use. Marcus squatted over the box, his free hand going through the wealth of the bank quickly but with consideration.

"Less than it was when we came," Yardem said.

"That's to be expected," Marcus said. "Most of it's tied up in loans and partnerships. There's enough, though. Maybe not for a full company and full season, but a couple hundred sword-and-bows. We'll move faster on the road that way too. Won't have the long supply lines to slow us down."

"I'm going to ask you for a favor, sir."

Marcus looked up. The lantern cast the shadow of Yardem's chin up over his face, hooding him with it. In that light, he could have been someone else entirely.

"What is it?" Marcus said.

"Once we put that in the cart and walk out the door, it's done. This is the last chance to reconsider. I'd like you to take a moment and pray with me on this."

Marcus laughed.

"I'm serious, sir."

"God's not listening," Marcus said. "It's not what he does."

"I think we might be the ones meant to listen, sir."

"Get it over with," Marcus said.

Yardem bowed his head, the black eyes closing. Marcus shifted from foot to foot, waiting. It was seven streets to a stable. More than that to the port. But with what he'd have in hand, buying a way out of the city would be easy. Between the gold and their two swords, the morning would find them elsewhere. Yardem opened his eyes.

"Change your mind, sir."

"Nope, the spirit didn't speak. Enough theology," Marcus said, tossing a small leather sack of gems. Yardem caught them overhand. "Help me load this up."

Yardem's hand closed on his shoulder, and the world spun. The stone wall of the basement struck his back like a hammer, and he fell to his hands and knees.

"What in—"

Yardem stepped close, his wide hand on Marcus's neck. Marcus rolled, pulling his sword free as he did it, but the Tralgu's other hand clamped on his wrist and twisted. The hand around his throat lifted, and Marcus's feet lost the floor. As the world began to go red and hazy, he brought a knee up hard into the soft spot just under Yardem's ribs. He felt something give way and the grip on his throat eased enough that he could draw in a sip of air. There was desperation in the way Yardem pulled at Marcus's sword arm, working it like a lever, but Marcus went with his momentum and broke the hold.

He swung around, blade at the defense half a heartbeat too late. The hammer he'd bought to break the lock came down gracefully on the bridge of his nose. Something cracked wetly and the world dissolved in pain. He felt his sword wrested from his grip as if it were happening to someone else. He bulled forward blind, his shoulder finding something soft and pushing Yardem back to the ground, but the Tralgu slipped to his left and got an arm around his throat. Marcus kicked, trying to twist his head down low enough to put his teeth on Yardem's arm, but he couldn't. His mouth tasted of blood and he couldn't breathe through his nose. His fingers dug at the thick, strangling flesh. Something smelled like smoke. His leg kicked out from under him, and the world narrowed to a greyish point far away before him and then blinked out.

When Marcus came to, his legs and arms were bound behind him and a cloth was pushed into his mouth and tied there with a leather thong. A sack was pulled over his head, making the process of breathing even more difficult. He was in the handcart, and its wooden wheels were rumbling against the cobblestones. His nose throbbed, sending stabbing pain back into his skull, and he tried to twist into a position where he could rise to his knees or shout for the queensmen. Anything.

"That the package?" an unfamiliar voice asked.

"Is," Yardem said. "You know where to take it?"

"Do. But I'm not going to vouch for a damned thing if he gets loose along the way. I'm no soldier."

"I am a soldier," Yardem said. "He won't get loose."

Something lifted him around the middle and dropped him hard against boards. Chains rattled and a wide leather strap wrapped him like a girth. The sack slipped, and Marcus saw the bed of a cart, a wide iron ring set into the planks, and Yardem fixing the chain to it. Rage and willpower lifted him to his knees, and Yardem casually pressed him back down.

"How long are you going to take back there?" the carter asked.

"Almost done," Yardem rumbled. He pulled at the chain, and Marcus slid down to the boards. His shoulder and hips screamed in pain. His labored breath started the blood flowing from his nostrils. Again. If he craned his neck, he could see the Tralgu's stoic face looming over him. There was fresh blood on Yardem's hands and a cut on his ear that Marcus didn't remember making. Part of Marcus still expected to be released. That it was a joke or a lesson or the start of some overblown religious statement.

The other part of him, that part that understood, stared up and thought, *I will kill you for this*.

When Yardem spoke, his voice was calm. He might have been talking about the weather or the prospects of a new recruit. He might have been talking about anything.

"The day I throw you in a ditch and take the company, sir? It's today."

Geder

They went underground.

His first thought had been to follow the paths and gantries that clung to the side of the Division, working their way down until they found a passageway that led into the ruins beneath the city. The pale woman, Cithrin, had seen the problem with that: following paths that people were already using meant running across the people who were already using them. Safety meant finding places that no one went, making passageways where there had been none before. The idea seemed second nature to her. It scared him to death, but he couldn't deny the wisdom of her words. It took the better part of a day for the actors to find an abandoned corner of the city, but they did. An old warehouse that had fallen into disuse and partly collapsed in on itself, the walls sinking into the city below.

The building had fallen because there was something beneath it to fall into. Geder, dressed now in rough grey clothes that stank of perfume and greasepaint, had let himself be led into the fallen house, and down to where an ancient archway still held the stone above it at bay. There was only a foot or so of open air between the rubble and the archway's top, but cats went in and out through it freely. Cithrin had gone first, crawling into the darkness with only a small candle carried in a thick glass lamp. The hole was so small, she had to pull herself along by the elbows, but when she'd gone in a half dozen yards, she called back. It opened wider. There was space. They should join her.

Aster had gone next, the stones scraping under him. Cithrin had kept calling until he found her.

And then it was his turn.

When he'd been a boy Aster's age, he had been the son of the manor in Rivenhalm. There had been no boys of his station within a day's ride in any direction. Climbing trees, leaping from precipices into distant water, crawling through caves. These hadn't been the things of his childhood. He had no experience of adventure to draw from. Inching forward, the daylight fading behind him, Geder was aware of the great weight above him. The old stone pressed on the air, thickening it. The rubble grew deeper, pressing his back against the ceiling until he almost had to slither, snakelike. The stink of cat piss grew stronger. At one point, he felt sure that he'd turned the wrong way in the darkness, that he was lost and buried alive.

But then the glimmer of Cithrin's candle caught his eye. When he tumbled down into the half-filled chamber, he was sure there would be blood soaking his knees and forearms, but the candle revealed only a few pale scratches.

Aster had volunteered to go back out to the actors waiting under the open sky. His eyes had been bright and excited. When he came back, he had a string tied to his ankle. Together, they pulled a tray through the tiny crawlspace: candles and blankets and sealed jars of raisins and water and dried meat. It wasn't enough to live on for long, but it would get them through the day. Cithrin shouted her thanks, and the faint voices of the others answered and then went away.

The room was part of a buried garden. The flowerbeds

were still visible between ancient columns. An open turning led to a smaller space where the corpse of a tree lay against the still-standing stones of a great wall. A crushed doorway led deeper into the bones of the city, rooms that might once have been a house. The space was too small for anything that wasn't a cat, and the dust on the ground was thick and undisturbed by human feet. Everything stank of cat, but Geder found that the scent faded with time.

"Well," Cithrin said. "This will do nicely."

"We should look more in the back," Aster said. "Might be another way out."

"Better that we don't. It's not on anyone's path. If we go farther in and find a space that people are using, we might be discovered. Better that we stay here where nobody goes."

"Who would be down here?" Geder said. "This place is a hole. Literally. It's a hole in the ground."

"Every city in the world has its poor," Cithrin said. "And say what you want about this. It's shelter. That's why we're here."

More than the violence, what haunted Geder was the betrayal. He lay in darkness, hands behind his head. Cithrin had gone out for food and news. The cats whose lair they'd appropriated were staying away except for the occasional distant scratching of claws on stone. Aster's deep, regular breath said the boy was sleeping. He wished he could sleep too.

When he closed his eyes, he saw Dawson Kalliam. He saw the knife in his hand and the blood on Basrahip's fingers. It didn't make sense. This was Jorey's father. Geder had helped the man expose and destroy Feldin Maas. He'd trusted Dawson with his armies. Dawson Kalliam was a friend. A patron. He saw the knife again, the cold hatred in Dawson's eyes.

If Dawson was an enemy, then anyone could be. For any reason or for no reason at all.

It was terrible and crushing, and since Aster was asleep and couldn't know, Geder let himself weep a little from the fear and desolation.

There were small noises here. The cats who still stalked the deeper ways, tentative scouts coming near and then scrabbling away in panic. There were neither rats nor mice, the prey kept away, Geder assumed, by the stink of the predators. Now and then, he also heard the ticking of pebbles and flakes of rock as something small dislodged. Over years and centuries, those tiny bits of stone and rivulets of rainwater would fill in the spaces like this. Once, men and women had walked on these stones, admired the violets in these beds. Now even the open sun was gone. And one day the sand and stone would claim even this small bubble of air. Anything could be buried below Camnipol, and no one would ever find it. It was a city built on lost things.

Someone grunted. Stones shifted in the little crawlway. Geder sat up, licking his lips nervously. He couldn't see anything. The darkness was perfect. He drew his little dagger, his breath coming ragged.

"Are you awake?" Cithrin asked, and Geder heaved a sigh.

"I am," he said, softly. "Aster's sleeping."

"All right," she said. "Light a candle for me, will you? I didn't dare while I was outside."

"Why not?"

"It's night. Someone might see."

Geder lit the candle, and the woman slipped down into the buried garden. Her hair was pulled back in a fierce ponytail, and grime and dust covered her hands and knees. Her skin, pale as a wraith, seemed almost to glow in the candlelight.

With the thinness of her mixed blood, she seemed fragile, weak. It was only the way she held herself and the confidence of her movements that gave that the lie. If she'd been a Firstblood, he would have thought she was little more than a girl, at least from the smoothness of her skin. But she was the magistra of a bank, and likely older than he was. A woman who traveled the world. She knelt, untying the rope at her ankle, and pulled. The tray skidded and scraped as she pulled it toward them.

"The news isn't good," she said softly so as not to wake Aster. "There's still fighting in the streets. Some of it's private guards and noble houses, but there are looters too. Gangs of them. If it looks like a nobleman's house is standing empty, they'll strip it to the walls. And there seem to be some old vendettas coming due. Five men in masks took away a merchant named Deron Root and threw him off a bridge this afternoon, and no one seems to know why."

"What about Basrahip?"

"The temple's scorched, but it's still standing. Mikel and Sandr didn't find anyone there, but they didn't find any bodies either. Some got killed, there doesn't seem much question. There are also stories that people have seen the priests about, but so far we haven't found any."

He sat forward, shaking his head. The tension in his shoulders ached. It was all too much. It was falling apart. And if he didn't have Basrahip or Dawson either, he couldn't imagine what he would do if he ever rose back up out of the earth.

"What about the city guard?" he asked. "What are they doing?"

Cithrin reached into the darkness of the crawlway, grunting, and pulled the tray back with her.

"They've got their hands full," she said. "There's no law

out there right now. Honestly? We three are probably the safest people in Camnipol tonight."

"Unless your friends betray us," he said.

"Unless that," she agreed, taking something wrapped in cloth from the tray and setting it on the ground at her feet. "They're not likely to, though."

"Why not?" Geder said, thinking of Dawson Kalliam's face again. The blood on his knife. "Any of them could. Why wouldn't they?"

"One of them did before," she said. "They saw how that ended."

She took a jar down from the tray, and then three wineskins. The last thing on the tray was a tin chamberpot that she held up in the candlelight with a rueful smile.

"Very nearly forgot the necessities," she said. "Do you think we set up the tree over there as the privacy room, or should we push in and see if we can't find someplace a bit farther from nose range."

Geder tried to imagine relieving himself where she could hear him, and his blush felt hot.

"Farther in would be better, don't you think?"

"All right," she said. "The first one who needs it picks the place."

By the light of the single candle she unwrapped the cloth. There was enough food for several small meals: roasted chicken, raw carrots no thicker than her fingers, half a rabbit boiled in wine, hard rolls so stale they sounded hollow when she knocked them together. They sat together in the gloom. She drank wine with the certainty of long acquaintance, and Geder found himself pushing to keep up. When the last of the chicken was reduced to bones and gristle, they had just cracked the third wineskin's neck, and from the way she held it, he was certain it would be empty before she slept.

Aster snored gently in his blankets and murmured to himself.

"He's taking all this well," Cithrin said, nodding toward the sleeping boy.

"He puts up a good front," Geder said. "It's been hard for him, though. He lost his mother young, and now his father. Add the weight of the crown."

"It doesn't seem fair that being born to the throne should make things so much harder," she said. "You'd think power would have more to recommend it."

"What? You don't think things are going well?" he asked. She didn't laugh for a moment, and he was relieved when she did.

"I assume this is an aberration for you, Lord Regent," she said. "But you've grown up noble, just like the prince. You understand what he's carrying."

"I really don't. I mean, I suppose I'm in the same place with him now, but I was very low before. He's known from the time he could talk that he was destined for the throne. I've known I was going to have a tiny little holding in a valley with too many trees and not enough farmland."

She tilted her head, considering him. The wine brought color to her cheeks. A stray lock of hair drifted onto her lips, and she blew it away.

"What happened, then?" she asked. "You've moved up in the world. You're practically the king."

"It's a long, complicated story," he said.

"You're right," she said. "We might run out of time."

He began at the beginning. Rivenhalm, with its fast, small river and the library his father had built up. He remembered a little of his mother, and told what there was. His imaginings of Camnipol when he was young and it had been a magical city that his father spoke of, where noble lords and ladies danced and spoke wise things and dueled for love and honor. He laughed about it now, but it had seemed powerful and important at the time.

And then his first entry into the life of the court. His first campaign.

When he mentioned Vanai, she went still. It wasn't that her expression closed so much as that it turned inward, became somber. Something in the back of his mind told him to stop, but the more quiet she grew, the more he wanted to pull her out, to make her laugh. The anxiety drove him on. He exaggerated his own failures and shortcomings for comic effect. Everyone else laughed at him, so maybe she could too, but she only nodded. He knew he had to change the topic before he got to the burning, but the tale and the wine had taken a life of their own and he listened to himself in growing horror as Ternigan took the city and named Alan Klin its protector. He told of his own role as petty enforcer of Klin's will.

When he mentioned the caravan that was supposedly smuggling the wealth of Vanai, she roused a bit. When he told how he'd drawn the improbable range south of the dragon's road, slogging through ice and mud with a troop of disloyal Timzinae soldiers, he had her full attention back. He even let himself confess—for the first time to anyone— that he'd found the treasure and let it go. Her expression of disbelief was almost comic.

"I know," he said, shaking his head. "It was petty of me. And probably disloyal, but Klin was such a pompous...I don't even know the word."

She was looking at him as if she were seeing him for the first time, and her smile was like pouring water on a burn. He grinned and shrugged.

"I only took a bit," he said. "Enough for some books when I got back to Vanai."

"Of course you did," she said and shook her head in amazement. The way she said it made it flattery, and he looked down, suddenly proud of his own daring. "You were there for the burning."

Geder took a deep breath. The dread welled up in him. He ignored it well, but it was never far away.

"I was protector of the city," he said.

Her face went very still.

"Was it your order, then?"

The truth was on the edge of his mind. It would have taken so little to say yes. But he wanted her to like him.

"No," he said. "The command came from higher ranks. But I didn't rise against it. I should have. It was a mistake. It was a terrible, terrible stupid mistake. Whoever did give the order, he can't have understood what it meant. Not really. I still have nightmares about it sometimes. You...you knew Vanai?"

"I was raised there," she said. "My parents were buried there, and the bank took me in. I lost everyone there."

Geder's belly felt hollow with fear, and he quietly thanked God that he'd chosen against the truth. Guilt washed over him like a wave.

"I'm so sorry," he murmured, looking away.

"I don't know," she said. "I loved them, but they didn't love me. Cam, maybe. But Magister Imaniel didn't love anyone, I don't think. He wasn't that kind of man. It hurt me when they died, but..."

"But?"

"But I don't know who I'd be if they'd lived," she said. She spoke with the clarity of being just drunk enough to know she had to try not to slur her words. "I missed them. And I mourned for them, I think. But I like who I am. What I do. I'm looking forward to everything. The things that happened to bring me here? I can't judge them. Good. Bad. Who would I be if I'd had parents? Who would I be if I'd gone to Carse? If something terrible leads to something good, where does that leave you?"

"I don't know," he said, though he didn't understand the part about going to Carse. She'd come from Carse, so she must have gone there at some point.

She put the wineskin to her mouth, tilting back her head. Her throat worked, once, twice, last. A tiny red trickle slipped from her lips, and she wiped it away with her sleeve. When she smiled, the expression was lazy and joyful, utterly out of place in the ruins of a city at war.

"I," she said, putting the empty skin on the ground, "am drunk enough to sleep now."

"Well, then. Good night, Magistra."

She nodded an unsteady bow, but her eyes were bright and merry.

"Sleep well, Lord Regent. We'll see who has to find a home for the piss pot," she said, leaned forward with pursed lips, and blew out the candle.

The darkness was utter and absolute. Geder found a blanket by touch and curled himself into it. The welts on his arm were itching, but not badly. He heard her struggling with her own blanket, muttering small curses, shifting, cloth moving against cloth. Her breath was shallow and impatient, and then softer, deeper, fuller. She snored a little, the rattle high in her throat. Geder lay on the dirt, his own arm for a pillow. He heard the patter of soft cat feet, one of the previous owners drawn by the smell of the chicken. The frantic licking of a small, rough tongue. When he moved, the cat fled, and he was sorry that it had. He didn't mind sharing what was left of the meal.

He hadn't realized how much the tiny candle flame had

warmed the little room, but the air was growing steadily colder. He willed himself to sleep, counting his breaths to himself the way he had when he was younger. Going through his body, forcing each muscle to relax, starting with his feet and ending with the top of his head. It grew colder, but he minded it less. Slowly, by inches, he felt his mind letting go, slipping apart into the quiet darkness. When she shifted against him, he only half noticed she was there.

His last coherent thought was that he was sleeping beside a woman and it didn't seem strange at all.

Dawson

The battle of Camnipol had raged for more than a week now, violence following violence, attack calling forth reprisal calling forth reprisal of its own. Twice now, someone had tried to open the gates, and both times they had been driven back. The city's food supplies were growing shorter, the water in the cisterns lower. The high summer sun had joined the battle with the worst heat in years. It beat down from an implacable blue sky, turning all the roofs to a burning bronze, wilting the flowers, and driving men to madness.

Dawson stood on the rooftop of Alan Klin's estate, his arms behind him, his chin jutting forward with a confidence he didn't feel. His city was suffering. His nation was suffering. Asterilhold could have reassembled its army and stood outside the walls right now, and not only would Dawson not know it, it wouldn't have made any difference. The siege they held themselves under was as vicious as any enemy could devise. It was like watching a beloved dog going slowly mad, biting itself to death while Dawson could only look on in horror and sorrow.

Behind him, Alan Klin cleared his throat. And Mirkus Shoat, never a man of particular originality, did as well. Dawson turned to his council. The patriots being mistaken for traitors. Estin Cersillian was dead, caught by a blade in the street. Odderd Mastellin looked small and sheeplike and weary. Only Lord Bannien lived and was not with them. He'd gone in the morning with a dozen men to salvage what he could of his mansion, burned in the night.

"We can't keep this going," Klin said.

"I know it."

In the street below them, there should have been men and women, dogs and children. Servants should have been carrying their masters' clothing back from the launderer. Horses should have pulled carts of turnips and carrots to the market square. Instead, men with swords walked in groups, wary-eyed. His men, Klin's, Bannien's. Aster's banner flew over the house as well, a visible claim of loyalty that seemed to matter less and less with every passing day.

"If we have King Lechan," Mastellin said, "we can lay claim to being the legitimate protectors of the throne. We'd hold the enemy of the crown as an enemy."

"Are we sure no one's killed him?" Mirkus Shoat asked. Klin's laugh was low and nasty.

"We're not sure anyone's *fed* him," he said. "He could be gone to the angels and not a dagger in sight."

"Then we have to surrender," Shoat said.

"Never to Palliako," Dawson said. "If we lay down arms, it must be to the prince. Otherwise everything they say about us will be true."

"I think you underestimate what they're saying about us," Klin said. "And it hardly matters. Until we find one or the other of them, we might as well give arms to Daskellin or Broot or whoever we find walking down the street. There's no one we can surrender to that can guarantee our safety as far as from here to the gallows."

"Why not?" Shoat demanded. "Those others could surrender to us."

"But they won't," Klin said, his voice the melody of despair. "They're winning."

"What about the priests?" Dawson said. "Have we tracked any of them down?"

"A few," Klin said. "Not all. The high priest especially can't be found. We've rounded up six or seven of the bastards."

"Where are they now?" Mastellin asked.

"Bottom of the Division," he said. "We threw them off a bridge. I talked to one of them for a while first. They tell interesting stories."

"I don't care what pigs mean when they grunt," Dawson said, but Klin went on as if he'd been silent.

"They say Palliako's running the whole damned fight from a secret tower in the Kingspire. He's supposed to have some kind of magical protection. When the blades hit him, they passed right through like he was mist."

"It's shit," Dawson said. "The only thing my blade passed through was the priest."

Klin shook his head. When he spoke again, his voice was harder.

"They say he planned all this. That it's part of the purge he began with Feldin Maas, and only he knew how deep it really ran. They say the fighting now is all him putting a hot cloth on the wound so he can draw up the pus." Klin looked around the rooftop. "We're the pus, in case you missed the metaphor."

In the street, someone shouted and half a dozen men drew blades and ran to the sound. Dawson wished his eyes could turn the corners and follow them instead of standing up where he could see so much more of the city, and still too little.

"You don't believe it," Dawson said.

"I don't know," Klin replied. "I didn't, but even wild tales can have a grain of truth to them. Palliako knew we were coming."

"He was suprised," Dawson said.

"He didn't know it was you, maybe," Klin said. "But he does now. Maybe it was all built to see who was against him. It worked out that way, didn't it?"

Sweat trickled down Dawson's back and stuck his sleeves to his arms. The shouts in the streets below were growing louder, and the sound of steel against steel rang with them. Klin ignored that too.

"I don't think he's become some sort of master cunning man who turns to mist and knows the hearts of all his subjects. But some people do, Kalliam. Some people think that's true."

"There are always idiots," Dawson said as a rough knot of melee pushed its way back round the corner and toward Klin's courtyard. "And you're one for talking to them. Damn it, they've come back. Sound the defense."

"What's the point?" Klin asked.

"That they don't kill us," Dawson said, speaking each word individually. Klin only smiled.

"Every man dies sometime," he said. "At least it won't be in that swamp."

At last, the drums beat out the defense. The men at rest came out from behind Klin's walls, pressing the attackers back to the barricades Dawson's forces had made. He was going to have to pull back farther still. With Bannien gone, he had too few men to command all the streets around Klin's estate. And God alone knew when Bannien would return.

And if.

*   *   *

The halls of Klin's estate were frankly ugly. Like Issandrian and Maas and all of that cohort of young iconoclasts, the old aesthetics were lost on them. There were no clean lines here. No austerity or dignity or gravity. Nothing held the beauty of classic architecture. Instead, the doorframes were carved into small riots of form: monkeys lifting frogs, frogs with lions on their backs, lions pawing at stretch-winged herons who were also the lintel. The tapestries were gaudy, busy things that dripped fringe like a drool from a man with a bad tooth. No floor could be left alone. They had to be inlaid with different colors of stone and chips of stained glass.

Sitting in the withdrawing room, Clara was like a gem in a pile of stones. The bed that Klin had supplied took up the better part of the room, but she sat on it as if it were the most elegant silk divan. The interior of the house was viciously hot, and without even the advantage of the smoky breeze, so she had the shutters cracked open, the soft daylight on her needlework. The web of pink threads and yellow and green were growing together into a pattern he couldn't yet make sense of. He'd always had the sense that she complicated the work intentionally, putting the thread together as a puzzle for her to resolve. In the end, it would be as if each step had been perfectly straightforward. Elegant.

"You shouldn't be here," she said without looking up. "You'll only make me feel guilty for distracting you."

"And if I told you I was looking for Jorey?"

She smiled. Clara had always had the talent for looking pleased without denying that she felt weary.

"I'd ask why you weren't looking in his room or the barracks."

"I was going to," Dawson said. "But I got distracted."

She put down her work and patted the mattress at her side. It was too soft, of course. Klin was a weak man at heart, and always had been.

"Tell me again," Dawson said, "what happened when Phelia Maas died."

"Well, you recall we were in the drawing room, you and Jorey and Geder and that very large religious friend of Geder's. And poor Phelia was in a state of nerves. When Palliako began unveiling everything that had been going on with Feldin, the poor thing fell apart..."

She told it all again, as she had before. The pretended errand to Maas's mansion, the priest's insistence when challenged that they were there at the baron's request. Then the letters that proved his conspiracy, and the discovery. Phelia's death.

And after, when Vincen Coe had stood against the baron and his men in the corridor while Basrahip the goatherd priest hectored Maas into walking away. Dawson tried to picture it, and failed. He had fought Feldin Maas many times, and more than one of those had been with a blade. To go meekly. To drop his sword and turn away.

"They have some evil magic," he said. "It breaks men. It broke Maas and the men in the keep at the Seref. And it's breaking Klin. I can see it in him. He spoke to them, and it's drowned the fire in him just the way it did for the others."

"Are you sure it isn't the fever and fighting that's doing it?" Clara asked. "It doesn't take magic to break someone's spirit. The world can be enough."

There was a truth in her words he didn't want to acknowledge, but it was there, patient and implacable. The exhaustion pressing down on his shoulders drew from more than the battle dragging on. More than his frustration and fear. It was also grief. He had done his best for his kingdom. He had done his duty as he saw it, standing bulwark against the small, shortsighted men who would change it. If Simeon had lived only a few more years, enough to give Aster the throne without a regency...

Clara took his hand, and he tried to muster some hope.

"Skestinin's got to be getting close by now," he said. "Once he brings his men south, he'll get the gates opened. We're too evenly matched now, and he can tip the balance."

"Will that be a good thing?"

"If it was only Barriath being under his command, no," Dawson said. "But there's Sabiha. Skestinin's family now. With his reinforcements, we can turn this. We'll get you and the girl out. Jorey, if he'll go."

"And you?"

The drums sounded, deep and dry. He saw Clara shudder. The defense again. Another wave of attackers come to erode their strength. They were coming more often now. They weren't coming to win, but to keep Dawson's men from resting. A siege within a siege.

"I have to be there," he said. "I am sorry the world came to this, love. It ought to have been on better behavior with you in it."

"How eloquent," she said, only half mocking. "You're a flatterer, you know."

"You're worth flattering," he said, rising from the bed.

By the time he reached the street, the men had already pushed back the latest assault. The sun had turned the cobbled streets hot. Even after sunset came, the heat would be rising up out of the land for hours. In better years, he would have been setting out for the Great Bear now, preparing himself for an evening of cooled wine and debates, contests of poetry and rhetoric. In better years, the summer would not have been so hot.

In the yards, men had built tents and defenses like an army on campaign. Klin's gardens were pounded into dust by boots. The roses had been cut down to make room, and a wide arbor where grapevines had hung down, dripping with wide green leaves was a pair of broken stumps, the body of the thing part of a street barricade. The men themselves slept on cots, torpid in the heat, or paced to and from the water trough. Their faces were dirty and closed, their movements defensive. Even in the way they drank a tin of water and nodded to each other, they were the image of a beaten army.

It wasn't true, of course. In the other mansions and squares, there would be other men who'd taken the other opinion who were just as hot and just as tired, who saw the damage being done to the city and felt its loss as deeply. There was no reason that Dawson's men should be hanging their heads. The battle wasn't lost as long as they stood.

He walked the perimeter with the captain on duty. The barricades had been set three and four streets out from Klin's, proclaiming the squares to be territory of Dawson's men, but under the constant and shifting attacks they were being eaten away like sandcastles at the change of tide. Where once they had been walls, they'd degraded into hills, or worse, mere collections of refuse, some stacked on each other, but hardly enough to slow an advancing force.

"We can't keep holding where we've been, my lord," the captain said. "The men don't say it, but they know. And once they know, it's hard to feel much enthusiasm for rebuilding. We need to pull in a way, eliminate two or three places that we have to defend."

"And the attack?" Dawson asked.

"I'm sorry, my lord?"

"The attack. How do we take this to them?"

The captain's cheeks ballooned out as he considered the question.

"We've got hunting patrols out. Four of them in rotation, looking for the prince and the Lord Regent. And those priests you wanted."

"It isn't enough," Dawson said. "We're sitting here like criminals waiting for the magistrate's blades. The men need glory. Pull back the barricades, and place archers on the rooftops in the new positions. Tell the men to rest tonight. In the morning, we take the fight to the enemy."

"Yes, my lord," the captain said, but there was no joy in his voice. After a moment's hesitation: "Lord Kalliam, which enemy are we speaking of?"

"Palliako and his Keshet cultists," Dawson said.

"Yes, but Lord, that's who we're hunting now. If you mean instead that we're going to draw arms against Ternigan's men or Daskellin's or some such, that changes the look of things. It may not be easy to arrange this well."

Dawson could hear how carefully the man was choosing his words.

"They have been attacking us," Dawson said. "And we're curling up and taking the blows. It's no way to win a fight."

"Yes, my lord. I mean no, sir, it isn't. But they aren't the enemy. All of us know men on the other side. We served with them. Fought beside them, a lot of them under your command. It's not the same as marching on Asterilhold or Sarakal. These are Anteans we're be fighting. It's not the same."

"They're the servants of the priests now," Dawson said. "They're corrupted."

"Yes, my lord. It's just hard to see that when you're looking at a man who maybe saved your life in Asterilhold. It's not as though those men crossed us personally. They're only following what their lords are telling them to do, sir."

Just as we are, hung in the air between them. Dawson heard the warning in it. It wasn't only hope that was fading, it was also loyalty. The glory of battle required an enemy they could hate, and apart from the priests and Palliako, Dawson didn't have one. He wondered whether the others—Ternigan, Daskellin, Broot—were suffering the same problem. He hoped they were.

"Thank you for your candor," Dawson said crisply. "Let's have those barricades remade. If we can defend the position with fewer men, we can send out more hunting parties, yes?"

"Yes, Lord. I believe we could do that."

"We'll do that, then."

The sun moved slowly in the great arch of sky above the city. Dawson found himself resenting it. It and all the stars hiding behind its skirts. The Kingspire caught the light for a moment, flashing like a bolt of lightning that didn't fade. He could imagine Palliako up there in his secret rooms, looking down at Dawson, at the city. That was where to go. If there was an attack to be made, a final assault, it would be to root Palliako out of his perch on the Kingspire. To haul him off the Severed Throne and put Aster there in his place. Already the boy would be a better king than Palliako...

A voice boomed out. The echoes bouncing from the canyon walls of the buildings made the words indistinct, but the timbre of it was familiar. Dawson's gut went tight as he walked and then trotted to where the new barricades were taking shape. His men were divided: half went on piling logs, tables, upended carts in the street, building defenses against the blades of their countrymen, and half stood silent, hands on their bows and swords, ready to push back when the new assault came.

But it didn't come. No melee. No blades.

In the square they had just withdrawn from, a siege tower

stood on massive wooden wheels, pushed by a company of slaves at the back. Fifty swordsmen at least marched at its base, but didn't call the charge. At the tower's head, almost as high as the roofs themselves, an archer's house stood, its thick wooden sides proof against incoming arrows and bolts. But instead of archers leaning out from its window to rain down upon them, there was the grey cone of a caller's tube. The words booming out from it were the deep, rolling voice of Basrahip, the high priest of the spider goddess. Geder's puppetmaster.

"Listen to my voice," he called. "You have already lost. Everything you fight for is meaningless. You cannot win. Listen to my *voice*..."

Cithrin

Y ou need a bath," Sandr said, prodding Charlit Soon
with his toe. And then a moment later, "*I* need a bath."

"I think we can say we'd all do well with baths," Cary
said. "And fresh food. And maybe a rainstorm."

Cithrin squatted on the back of the cart, a bowl of stewed
barley in her hand. She hadn't come out of the hole until just
after midday, and even after the walk to Yellow House, the
sun seemed too bright. Twelve days in the darkness. So far.

"Well, the good news is we found your high priest," Cary
said. "The bad is that he's holed up in the middle of an army
and won't let anyone come near him. I thought about passing him a letter, but I wasn't sure you'd want that."

Cithrin frowned. The truth was, she was of two minds.
Several times in the last week, she'd have offered to cut off a
toe if it meant a warm bed, a good meal, and five hours in a
bathhouse. When Geder and Aster emerged from the hole,
there would be no reason for her to be down in it with them,
and she was coming to truly loathe that place. But when the
time came, Geder would become Lord Regent Palliako again.
Aster would be prince and king. Everything would change.

She'd been sent here to find out what she could about
Antea in the face of its war with Asterilhold. Now she was
hiding with two of the most important leaders, present and
future, that the kingdom would have. What she'd learned

was that Geder Palliako was a funny, somewhat awkward man who loved books of improbable history. That Aster hadn't known how to spit for distance, and now—thanks to her—he did. She saw the affection between the pair of them, and the enthusiasms. And the almost physical shared sorrow that neither one of them acknowledged, or even recognized. When they rose out of the ground, they would leave her, and her chance to learn more of them both would vanish.

"I'll talk to Geder about it," she said, scooping up the last of the barley with two cupped fingers. "Anything else?"

"The usual human landscape of lies and folly," Cary said. "Did you know that Geder commands the spirits of the dead, and that at night ghosts stalk the streets rooting out his enemies?"

"He hadn't mentioned that," Cithrin said. "Good to know. All right, then. If that's all—"

Mikel grinned.

"Well," he said, "as a matter of fact..."

Cithrin lifted her eyebrows.

"You always do that," Charlit Soon said. "That's exactly what I was talking about with A Tragedy of Tarsk. You always play the pause for effect."

"Has an effect," Smit said.

"Yeah," Charlit Soon said, "it prolongs and annoys." She tossed a pebble at Mikel.

"As a matter of fact," Cithrin prompted.

"As a matter of fact," Mikel said, somewhat abashed, "I found where your Paerin Clark's been hiding. Went to ground in a guesthouse of Canl Daskellin's, which was a pretty good idea since the inn you were staying in burned."

"It burned?" Cithrin said.

"Fourth night after," Cary said.

"My clothes were in there," Cithrin said.

"Twelve people were in there," Sandr said. "Two of them children."

Cithrin considered Sandr. There had been a time not all that long ago when she'd very nearly taken him as a lover. From where she sat now, the wisdom of her decision not to glowed like a fire in the night.

"Yes, I am a small, petty woman," she said, "and I mourn for the dead and the suffering, but I really wanted to get my own damn clothes back. Can you reach Paerin, or is he as guarded as the priest?"

"He's not taking visitors he doesn't know," Mikel said.

"All right," Cithrin said. "I'll need something to write on."

The company cipher was still clear in her mind, and the note was a brief one: *Have access to Lord Regent and Prince Aster. What questions do I ask? Reply by same courier.* She considered adding something that would say where she was, where Geder and Aster were, and she didn't. If he wanted Geder and Aster, he could come to her.

It was one of the great and powerful lessons of finance. The key to wealth and power was simple enough to state and difficult to employ: be between things. Narinisle was a chilly island with barely enough arable land to support its own population and no particular resources to offer, but the currents of the Ocean Sea put it between Far Syramys and the rest of the continent. And so it was vastly wealthy. Now Cithrin had fallen into Narinisle's position, and while it wouldn't last, she could gain more the longer she remained in place.

"All right," she said, handing the paper to Mikel. "I'll come back as soon as I can for the reply."

"How are things going underground?" Cary asked.

"Frightened and bored and ready to be done with this.

But we let Aster sneak up to the mouth and look out at the daylight. It seems to help."

"Good. When this is over, though, I hope the Lord Regent remembers who his friends are. I'm almost through all the stones the prince brought with him."

"Really?"

"I could buy more with a ripe orange than with one of those pearls," Cary said. "It's already starvation time in some quarters. If this all doesn't break soon, we'll start seeing a lot more people dying. And they won't be lords and nobles falling in glorious battle."

When there was nothing more to be said, Cithrin pulled a sack over her shoulder with four fresh wineskins, a palm-sized round of hard cheese, a bottle of water, some stale bread, and a double handful of dried cherries harvested at least a year before and hard as pebbles. She paused before she started the walk back, looking out over the Division. The air was hazy, the far side of the span already a bit greyer than things closer to hand. Nothing was burning at the moment, but there was no reason to expect that would be true through the night, for instance.

She hadn't been there for a half a season, but Camnipol had gone from the heart of an empire to a city of scars. It was in the scorch marks on the buildings and the faces of the men she passed in the streets, the empty market squares and the gangs of swordsmen moving together like packs of wolves. She walked quickly and with her head down. She was too clearly not Firstblood to be mistaken for someone with power in the city, but she could play the servant. There were any number of lower-class people of the crafted races, and if she were one of those, no one would wonder particularly where she was going or why.

On her solitary way back to the warehouse and the hole,

three men followed her for nearly half a mile, calling out vulgarities and making crude suggestions. She kept her eyes low and kept walking. She told herself it was a good sign, because it was how the men would have treated a servant girl walking alone through the streets, but she still felt the relief when they lost interest and wandered on.

At the warehouse, she stopped, turning slowly in all directions. There was no one there to see her. She went through the usual ritual, tying the length of rope to her ankle and crawling in. The others hadn't come with her this time, so she didn't bother using the tray. Everything she had already fit in the sack.

The first time she'd crawled through the black passage, it had seemed to go on forever. Now it felt brief, trivial. When she reached the dropoff where it broadened out into the sunken garden, Geder and Aster were sitting beside each other, drawing patterns in the dirt by the light of a candle.

"Has that been burning since I left?" Cithrin asked.

Geder and Aster looked at each other, an image of complicity. Cithrin sighed and began pulling in the pack.

"It's going to run out, you know. And won't get another one until tomorrow at the earliest."

"Dark now or dark later," Aster said. "It's not a great difference."

"The difference is dark now would be a choice," she said. "Dark later's by necessity. What are you playing at?"

"Geder was showing me Morade's Box," Aster said.

"It's a puzzle I found in a book," Geder said. "It's about the last war."

"We had a last war?" Cithrin asked, pushing back a lock of her greasy hair. "I'm not sure everyone knew to stop."

"The dragons, I mean," Geder said. "Here, look."

Cithrin came and sat beside them as Geder drew out the problem fresh. Morade was a dot in the center, his clutch-mates were set one on either side. And three stones were the places Drakkis Stormcrow might be hiding: Firehold, Matter, and Rivercave. The puzzle gave each of the dragons rules on how they could move and in which order, and the puzzle was to find how Morade could check all three hiding places while blocking his clutch-mates.

"What if Stormcrow's in the first one?" Cithrin asked.

"No, you don't ever find him," Geder said. "It's only to look in all three places."

"What if…" Aster reached for the little improvised board and tried a series of moves that didn't work. Cithrin left them to it, opening the pack and putting everything out where she could locate it again by touch. The candle wasn't going to last all the way to nightfall. Not that day or night meant much in the darkness.

They ate their dinner in darkness, and Aster crawled up through the dark tunnel to watch the sunset fade at the bottom of the ruined warehouse. Cithrin sat against a wall of stone and earth, her wineskin in her hand. Geder, invisible, was before her and to the right.

"Do you think they really all died?" she asked.

"Who? The dragons? Of course they did."

"I went to the Grave of Dragons before I came out here. The man I was with was saying that Stormcrow would put pods of them to sleep, hide them away so that they would wake behind enemy lines and attack from the rear."

"I've read about that," Geder said. "They had ships too that would carry people into the sky. They had spines of steel and knife blades as long as a street. They'd fight dragons with them."

"Did they ever win?"

"I don't think so," Geder said. "If they did, I never read about it."

"When I was a girl, I dreamed about riding dragons. Having one as a friend who could carry me up and away from Vanai and everyone I knew. Everything. I had these elaborate stories about how it would obey me and let me do whatever I wanted. And then..." She laughed, shaking her head though no one could see it.

"What?" Geder asked.

"And then the dragon turned out to be money," she said. "Coin and contract and lending at interest were what let me fly. Who would have thought that was what I meant by dreaming of dragons?"

"It makes sense," Geder said. "I mean, it wasn't really gold either. Dragons or coins or riding off with an army at your back and a crown on your head. It's all the same. It's power. You wanted power."

Cithrin sat with the thought for a moment.

"Did you want power?" she asked.

"Yes," Geder said. She heard him shifting his weight in the earth. "I wanted to see everyone who laughed at me suffer for it. I wanted every humiliation answered for."

"And now that you have the power, you're living in a ruin that stinks of cat piss and eating whatever an acting company can scrounge for you," Cithrin said. "I'm not sure the plan is going well."

"This isn't a humiliation."

"No?"

"No, you're here. And anyway, it isn't over. We won't die here. The people who started this will answer for it." He said it calmly and with confidence. He wasn't bragging, just saying what he saw. "So. Who was this man you were with? When you saw the Grave?"

"Komme Medean's son," Cithrin said, and took another mouthful of wine. "It's hard, I think, for Komme. He built the bank from a small concern that his grandfather had started, and he made it into this grand system that covers the world. A lot of it, anyway. And then he had a son who doesn't understand anything."

Geder's laughter was warm and rich and oddly cruel, as if hearing her casually insulting Lauro pleased him.

"His daughter's smart, though," Cithrin said. "Paerin Clark's wife. If Komme wants to see the bank last another generation, he'll give it to her."

A gentle scraping announced the return of the prince, and the scattering of stones fell to the ground.

"How was it out there?" Geder asked.

"There was light," Aster said. "And I heard some men on the road. They sounded angry."

"Did they see you?" Geder asked a moment before Cithrin could.

"Of course not," Aster said, and she could hear the grin in his voice. "I'm the prince of ghosts. No one sees me."

That night was cooler than usual, though she couldn't tell any difference from the steady depth of Aster's breath. The wine had blunted her anxiety, but she hadn't drunk all she had to hand. One more skin lay on the ground just out of reach, and lying in the darkness beside Geder, she thought about reaching for it. But the fact that she wanted it was its own argument against.

The combination of enforced quiet and fear were, she knew, an invitation to overindulge. If she were honest with herself, she had probably already missed an opportunity somewhere in the dark nights with Geder and Aster simply by letting the wine blunt her. On the other hand, sleeplessness wasn't a very good way to stay alert and focused either. Somewhere in the middle there had to be a balance, a way to calm her nerves without softening them. She didn't want to grow old and find herself one of the wasted, bleary-eyed drunks living in the taprooms. The potential was in her, and so she lay in the darkness and didn't reach for the wineskin.

Geder rolled against her, his arm falling across her belly, his face turned to the place between her shoulder and the floor. He was warm, at least, and her mouth didn't smell better than his. The pattern of his breath told her that he was pretending to be asleep, and she let herself smile at that. It took him time to work up his courage, and she wasn't at all surprised to feel his hand cupping her breast.

She closed her eyes, thinking through what she ought to do. No, more than that, what she *wanted* to do. Aster had already proved that he could sleep through hours of candle-light conversation, and even laughter. But what was the protocol about sex with a king? Or a Lord Regent, anyhow. She could refuse him, and her guess was that he would take the rejection gracefully and with apologies. Or at least that's how she expected Geder to treat Cithrin. If he chose to react as Lord Regent Palliako, that was something else. It would be interesting to know which of his different roles he adopted, but the price of finding out might be unpleasant.

Almost as if at a distance, she noticed her own breath growing shallow, which she thought was odd. And, unfortunately, it removed the option of feigning sleep herself. Surely she couldn't want him. Could she? She'd only had one lover before, and she remembered reacting this way to his touches, more or less. She shifted her mind, by conscious effort attending to her body. The weight and warmth she found was surprising. Geder's hand had shifted, his fingers pressing tentatively against her belly, inching slowly down, and instead of awkwardness or discomfort, she mostly felt impatience that he was being so hesitant. Either he was doing this thing or he wasn't; hovering awkwardly at the edge was undignified. What was he going to do? Pretend his hand had just landed by chance? *Oops, how did that get there?*

Her laugh was unintentional and deep in her throat. He went perfectly still, like one of the cats trying to sneak past in the dark, pausing in fear.

This was a bad idea. On every level, this was a terrible, awful, awkward, improbable impulse, and the right thing to do was turn to him and tell him so, and make whatever peace they could salvage from having come so very near to catastrophe together. She shifted, her betraying body moving to keep his hand against her. She opened her lips to speak, but somewhere along that path, she was distracted, because instead she kissed him.

Oh dear, she thought as his surprise faded and his mouth softened against hers. *That didn't go well at all.*

His hands rose to her, and his breath was shuddering. He was trembling.

"I..." he whispered. "I haven't..."

"It's all right," she said. "I have."

Cithrin!"

The whisper was like paper tearing. She struggled up from a sleep so profound that she didn't remember at first where she was or why opening her eyes didn't have any effect.

"Geder?" she said.

"Cithrin, it's me!"

Not Geder. Not Aster either.

"Hornet?"

"Do you have a candle?" the actor asked. "It's near midday and I didn't think to bring one."

"No," she said, sitting up. Oh God, where was her robe?

She patted the dusty earth around her quietly, and Geder found her hand, pressing a familiar wad of cloth into it. "No, we used our last one yesterday tracking down Drakkis Stormcrow. Why are we whispering?"

She used the pause to pull the garment over her head.

"I don't know, now you put it that way," Hornet said. "Just seemed a whispering sort of place."

"We talk here too," Cithrin said.

"We do," Geder agreed.

Aster chuckled from somewhere off to her left. She fit her arms into the sleeves. There. Decent now.

"I came to call you back," Hornet said. "It's over."

"What's over?" Geder asked.

"Battle of Camnipol," Hornet said, rounding the vowels with an actor's pride. "Dawson Kalliam's in the gaol and his allies are falling over themselves looking for someone to blame or apologize to."

"Kalliam surrendered?"

"Odderd Mastellin turned on him. Anyway. Thought you'd want to know, yes? Get yourselves out of here and back to the world."

"Of course," Geder said, and she heard the complexity in his voice. Pleasure and regret. The ending of something. "Back to the world."

Marcus

All through the long night's ride, Marcus had looked for his escape. He'd strained at the ropes wound around his wrists and ankles. He'd tried gnawing at the leather thong that held the cloth in his mouth. He'd rolled to the limit that the ring and chain allowed. When they came to a stop—the first birds singing up the dawn—his only achievements were that he'd made the bones of his wrist pop painfully and the blood from his broken nose was spread more or less evenly throughout the cart.

The voice that hailed the carter was familiar, but he didn't place it until the man rose up beside him and smiled with a mouth overfilled with teeth.

"Yes, this is the man," Capsen Gostermak said, shaking his head sadly. "Good morning, Captain Wester. I'm sorry that we have to meet again under these unpleasant circumstances."

Even with his teeth, his smile managed to seem world-weary and amused. So at least his gaoler was a sophisticate.

"There was supposed to be payment sent with him," Capsen said.

"Ah, right," the carter said. "Forgot."

"Certain you did."

Marcus heard a purse change hands, and then the pair of them hauled him out of the cart and marched him through the darkness, carrying him like a slaughtered pig. His shoulders lit up with pain and whatever he'd pulled out of place in his wrist snapped back. It hurt just as much going the other way. The dovecote was rough and unfinished stone, so when they leaned him against the wall, Capsen fumbling with a wide iron key, Marcus was able to scrape his cheek against it and dislodge the gag. He spat the wet, bloody cloth to the ground.

"I'll double it," he said. "Whatever he's paying you, I'll double it."

Capsen chuckled ruefully.

"You're already paying me quite handsomely, Captain," he said. "I'm not a greedy man."

The interior was less than twenty feet across. The doves fluttered, asking wordless questions with their coos. Capsen and the carter hauled him across to a wide iron bar set diagonally across a corner, the ends of the bar deep in each wall. The leather strap was chained to it, and Marcus left to kneel on the flagstone floor. The carter trundled away, and Capsen drew a thin, wicked knife. The doves fluttered as if concerned on Marcus's behalf.

"I have some experience with this," Capsen said, slicing through the ropes that bound Marcus's legs. "Turn around. Thank you. There are two ways that this can go, and I will be paid the same in either case. You can have the admittedly limited freedom of the chain there."

"Five feet of freedom," Marcus growled.

"It's a relative term, granted," Capsen said, sawing through the ropes on Marcus's wrists. "Or else I have a set of old manacles. They chafe and they were meant for Cinnae, so they'd likely be a bit tight on you. But if you insist, we can use them."

"I'll kill you," Marcus said.

"And I'm not much of a fighter," Capsen said. "So if you tried, I would have to act definitively. I don't really know enough to manage simple restraint against someone as experienced as yourself. Mealtimes are first thing in the morning, a snack at midday, and another full meal just before sundown. I'll empty the night pot once a day. The door will be locked from the outside always, and you're too large to fit through the doves' holes. If you make things unpleasant for me, I will make things unpleasant for you."

"More unpleasant than being chained to the wall of a dovecote, you mean?"

"Unpleasant's another relative term," Capsen said. His smile seemed genuine.

"Why are you doing this?"

"I raise doves and write poems. Something has to pay the taxman."

He stood back, and Marcus staggered to his feet. Everything from his knees down was numb as the dead.

"I'll let you try to escape for a while if you'd like," Capsen said. "Breakfast will be in an hour or so."

For the next week, Marcus tried everything he could think of. He tried to twist out of the leather restraints. He tried to find how the chain was fastened, reaching behind himself until his shoulders and elbows ached. He ran from the wall, putting his full force behind each charge in hopes of breaking something loose, and then tried everything he'd done before again. One day he tried shouting for help. On the sixth day, he remembered something he'd heard about twisting rope out of cord, and turned himself head over foot, winding the chain tighter until it was a single, solid thing four times as thick as the original restraint and unable to move further. He used all his strength to force it on, to crack one link loose.

"Ooh," Capsen said when he brought the evening meal that day. "Haven't seen that one before. You're very clever."

"Thank you," Marcus grunted. Unwinding himself took a long time, and when he had enough slack in the chain, his dinner was cold.

As the second week of his captivity began, Marcus found his anger and outrage fading. The world narrowed to a small, insoluble problem. It consumed him. Long after he'd convinced himself that the mechanism was inescapable, he kept trying, doing all the things he'd done before, expecting them to be the same as they had been, but open for a pleasant surprise. No matter what happened next, his first job was to escape.

The doves seemed to look at him as free entertainment, shifting on their perches and turning first one eye and then another. Capsen's children would sometimes peek in at the doves' holes high in the wall, stare at Marcus for a few minutes, and then flee, laughing. At night, Marcus took his revenge by tossing pebbles and small clods of dirt at the doves until they puffed up and turned reproachful backs.

At night, he had nightmares. That wasn't new.

Dawn came in at the windows, a rising blue-white light. The doves commented to each other in a chorus of interrogative coos. The rattle of the lock came earlier than usual, and when the door swung open, it wasn't Capsen who ducked in.

"Kit?"

"Marcus," the actor said cheerfully. "I've been looking for you. I think I see now why you were so hard to find."

"You have to get me out of here."

"I do. But I wanted to speak with you first."

Master Kit sat with his back to the rough stone wall. He looked older than Marcus remembered him. There was more white in his hair, and he looked thinner than he had even on the long caravan road from Vanai to Porte Oliva. Marcus pulled at his chains, setting them to rattle.

"I can talk to you without being strapped to a wall," Marcus said. "We could skip to that part. I wouldn't mind."

"Do you know why we cut thumbs when signing contracts or treaties?" Kit asked, drawing a dagger from his belt. It was a simple huntsman's blade, but sharp.

"Because that's how you sign a contract," Marcus said.

"But how did it get that way? Why blood and not...I don't know. Tears. Spit. The story is that it's been that way since the dragons, but it wasn't always. That it began during the last war, when Morade forged his Righteous Servant and his clutch-mate built the Timzinae. Last race of humanity."

"All right," Marcus said. "I've never heard of a righteous servant apart from someone trying to convince me to buy a squire, but I'm going to assume you're going somewhere with this?"

"I believe it was meant to show that neither party was tainted. If one or the other had been able to cheat, to force the other into agreement, the blood would show it."

"And I'm sure you're right. Kit? Unchain me now?"

"Come. Look at this."

Kit pressed the blade to his thumb until a tiny drop of red appeared. The cut was tiny, no more than a pinprick, but the deepness of the blood made it seem almost black. No, there was a knot at the center of the drop, a tiny dark clot like a flake of scab that was forcing its way up through Kit's skin.

The scab rolled to the side, tracking bright red behind it, and extended tiny legs.

"All right. That's odd," Marcus said.

"Don't touch it. They bite. I find they're poisonous in more senses than one."

"Not to be rude, Kit, but you have spiders living in your *blood*?"

"I do. I have since I became a priest of the goddess many, many years ago. I believe we all carry the mark, though I haven't tested it." Kit caught the tiny spider and cracked it between his thumbnails. "I had a falling-out with my brothers. I'm afraid I lost my faith, and I found there was very little room for dissent. You may recall that before I left Porte Oliva word came of a new cult, drawn from the mountains east of the Keshet. It was mine. It was men who bear the same taint that I do. The war with Asterilhold and the unrest in Antea are, I think, the first, stumbling steps toward something much larger. Much worse." Kit held up his bleeding thumb. "And that is why you cut thumbs on a contract. Because of men like me."

Marcus ran his fingers through the beard that had grown during his captivity. His skin was crawling, but he kept his voice steady.

"This is the thing you were talking about. The evil that got loose in the world. It's *you*?"

"It's men like me. The taint in my blood is the sign of the goddess, but it isn't her power. Her priesthood is given gifts by her. We are the masters of truth and of lies. I told you once that I could be very persuasive and that I was very difficult to lie to. It is this way with all of us. Tell me something I couldn't know. Tell me true or lie. It doesn't matter."

"Kit, I don't think that parlor tricks—"

"I don't think you'll find this a cunning man's small magic," Kit said.

"All right. Ah. I stole honey stones from my friend when I was a boy."

"You did," Kit said. "Try again."

"The first battle I was in, I lost my sword."

"You didn't. That's a lie. Try again."

Marcus frowned. Something was shifting in the pit of his stomach, and it took him a moment to recognize it as fear.

"About a month ago, I found a silver coin in the street outside the counting house."

"No."

"It was copper."

"Ah. Yes. So it was."

Marcus let his breath out.

"That's a good trick," he said. "Could see how a man might be tempted to use that."

"I don't think it's the worst thing I can do. I find the spiders can make me impossible to disbelieve. With time and repetition, I can make anyone believe anything. However ridiculous or absurd or dangerous. If it were in my interest, I could convince you that you were a god. Or that your family was still alive but hiding from you. Even if you knew better, even if your mind knew better, your heart would lead you wherever I told it to go. I can do that, and so can they."

"And they're in Antea?"

"And very close to the throne."

Marcus sat for a moment, considering it. The corruption of kings and princes was nothing new. The twist-minded cunning man was a standard character in a thousand songs. And still, there was something about the tiny spider birthing itself out of Kit's skin that made Marcus shudder.

"What do they want?"

Kit considered his thumb. The cut was already closed, neither blood nor spiders leaking out of his body. His voice was almost contemplative.

"When I was there, I was taught that the goddess would

return justice to the world. We were to keep faith and wait for the day when she would send us a sign. A leader whose Righteous Servant we would be, and through him, the goddess would free the world from lies."

"That's a bad thing?"

"Probably, yes, but I also decided it might not be true," Kit said with a smile. "I was a very junior priest when I left. Many of the menial, small tasks fell to me. One was to be sure the temples were swept. I didn't actually sweep. There was an old man who did that. I don't even remember his name now. But I asked him one day whether he had swept, and he said yes. He had. And he was telling the truth. Do you see? I felt it in my blood, just the way I did with you. Only he was confused. He was mistaken. He thought he had. He was *certain* he had. He hadn't.

"And so I fell from grace."

"Over an unswept floor?"

"Over the proof that someone can be both certain and wrong. In my mind, I began to reserve judgment even on the revelations of the goddess. I cultivated the word *probably*. Was the temple swept? Yes, probably. But perhaps not. The goddess was eternal and just and immune to all lies, probably. We were her beloved and chosen, probably. But perhaps we weren't. I became very aware of the division between truth and certainty. I began to doubt. And once I was on that path, there was no hiding it.

"One day the high priest came to me. He had found a remedy to my unfortunate predicament. I was to be taken to the goddess herself. Deep in the temple, through the secret ways, to her holy cavern. Only the high priest was ever allowed to commune with her directly, you see. But now I was to have that honor."

The doves shifted, as if made uneasy by Kit's voice.

"Didn't like what you saw of her?"

"I ran," Kit said. "He told me that no harm would come to me, and I believed him. I knew he was lying to me, and I believed him anyway. I told myself that no harm would come to me. That she wouldn't harm her own. I had faith that what they were doing came out of love for me. As long as I had faith in her, she would not hurt me. And then, like a reflex in my mind, I thought probably. *Probably* she won't. But she might. And as soon as that doubt was there, I saw how likely it was that I was being sacrificed. I found I wasn't interested in finding religious completion. So I left."

"I get the feeling it wasn't as straightforward as that."

"It wasn't. I've spent years, decades now, in the world we never saw. It is more complicated than the priests of the goddess taught. Truth and lies, doubt and certainty. I haven't found them to be what I thought they were. I dislike certainty because it feels like truth, but it isn't. And I think I have had some inkling what it is for a whole people to become certain."

"And what's that like, then?"

"It's like pretending something, and then forgetting you were pretending. It's falling into a dream. If justice is based on certainty, but certainty is not truth, atrocities become possible. We're seeing the first of them now. More will come."

"Probably," Marcus said, and Kit's laughter startled the birds into flight.

"Yes," Kit said as a dozen small feathers floated down around them. "Probably. But it seems likely enough that I feel obligated to stop it. If I can."

"And you'd do that by...?"

"There are swords. Dragon-forged and permanently venomed. We had several at the temple, but I have found the location of another. I believe that with it, the goddess can be killed, her power broken. And so I am going to find it and go back to my home. And I will go to that sacred cavern at last."

"That's a stupid plan," Marcus said. "It's more likely to get you killed than anything else. How am I supposed to fit into this?"

"As my sword-bearer. The spiders in me dislike the blade. I don't believe I could carry it all the way back myself. I think you could. Of all the men I've met in my years after the temple, I believe that you particularly could."

Marcus shook his head.

"It all sounds a bit overheated and dramatic, Kit. The paired adventurers rushing to find the enchanted sword? Are you sure this isn't an outline of some old play about defeating a demon queen?"

Kit chuckled.

"I have spent a certain amount of time onstage. My perspective on the world may come from standing on the boards. But I believe I'm right all the same," he said. And then, gently: "Come with me. I need you."

"You've got the wrong man, Kit. I'm not some sort of chosen one."

"Yes you are. I've chosen you."

The excitement—the joy—that woke in Marcus was like being pulled by a wave. It was what he'd wanted, what he'd been wordlessly longing for all the dire, grinding weeks in Porte Oliva. And now God was giving it to him on a gold plate. He dug in his heels.

"I can't. Cithrin's in Camnipol. I have to protect her."

"Do you think you can?"

"Yes," Marcus said.

Kit raised a finger. His smile was gentle, half amused and half sorrowful.

"Remember who you're talking to. I know parlor tricks," he said. "Do you think you can?"

Marcus looked down at his filthy hands. The nails were cracked and broken from scrabbling at his restraints. He didn't have a blade or enough coin to buy a meal. Something thickened his throat.

"No."

"Neither do I," Kit said. "Neither does Yardem or that unpleasant notary the bank brought in. And I would be willing to wager that Cithrin doesn't expect it of you. If she's in need of rescue, I don't think her strategy will be to wait meekly for her adoptive father to fix things."

"She's not my daughter. I don't think of her that way."

"If you say so," Kit said.

"All right, that's going to get annoying," Marcus said.

"Marcus, it seems to me your life in Porte Oliva is over. Perhaps there's a way to return to it, forge it into armor that doesn't bite when you strap it on, but I don't see how."

"When Cithrin's back. When she's safe."

"No one's safe, Marcus. Not ever. We both know that. I believe you're looking for a noble cause to die in," Kit said. "As it happens, I have one. If we win, it will save Cithrin and countless other innocents besides. Or tell me you'd rather go back to enforcing loans, and I'll leave you."

His belly felt heavy, the truth of his situation pressing against him like being buried in sand. Still, he managed a smile.

"Unchain me before you go?"

Kit rose, put his hand on Marcus's shoulder, and turned him around. It took only a few moments, and the leather strap that had bound Marcus for what seemed like a lifetime fell away. Marcus scratched at the skin where the restraints had been, reveling in the freedom of being in command of his own body. One of the doves hopped back in through its hole and took a place on its perch.

Kit stepped back. The silence between them was woven from light and dread. Marcus had put his life in this man's hands more than once. He knew he could turn away now, go and exact vengeance on Yardem and try again to find Cithrin. The idea was still profoundly pleasant, and like all pleasant things, suspect. Kit waited.

It was idiocy. It was doomed from the start. Diving into ancient mysteries and solving the problems of the world in some grand, transforming gesture was something for the daydreams of children who didn't know the world.

"These priests. Their goddess. They're as bad as you make them out?"

"I believe they are."

"And this magic sword of yours. Where is it supposed to be?"

"In a reliquary on the northern shore of Lyoneia."

Marcus nodded.

"We'll need a boat," he said.

Dawson

Dawson locked his jaw shut as they beat him. They were young men for the most part. He knew their names, he knew their fathers. Two at least had played games with Vicarian when they had all been children together. There was a bowl of water beside the entrance, and the strips of wet leather cut more than dry would have. Others carried sticks or the wide wooden handles of axes without the metal head. It had taken so little time to take the youth of the empire, noblest blood in the world, and turn them into thugs. Dawson stood until his knees buckled. Laughter filled the air. He couldn't defend himself. Couldn't shout them down. So instead he locked his jaw and denied them the pleasure of hearing him cry out. Likely it only goaded them to worse violence. That was fine. He wasn't here to take the easy path.

He found himself on the floor, the water pail pouring over him. He sputtered, trying to draw breath from someplace in between the deluge and the stone. A voice he didn't recognize called the halt, and someone kicked his side as casually as he might have punished a lazy dog.

Hands gripped him under his arms and lifted him up. His mind felt fuzzy, confused, and distant. He was being carried somewhere he didn't want to go, and all he could remember was that it would be beneath his dignity to complain. A door opened somewhere and he landed on filthy straw that despite its thinness and the stink of it felt as comfortable as his own bed. His mind failed him for a time. Next he felt anything, it was a soft cloth cleaning the raw wounds over his ribs where the skin had split. Everything hurt. The old man tending to him wore chains on his wrists and neck and a filthy smock. It took Dawson what felt like a great deal of time to remember where he'd seen that face before.

"My thanks, Majesty," Dawson managed. His throat seemed to have spasmed at some point, and his voice sounded strangled though there was no one touching it.

King Lechan nodded.

"Don't speak yet," he said. "Rest."

There were no marks on the king of Asterilhold. No bruises on his face or old blood blackening his prison garb. Here was the man who had plotted to slaughter Prince Aster, and it was Dawson whom they tortured as a game. He wanted to find it unfair, but he didn't. He understood the difference between how you treated an enemy and how you treated a traitor. They didn't see that *they* were the ones betraying the traditions and nobility of Antea. They were the ones handing the throne to a bloodthirsty clown and his foreign masters.

Only, of course, it had been his fault as well. He should never have agreed to let Palliako be protector to the prince. It had only seemed convenient at the time. It had seemed innocuous. How could he have known it was the stray spark in a dry forest?

He rolled to his side as the enemy king protested, and forced himself up to sitting. He almost vomited. He would have if there'd been more in his belly. The cell was smaller than he'd thought. Ten feet from side to side, twelve deep. His kennels were larger.

The door opened and the high priest stepped in. The congenial smile was gone as if it had never been. No scowl took its place, and no frown. Basrahip might have been wearing a mask of himself cast from stone. Nothing about him moved. Dawson was gratified to see the lump of a bandage under the priest's cloak where the knife had bit. Four men in leather armor with swords and daggers at their sides followed him, taking the door like the personal guard of a king. Dawson turned his head and spat out a bright red clot of blood.

"Where is Prince Geder?" Basrahip asked. His voice was distant thunder.

"There is no Prince Geder," Dawson said.

"You've killed him."

"No. He's not a prince. He's Lord Regent. That's not a prince. Aster is prince and king, and Palliako is nothing more than a placeholder until he takes his father's throne."

The priest's eyes narrowed.

"Where is Geder Palliako?"

"I don't know."

One of the guards drew a dagger. More torture, then. Dawson was ashamed to feel himself drawing back from the prospect.

"And the little prince? Aster?"

"I've been looking for him since this began."

"To kill him."

"To give him my loyalty and my sword against you and Palliako."

Basrahip finally managed an expression. His wide brow kinked and furrowed. He sat on the ground in front of Dawson, his legs tucked under him. Dawson saw the guards glance at one another, confused.

"You are speaking the truth to me," the priest said.

"You're not worth lying to," Dawson managed.

Basrahip's amazement was almost comical.

"You treat truth as a kind of contempt? Oh. You are corrupt to the soul, Lord."

"I don't answer to you," Dawson said. "You're a bit of dirt that pulled itself off the riverbeds of the Keshet and started taking on airs. You aren't worthy to clean my shoes. You don't belong in the same city as Simeon. You don't deserve to breathe the air he breathed."

"Ah," the priest said, as if understanding something. "You are in love with this world. You fear the coming of justice."

"I don't fear you or your whore of a goddess," Dawson said.

"You don't," Basrahip agreed. "That is another mistake. But you cannot tell me where Prince Geder is, so you are insignificant. You have lost, Lord Kalliam. Everything you love is already gone."

Dawson closed his eyes. He had the urge to roll to his side, pressing hands over his ears like a schoolboy refusing to hear a scolding, but he knew the priest was right. He had wagered everything that Palliako could be stopped. He'd lost. It didn't matter that he'd be remembered as a traitor. To live for the legacy was only a way to pander to men as yet unborn. All that mattered was that his nation had been taken from its rightful rulers. Not even taken. Given away.

It was over.

The assault on Klin's estate had been brutal. No swords rang, no arrows flew. But for two days, the priests had shouted at them. Their voices grew more annoying than flies. The same words, again and again: *You have already lost. You cannot win.* At first, Dawson had led the others in their refusal and mockery. As if they could be talked to death. Let them waste their breath until Bannien returned.

Or if not Bannien, Skestinin. Every hour the priests spent talking was one less that they had to live.

But slowly, unmistakably, the laughter and bravado had hollowed out. Dawson had felt the growing suspicion that perhaps hope was fading. Perhaps time was allied to the enemy, and another passing day wasn't something to welcome or hope for. He didn't say it, nor did any of the others. It was in their eyes.

He'd been asleep when they came for him. The door of the withdrawing room had burst open in darkness, guardsmen with swords drawn pouring in. He'd leaped up. Even now, he could hear Clara screaming his name as they hauled him down the corridors, through the courtyard, and to the night-black streets. Odderd Mastellin had led them, his jutting chin making him look belligerent without seeming any less sheeplike. In the square, the siege tower was quiet. The priest stood before it. Behind him, in the light of the torches, the common men and women of Camnipol stood silently, like a collection of statues constructed at Basrahip's whim. The sky above was black, and the torchlight drowned the stars.

"I've brought Kalliam," Mastellin shouted. "I've brought him. Me. It's the proof that I'm loyal. I've captured the enemy of the crown."

"Congratulations," Dawson had said loud enough to reach Mastellin's ears. "You're about to be the most loyal chicken in the wolf den."

In truth, though, if Mastellin hadn't broken, another of them would. Dawson understood that. It was the unholy power of their voices, insinuating their lies until they were indistinguishable from truth. Dawson had struggled against it. What hope was there for a weak-minded man like Mastellin? Or Klin. Or any of the others.

The enemy guard had accepted Dawson as a prisoner, and he'd been hauled away to the gaol and a day of beatings and humiliations ending here, in the same hole as his own captive and hoping that somehow Clara and Jorey had slipped the cordon. If he died, he died for his own judgment. But Clara...He'd have spared her that, if he could.

"Don't blame yourself," King Lechan said. "He's more than either of us could have stood against."

"What?"

"Palliako. Geder Palliako. He isn't human. The dead walk with him and tell him their secrets."

Dawson laughed, but it made his ribs ache and he stopped.

"Have you met him?" Dawson asked. "He's a tool. He'd have been a scholar but he didn't have the discipline for it."

"I heard the guards talking about it. The one who brings the food? His brother saw Palliako by the fountain sitting with the dead king. He saw dead Simeon bow to him. This Palliako is a wizard, I think. Or a dragon in human skin."

"He's nothing like that. He's a hobbyist. He didn't command the death of your noblemen out of bloodthirst. He did it out of fear. The idea that if he could just cut off enough heads, he'd be safe. If he'd had to wield the axe himself, he'd have turned white and decided on clemency. He's petty and a coward. He's not even grand enough to be evil."

King Lechan shook his head.

"He has defeated us."

"No," Dawson said. "*I* defeated you, and that hell-born priest defeated me. Palliako may have succeeded, but he's never won anything. And he never will."

They found him," Lord Skestinin said. He sat on a small three-legged stool the guards had brought for the purpose. The prisoners were consigned to the floor, but Dawson didn't take the slight personally. He was well beyond that now. "They said he rose up out of the ground with Prince Aster at his side. Walked back to the Kingspire dressed in robes like a commoner. He'd been on the streets the whole time, but no one knows where."

"I'm surprised they aren't saying he was killed in the original attack and rose up from the grave to preserve the kingdom," Dawson said dryly.

Skestinin's chuckle had a nervous edge.

"Odd stories do seem to find ways to attach to that man, don't they?"

"You've seen him?"

"I have," Skestinin said. "We would have been here sooner, but as soon as news of the trouble came, there were uprisings all through the north. I had to decide whether to risk losing all we'd gained in Asterilhold. And I..."

You waited plausibly and at a safe distance until you saw who won, Dawson thought, but he didn't say it.

"Thank you for being my chaperone today."

"Least I could do," Skestinin said.

He wouldn't meet Dawson's eyes. It looked much like shame.

"How are Barriath and Jorey?"

"They're well, considering. They're free, for now, though Palliako's personal guard is watching them like cats stalking pigeons. It's a different city than the one I left after the wedding."

"Sorry about that," Dawson said. "The renovations I'd planned turned complicated on me."

"Don't joke about it," Skestinin said. His voice was hard now. "You'll be heard, and I'm risking enough by being here. If they hear I was cracking jokes about assassinating Prince Aster and the Lord Regent, it won't go well for me."

"I apologize," Dawson said. "Gallows humor."

The door opened and a young man—one of the group that had beaten Dawson on his arrival—looked in.

"It's time," he said. "You can bring him."

The audience chamber was packed full. The summer heat still hadn't broken, and with the press of bodies, the air felt as if it had all been breathed through twice already. Dawson had to sit on the floor behind a screen of woven iron, invisible from the court. Palliako was already on the throne on his raised dais, the crown of the Lord Regent on his brow. Aster sat at his side. Lechan, King of Asterilhold, knelt on the hard stone without so much as a cushion for his knees. From behind the screen, everything seemed in shadow, and Dawson found himself rocking from side to side trying to see the details better.

He found Clara. She was standing in the second gallery with Barriath and Jorey at her side. Good boys. Sabiha wasn't there. He found her on the first level, standing beside her mother. Basrahip was, of course, at the side where Geder could look to the man for his orders. Dawson wasn't sure how many of the spider priests he'd had killed in the final account, but he wished they'd managed one more at least.

"Watch the priest," he said softly.

"What?" Skestinin said.

"When the time comes, Palliako will look to the priest for permission. If you watch you'll see it."

"Enough, Dawson. We aren't supposed to be speaking."

"So we won't discuss it. Only keep your eye on them. You'll see what I saw."

Geder rose and the hall grew quiet. King Lechan met Geder's scowl with equanimity.

"I'm Geder Palliako, Lord Regent of Antea. Lechan of Asterilhold, you are before me now as prisoner and enemy."

"I am," the king said. He had the actor's trick of speaking in a conversational voice, only loudly enough that it carried to the farthest ends of the hall.

"I have only one question before I pass judgment upon you," Palliako said. "Were you aware of the plot within your court to see Prince Aster dead in hopes of placing a man loyal to Asterilhold on the Severed Throne."

"I was," Lechan said calmly. "I claim sole authorship and responsibility for the plan. The intention was born with me. The men in my court who took part did so only out of love for me and loyalty to my words and commands. Most were ignorant of my final design."

Palliako looked as though someone had struck him on the back of the head. When he shot a glance at Basrahip, Dawson tapped Skestinin's knee. The huge priest shook his head. No. Geder licked his lips, obviously confounded. Dawson understood, of course. It was Lechan's duty to protect his people as much as it was theirs to protect him. Battle and war were lost, and now Lechan would do all he could to eat the sins of his people and carry the retribution to the grave with him. Dawson felt a surge of respect toward this man, his enemy. If Simeon had had half the spine of Lechan, what a world he and Dawson could have made.

Geder's face was growing darker than a stormcloud. When he spoke again, his words were clipped, narrow, and rich with anger.

"All right," he said. "If that's how you want it, that's how we'll have it. Lechan of Asterilhold, for your crimes against Antea, I declare your life and your kingdom forfeit to the Severed Throne."

Lechan didn't move. His face was calm. Geder raised a hand, and the call went for the executioner. The man who came out wore the white, faceless mask. He bowed to Geder and again to Aster, then drew his sword and walked to the prisoner.

The crowd gasped when the blow struck, and then they cheered. The chorus of voices raised in joy and bloodlust was like a waterfall. It deafened. Dawson watched in silence as one enemy of his kingdom bled dry at the feet of another. The claiming of responsibility had been a noble gesture, he thought, but doomed. Palliako's wrath wouldn't be restrained by it. If he chose to spill every drop of noble blood in Asteril-hold, he would do it. There was no one left to stop him.

The guard tapped his shoulder, and Dawson realized it wasn't the first time he'd been told to stand. He rose to his feet and began the walk back toward his cell. Skestinin walked at his side, his gaze cast low. The halls of the King-spire seemed different now. Smaller, darker. It wasn't that they had changed—the structures were all just as they had been since the day they'd been built. But it also wasn't the Kingspire any longer.

As they walked out into the open air, Dawson looked to his left, craning his neck to see the dueling grounds, and beyond that the Division, and beyond that the buildings and mansions, one of which had been his. The wind was picking up, pressing a warm hand against him. It smelled of rain. He paused, looking for clouds on the horizon, and the guards shoved him.

His cell seemed larger now that he was its only occupant.

"Well," Skestinin said.

"Thank you for that," Dawson said. "And give my family my regards."

"I will."

Skestinin hesitated, desperate to leave and unable to. Dawson lifted his eyebrows.

"About Barriath," Skestinin said. "He's a good man. I've

been proud to have him. But as things are...I've asked him
to step down, and I'd rather you got word of it from me. It's
not wise right now to have a Kalliam commanding swords
or ships. Not good for him and not good for the court."

The anger came fast and clean.

"Are you going to have your daughter step down from her
marriage?" Dawson said.

Skestinin's contrition blinked out as if it had never been
there.

"Might if I could," he said. "I don't agree with what you
did, Dawson, but you'll face your judgment and take the
consequences. My Sabiha didn't have the choice. They said
she was a slut. Now they're going to say she's a traitor too."

"But she isn't," Dawson said. "Truth isn't what other people say. Sabiha isn't a traitor, and she isn't a slut. If she
doesn't know that without someone telling her, you've done
a poor job as a father."

For a moment, Skestinin didn't answer. His expression
was incredulous, fading slowly to disgust. Or worse, pity.

"You don't change, Kalliam."

"No," Dawson said. "I don't."

Geder

Geder stalked through the halls of the Kingspire. He had expected that the death of King Lechan would leave him feeling better. Relieved, perhaps. Victorious, certainly. Instead, he felt grumpy. He'd thought that returning to his bed and his place in the Kingspire would be more of a homecoming, the end to his time in exile. If anything, he felt less at home now than he had before.

When he'd been his own man, back before King Simeon had died, there had been days spent in his library, immersed in a translation, his mind utterly focused. He would forget to eat. He would forget to rest. Everything in him would come to a single point, a perfect kind of clarity. And when, as inevitably happened, something broke the trance, he would discover that he was hungry, thirsty, exhausted, and in the ragged edge of pissing himself. And even when all his bodily needs had been satisfied, he would still feel displaced, still reaching for that next word or phrase, the nuance that best captured what he thought the original author had intended. Everything around him—walls, chairs, people— could seem unreal.

The Kingspire, and in truth all of Camnipol, felt odd and unstructured. Out of joint. His mind and memory were aimed behind him, at a dusty, stinking ruin. Days in darkness with nothing to do but play simple puzzle games by the light of a candle and talk to a part-Cinnae banker. Cithrin bel Sarcour. Part of him was still there, with her, in that darkness. All the rest was distraction.

Geder knew he was the most powerful man in Camnipol, in Antea, quite possibly in the world. He could command the death of kings. The men who had mocked him once lived in fear of him now. It was everything he'd wanted. Everything he'd hoped for. Only now, he found, he wanted more. He wanted to wake in the morning and dress himself. He wanted to sit in his library and read until he slept. He wanted to sit and talk with Aster, or with Cithrin. He wanted to feel her body against his again.

And why not? Why couldn't he have these things? And more than that, why *shouldn't* he?

The chief valet was an older man with powder-pale skin and a fringe of hair around an age-speckled pate. He answered to Geder's summons immediately, bowing his way across the chamber.

"You called for me, Lord Regent?" he said.

Geder felt the unease in his belly and tried to put it aside.

"I don't...I've decided I don't want to be dressed anymore. I don't need people to put my clothes on me or bathe me or trim my toenails. I've done all of that myself for years, and I managed."

"The dignity of the regency, my lord, like the dignity of a king, is not—"

"I didn't call you here to be lectured," Geder said. "You're here so that I could tell you something. I don't want people to come dress me in the morning. Bring the clothes, draw the bath, and get out. Do you understand that? I want my privacy, and I'll take it."

"Yes, Lord Regent," the older man said, his lips pressed together in disappointment and disapproval. "As you see fit."

"Is this a problem?"

The man practically vibrated, conflicting impulses warring behind pale and watery eyes.

"Tradition, Lord Palliako, and the dignity of the throne argue against a man of your stature and position acting as his own servant. It diminishes—"

"Strip," Geder said.

"My lord?"

"Your clothes. Take them off."

"I don't—"

Geder rose up, gesturing at the impassive faces of his personal guard.

"I have men with swords at my command. I am the regent of Antea. I sit the Severed Throne. When I tell you to do something, I'm not opening a debate. Take off your clothes."

Trembling, his cheeks burning scarlet, the old man undid his robes. His undershirt was a pale yellow silk. His undergarments showed a spot of blood at the flank where the old man had a small round scab, a blemish that would not heal. His pubic hair was the yellow of white cheese and his belly sagged. Geder stood up. There was neither disappointment nor disapproval in the man's face now.

"Why my good sir," Geder said. "What ever is the matter? You don't seem to enjoy this."

The servant didn't speak.

"Do you?"

"Lord?"

"Do you enjoy this?"

"I do not, my lord."

Geder walked up, putting his face inches from the old man's. With each word he spoke, the servant winced.

"Neither. Do. I."

Geder turned on his heel, walking out of the room. Behind

him, he heard his personal guard following and the soft sounds of the servant picking up his fallen clothes. And that simply, it was done. The ritual morning humiliations were over, and no one was going to laugh about it. Now the relief that killing King Lechan hadn't provided flowed into him. Odd how the important things in life could be the smallest ones. He considered whether to clear his schedule, take all the audiences slated for the day, and set them to the winds. He could take his books to a comfortable place and have food and drink brought to him. Now that he'd done some—one—small thing genuinely for himself, anything seemed possible.

But no. Not yet. All of that could come on another day.

The banker looked perfectly at home in the grandeur of the meeting chamber. Canl Daskellin sat at his side, the pair of them smiling and joking as if they hadn't seen the king of Asterilhold die that morning. Paerin Clark wore modest clothes of simple cut that looked understated rather than plain. Basrahip sat at the foot of the table, his genial smile the same as ever. Geder looked for Cithrin, but she wasn't there. He tried to keep the disappointment from showing.

"My Lord Regent," Daskellin said as all but Basrahip rose. "Thank you for making time."

"Pleased to do it," Geder said. "I've been looking forward to meeting you. Cithrin speaks highly of you, even behind your back."

"I'm gratified to hear it," Paerin Clark said. "She sends her regrets, my lord. We suffered certain losses in the trouble, and Magistra Cithrin's particular attention was needed to address some of them. I'm sure she would have come if circumstances had been different."

Geder glanced at Basrahip, who nodded. A twist of anxiety Geder hadn't known he was carrying relaxed. He was glad she wasn't avoiding him. And he hadn't made an effort to seek her out, as full as everything had been on his arrival. There would be time. The thought of seeing her again left him feeling a little breathless.

"Tell her I'm sorry she wasn't here," Geder said, smiling. "And I'm very sorry that all of this happened when you were in Camnipol. Really, armed insurrection isn't as common as it's seemed these last couple of years."

Paerin Clark laughed, and Daskellin followed along.

"That does bring me to the reason we came in the first place," the banker said. "Antea is in a difficult transition. The passing of King Simeon followed by the war, and now all of this. Any one of these could shake a kingdom. All three coming as they have are certain to."

"Yes, I'm told that the harvest's going to be a bit thin this year," Geder said. "But it won't be a problem."

"You sound very confident. That's good. Antea will want a steady hand. In that regard, I'm here in part to—"

"Oh stop it," Daskellin said, with a chuckle. "Clark's here to say that his bank would want to put their toes in Camnipol. They don't lend to the nobility. It's policy, and likely a wise one. But they can bring in gold to lend to artisans and merchants. When I went to Northcoast, I thought we'd still be fighting a war when I got back."

"Banks are at their best when there isn't war," Paerin Clark said. "Trade in peacetime is always more reliable and regular. And stabilizing."

"Have you thought about opening a branch here?" Geder asked.

For the first time, Paerin Clark seemed at a loss.

"Yes, actually," he said. "But the climate of court didn't seem open to the idea."

"I think you should," Geder said. "Camnipol's the center

of the world. Antea's the greatest empire there is. Seems silly that you shouldn't be here. More trade, right?"

"You heard the part about not lending to nobles?" Daskellin said, and Geder waved the comment away.

"Lend to other people," he said. "Then they'll have enough money on hand that we can tax them."

"Well, if that's something we should consider," the banker said, "perhaps we can talk about the challenges facing Antea in the coming years, and how we might be able to help."

The meeting went longer than Geder had intended, the conversation ranging from the division of Asterilhold into new baronies and holdings under the control of Antean noble houses to the possibility of buying up grain supplies from Sarakal to ease the coming harvest to the new Antean border with Northcoast and the changing diplomatic position with King Tracian. In truth, Geder didn't care deeply about any of it, but Paerin Clark knew Cithrin, and so Geder wanted the man to think well of him.

When at last the meeting ended, Geder made his farewells and walked back to his private rooms, Basrahip at his side.

"So?" Geder asked. "What do you think of him?"

"He means the things that he says," Basrahip answered, "but he chooses what he says very carefully. He is a wise man, but not holy. We will be careful of him."

"Good idea," Geder said. "I agree."

"There is another matter."

"Kalliam," Geder said.

"No. With him, nothing need be said. All his roads have ended. But in his fear of the coming justice, he made the servants of the goddess his targets. His hatred of us has taken its toll. We have lost many, my lord. With the new temples you are sworn to build in these cities that fall before you, I must ask that more of my brethren are permitted to join us."

"How many more?"

"I would send for ten cohorts of ten," Basrahip said.

"A hundred?" Geder said. "Is that all? Of course you can. If it's a question of seeing them with food and shelter, I can send a hundred servants away tonight and not miss them tomorrow. In fact, why not take Kalliam's mansion? I mean, it won't be enough space, I don't think, but there's a poetry in it."

They paused at a small fountain, water pouring over the shoulders of an ancient king and flowing down the half-sized noblemen and -women at his feet, and then a miniature horde of carved-stone peasants. Political philosophy as decoration.

"I am grateful to you, Prince Geder."

"You don't need to be. I couldn't do any of this without you."

The fear came with night. He couldn't think why that would be. Darkness had been the best part of all that had come before, but now when the sun failed, Geder found the face of Dawson Kalliam coming to him. The flash of the blade. The blood on Basrahip's hand.

Sitting in his library now, his personal guard discreetly at a distance, he knew he was in no danger. But he hadn't seen danger in Kalliam's revel either. If there was one thing to learn, it was that danger came at any time and from any quarter. He fought the darkness with light. Lamps and lanterns and candles glowed in among the papers and piles of books, pressing back the night.

His own collection, product of a lifetime's gathering, wasn't so much as a quarter of what stood in the royal archive, but the archive reflected the tastes and opinions of any number of scholars. It had all the genres in some degree—

poetry, moral tales, histories—but speculative essay, his own particular favorite, was thin. And besides that, there was a comfort in reading again what he already read, and he was here for comfort.

The pillow essays traced back to the reign of the second Queen Esteya and addressed everything from points of court politics and rivalries between people whose names were now otherwise forgotten to speculations on the sexuality of the various races. The dialect was simple enough to follow, especially since he was used to translating from other languages. When he'd read it before, it had been a guilty pleasure. Titillating and embarrassing. What he knew of women and their bodies had, for the most part, come from this book and others like it.

It is the nature of women or any race except the Firstblood to be attracted to men most like the original forms of man. The Jasuru find most pleasing men with the thinner scales of colors more near to flesh. Southling women, apart from those given over to being their pod's breeding stock who need not concern us here, choose men with smaller, lighter eyes. Women of the Yemmu will, given the option, provide themselves to males of slighter frame and more upright stance. Indeed the races would, in time, fade back into a single form if it were not for the masculine drive to explore carnally the exotic.

The scandals of Robbe Sastillin are the classic example. Here was a man of noble frame and blood, a man with real possibilities and prospects in the court who took a series of Cinnae girls to his bed. It debased him and ruined the girls, but in the moment each was acting from the base impulse natural to them.

Geder put a fingertip on the passage, leaning back in his chair. It didn't seem plausible to him. Not for the first time, he wished that Basrahip and the goddess could speak to the truth of written words as well as those that were spoken.

Was it true? he wondered. Would a woman of one of the crafted races be drawn to a Firstblood man simply because of his race? Had Cithrin bel Sarcour chosen him because he was himself, or because he was Lord Regent, or because he was a Firstblood? Was there any way to tease apart the logic that had brought them to that singular moment in the darkness? He wondered what Basrahip would tell him if he could bring her to speak of it in the priest's presence. Not that he ever would, but it was hard not to speculate.

He wondered whether she was thinking of him.

Aster's voice startled him.

"Here you are."

Geder clapped the book closed and turned to the prince. Aster looked older now. As if the days underground had sharpened his cheeks. Geder wondered if that was normal. He would have guessed that children grew to adults imperceptibly, each day's change too small to see, each week too small, each month. The changes may be clear if seen year by year by year, but maybe that was wrong. Maybe people stayed just the same for long stretches of time, and then shifted suddenly, becoming someone different than they'd been. Or not different, but older. More mature. More themselves.

"Yes," Geder said. "I was reading. It's a long day, and I thought..."

Aster nodded. His face might not have changed shape. It might only have been the solemnity of his expression that had changed, though why their time with Cithrin would have done that and the death of King Simeon hadn't... Or maybe it was one thing coming as it did after another.

That was certainly how Geder felt about himself.

"You haven't done anything about Kalliam yet."

"I know," Geder said. "I mean, I have. I've given his estate to Basrahip. For priests. That's something. I did something."

Aster sat on the table, his legs swinging under it. His silence was reproach enough.

"It's Jorey," Geder said. "Dawson's his father. I can't execute my friend's father."

"Are you certain he's your friend?"

Geder looked out toward the gardens, but the light had turned the glass to a dark mirror and all he could make out was himself and his books. Piles and piles of words that were neither truth nor lies.

"No," he said. "And I know that I could just ask, and Basrahip would tell me. But I don't want to. Because what if he isn't? What if it all runs so deep that I don't have anyone left? No, don't. I know it makes sense to do the thing. I know I'd be better off knowing. Only, I could read a book first. Or talk with one of Cithrin's bank people. Or anything, really. In any given hour, I can find something I'd rather do than know."

"Why aren't you angry at him?"

"Jorey?"

"Dawson. The father. He tried to kill you."

"I know. And I should be. Maybe I am, just...I mean, it's not like he laughed at me. He takes me seriously enough to think I'm worth killing. It's just that I liked him. I did. And I wish he liked me too."

"I don't think he does," Aster said.

Geder laughed.

"I think you're right. I'll do what needs doing. And I won't die. I promise."

Geder wondered whether this was what it was to have a

son. He didn't think so. It was too much like having a friend, and father and sons were something—many things—but not that. Perhaps it was that they both knew what it was to lose someone important. Or that they were the two men in Antea so wrapped in power and privilege that it isolated them.

"What are you going to do?" Aster asked.

"I'll see him punished," Geder said. "I'll see all of it stopped. Whoever it is. And I'll see that this never happens again. Agreed?"

Aster considered silently for a moment, then nodded. Geder put his book on the table, stood, and blew the first candle out. Aster joined him, snuffing each wick until darkness and a breath of smoke was all that was left of the library.

"So," Geder said as they walked out, man and boy side by side, together but not touching, "I know nothing would be possible so long as I'm Lord Regent. But once I'm done with my watch and the throne's yours? How bad do you think the scandal would be if I married a banker?"

Cithrin

Cithrin walked through the charred ruins of the inn. It was dreamlike. Strange. She'd stood there not a month before and heard Smit's voice again. When she had, the stone walls of the inn had been as strong and permanent as mountains. Now soot stained them, and the roof had fallen in where the supporting timbers had burned out. It seemed unlikely that this was the same place. Or even the same city. Perhaps it wasn't.

"I went through it all as best I could, Magistra," the woman said. She was Firstblood, thicker than Cithrin. Darker-skinned with ruddy cheeks and dark smudges of exhaustion and loss under her eyes. "I found what I could, but it was little. They took a good bit before they burned it, and the fire took the rest, most part."

"Show me," Cithrin said.

The little courtyard was laid out in squares now. A bit over two dozen of them. At a guess, they were the men and women who'd paid for the woman's hospitality and been overtaken. The woman stopped at a square of blackened cloth.

"This was in about the right place, Magistra," she said. "It was in the corner away from the worst of it. There's a few things might be worth keeping."

Cithrin squatted down. Everything smelled of smoke and

ash. Yes, here was the green dress she'd brought from Carse. Here was a thin silver necklace, the links fused. If this had been in the corner farthest from the fire, it had still been a kiln. The notebook she'd kept had burned along all its edges, but the center pages had only yellowed and curled. When she flipped through them, the reek of smoke was overwhelming. She tossed it aside. The blue silk cloak, ruined. The wool, ruined. A ring of gold and gems that wasn't hers she put aside for the innkeeper to either find its right finger or keep for herself.

Moving the ruined scraps of cloth, her fingers touched something hard and solid as stone. She pulled the dragon's tooth free. It was perfectly white. The complicated roots looked like a sculpture of water. Amid all the human destruction, the dragon's tooth stood untouched. She wasn't sure whether she found the idea reassuring or eerie, but either way, the tooth was hers. She slipped it into her pocket.

Another man came, and the innkeeper went to speak with him. Not another guest of the ruined house, but a tax assessor come to negotiate. The small people might suffer their tragedies, but the taxmen had bought the rights to collect, and if they couldn't make back the contract, their own children would go wanting. And so it all went on, endless and merciless and unyielding.

Cithrin stepped out to the street. The necklace she could sell as silver. The tooth was as uselessly beautiful as it had ever been. Everything else was a loss.

The tailor's shop was across a wide courtyard from the bathhouse where Cithrin had spent a full day after rising up out of the bolt-hole. She'd washed in the wide copper tubs, scrubbing her hair until it stood wide and unruly as a dandelion puff. She'd scraped herself with the wooden slats until her skin was pink as a newborn mouse. And still, when she'd walked out to the street, she'd felt the grit at her scalp and smelled the cat piss on her skin. In the end, she'd been forced to conclude it was all an illusion of habit, and she'd best just pour on the rosewater and wait for the feeling to fade. But in leaving, she'd seen the tailor's and made note of it.

Part of what made the place stand out was that the proprietor was Dartinae. Camnipol was a Firstblood city, and while there were a few people here and there of many of the races, to see a Dartinae with a business of his own was strange enough to make Cithrin well inclined toward him even before she went in.

"Yes, miss," he said as she stepped in from the street. "Can I help you?"

"I hope so," she said. "I am here from Porte Oliva, and my entire wardrobe has been reduced to ash. I'm going to need several pieces and I'm in a bit of a rush."

It was, she knew, the unsubtle merchant signal that she was willing to pay a little more coin if he was willing to give her a little more of his attention. It worked as she knew it would. He took her measurements with string and wax, making small notations in a system she'd never seen, and then bringing out samples of his work. She commissioned two dresses formal enough to stand before a king, or in this case Lord Regent. It was odd to think of dressing formally to attend Geder, but that was the world now. They weren't living like beggars and refugees, so she couldn't dress like one.

She'd also need something warm and sturdy for the journey back to Carse, but for those she'd check the rag shops and talk with Cary about where the company was getting its costumes. Maybe she could even commission something very simple from Hornet. He had a decent eye as a costumer, and despite the riches from Aster's clothes, a theater company was never so well off that it would turn away the coin.

"And perhaps a cloak, miss?" the Dartinae said, holding up what seemed a massive expanse of sewn black leather. "It is the fashion."

On whim, she tried it. It felt like she was swimming in a night-black sea and looked like she was being eaten by shadows. She shook her head and handed it back.

"Just the others, thank you."

"You're sure?" The tailor's eyes glowed a bit brighter. "It is the fashion."

When she found her way back to Lord Daskellin's mansion, Paerin Clark was waiting with an odd expression. The baron had been kind enough to offer lodging to the members of the Medean bank in no small part because of the extraordinary circumstances and his role in bringing them to the city. The understood message being that their welcome shouldn't be taken as precedent. Daskellin was, after all, a Baron of Antea. They might break bread in a peasant dining room in Carse, but this was Camnipol and his home. There were standards and boundaries. For instance, she went in by the side doors.

She walked up the wide stone stairs, her eyebrows raised in query. Paerin's smile was calm, disarming, and so practiced that she was sure he was unaware of it.

"I've just come from meeting with the Lord Regent," he said, opening the door for her.

"Yes?"

"He is in an astoundingly companionable frame of mind," Paerin said. "He suggested that the Medean bank might consider opening a branch in Camnipol."

"Really," she said, stepping into the hallway. The rooms they'd been given were the largest in the servants' quarters, and reaching them meant walking through the kitchen. "That doesn't seem likely, does it?"

"I wouldn't have thought so. But I also wouldn't have expected to be asked. And not only that, but he seemed very reluctant to have me leave. We talked for easily twice the time allotted for the audience. I almost had the sense he was working from some other agenda."

Cithrin laughed low in her throat.

"And what sort of agenda would that be?" she asked.

"That was what I wanted to ask you. You've become the bank expert of Geder Palliako. Why would he want a branch of the bank?"

Cithrin paused by a thin black doorway so unobtrusive it apologized for itself. Outside the servants' door, the voices of young women of the court floated like birdsong, beautiful and rich and essentially empty of meaning.

"I can't say for certain," she said, "but I would guess that he was hoping I might be set to watch over it."

"Really now," Paerin Clark said. "And you wouldn't have put that thought in his mind, would you? I only ask because your interest in running a branch is fairly well known."

"I don't want just any branch," Cithrin said. "I want mine. If you offered me Camnipol...well, I might accept, but you'd have to pay me a great deal more."

"His idea, then."

"His."

"That's quite interesting too. Is there anything you'd like to add to your official report?"

"No," Cithrin said. "There isn't."

"Where are your loyalties?" he asked. His tone of voice was precisely the same, but she could sense that the question was deeper, and she thought for a long moment before she answered.

"I don't know. I think we're in the process of finding that out, you and I. Don't you?"

"As a matter of fact, I do," he said. "Oh. And there's a letter come from dare I call it your branch. From a Yardem Hane? Nothing critical I don't think. Only that Captain Wester resigned. This Hane person was his second, and he's stepped in the role."

"What?"

He looked up at her, concern in his eyes.

"Is that a problem?"

Cithrin felt shocked and hollowed. He wouldn't be there when she went back. She tested the thought and found it implausible. Of course Marcus would be there. He was *always* there. Something must have happened, but she couldn't think what it would be, of what could make it all right.

"Not a problem," she said. "Only a surprise."

I might be able to get you some interest from Geder," Cithrin said. "Having the patronage of the Lord Regent could make you all quite fashionable."

"You're moving," Hornet said around a mouthful of pins. "Stop moving."

"I'd be quite happy for whatever patronage we could find," Cary said, lifting one of the mock swords and considering it. "But I'm not sure how much the Lord Regent is going to want to remember his time with the company."

"Don't know about that," Sandr said. "It was an adventure, wasn't it? It isn't like it's a thing everyone in court will have done."

"I don't think court grandees score points off each other by bragging on who's lived in the most squalid filth," Cary said. "Really, that hole reeked."

"I suppose it did," Cithrin said. "Well, if you don't make yourselves the favorite company of the noble classes of Camnipol, then what? Come back south?"

"Anyplace that's not so hot the stones sweat would be fine with me," Sandr said.

"Oh, don't bother leaving for that," Smit said. "This heat's about to break. You can smell it, if you know how."

Sandr snorted and rolled his eyes.

"You can't call the weather," he said.

"Sure I can," Smit said.

"No you can't. You always say the same thing. It's always that there's a storm coming. You'll go on for weeks that way." Sandr shifted his face, lengthening his jaw and pulling down in the eyes somehow that Cithrin didn't entirely understand. The imitation was so good, he seemed like Smit's brother. When he spoke, the voice was Smit's. "Storm's coming. Mark me, storm's coming."

"And I'm always right," Smit said. "Sometimes it just takes a little longer for it to get here."

"But you could just as well say snow's coming and claim every winter proved you right."

"I would be," Smit said. "And besides that, storm's coming."

Cary turned, catching Cithrin's eye. They smiled at each other. This was Cary's family, and she loved it. Cithrin loved it too, though it wasn't hers. They were friends, some of them dear, but her home wasn't in the cart or on the stage or sleeping in the hayloft above some new stable. Hers was in the counting house and the café.

"All right," Hornet said. "Let me throw some stitches on that, and you'll have a nice simple traveler's dress, perfect for any occasion involving mud, mules, and mischief. And I've put in a little pocket here you can hide a knife in case the caravan master sets his aim for your virtue."

"I will fear no caravan master," Cithrin said in an artificial voice, the parody of stagecraft. Her bow was florid and unlikely to match. "My eternal thanks."

Hornet returned the gesture in kind, perfectly, and they both laughed.

Cithrin knew the rule from the first time she'd traveled with the company, back when Master Kit had been its control: run against the stream. In a city struck by plague, comedy. In a rich city in prosperous times, tragedy. The power of the stories they told was in the distance they took the people standing in the audience. Tonight, they were doing The Dog Chaser's Tale, which was about as low and bawdy a farce as Cithrin had ever seen. They did it well. Sandr's delivery of the lines had, she was sorry to admit, a certain genius to them. But her attention wasn't on the stage, but the men and women looking up at it.

When Smit leaped to the stage with the enormous leather phallus bulging out of his costume, the crowd roared and pointed. Tears streamed down their cheeks. They were hungry for this, Cithrin thought. They were desperate for pleasure, joy, laughter. And of course they were. They'd faced a conspiracy by their neighboring kingdom, the death of their king, war, and now a vicious battle on their own streets. They had earned their desires.

But she couldn't look away. A boy barely old enough to shave was laughing so hard he rolled back on the stone-paved ground. On the stage, Charlit Soon pretended to be a cunning man changing his shape into a woman and then being wooed by another man, and an ancient-looking toothless woman slapped her knees and roared. It was too much. The laughter bordered on the grotesque. Cithrin sat on the side of the crowd, stage and audience equally in her view.

There was no sense of victory. There had been when she'd first arrived. There had been banners and cloth, and children running in the streets throwing handfuls of bright and shining confetti. When Antea had conquered Asterilhold, the empire had been giddy and drunk. The defeat of Daw-son Kalliam had no joy for them. The hilarity wasn't a mask. It was one side of a coin, and Cithrin had the growing suspicion that the image on the coin's other side was a bleakness that Camnipol would be a long time in shedding. It would be comedy along the Division's side for more than this season. The prospect left her with a feeling of dread and anxiety that was more personal than she liked.

Cary strode forth on the stage, the mock sword in her hand going limp and flaccid in the middle of her dueling challenge. The crowd laughed, and Cithrin didn't. She gathered herself and walked along the side of the crowd and into the common room of Yellow House.

The press of bodies wasn't as bad inside as out, but the heat was worse. The high summer of Camnipol meant a sunset that lasted until the early dawn was almost beginning. That it was dark now meant it was very late. There were a dozen men and women sitting at tables, drinking cider and beer out of brown mugs and eating hard cheese and twice-baked bread. The lovers of laughter had been drawn outside by the show. The ones who remained in the swelter were a somber bunch, which fit Cithrin's mood nicely.

The beer was rich and thick, and the alcohol in it bit at the soft flesh inside her mouth. It was a beer to get drunk with, and tempting as it was, she wasn't ready to lose herself. Not yet. Something was turning restlessly in the back of her mind. A thought or insight fighting its way into being. She looked down at the rough planks of the table and listened.

"He was with Asterilhold from the start," a man behind her said. "You think he was really able to make it to Kaltfel so easy without old Lechan giving permission, may God piss on his dead heart."

"But the Lord Regent knew, didn't he?" the woman beside

him said. "Flushed the traitors out. Killed Lechan, and he'll break down the rest of them when he's ready. You watch."

"You heard what he was doing while the battle was on?"

"Up in the Kingspire calling the whole damned thing like he was a kid playing sticks."

"No," the woman said. "That's what they want you to think, but he was out in the streets the whole time. Dressed like a beggar, and he'd go right into the enemy lines and see what they were planning. No one looked at him twice."

"That's true," another man said. He was older, with a white mustache and bloodshot skin. "I saw him. Knew him. I mean, didn't know it was him. Old Jem, he called himself. I knew there was something odd up with Old Jem, but I never guessed the truth."

"And he talks with the dead," the first woman said. "My cousin guards the tombs, and the thing all his men know that no one talks about is how the Lord Regent goes there all the time. All the time. Twice a day, sometimes. Walks right into the tombs. My cousin says if you go listen, you can hear Palliako talking just like he was sitting here like we are. Joking and asking questions and having his half of a debate. And sometimes you can hear other voices too, talking back."

"He's no cunning man," the first man said. "I've known cunning men. Half of them couldn't magic up a fart. Palliako's something else, and we're damned lucky to have him on the throne. Damned lucky."

"No one else could have seen through Kalliam," the man with the white mustache said. "I sure as hell didn't. And you know what else no one talks about? Kalliam's advisors? They were all Timzinae. Now you tell me that's coincidence."

Cithrin listened, her hand around her mug. She forgot to drink from it. Instead, she listened to story pile upon story pile upon story as Geder Palliako grew toward legend.

Clara

The soldiers came with an edict from the Lord Regent. It wasn't that Clara had expected it, so much as that she wasn't surprised when it happened. Indeed, there was a level on which it was a relief. The long days of anticipation after Dawson's capture had been perverse in their normalcy. Waking in her room without him, speaking with the servants and the slaves, walking through the gardens. It was the same routine that she'd kept while he was away leading the war on Geder's behalf. Only instead, her husband was in the gaol. The anticipation of consequences had been so terrible that when the first one came, it felt almost like relief.

She stood in the courtyard before the house as they took her things away. The bed that her children had been conceived and born in. The violets from her solarium. Her gowns and dresses. Dawson's hunting dogs, whining and looking confused on the thin leather leads. She had a purse of her own and a bag she'd put together during the grace period the captain had allowed her. It wasn't in the order. If he'd lifted her on his shoulder and thrown her to the street, he would have been within the letter of Geder Palliako's law. He hadn't, and she was grateful.

"They can't do this," Jorey said. His voice was tight as a violin string. Outrage made him taut.

"Of course they can, dear," Clara said. "You didn't think

they would let us go on living the way we'd been, did you? We're disgraced."

"You didn't do anything wrong."

I did, though, she thought. *I loved your father. And that is a treason in which I persist.* She didn't say it. Only took her youngest son by the hand and led him away.

The staff of the mansion, servants and slaves, stood at the street, their personal belongings in their hands. They looked like survivors of a cataclysm. Clara went to them, their mistress for the last time. Andrash still had the chain around his neck; his eyes were wide and horrified. Clara raised her hands.

"I am afraid that, as I think you've seen, the needs of the house have been somewhat reduced," she said. There were tears in her eyes, and she clenched her jaw against them.

Lift your chin, she told herself. *Smile. There, like that.*

"If you have been a slave of the house, I release you from your indenture. I hope your freedom treats you at least as well as your captivity has. If you have been a paid servant, I can offer letters of recommendation, but I'm afraid they may not carry much weight."

Someone was sobbing in the back. One of the cook's girls, Clara thought.

"Don't be afraid," Clara said. "You will all find your new places in the world. This is unpleasant. Painful, even. But it is not the end. Not for any of us. Thank you all very, very much for the work you've done here. I am very proud to have had such wonderful people working for me, and I will remember all of you fondly."

It took the better part of an hour, going through the whole crowd, saying her goodbyes to each of them in turn. Especially at the end, they kept wanting to embrace her and swear that they'd always be loyal to her. It was sweet, and she hoped at least some of it was true. She was going to need allies in the days ahead. She wasn't in a position to turn away the kind opinion of a third footman.

Jorey slung her bag over his shoulder and took her arm. They walked through the streets together. She stopped at a corner stand and bought candied violets from an old Tralgu man with a missing foot. The petals softened against her tongue as the sugar melted. She steered them south, toward the Silver Bridge. Lord Skestinin's house was on the opposite side of the Division, and Sabiha, bless the girl, had gone ahead to see that they were made welcome.

"I think this must be seen as an indication that your father will be called to account soon," she said. "This won't be easy."

"You don't have to worry, Mother," he said. "I won't disgrace him. He won't have to stand alone."

She stopped. Jorey went on another few steps before he realized that she had.

"You *will* disgrace him," she said. "You will renounce him and deny him. Do you understand me? You will turn your back on him and let the whole world see you do it."

"No, Mother."

She raised her hand, commanding silence.

"This isn't a debate at the club. Filial piety is all well and good, but that isn't the time we're living in. You have obligations. To Sabiha and to me."

He was weeping now too, and in the street. Well, if they were going to make a spectacle of themselves, she supposed this would be the day for it. A cart rattled past them and she put her hand on his arm.

"Your father knows that you love and respect him. Nothing will change that. And he knows that you have a wife of your own. A life that he helped to give you. He won't resent your protecting that. We don't have very much left. We aren't giving away what we do."

"Father deserves to have someone beside him."

Clara smiled, her heart breaking just a little more. Her son, loyal as a dog. *We raised him well*, she thought.

"He does deserve that," she said, "but he wouldn't *want* it. I'm only his wife, but he deserves to have his sons by his side. Only then he'd be distracted trying to protect us all. He knows you love him. He knows that you honor him in your heart. Seeing that you were suffering with him and because of him would make whatever happens to him worse. So you will renounce him. Change your name, likely. Do whatever you have to do to be as good a man to your Sabiha as Dawson has been to me."

"But—"

"That's what you will do," she said. "Do you understand?"

"Yes, Mother," he said.

"Good," she said.

Lord Skestinin's mansions in the city were modest at best, a nod to convention more than an actual working household. He was a naval man. His summer seasons were spent on the sea, not in the court, and his winters were at his holding or, rarely, on the King's Hunt. Clara stowed her few things in a cell hardly larger than her dressing room, made up her face and straightened her gown, and went immediately back out to the street. The hour was almost upon her, and the shock of losing her home pressed her into action.

Curtin Issandrian's mansion looked somewhat reduced, partly because it shared a courtyard with the house that belonged to the Baron of Ebbingbaugh, Geder Palliako. When Aster ascended, Palliako would retire there, and in the meantime it was being kept up as a point of pride. Any mansion would pale if compared to the Lord Regent's, and Issandrian had fallen on hard times.

The door slave announced her, and almost at once, Curtin Issandrian led her into his withdrawing room. She was about to take her pipe from its holder when she realized she'd left all her tobacco at the house. She didn't have any, and she didn't feel right begging that when she'd already come to ask so much of him.

"I heard that your mansion has been confiscated," he said. "I am truly sorry."

"Well, I could hardly expect to keep it. The holding in Osterling Fells is gone too, of course. And I don't think Dawson was actually Baron of Kaltfel for long enough that I'll feel that loss. I'll miss the holding, though. It's a pretty place in winter."

"I recall," the man said, smiling. "Your hospitality was always excellent. Even to your husband's rivals."

"Oh, especially to them," Clara said. "What sort of virtue does it take to be nice to your friends?"

Issandrian laughed at that. Good. He might be willing to hear her out. They talked about small things for a few more minutes. The heat of the day wasn't so bad yet that the withdrawing room became unpleasant. It would come, but not yet.

"I confess I've come for more than kind words and comfort," she said, "though you're quite good at both of those."

"How can I help?" he asked.

"You and my husband are acknowledged enemies."

"Not so far as that, I hope. Rivals, perhaps."

"No. Enemies. And there's a sincerity in being a man's enemy. It puts you in a position to help me. I have nothing to offer you in exchange, but if you can, please speak on behalf of my sons and daughters. Not formally, but in the Great Bear and privately. I should be very grateful."

"Daughters? I thought you only had one."

"Elisia and Sabiha," Clara said.

"Ah," Issandrian said. He didn't look so bad with his hair

cut short. Now that he'd worn it this way for a time, it became familiar. The difference was only a difference after all.

"You have always been very kind to me, Lady Kalliam," Issandrian said. "Even when your husband was hoping for my death. I have very little influence anymore, but what I have is yours."

"Thank you," Clara said.

After the first, the rest were easy, or if not easy at least inevitable. If she could go begging to Curtin Issandrian, surely her cousin Erryn Meer would be simple to appeal to. And the women she'd had for needlecraft demonstrations, and the poetry group that Lady Emming had arranged, and so on through the city and through the court and through her day.

She was no stranger to these sorts of little informal audiences, but she'd always been on the other side. Offering sympathy with cookies and support without promises. The form was familiar. The only change was the role she played and the stakes she played for.

Elisia, thankfully, had already shed the Kalliam name. Safe in the bosom of Annerin, she could still be seen in court and her position was secure. Vicarian was less secure, but still better than he might have been. He'd been out of Camnipol for the trouble. He hadn't served in the field. His loyalty was to God and the priesthood of the kingdom. He would have to renounce Dawson, but as long as he did, he should be safe.

Barriath and Jorey were in the greatest danger, and so she concentrated her work there, doggedly calling on everyone she knew, everyone she could think of who might still accept her socially. Anyone to whom she had once been known. She used all those past moments of grace and unnecessary kindness as a tool now. And like any untested tool, sometimes it would work as she hoped. Other times it would fail under strain. She might never know which was which. Nor did it matter, so long as her children were safe.

She stopped at the beginning of evening meals when she could no longer politely intrude uninvited and found a small baker's shop that sold yesterday's rolls with sausages and black mustard and beer. She reached for her pipe again and put it away cursing under her breath. She would have to find a way to afford a bit of tobacco. And for that matter, a bit of food. And whatever shelter she could manage after Lord Skestinin's hospitality came to its inevitable end. One didn't take in the wife of a traitor indefinitely. If Barriath became commander of the fleet or Jorey won a war in the field, she might remake herself as the mother of a respectable man. But for the future that she could imagine, she was doomed to be her husband's wife.

For a few minutes, sitting at the little stall with its splintering wooden tables and unsteady chairs, she let herself stop smiling. She was lost now, and emptied in a way she hadn't ever imagined she would be. Her marriage, her family, the small and peaceable intrigues of the court, and Dawson with his archaic love of duty and his blindness to the inconsistencies of his application of it. Those had been her life since she'd left her own mother's house. She hadn't built that life, but rather grown in it.

Now she felt like a flower plant that had been dug up gently and washed in water. She wasn't injured precisely, but her pale roots were all exposed. If she couldn't find soil, that would be enough to kill her. She knew it like she knew the sun would rise and the autumn would come.

And the center of it all was the powerful absence of Dawson Kalliam. The man who had loved her better than he had understood her. The constant in her life. She could still remember what he had looked like the first night she'd kissed him. The way he'd hidden his fear behind chivalry and she'd wrapped hers in modesty until she was more than half certain neither of them would do anything, and they would sit in that garden, aching for each other until the earth itself grew old. He'd been young and handsome. The best friend of Prince Simeon. And who had she been? The girl that his father had chosen for him. The marriage arranged before either of them had had the chance to refuse it.

She wondered if there might have been something that she could have done that would have changed his course. She wanted there to have been something. If all this disaster was her fault, at least she would have had some control. But it was a fantasy. There was no dinner party or distracting conversation that would have reconciled Dawson to being ruled by Geder Palliako's priests. Stones would fly like birds first.

It had been inescapable. And even if there had been something, it was gone now. She sighed and took a bite of the sausage. Too much gristle and oregano, but otherwise perfectly acceptable, and the black mustard hid an abundance of sins. She wept quietly while she finished her little meal and beer, then gathered herself, regained her smile, and returned to the world. She was heartbroken, and she would be for a very long time, but she needn't be ineffective.

She came back to Lord Skestinin's house near nightfall. Her feet ached and her back. The hem of her dress was filthy from walking in the common street with the dogs and horses. The smell of animal shit seemed a part of the life of the city she might have to get used to. She bore worse. It was nothing.

As she came into the house, she heard Barriath's voice raised in anger and Jorey's responding in kind. Her lips pressed thin, and she followed the sounds of fighting through the dim hallways and into the dining room lit by cheap tallow candles and decorated for a family that didn't live there.

"He's my wife's father," Jorey said.

"And I'm your brother," Barriath roared, his face red to the edge of purple. "When did that stop mattering? Next you'll be cozying up to that son of a whore in the Kingspire, asking him if he'll give you room and a scrap of meat."

Sabiha stood in the doorway at the far side of the room, her knuckles white around a bit of lace handkerchief. Her expression told Clara how much damage Barriath had already done.

"Good God," Clara said, stepping into the room confidently as a bear tamer walking into the pit, "I'd think you were children again and someone had taken your best toys. What is this about?"

"You're taking shelter with Skestinin," Barriath said, turning his wrath on her. "I won't have it. He took my position with the fleet. I served him for years, and as soon as there's a bit of trouble, I'm overboard like old fish."

"There are certain realities—"

"I'm the eldest man in this family. That makes me responsible for our name," Barriath said. "And I won't have my dignity compromised by this."

Clara didn't know what change of expression came to her face, but she saw Jorey's eyes go wide and Barriath's blood-thickened face grow apprehensive. A faint smile touched Sabiha's lips. Clara met her firstborn son's eyes. One day, he would have been Baron of Osterling Fells, she thought. His future had gone away without warning or reason, and grief made people mad. They did things they would never have otherwise done.

She began to speak, paused, and began again.

"My husband," she said, softly and with terrible precision,

"is not dead. You are my son. Jorey is my son. Sabiha is my daughter. Lord Skestinin is your family, and it would be best for all of us if he found that burden light."

Barriath scowled, but he looked away. The bear tamed, for the time being.

"Jorey's going to renounce Father," Barriath said. He sounded peevish.

"I know he is, dear," Clara said, sitting down at the table with a sigh. "So are you."

Under Clara's eye, Lord Skestinin's house kept its uneasy peace for the night. Barriath sulked and pouted the way he had since the day he'd drawn breath. Jorey brooded more subtly, and with greater consideration for those around him. Clara sat by an unfamiliar window that looked out on a garden not her own, knotting lace because her needlework was lost to the Lord Regent's justice. Just before bed, Sabiha found her, a small leather sack of pipe tobacco in her hand. Clara had kissed the girl's cheek, but they hadn't said anything. Some nights, Clara decided, were too delicate to risk with words.

In the morning, the news came that Lord Geder Palliako was prepared to announce his judgment on the traitor Dawson Kalliam.

Cithrin

If Cithrin had known when she went to the tailor that she would be dressing for an execution, she might have made different choices. In Vanai, the gaol had been open, and those waiting to see the magistrate could be seen and mocked, but the justice of the prince was done in private, the bodies of the condemned buried if they had families to watch over them and bear the cost or left on the hills outside the city if not.

Porte Oliva was just the reverse. Waiting to be judged was a private matter, but once the sentence was passed, or the enforcement fees paid, the punishment was open for anyone walking by to see. The idea of holding a ceremony with all the highest levels of the court in attendance in order to carry out a slaughter that everyone knew was coming seemed perverse, and her limited wardrobe didn't support it.

In the end, she chose the darker of her two dresses. The lines of the lighter one were simpler and more sober, but even after consulting with Paerin Clark, she wasn't certain how much of the day was supposed to be a celebration. A bit of face paint to give definition to her eyes, but not so much that she'd start to look like she was melting if the room was too warm. Two bits of jewelry that she'd acquired since the fire she tried in every combination, eventually settling on a thin silver necklace and no bracelet. She didn't want to appear to compete with the nobility. Simple, understated, formal.

She was on the edge of reconsidering her choice of dress when it occurred to her that she wasn't concerned about the opinion of the court. To them, she was a foreigner, a half-breed, and a merchant. If she'd worn the perfect clothes with the ideal jewels, the ones who had use of a banker would treat her nicely to her face and the others would ignore her.

No, she was worried because Geder would be there. And that had to stop at once. She wasn't a child or one of Sandr's easily impressed stage followers. Something had happened once if they chose to agree that it did, and nothing had if they said it hadn't. Going to court as if he would have time, interest, or attention for her was idiocy. And still, he had talked of allowing the bank to open a branch, so perhaps wanting to dress well in his presence wasn't entirely dim.

Still, she put on the bracelet before she stepped out to the gathering. Not for Geder or Paerin Clark or anyone else. She just liked it.

The heat of summer was losing its grip on the city. The sky overhead was blue, but not rich, and she wouldn't have been at all surprised if Smit's eventual rain came in the next day. She went out to the kitchen where the lowborn among the party were waiting. Elsewhere in the mansion, Baron Watermarch and his wife and daughters were making themselves ready, and no one would be leaving the courtyard until the family was prepared. Fortunately, the cook had put a plate of biscuits and cheese out for the guests to eat before they left.

Paerin Clark was in a simple tunic and hose with a narrow leather belt. Seeing him, she felt more comfortable with her own decision. He smiled and offered a half bow, which she returned, reaching for a biscuit as she did.

"Well, this should be interesting, at least," he said. "It isn't every journey we begin with the celebration of a war hero and stay for his execution."

"Do we know anything about him?" she asked around a mouthful of salt and butter with just enough flour to hold it together. Whatever shortcomings the hospitality might suffer, Daskellin's cooks spared little and the results were lovely.

"I've met him several times. He was important to putting Palliako on the throne and he's been swimming-deep in court intrigue since I met him. Rigid thinker, no use for us or our kind."

"I'll keep my mourning short," she said. "Anything I should be watching for?"

"I don't know," Paerin said. "Listen to what people say about the insurrection. If Kalliam has partisans, this will be the time to catch them upset."

"I will," she said. "I would have thought that there would be more punishments. Kalliam wasn't the only house involved in the thing."

"No, it wasn't, but it was the leader. And some of the others made peace. Kalliam was captured. It makes him the extreme case."

The door opened and one of the junior footmen leaned in.

"The lord and lady are walking out," he said. "Come on along or we'll be left behind."

"And here I thought we were waiting for them," Cithrin said.

"Noble blood flows by different rules. Best to nod and bow and be patient."

"And piss before you leave," Cithrin said sourly.

"Yes," Paerin said with a smile. "And that."

Canl Daskellin and his family rode a palanquin with a dozen bearers while Cithrin and Paerin followed at a polite distance in a cart pulled by horses. As they came near the Kingspire, the magnitude of the crowd became clear to her. Every street and alley was packed with the powerful. Their servants shouted and fought, pushing for advantage and arguing precedence and points of etiquette like fishermen coming in from the dock shouted about nets. Their own cart didn't come near the great tower itself, but drew aside perhaps a quarter mile away and stopped.

"My thanks," Paerin Clark called to the carter and tossed a copper coin through the air to him. Cithrin slid down at his side.

"Walking the rest of the way?" she said.

"As befits our station," he said, offering his arm.

The architecture of the chamber was marvelous. No matter where people stood, no matter how tall the person before them was, the view of the raised dais at the end was clear. Geder sat on a plush chair and Aster at his side. Cithrin felt a passing urge to wave to them. Seeing the pair of them together gave everything the feeling of theater. Though of course that wasn't true. Geder wasn't simply playing at Lord Regent, that was who and what he was. Or perhaps playing at it and being it were the same thing.

The priest Basrahip stood to the side, his head bowed as if listening. Cithrin had the irrational sense that he was aware of every conversation in the hall, however quietly spoken.

"You see the woman on the far left in grey?" Paerin said softly enough that the words were almost lost in the murmur of a hundred small conversations. Cithrin craned her head. She saw Canl Daskellin and his family, but none of them wore grey. The daughter especially seemed to be dressed for a celebration. She shifted again, and then found the one Paerin meant. She was in the first part of her early middle years with a face that seemed to be made without angles. The cloak she wore was the grey of ashes. Two younger men stood at either side, the taller, thicker of the pair affected a full sailor's beard. The smaller had a beard of more recent vintage.

"Kalliam's wife and sons," she said.

"Ah, you've seen them before, then."

"No," she said, and began looking at the people around them. The disgraced family stared straight ahead, expressions empty or despairing or thick with dread, and the people nearby pretended not to notice them. The three might have been ghosts. No one saw them.

No, that wasn't true. Geder did. Cithrin leaned forward. Geder was looking at them, and his expression wasn't angry or vengeful. That was interesting. Down in the darkness, he'd said he wanted every humiliation answered for, and she believed him. But now he looked anxious.

The beat of a drum announced the arrival of the prisoner, and a small wooden door opened not far from Geder and Aster. The man who came through had grey hair pulled back from his face. He wore peasant canvas with smears of dirt and filth on the tunic and legs. His feet were bare and the soles black. He bore himself more regally than Geder, so much so that she felt a little pang of embarrassment on Geder's behalf.

Dawson Kalliam, patriot and traitor, was made to kneel in the center of the room, guards with drawn blades behind him either side. Aster glanced at him nervously.

Cithrin bit her lip. What was she seeing here? Geder's reluctance was written in every angle and underscored each movement. When he cleared his throat, the court went silent.

"I have been petitioned by the...sons of House Kalliam for permission to speak. I hereby grant this to Jorey Kalliam of House Kalliam."

The crowd murmured as the younger son walked out.

This wasn't expected, then. Geder was giving something to the family of the man who'd tried to kill him. She couldn't guess what he wanted in return. Lady Kalliam's eyes were closed, her face nearly the grey of her clothing. The larger of her sons held her hand.

"Lord Regent Palliako," Jorey Kalliam said. He had a nice voice. Strong without being overpowering. "My prince, I have come to speak before you. Please know that I love my father much, and that I respect him for the honest service he has given the crown in the past."

The rumbling of the crowd told her that the sentiment wasn't widely shared, but the man lifted his chin and his voice, pressing on.

"However this most recent endeavor was..." The word was lost, the youngest Kalliam choking on it. "This most recent endeavor was treason. And I on behalf of my house renounce my father, Dawson Kalliam. I reject his name and reaffirm my loyalty to the crown."

Jorey Kalliam bent his knee and bowed his head. A glance at the crowd showed that all eyes were on the father whose son had just refused his name, but Cithrin was more interested in Geder. He wasn't looking at the young man. His eyes were on the priest, and they were anxious. Basrahip gave some sign too small for her to make out, but the relief that flooded Geder's frame was perfectly clear. Beside her, Paerin made a small click between tongue and teeth that meant he'd seen the same thing.

"Did Jorey Kalliam just give the Lord Regent permission to kill his father?" Cithrin muttered.

"Don't know," Paerin said. He had the trick of not moving his lips at all when he spoke. "But he got his permission from somewhere. Look how solid he's turned."

It was true. The way Geder held his body had changed

profoundly. The anxiety and uncertainty were gone. He looked as if he might start grinning at any moment.

"I would speak," Dawson Kalliam said.

"You don't have leave," Geder said.

"Your leave is shit, you doughy little coward. I won your wars for you," Dawson said and tried to rise to his feet. The guards moved quickly forward to pull him down. The crowd fixed their attention on Dawson or else Geder, but Cithrin turned to watch the family. Lady Kalliam was nearly white now, her eyes pressed closed. The older son's eyes were wide and his nostrils flared wide. Not the image of a family looking forward to the death of their patriarch.

"I am the one who lifted you up," Dawson shouted from his knees, "and you have betrayed everything that my kingdom and my friend Simeon stood—"

"I didn't give you leave to speak," Geder shouted. Cithrin was watching him now. His face was darkening, and the relief was gone. "You will be *quiet*!"

"Or what? You'll kill me? You're a buffoon. I see how you've sold the throne. I stepped forward, and know this, Palliako, when we start to rise, you won't be able to kill us fast enough. The true men of Antea will—"

It happened quickly. There were executioners at the ready, dull and rusted blades in their hands. Geder ignored them. His face a mask of fury, he strode out to where Kalliam knelt, arms chain-bound. Geder walked past him, plucked the blade from the guard's side, and swung it hard and artlessly as a child hewing wood. The sword took Kalliam in the face, shearing off a great slice of his cheek. He stumbled back, lost his footing, and fell. Geder stood over the fallen man, swinging the blade up and down again, soaking himself and the guards in the dying man's blood.

"You will speak when *I say you can*!" Geder screamed.

Cithrin almost laughed at the unintended, bleak comedy of it. No one would ever successfully command Dawson Kalliam to speak again.

Geder stood, looking out at the crowd as if seeing them for the first time and unimpressed. At his feet, Dawson Kalliam spasmed once, then again, bare heels kicking at the floor. He went still.

"It's over," Geder said. "You can go now."

He walked out quickly, the bloody sword forgotten in his hand.

"I do believe that man is about to vomit," Paerin Clark said.

"I think we should leave," Cithrin said.

The court left with them. Men with wide eyes and women with tight mouths. They'd come to see a death, and there had been one, but the form of it had been wrong and it left them shaken. If Dawson Kalliam had been stabbed with thirteen dull, rusted blades, there would have been no discomfort. Instead, Geder had lost his temper and taken the thing in hand and anything was possible. And she'd have bet a month's salary that by nightfall, the story in the taphouses and alley mouths would make it sound like something out of a drama. The righteous king taking the executioner's sword in his own hand.

The day gave no hint at the violence that had just taken place. Birds still sang, and the breeze smelled of flowers and smoke and the promise of rain. As she and Paerin walked down the flagstone pathway past sprays of midsummer blooms, she caught sight of the woman in grey. Lady Kalliam. On impulse, she took Paerin's hand and dragged him with her as she threaded her way through the crowd.

"Lady Kalliam," she said as she drew up beside the woman. "Yes?"

"My name is Cithrin bel Sarcour. I'm voice of the Medean

bank in Porte Oliva. I wanted to give you the bank's sympa-thies and my own. This can't have been a good day."

Lady Kalliam lifted her chin and smiled. She looked younger than Cithrin had thought. And on a better day, she would have been beautiful.

"That's kind of you," she said. "Very few people seem to feel that way."

Cithrin put her hand on the woman's arm, and Lady Kal-liam covered Cithrin's fingers with her own. It was less than a breath, and then the crowd parted them again.

"And that was for?" Paerin asked.

"Her son's important enough to Palliako that there was spe-cial dispensation to speak at the execution," Cithrin said. "May be useful later, it may not. Either way it costs us nothing."

"Well, I suppose that's one—"

"Cithrin!"

She stopped, looking back. The crowd between her and the Kingspire was splitting apart, highborn and low, noble-men and servants, all of them stepped off the flagstones and into flowerbeds or grass or mud. Geder Palliako was racing toward them, his face red. Blood still spattered his sleeves and face. She waited for him. The eyes of the court were on her like hawks considering a rabbit. Paerin Clark's eyebrows were crawling up his forehead. This was a problem, and she couldn't solve it.

"Oh dear," she said. Then, stepping forward. "Lord Regent. You're much too kind."

He stood before her now, his chest working like a bellows.

"I'm sorry," he said. "You shouldn't have had to see that. I shouldn't have...I meant to invite you. And Paerin. Both of you. After it was done, I wanted you to join me for a meal. Some conversation. I have a book of poems that I got in Vanai, and I wanted you..."

Paerin Clark, beside her, said nothing. She didn't think a little help here would have been too much to ask, but she also knew he wouldn't give it.

"You are very, very kind to make such an offer, my lord," she said. "But it occurs to me that you are presently soaked in a dead man's blood."

"Oh," Geder said, looking down at himself. "I am. I'm sorry about that too. But if you'll wait, just a few minutes."

"There will be better days for it, my lord," Cithrin said. For a heartstopping moment, she thought he was going to kiss her, but instead he only bowed much more deeply than the head of an empire should ever do before a banker. The looks of surprise and outrage traveled out from him like a ripple in a pond, but she only kept her smile in place as he made his way back toward the Kingspire. When she turned to leave, Canl Daskellin's daughter was looking at her like the promise of an early death. Cithrin bowed to her as well, and took Paerin Clark by the arm.

The crowd re-formed, high men scraping mud off their best leather boots, and the tittering and laughter and scandalized eyebrows swarming among them. Cithrin cursed quietly under her breath, repeating a nearly silent string of obscenities until they were nearly at the cart. She was embarrassed. She was horrified. And more deeply than any of the rest, she found she was afraid. Afraid in particular of Geder Palliako.

The carter started them off into the press of the street. No one was moving quickly. It could take them hours to get back to their rooms. Cithrin wished deeply for a way to clear their path, and not just here on the street.

"So," Paerin Clark said. "Did all of that mean something?"

"It meant it's time for us to get out of Camnipol," Cithrin said.

Marcus

It had been years since Marcus had traveled the coast of Elassae. He'd forgotten how beautiful it was. Just after Newport, the ground became rough, the coastline ragged and craggy. Mountains rose up, dead volcanoes with caldera lakes. They marched along north to south like soldiers marching into the sea. The string of islands leading south into the Inner Sea was their heads as they sank deeper and deeper. The water had none of the greenish tint and cloudiness of the colder climes. Sailing a boat on these waters would be like taking wing and flying.

There was no dragon's road along this coast, or rather there were rumors that once there had been one, and the spill of the molten rock had covered it over back before the volcanoes had gone into their torpor. Somewhere deep under the rolling black hills, a thread of eternal green about as useful now as a fishhook in the desert. And Marcus found he didn't particularly care. The path before them was clear enough: don't walk so far north that you were going uphill, don't walk so far south that your feet got wet. Soon enough, they'd reach the inner plains, and then Suddapal and then south across the Inner Sea to Lyoneia. And after that, it was too far ahead to figure.

The grass on the hills they rode was so green it hurt to look at. So intense that there were times Marcus felt that he was dreaming or hallucinating, and the sun and the tall blue air left him feeling that he could stretch up his arms and take it all into himself. Small villages studded the coastline. Timzinae fishermen, their black, insectlike chitin greyed and cracked by years of brine. When they were asked, Master Kit told a story about being a naturalist for the queen of Birancour searching for a rare kind of singing shrimp. He told it well enough that Marcus had found himself wondering sometimes whether the next cove might have them. Or perhaps it was the power of Master Kit's strange blood that made him so convincing.

They were asked less often than Marcus had expected, though. The more usual case was that they were offered a bowl of the potluck stew that every fishing dock kept cooking all through the year, each man paying in something from that day's catch in return for a bowl that had been simmering since before some of them had been born. The fishermen of the coast were dour and gruff and friendly. The women, apart from being Timzinae, were beautiful. The scales were more than enough to keep Marcus from repeating his error from Porte Oliva, though. And Master Kit, while a vicious flirt, never seemed to follow along as far as a woman's bed.

Suddapal was a complex of five coastal cities, the largest of which spread out black and tan against the unreal green of the countryside. Where there should have been farms, sheep, goats, there was a vast swath of wild grassland, untouched and unhunted except at religious festivals. It struck Marcus as a terrible way to assure a steady food supply, but he had to admit it was beautiful to look at and walk through. A dragon's road led east from its main square, but they'd gone as far east as they were going to go.

Which meant finding a boat.

"Are you sailors, then?" the Yemmu man asked.

"I've been known to haul a rope a time or two," Marcus said.

"I've been known to pray a time or two," the man said, the words surprisingly clear around the massive bulk of his tusks. "Doesn't make me a priest."

The docks of Suddapal spread out before them, piers running out into the wide blue water like bridges so long that Marcus could imagine walking to Lyoneia. After Timzinae, the most common race in Suddapal were the Yemmu like this man, thick, strong, intimidating to look at, but for the most part nicer than Pyk Usterhall. It was good to be reminded that the woman's irritating nature was her own and not her people's.

"We aren't expecting difficult waters," Master Kit said. "I understand that the worst of the storm season is over, and the maps I've seen show the current carrying us quite near our destination."

"Maps you've seen," the Yemmu said. "So you've never been there."

"No."

The man nodded his massive head.

"You're a pair of idiots," he said.

"Friendly, though," Master Kit said. "And I do have a certain amount of gold."

"Gold sinks," the Yemmu said. "I don't mind taking your coin, but I start feeling guilty when I let idiots die. Here's what I will do, though. Small finder's fee. Nothing you can't afford. I'll find you a ship and someone that knows how to use it."

Marcus looked at Master Kit. The actor frowned.

"I hesitate to take anyone with us," Master Kit said. "Our business is sensitive."

"You know what else is sensitive? My—"

"I'm afraid that what we're doing might be dangerous," Master Kit said.

"That's what I'm trying to tell you."

"Kit," Marcus said. "Give the man his fee. If we find something that'll work, we're not obligated to wait. If we don't, that's a fine second best."

Kit sighed, counted out seven silver coins, and pushed them across the table. The Yemmu man took them, nodded once, and heaved himself up and away. Marcus watched him lumbering away from them down the docks.

"You think he'll really look for someone?" Marcus asked.

"He will," Kit said. "I wouldn't have given him the money otherwise."

"Right, you can tell," Marcus said. "I keep forgetting about that."

One of the curiosities of Suddapal was the utter lack of inns and wayhouses. There were travelers, but negotiating shelter was a matter of knocking on doors until someone with a spare room or space in a shed was willing to reach agreement. In good weather, they went to a great common green in the middle of the city and set up camp there just as they would have on the road. Timzinae boys walked the green from dusk until late into the night selling baked fish and goat in bowls made from turtle shells. The horizon was clear and the smell of the sea air so clean and unthreatening that they put their bedrolls out without the bother of the little lean-to tent. The horses, they stabled, though other people had let theirs wander the green, cropping the grass and sleeping in a great and temporary herd.

Marcus traced the constellations, his fingers laced behind his head. It had been a long time since he'd just looked up at the stars. Beside him, Master Kit sighed.

"Maybe we should have started by sea," he said. "We

could have gotten a boat in Maccia. Or gone west to Cabral and made up the time by sailing."

"I thought the currents wouldn't have done the right thing."

"But if we're going to end up hiring on help anyway," Kit said.

"We couldn't have known. It was the best guess we had. Not like there's much else we could go on."

"No," Kit said. "I suppose there's not."

Across the green, someone struck up a tune on a small harp.

"Are you still worried about her?" Master Kit asked.

"Cithrin, you mean?"

"Yes."

"Yes," Marcus said. "But I think you were right. She wouldn't have been counting on me to come save her. So at least I won't have disappointed."

"You sound bitter."

"That's because I'm a mean bitter old man. Do you see those four stars in a row? The ones right there near the horizon?"

"I do."

"You can't see them where I was born. Too far north. There are a lot of stars you can't see from there."

Kit made a small grunting sound by way of comment.

"You've traveled the world," Marcus said. "What's the strangest thing you've ever seen?"

"Hmm. Let me see. There's a lake in Herez. Lake Esasmadde. It's huge. And in the center of it, there's a whirlpool like when the last of the water is leaving a drain, but the lake never empties. And in the center of the whirlpool there's a tower. Five stories tall, and utterly unreachable. As far as I can tell, it's been that way since the dragons."

"What do you think it is?"

"It could be a prison. Someplace that the dragons dropped their bad slaves. Or the last retreat of Drakkis Stormcrow. I really couldn't say for certain. What about you? What's the strangest thing you've seen in your travels?"

"Probably you."

"Well. Fair enough."

The harp tune changed, shifting to a soft melody that the night seemed to carry on its own.

"I think the third string's out of tune," Kit said.

"Only a bit," Marcus said. "And you aren't paying for it."

Sleep hovered at the edge of Marcus's mind, but never quite descended. Kit shifted in his bedroll, and a falling star flashed overhead, there and gone before Marcus could say anything.

"You know," Kit said, very softly. "I think I could make the nightmares go away. If you wanted me, I could try."

"And how would you do that?"

"I would tell you that it wasn't your fault, what happened to them. I could tell you that they forgave you. Given time, you would believe me. It might afford you more peace. Some sleep."

"If you tried, I'd have to kill you."

"That bad?"

"That bad," he said.

"It wouldn't take your memory of them."

"It would take what the memories meant," Marcus said. "That's worse. Besides, they're not bothering me right now."

"I'd noticed that," Kit said. "I thought it was a bit odd. You've seemed almost content. It's unnerving."

"I had everything in Porte Oliva," Marcus said. "Steady work. A company that respected and followed me. I didn't work for a king. I had Cithrin and I had Yardem. I am, by the way, going to kill him when we're done with this. He betrayed me, and he'll answer for it. You can try your little magic on that if you want."

"I believe you," Kit said. "But you've lost all of that now, haven't you?"

"I have," Marcus said. "I'm finishing up my fourth decade in the world sleeping on dirt and grass beside a man with spiders crawling though his veins. I have to get across the Inner Sea, and I don't know how I'm going to manage it. If I do get there, I'm not certain yet how I'll get back. And when I do, I'll most likely be killed trying to slaughter a goddess. And I feel better than I have since Cithrin beat her audit. When I have something, I worry about all the things I'd have to do to keep it. Out here, I've got nothing. Or at least nothing good. And so I'm free."

"That sounds like a complex way of saying that your soul is in the shape of a circle, turned on its edge," Kit said.

Marcus nodded.

"You know I respect your wisdom and enjoy your company, yes?"

"Yes."

"Nobody likes you when you're being clever."

Marcus drifted to sleep even before the harpist quit for the night. He woke in the morning with dew in his hair and the blue-yellow light of dawn reaching across a perfect blue sky.

Two days later, they were walking past a small streetside café when Master Kit suddenly paused, his eyes narrowing at the worked iron sign of a dolphin above the door.

"Something?" Marcus said.

"Perhaps," Kit said. "It's been…Just a moment, would you?"

Inside, the café was dirty and close, the walls stained by years of smoke that came even now from the kitchen, leaving the place in a haze of charcoal smoke, seared fat, and spices that made Marcus's mouth water just smelling them.

A young and angry-looking Timzinae man barreled out toward them, waving black hands.

"Not open yet," he said. "Come back in an hour."

"Forgive me," Master Kit said. "Your name wouldn't be Epetchi, would it?"

The Timzinae's eyes went wide, and then disconcertingly did it again as his nictitating membrane slid open with an audible click.

"Kitap!" he shouted, leaping to put his arms around Master Kit. "Kitap, you old bastard! We all thought you were dead by now. You and your friend come back to the kitchen. Ela! Kitap's here, and you won't believe it. He's old and fat."

Marcus found himself carried along on a wave of other people's enthusiasm, seated at a cutting table, and eating from a bowl of something that looked like the waste scraped off a cooking grill and tasted better than anything he'd had in years.

All around him, Timzinae men and women were smiling, and little boys and girls so young that their scales were still light brown were trotted out bored but patient to Master Kit, who delighted over each one. When he introduced Marcus by his full name, he could tell that the first man—Epetchi, his name was—was skeptical. But if old Kitap wanted to travel with a man who pretended to be the murderer of kings from Northcoast, it was apparently fine by him.

They weren't permitted to sleep under the stars anymore. Instead, they had a room in the back of the café and bedded down on a thin cotton mattress that had seen cleaner days.

"Friends, I take it?"

"When I first came into the world, I spent the better part of a year in Suddapal," Master Kit said, laying his bedroll out over the mattress. Probably wise. At least all the insects living in their bedrolls were familiar. "I stayed here. Epetchi was just a boy then. Thin as a stick and couldn't think about anything but girls."

"Do you think they can help us, then?"

"I think that if they can, they will. That may not be quite the same thing. But I have more faith in goodwill built with meals and shared stories than goodwill bought from strangers with coin."

"You know," Marcus said, "I didn't force you to pay the finder's fee."

"The world's an odd place," Kit said, and sat down with a grunt. "The last time I was here, everything was different. I was different, they were. Even the building's changed. There wasn't a wall there, at least not that I recall. And yet it was all related. It's as if the world was a stone, hard and unchanging as we lay paint over it, one layer and then another and then another. We change it by the weight of the stories we bring to it, but we only change what's there. Not the stone nature of the world."

"That sounds very deep," Marcus said. "Don't know what the hell it's supposed to mean, though. Do you think they know someone with a good boat?"

The captain of the little sailing boat was a Timzinae woman with a broad face and a wicked smile. At Epetchi's instructions, they met her near the end of one of the long piers. So far from the shore, Marcus felt he'd already left the city. She sat in the back of her boat, wrapping long, braided ropes in patterns that Marcus, in another context, would have mistaken for art. Her name, they'd been told, was Adasa Orsun.

The boat itself was small enough for one person to manage, large enough to carry five if they didn't need to lay in provisions for a long trek across open water. The deck was white as snow and its sails were square sheets of thick canvas dyed the blue of the sea. It bobbed with the waves, a little up, a little down. As close as it rode to the waterline, Marcus couldn't imagine how it would keep from being swamped in a storm. But there were at least a dozen other boats similar to it tied to the pier, so there was something to the design or the handling that made it possible.

That or they just didn't put out to sea if there was weather.

Master Kit made the introductions.

"We were led to understand you might be willing to take passengers south to Lyoneia," he said.

"Might be," the woman said. "For the right price. When are you wanting to leave?"

"Sooner would be better," Master Kit said with a smile.

"Can't go for a month," she said with a shrug. "Other work already agreed to."

Marcus didn't need little black things living in his veins to know it was a lie. The woman smiled up at them. The next move was theirs.

"I am a friend of Epetchi's," Master Kit said.

"And so I'm talking to you," she answered. The rope flowed in loops over her arm and cascaded down.

"I can pay," Kit said, tossing her a small leather purse. She didn't open it, just tested the weight in the palm of her hand.

"This gold?"

"Silver. Some copper."

"And a pretty stone I put in," Marcus said. "If we can stop dancing, what's it going to take to get this"—he pointed at the deck—"there?" He pointed at the sea stretching away to the south.

The woman looked at him, then turned back to Kit.

"Who's he?"

"My name's Marcus Wester."

"Sure it is," she said, not looking at him.

"His name is Marcus Wester," Kit said. "And yes, he's that Marcus Wester."

"Is not."

"Listen to me," Kit said with a sigh. "Listen to my voice. This man is Marcus Wester. He is."

"Have been since before people thought much of it," Marcus said.

Adasa Orsun tucked the purse into her jacket.

"All right, then," she said. "Bring your things. The tide's in six hours, and we'll be out on it."

"Because everyone wants to travel with me?" Marcus said.

"Makes a good story," she said, turning back to her ropes. "You best hurry. Get some good food while you're at it. I've got enough to keep everyone alive, but I run a ship, not a kitchen."

As they walked back down the long stretch of tar-soaked logs that made the pier, Marcus shook his head.

"I don't like that," he said. "She doesn't know us. Not really. What if I was a terrible, violent, mean-spirited person? I mean, I'm mostly known for killing my employer. You wouldn't think that would make traveling with me more attractive."

"I think we are the stories people tell about us," Kit said.

"No," Marcus said. "We aren't. We're more than that. And our friend on the boat there is taking a stupid risk by going with us."

"I suppose so," Kit said. "But I'm still glad she is."

Clara

Clara could not tell whether the darkness had taken the city, the kingdom, the world as a whole, or only her. When she rose in the morning, the sky seemed dimmer than it had before. When she ate, the salt seemed both weaker and less palatable at the same time. She slept little, waking in the middle of the night and staring up at the ceiling that wasn't hers. Sometimes she forgot why Dawson wasn't beside her, and then recalled, and felt the despair roll over her afresh. As if it were all happening again.

But she didn't allow herself to stop. If she stopped, she was certain she would never start again. It wasn't even that she would die. She would simply be, still and grey and unmoving. A statue of herself in stone.

"Good morning, Mother," Barriath said as he stepped into the little dining room. "There's eggs ready."

"Thank you, dear," she said. "You rested well, I hope?"

"Well enough."

In a better world, he would have been gone again by now. Back to the north and the ships. His place with the navy. Instead, he would spend the day brooding, going to taphouses. And she would go instead along the streets and into the courtyards where she was barely welcome and see to it that her family survived this all as best they could. Or at least that part that hadn't died.

The rain, when it came, hadn't been a massive cloudburst, but a slow, low drizzle that made everything damp without cleaning anything. It did, however, bring the colors of everything out: the red stone arches of the Lias Gate looked like the coals from a fire that had almost burned out. The carving of the bear outside the Fraternity of the Great Bear looked less like a dust-colored dog on its back legs and more like a predator. Even Issandrian's overly carved and decorated mansion was lent a kind of beauty by the rain. She would have to tell Dawson about that, only she wouldn't.

Issandrian received her in his withdrawing room, offering her coffee and baked cheese and even a pipe's bowl of tobacco. Clara forced herself to accept less than she wanted. When she sat on the little white-upholstered divan, she could already see from his expression that the news was bad.

"My lady," he said. "I am doing everything in my power, but I warned you at the start how little influence I have. And forgive my saying so, but the Kalliam name is tainted. It's being used among the court members as another way to say traitor."

"Still, there must be something, mustn't there?" she asked, sipping at her coffee. "There were houses who fought at my husband's side. He had those sympathetic to him."

"Not the way the story goes now," Issandrian said. "To hear it, he fought the throne single-handed. The houses whose banners flew by yours were all neutral now and never took arms, and the houses that weren't in the streets at all were fighting on the side of Palliako. Not all will escape judgment, but they will all try to."

"I see," she said, and she did. Court life was always a tissue of reputation and rumor. This was no different.

"I haven't given up all hope," Issandrian said. "There is discussion of an expedition to Hallskar. It's possible that if they go by water, they'll need a captain. I can't get Barriath command of the ship with the actual members of court sailing on it, but there may be cargo ships, and with the right word in the right ear, Barriath could be hired on to take that."

It was, she thought, a terrible lot of conditional phrases for a single statement. Still, she smiled the gratitude that she knew she ought to feel. They chatted for a few moments more, Clara savoring coffee and pipe, and then it was time to keep on. Time to not stop.

House Annerin was gone, leaving the city even before the close of the season and taking her daughter and grandson with them. The intention was to avoid precisely the kind of social call Clara was making, but still, she walked to the door slave and made her enquiries. No, my lady, the family had not returned and were not expected until after the winter. But yes, he could accept yet another letter and see that it found its way to her daughter. At Canl Daskellin's mansion, they were very sorry, but the whole of the family was indisposed. Perhaps if she called another day.

She walked for most of the morning, stopping at half a dozen houses, and hoping without reason to hope that by her presence she could force the world to open a place for her boys.

When, near midday, she returned, feet aching, to Lord Skestinin's house, the fight was already under way again.

"I'm a sailor," Barriath shouted. "I could drink three times that and be more sober than you are waking up."

She was accustomed to the sound of fraternal battle, but the voice Jorey spoke in now was low and cold and unfamiliar.

"You've disrespected my wife in her own home," Jorey said. "You have to leave."

Clara walked through the hall, her spine straight. Not here too. She could stand to fight the world, if she had to.

She would endure the pain of waking alone in her unfamiliar bed with the echoes of her husband's death still in her ears, but she couldn't do it all here too. There had to be one place—one—where she could rest and draw strength. If it wasn't her family, she didn't know where it could be.

"I'm not staying," Barriath said as she stepped into the room. "Wouldn't do it on a bet. But take it clear, I'm not the one looking down on Sabiha. She's your wife and so she's my sister, and it's her fair-weather friends you're talking to. Not me."

Both her boys turned to her.

"What," Clara said. The exhaustion in her voice weighted the word so heavily that it was all she could manage. "What?"

Jorey looked to his brother, then down. When he spoke, his jaw was set forward. It was something Dawson had done too. Clara wondered whether it was the boy imitating the man, or if there was something in the blood that would have made Kalliam men do that even if they'd never met.

"Sabiha arranged a garden party," Jorey said. "A half dozen of her old friends. Some that had stayed by her even through the...last scandal. They all sent regrets."

"And he's blaming me," Barriath said. "I wasn't rude. I didn't track these girls down and tell them to turn their backs on Sabiha."

"You didn't need to," Jorey said. "Everyone knows we're here."

"We're not," Barriath said. "You are, but I'm elsewhere. I'm sorry, Mother."

She wanted to ask where he was going. How she would reach him. All the thousand questions that would have let her keep some semblance of family together. But she was too tired, her mind too scattered. He brushed past her as he walked out the door, and she felt like the motion of his passing could have knocked her over. Jorey hadn't moved. His face was pale and pained. Sabiha had appeared at his elbow.

"Mother, this isn't going to work."

"It will," she said. "It's only hard now, but it will work. Barriath is in mourning. We all are. You have to treat him gently."

"That's not what I mean," he said. "You said that you wanted me to be to Sabiha what Father was to you."

"That's right. I want that."

"Father put you ahead of everyone. Everything. If you'd asked him to, he would have done anything. There was no limit."

"That's true, I think," she said, but Jorey was shaking his head. Tears flowed down his cheeks the way they hadn't since he was a child. Not even on the terrible day when Geder had killed her husband.

"I can't do this," he said, and then again, more softly. "I can't."

"I will," Sabiha said, and put a hand on Clara's shoulder. "Please. Come sit with me for a moment, my lady."

Clara let herself be led to a window seat. Sabiha sat beside her, holding her hand. The girl looked thinner. And not just in her face and body. For a time just after the wedding, there had been joy in her. A hopefulness born of seeing the changes that her new reputation brought. That was gone now, and Clara knew why. She knew, almost, what Sabiha was steeling herself to say. The words that had defeated Jorey.

"We love you," Sabiha said, "and we will always be your family, but you need to leave this house."

It was strange. Clara actually felt the words cut into her. It was a physical sensation at the neck and heart.

"Oh," she said.

"It's hard enough for Jorey alone," Sabiha said, her fingers pressing Clara's hand. "But everyone saw him when he renounced Lord Kalliam. They're willing to give him a chance. Well, some of them are. But you didn't speak. Barriath didn't. And truly, even if you had, my lady, no one can see you without seeing your husband too. You were too much the same thing, and even with him gone, you carry him with. You see that, don't you? You understand?"

"I do," Clara said. "I feel him myself."

"Until the court forgets, at least a little, having you with us taints us more than it protects you."

"I will go," Clara said. "If there's room at the holding, I can...exile myself, I suppose."

"We were thinking that we could pay for a boarding house," Sabiha said. "Something that wasn't in my father's name. Something to give us a little distance in the eyes of the court."

Not even that much? Clara wanted to say. Can't you give me that one small thing? Must it be an anonymous grave of a room, in among people she'd never known?

"I can see why that would be wise," she said. "I'll gather my things."

"No, please," Sabiha said. "I'll have them brought. You shouldn't have to."

"None of us should have to," Clara said, patting the girl's shoulder. "But we live in a world of necessities. Don't bother yourself. I understand. I should go now."

"No, please," Sabiha said. "We'll have someone go with you to find the right place. And we'll bear the price of it."

Clara's smile almost felt real. She took her hands out from the girl's grasp and stood. She kissed Sabiha and Jorey both, each of them on the forehead, and took herself back out. There was no staying now. No sitting in the kitchen and discussing what sort of boarding house might be right for the widow of a famed traitor and enemy of the throne.

By renouncing Dawson, they were supposed to have gained something. Protected it. Kept it. And perhaps they had. Perhaps if Jorey hadn't said what he'd said, Clara would have even less than she did now. But she could hardly imagine it. She felt like the queen of nothing.

She walked without knowing where she was walking to. Her feet ached terribly, but she ignored the pain. Once, she'd ridden through the city as the small people in the street made way for her, and she'd thought nothing of it. Now she found that she was moving aside to let carts of meat or turnips pass. She was avoiding the eyes of the men and women she passed.

When the great arcing span of the Autumn Bridge rose up before her, she began across it, but at the midway point, she stopped. It wasn't even that she intended to, it was only there that she was when her resolve finally broke. Leaning against the great beams and looking down over the abyss of the Division, she felt something like peace come over her. Not peace, not really, but something like it. The world looked almost beautiful at this distance. The Kingspire. The walls of the city. The clouds scudding quickly overhead, caught in some unthinkably high wind that she herself could not feel.

She considered how little it would take to step over the edge. Not that she intended to. Self-slaughter was too easy, in its way. But it did have its appeal. She'd never been religious, but neither had she refused the priestly stories of life and justice on the farther side of death. Perhaps Dawson was there waiting for her.

But not yet. Vicarian's position wasn't assured, even now. And Barriath...poor Barriath, turned out of the house by his own brother. He needed her still. And Jorey would. Even Sabiha might. And how terrible would it be for the girl to have sent her husband's mother out, only to have her leap off a bridge. The poor thing would never recover.

No. Another day, she would. Later, when all her children were taken care of and no one would feel responsible for a decision that was utterly her own. Then she could come, dressed perhaps in bridal array, and take one last brief dance with Dawson. She was weeping now. She didn't know how long she had been. Days. Weeks. All her life, it seemed. All those years of content had been an illusion. A thin line that she had walked over an abyss. Without a home to go to, without a friend to rely on, she was reduced to the aspect of a madwoman wailing on the bridge, and she found the role fit well enough.

"My lady," a man's voice said, like warm flannel on a cold night. "No."

She turned, surprised. Some part of her that still cared about such things reached to straighten her hair and tug her dress into its best drape. The rest of her, the vast majority, collapsed in a hilarity of relief and embarrassment and an amused kind of dread that was much more pleasant than the sincere one she'd been inhabiting.

"Coe," she said, laughing and crying. "Oh, not this too."

He put a hand on her shoulder. His expression was so sincere. So open and concerned and young.

"This isn't the way, my lady. Come with me."

"I wasn't going to jump. I wasn't. I mean not now, not with so much to do. There's the boys, you see. And my daughter, my new one, you won't have met her. She's a dear child, but troubled. Troubled. And to go now, to leave now with everything in such a state." She had trouble with the words because the sobbing was so hard now that there was very little room for them. "I couldn't leave it all like this, so broken and so empty. Oh God. What have we done? How? How did I come to this?"

Somewhere in the middle of it all, he'd lifted her up, taken her in his arms like she was a child.

"You can't do this," she said. "I don't love you. I don't know you. I can't ever be what you want me to be. I'm married. I mean..."

"You don't have to speak, my lady."

"I'm poisoned," she said. "Everyone I know is tainted by me. My sons. Even my sons. They'll look at you and they'll see me. And if they see me, they'll see him, and they'll do to you what they did to him. I can't stop it. I can't even slow it down."

"I'm no one, my lady. I have nothing to lose."

"And I'm getting your shirt all wet. This isn't wise. You should go. You should go."

"I won't," he said.

She was silent for a long time. His arms weren't even trembling. She felt he could carry her forever if he chose to. He smelled like dogs and trees and young man. She laid her head against his shoulder and heaved a sigh. When she spoke again, the hysteria was gone.

"I'm not some fucking little girl who needs *rescuing*," she said.

"No, my lady," he said, but she could hear the amusement in his voice. She sniffed. Her nose was running. The streets around them were close and dark. Three men couldn't walk abreast through them. The poorest quarters of Camnipol closed around her like a blanket. Vincen Coe carried her through the shadows and the light.

"Shit," she said, and clung to him.

The rooming house was terrible. It stank of old cabbage, and the walls were stained green and black in drips that had dried solid years before. There was a wardrobe with a missing door and nothing inside, and the dirty little window no wider than her hand let in only enough light to condemn the surroundings. The bed was small and stained, but it had a mattress. He put her down on it, and she curled up. It smelled rank, but it was soft and her body curled against it with the weight of exhaustion.

He brought her a wineskin filled with water and a wool blanket that smelled more of him than of the room.

"There's no common room here," he said. "But there's a fire to sit near in the kitchen. The man across from you shouts sometimes, but he's harmless. If you need me, I won't be out of earshot."

She nodded.

"My family doesn't know where I am," she said.

"Should we send word, my lady?"

"No," she said. "Not yet."

"As you see fit."

He leaned close and kissed her once gently on the temple. He hesitated for a moment the way she would have if she'd been a man and she'd wanted to kiss a woman's mouth. She shifted her eyes to his, and he stood.

"I'm old enough to be your mother," she said.

"My mother's considerably older than you, my lady," he said.

"Why are you doing all this?"

"Because you've let me," he said. "Sleep now. We'll talk later."

The door closed behind him, and Clara lay in the dim and stinking gloom.

"*Well*," she said to no one, and didn't finish the thought.

Geder

*L*ord Palliako, the letter said, *I am very sorry to have been called away on such short notice, but word has come from the holding company that requires my immediate presence. Thank you very much for the offer of your hospitality and your company during my time in Camnipol. It has been a singular experience, and one I will recall fondly. The challenges of governing a nation as great as your own must take precedence over matters like small personal correspondence, but I will be paying close attention to the news from Antea.*

The chop was Cithrin bel Sarcour.

He'd read the words a thousand times already, and he expected he'd read them a thousand more. He could hear her voice as if the paper itself had soaked it in. The softness in her throat. The slight melancholy in her inflection of *fondly*. He had read love notes before, but usually in the form of poetry or song. To cast it as business correspondence was both odd and exactly what he would have expected of a banker.

He'd been worried after the execution of Dawson, that he'd offended her, either in the way the execution had taken place or from the way he'd reacted after. He'd often heard that killing a man was an upsetting thing, especially the first time, but he'd nearly been sick in front of the whole court. It hadn't been in keeping with his dignity, but he'd do better next time. And anyway, she seemed to have forgiven him if there was anything to be forgiven.

As he reached the door, he tucked the letter in his pocket. The voices of men so rough and grating by comparison to the woman he'd conjured leaked through the door. Geder motioned to his personal guard that they should wait for him to precede them, then pushed his way through into the meeting room. Basrahip followed on his heels and before the guard. That wasn't a matter of etiquette so much as the habit that they had all formed.

Maps littered the table, four and five layers thick in places. Canl Daskellin and Fallon Broot stood over the mess, scowling and angry-looking.

"Gentlemen," Geder said. "I take it we've made no particular headway."

"Asterilhold, in practice," Daskellin said, "is posing several problems we hadn't anticipated."

"You're damn near out of noble families," Broot said. "There were only about forty to start, and that's counting the eastern Bannien group as their own that just happen to have the same name. The ones we lost in Kalliam's rebellion, that's down to thirty-four, thirty-five."

"Broot wants to redraw the map of Antea while we're about it."

"Doesn't make sense for a man to have two holdings on different sides of the river. How are you to oversee them both? Spend half the winter one place? Only see a holding every second year? It's just sense to expand the existing baronies."

"These aren't just dots on a map, Broot. These are places. My family has lived on its holding for ten generations. My grandfathers are all buried there. It's not as if we can switch that to some field in the middle of Asterilhold and call it the same."

Geder raised his eyebrows. This wasn't the part of being regent he was best at, but they were right. It would need to be addressed.

"And there's the problem of the cities," Broot said, pointing an accusing finger toward the blotches of Kaltfel and Asinport. "We can't make them part of a barony and check in on them once a year. We could try it, but they'll revolt by spring and we'll be right back where we were when the whole damned thing started."

"There will be no revolt," Basrahip said.

"Easy for you to say, Minister," Broot said. "All respect, but you've never run a city. They're worse than children."

"They have the temple of the goddess within them," Basrahip said. "The Righteous Servant will keep them true."

Daskellin and Broot shared a glance. Daskellin looked away first.

"We did just have war in the streets for the best part of the summer," Daskellin said.

"Yes," Basrahip said, his smile broad. "The city was tested and purified, and note, Prince Daskellin, that we are here, and the enemy is slain."

"Speaking of slaying enemies," Broot said. "There is a third option, but it does mean abandoning the wholesale slaughter of the noble classes of Asterilhold."

"And means less reward for the people who stayed with the crown," Daskellin said.

"It's not a reward if you can't manage it, Canl. If you would stop thinking with your purse and see sense, you'd know that."

"Stop!" Geder shouted, and the two men went silent and abashed. "There's a third option. What is it?"

One of the maps slid to the floor, pooling in great loops and folds. Broot tugged on his mustache.

"We could keep Asterilhold under its own rule. Take men from their best stock, let 'em swear fealty to the Severed Throne. Not all that many. Just five or six to…well, to replace the ones we lost. As it were. Even if they weren't on our side before, it doesn't take a wise man to see where the power is now."

Geder stepped to the table and plucked one of the maps to the center where he could see the whole place at once. Asterilhold was much smaller than Antea, and with the marshes and mountains in the south, less of it was arable than a part of Antea the same size. Apart from the two great cities, it wasn't even a particularly great conquest.

"Have we started killing the noblemen yet?" Geder asked.

"No, my lord," Daskellin said. "Kalliam's insurrection threw the plans badly behind schedule."

"Hold off, then. I think I have an idea."

The ballroom where Basrahip had questioned the personal guard hadn't been used for dancing in some years. The boards were warped and uneven. The chandelier, though clean, was rusting at the joints. Geder walked through the space, his eyes narrow, seeing not what was before him, but what could be. Basrahip stood by the doorway, hands folded. If the big priest had an opinion, he didn't say it.

"The thing we did here," Geder said, nodding up at the steep tiered benches. "We could do that again, couldn't we?"

"If you like, Prince Geder, we could."

Geder stepped up two, three, four tiers, then turned, looking down at Basrahip and the ballroom floor from a height. The perspective made even Basrahip seem small. Geder felt a little bubble of pleasure rising in him. It reminded him of finding a new book on a subject he enjoyed.

"Not with the guards," Geder said. "With the nobles of

Asterilhold. We bring them here and question them. The guilty, we throw off a bridge, and the innocent we reward with lands and titles and control over their homeland, only with fealty to the Severed Throne. All the problems go away, yes?"

Basraship stepped forward.

"It can be done, my lord."

"Good," Geder said.

"May I suggest, my prince?"

"Yes? What?"

"We would not need to wait for the men of Asterilhold to arrive before we made some use of this plan."

It took a week to remake the room into something of the appropriate dignity. The walls, Geder stained black. The benches on the sides of the room, he left in place, but his carpenters removed most of the ones in the front, using the same wood to construct something almost like a magistrate's desk, only built higher. The sweet smell of their sawdust leaked out through the halls and grounds of the Kingspire. The rusted chandelier, Geder left in place, in part because it was thick-cast iron and in part because it would have taken the smiths another week to replace it with something better, and he was impatient.

When the remade chamber was complete, he brought Basrahip to it like he was presenting a present to a child.

"I hope you like it," he said. "I have the sense that we'll be spending quite a bit of time in here over the next year or so. The guardsmen stand on the benches to either side, you see? Rising up like that? And then I'll sit up there, and you can be down here near me, but where you can hear the prisoner talking better."

"The prisoner?"

"Or whoever," Geder said, waving the question away.

"It is majestic, my lord," Basrahip said.

"But?"

The priest nodded to the back wall.

"There is no banner," Basrahip said. "I would put the symbol of your house there on the right, and the sigil of the goddess there to the left. For balance."

"Brilliant!" Geder said. "We can do that. But...before that, I was wondering if you'd like to try it. In practice, I mean. Just to see whether the design works as well as I think it does."

"If you wish. I am here as your servant."

Geder arranged it all as carefully as a party. Which guards, with what arms and armor. The lighting of the candles. Everything. And then, when it was all as he'd hoped it would be, he sent out the guard into the city. Four hours later, they returned with the prisoner in hand.

Geder looked down from his heights. Barriath Kalliam looked small and frightened.

"My lord," Geder said.

"Lord Regent."

"Thank you for joining me. I apologize for the unpleasantness of your arrival."

"Think nothing of it," Barriath said, he looked from side to side, taking in the armed men arrayed at his flanks. "I may not be as formally dressed as the occasion calls for."

"I hear that you have left your brother's house," Geder said. "Is that true?"

Barriath shrugged.

"It wasn't what we wanted, so no. I'm not there any longer."

Geder shifted his eyes, and Basrahip nodded. It wasn't as easy to see, though. The angle wasn't quite right for it. He'd need to think about that.

"You had a falling-out with Jorey."

"Wouldn't go that far," Barriath said. The priest hesitated, and then nodded, but Geder realized he didn't know what that meant. It might be true that Barriath wouldn't go that far, but that wasn't the question he'd wanted answered. Below him, Barriath seemed less awed and humbled than amused.

"Are you loyal to me?"

"Excuse me, Lord?"

"Your brother renounced Lord Kalliam. You didn't say the words. I'm asking now, are you loyal to me?"

"I'm a proud servant of the Severed Throne and I always have been," Barriath said, throwing the words out like a challenge. Basrahip nodded. *Yes.* Geder felt a surprising bite of disappointment. Still, it was what he'd brought the man here to find out.

Only no. It wasn't.

"Are you loyal to me?" Geder asked.

"You're the Lord Regent," Barriath said. *Yes.* And yet.

"Are you loyal to *me*?"

Barriath shrugged, looking up at Geder the way a lumberjack might size up the tree he wanted to fell.

"I am," he said. *No.*

Geder chuckled.

"I am not a man easily fooled," he said.

"If you say so, my lord."

"You've lied to me. The last man that did that I cut his hands off. I have an offer for you. If it weren't for my friendship with your brother, I wouldn't offer this much. I am going to ask you the same question again. If you tell me that you are loyal to me and you are telling the truth, I will make you lord of Asinport and head of the fleet that was Asterilhold's. Tell me that you are loyal and lie, you will die where you stand. Or admit your disloyalty, and I will only send you into exile. You have my word on that."

"I don't understand," Barriath said. "Is this some kind of trick?"

"You know my terms," Geder said. "Now. For the last time. Are you loyal to me?"

Barriath was silent, his arms folded and his face bent in a scowl. He stretched his neck first one way and then the other. When he spoke, his voice was quiet and conversational.

"No," he said. "You're a small-hearted, small-minded prick and any man with a real love of Antea would want your head on a pike."

"As I thought. You are exiled from Antea and all its holdings beginning now and lasting until your death. Any man who finds you on Antean soil may kill you and bring your head to me for what reward I see fit."

"All right," Barriath said. "Wasn't as if I had much worth staying here for. We done, then, Lord Regent?"

"Captain? See him out," Geder said. "And put him on a cart for whatever border he chooses."

"Sir!" the guard captain said, and marched forward to lead Barriath Kalliam away forever. As the doors closed behind them, Geder allowed himself a wide smile.

"Oh," he said. "I'm going to enjoy this."

That night, Geder sat in the royal apartments talking with Aster about the issues and questions that surrounded the problem of Asterilhold. The decisions were, of course, Geder's, but since Aster would be inheriting the aftermath of whatever mistakes he made, it only seemed right to have him at least present during the deliberations. Basrahip wandered around behind them, drinking a cup of the foul-smelling tea that he liked.

"So assuming we can find five true-hearted men in Asteril-hold," Geder said, "I think we can hold everything more or less the way it was, only unified under the Severed Throne."

Aster nodded, paused.

"What about Osterling Fells?" he asked.

"Well," Geder said. "I've been thinking about that. I'm tempted to hold it for Jorey. Wait, wait. Hear me out. We can't just turn around and give it back. I don't want every-one thinking that they can assault the throne and their fam-ilies won't suffer for it. But he did renounce Dawson and he meant it. It was true. Wasn't it?"

"The words he spoke were true," Basrahip said.

"So I imagined that once you came of age, one of the first things you could do was restore him. Make things right again. It's symbolic."

"It's a thought," Aster said.

Basrahip cleared his throat.

"Forgive me my intrusion, Lord Prince," the priest said.

"Do you mean him or me?" Geder said. "I'm lord, he's prince."

"No one yet has discussed the greatest problem with this glorious conquest."

"You mean the harvest?"

"I mean the next war," Basrahip said. "You have won, but at a cost. Everyone knows this. The great empire has grown, but it has lost men. It has lost time. It has become richer and weaker. There are no greater incitements to war than wealth and the appearance of weakness."

Geder looked at the map again. It wasn't something he'd considered, but the border between Asterilhold and North-coast was not only wide, but accessible. Difficult to guard and patrol. He tapped at the page and traced the line between Kaltfel and Carse.

"No, my lord," Basrahip said. He still found the idea of maps very amusing, it seemed. "Your battle is on the other side of your paper."

"What? Sarakal?"

"Sarakal, the Free Cities. Elassae," the priest said. "The home of the Timzinae. With your armies drawn north, they will see the empty, rich fields of your south and know that there are no men to defend them. You must make a land between the lands. A way to keep your kingdom safe while its strength regrows."

"You think so?"

"You are the chosen of the goddess," Basrahip said. "All those who hear your name will fear justice. You must be always on your guard. Always at the ready, both in the borders of your nation and the people in your streets and the corridors of your great house."

"I suppose," Geder said. "I suppose that does make sense."

"But then we have another border to protect, don't we?" Aster said. "If you take Sarakal, then what do you do about Borja? All the histories say Elassae's vulnerable to the Keshet. There's always the next war."

"No, little prince," Basrahip said. "The goddess is returning, and her justice means an end to all wars. All cities will live in her peace. This part that you face now is the most difficult. Many will hate and despise and fear you. But you will win through. Your servants are with you."

After they took their evening meal, Geder debated going back to his room or staying up in the library. The books called to him, as they always did, but the day had been long and eventful, and as much as he regretted the loss, he thought it better to rest. Pleasure was for men with fewer responsibilities. And the books would be there when he had done his part, and could retire to a quiet life of scholarship, naps, and—was it too much to hope?—a little family of his own. A beautiful young woman beside him in the night and still in the morning. It was a thing he could develop a fondness for.

He hadn't understood, when he became Lord Regent, how much would be asked of him. How much would be required. It gave him, he felt, a real respect for King Simeon and all the other kings of Antea before him. Basrahip had been right. Antea would look weak and vulnerable, and it was Geder's place now to see that the kingdom was kept safe, whatever the cost.

Alone in his bed, by the light of a single candle, he took out Cithrin's note. He wished she'd been able to stay. That she'd seen what he was planning and arranging for Aster. She cared about Aster. He knew that. He could tell that she'd be pleased with all the things he had in mind.

He pressed paper to his mouth, breathing in through his nose in hopes of catching some slight scent that was her. All he found was ink and paper, but the thought of her was enough. He placed the letter carefully by his bed and lay back. Sleep was far from him, but it didn't bother him. His mind was full and awake and aware.

I will be paying close attention to news from Antea, she'd written. And what an amazing thing she would see.

He would bring peace to the world.

Cithrin

Cithrin and Paerin Clark had left Camnipol like thieves in the night. Much of King Tracian's party had escaped during the fighting, and those few that hadn't might stay on past the departure of the Medean bank. Cithrin found she didn't particularly care. With Asterilhold open, there was no call to ride north and take ship. Paerin used the money he had to buy a light cart and a fast, reliable team of horses, and they were off. She couldn't help but remember leaving Vanai, it seemed a lifetime ago. In a way, it had been.

The plains of Asterilhold were in ruins where Kalliam's army had passed. Grasslands had been churned to mud. Forests had been cut to the ground. The bones of the world were exposed here. The great wound was the aftermath of a short, successful war. Cithrin could hardly imagine what a longer one might have done.

Paerin Clark passed the hours with talk of finance and coinage, and Cithrin kept the pace he set. He told stories of how the Borjan kings had minted two separate currencies, one for trade and the other for tax, and that the two had been intentionally inconvertible. A man might accrue all the wealth the market could deliver and still not pay his taxes if that was in the interest of the Regos and his council. Cithrin told him about coming to Porte Oliva nearly penniless apart from the massive hoard of wealth she was smuggling and the creation of a fashion for Hallskari salt dyes out of a load of ruined cloth. The things they never spoke of as if by explicit consent were Antea, Camnipol, and what had happened during the long days of hiding.

Which wasn't to say that they didn't talk about Geder Palliako.

"So he never left the place?" Paerin Clark said. "You're sure."

"Fairly. I suppose he could have gone out while I was and gotten back before me, but he didn't say it. Neither did Aster. And I don't know why they'd have lied to me about it."

"Well, maybe they didn't," he said. "It's just that there were so many stories of people who saw him during the battle, it's astonishing that there wouldn't be one of them that was at least partially true."

"People see what they want to see, I suppose," she said. "I'd find the idea of a ruler skilled and dedicated enough to take to the streets in costume and defeat the enemies of the crown reassuring. Or terrifying. One or the other."

"Hmm," was Paerin's only reply.

Approached from the east, Carse looked like a different city. The farmhouses and hamlets gave way slowly to larger buildings with more families living in each, and then suddenly the towers that had been on the horizon were all about them, reaching up toward the hazy white sky. And only a little bit beyond that, the cliff and the Thin Sea. She had spent so little time in Carse on her way out. The quest to undermine Pyk Usterhall seemed like something another woman had done. Her relief at being back in the great fortress of the holding company was like coming back to the house of a dear friend. Even a lover.

But it was nothing like home.

Lauro and Komme came to greet the cart. The older

man's gout was between flares, and he looked ten years younger without the lines of pain in his face. Chana was at the market, and Paerin left the cart to a servant so that he could go out to find her there. Magister Nison also appeared, friendly and laughing, and digging for every scrap of information and gossip he could.

A room had been set aside for Cithrin, and she walked up the stairs to it gratefully. It wasn't large, but it was comfortable: a small bed, a writing desk, a lantern of glass and silver that managed to be both elegant and ornate. The rug was woven from reeds and felt surprisingly soft beneath her feet.

And beside the bed, a satchel made of red leather that she didn't recognize. When she opened it, a double handful of papers came out, along with a small lacquer box with the image of a stork taking flight inlaid on the lid. Most of the papers were letters from Porte Oliva and Pyk. Cithrin read through them. The loan to a new brewer had gone south, and the stock and equipment sold at cost to the other brewer with whom they had partnered. The ultimate loss was minimal. Dar Cinlama, the explorer who had given Cithrin the dragon's tooth that was still in her bags, had gone off into the Dry Wastes with a party of a hundred, and hadn't come back. Either he'd found something of interest or something had found him of interest. The way it was written, she could hear the contempt in the Yemmu woman's voice.

Certain belongings of Marcus Wester's had been taken from the warehouse and sold. The proceeds were being held by Yardem Hane. Nothing else was on that letter. No explanation of why Marcus had left or where he'd gone that he couldn't take his money with him. That was the first order of business when she got home, and no doubts.

The last report wasn't from Porte Oliva at all, but from the holding company itself. It included records copied from

Porte Oliva, and before that from Vanai. It was the complete accounting of the deposits her parents had put in the bank before they died, and how the money had been spent in the meantime. A depositor's report in the name of Cithrin bel Sarcour.

The lacquer box was listed among the assets.

"You forgot, didn't you?" Komme Medean said from the doorway. "Chana didn't think you would, but I knew. I knew."

"Knew what?"

"You've come of age. While you were in Camnipol hiding from God knows what with I frankly can't believe who, you became a woman. Chana thought that something that important wouldn't go unnoticed. I thought you'd already crossed that line in your own mind so long ago, it would matter very little to you."

Cithrin opened the lacquer box. Inside was a necklace of white gold with pale emeralds just the color of her eyes. Cithrin found herself moved.

"I think your mother must have had coloring very much like your own," Komme Medean said. "Would you like some help fastening it?"

"Please," she said.

The old fingers were steady and sure. The necklace lay against her collarbone. It wasn't the right length for the clothes she was wearing now, but the paler dress would leave it looking brilliant. She smiled and bowed her head.

"Thank you," she said. "I couldn't have asked for better parents than the bank has been."

Komme Medean smiled.

"You're a forger and an extortionist. From what I hear, you like wine entirely too much for your own good. And Pyk Usterhall thinks the part of your brain that measures risk was underfed when you were a babe. None of this has changed. Only one thing is different now than it was when you left."

"Yes?"

"Yes," Komme Medean said. "Now I can hold you to your contracts."

"Does that mean I can stop being the playtoy magistra with Pyk pulling my strings?"

"You hate that, don't you?" he said.

"I do."

"No. You're still too young. Too inexperienced. Four years, two of them in other branches where you can see an established magister. Then we can decide whether Porte Oliva is yours."

"Two years, six months with a different branch," she said. "I grew up in Vanai with Magister Imaniel. I've already seen a branch function from the inside."

"Two years, one of them with a different branch. You can't understand the whole cycle of a year until you've seen it start to finish."

"Done."

Komme Medean smiled.

"Well," he said. "I think I've just bought myself two years, don't you?"

Despite Paerin's comments about her being the new expert on Geder Palliako, Cithrin had been surprised to be included in the formal meeting. She'd assumed that she'd talk with Komme, Paerin, and Chana—possibly Magister Nison or Lauro—and then the information would be distilled and interpreted before it was presented to the king.

Instead, a massive carriage the green of summer leaves had arrived at the holding company. It bore the royal arms, but not the pennants of gold that would have meant King

Tracian had come to them. She and Paerin were bundled up
the step and into the dark luxury within, Komme following
behind. When the driver set them in motion, the whole thing
shook like a ship in a storm. By the time they arrived at the
palace Cithrin was feeling hot and sweaty and less than well.
A servant whose rank she couldn't divine led them up a set of
white marble stairs to a building the size of a decent-sized
township. The king's palace. From its door, she could see the
sleeping dragon before the Grave of Dragons and the tower
of the Council of Eventide. It was a beautiful city in its way.

What she liked about it most, she thought, was that there
wasn't a hell-deep pit in the middle of it.

The meeting room was a balancing act of bragging and
understatement. The walls were hung with cloth dark enough
that she had to look twice to see its quality. The chairs were
all simply designed, but of rosewood and teak and upholstered with silk so soft she was worried that she'd split it
when she sat. Taken as a whole it painted the portrait of a
man who knew he was supposed to be grand without being
tasteless, and hadn't quite brought it off.

King Tracian was younger than she'd expected, though of
course he hadn't been the man Marcus had fought against.
That had been Lady Tracian. Still, it was strange to see him
appearing only a few years older than she was and think
that if it hadn't been for Marcus, this man wouldn't be here
at all. There would be a Springmere on the throne, and
Cithrin would have gone through her life without Marcus
Wester to protect her. And if Springmere hadn't frightened
himself into killing Marcus's family...

Too big. It was all too big, the good and the evil too much
mixed with each other. And in any case, King Tracian had
given his permission for them to sit.

"You're looking well, Komme," the king said.

"Some days good, some bad," Komme said with a shrug. "I hope your little problems are little too?"

"Much better," the king said with a sour little smile that told Cithrin she was better not knowing what the reference was to. Komme's smile was warm and apparently genuine, but she had the feeling it might always be.

"I've already heard quite a bit about our neighbors and cousins in Antea. This regent. How did we overlook him?"

"He wasn't anyone until recently," Komme said. "Minor house. Father of no importance."

"Fortunes change quickly," the king said, leaning forward. "What exactly have we found out?"

Paerin's barely audible exhalation made it clear he was to take the lead. Cithrin sat on her hands.

"The situation in Antea has been unsettled," Paerin said. "They've had two insurrections, the most recent of which led to a protracted battle and the collapse of several noble houses. They've conducted a particularly effective war against a traditional enemy. They've lost a king to the same ailment of the blood that took his father and which will, we must assume, eventually kill their next king as well."

His voice and demeanor changed when he spoke like this, and Cithrin watched him, fascinated. He spoke firmly without aggression. His gestures were controlled but flowing. She was certain that the delivery would have been precisely the same if he'd been talking to a man like the king before him or the lowest servant in his house. They had moved beyond class and status, if only for a moment, and they were in the realm where Paerin Clark was the master.

"Palliako has an uncanny talent for mythologizing himself. But ultimately, his personality is unimportant. There are constraints on him that he won't be able to avoid or to adjust to quickly."

"Tell me," the king said.

"He's lost most of a harvest in two kingdoms," Paerin said. "If he hadn't made the war with Asterilhold a matter of conquest, he'd have fewer starving people next spring. But now they're his, and they're *all* his. He's weakened his own support among the noble classes. He wasn't precisely one of them to begin with. That his own Lord Marshal led an attack against him and did it in the name of the prince shows just how much work he has to do, just to get up to being an effective leader.

"He is open in ways that King Simeon wasn't. There's been the suggestion of a branch bank in Camnipol, which I think worth looking at seriously."

Paerin folded his fingers together, and the king unconsciously mirrored him.

"Antea isn't going to collapse, but it isn't going to be stable either. I'd guess we were looking at five, maybe six years before Palliako poses any threat to trade or to his neighbors. I think he has a long memory, though. Anyone who crosses him while he's weak will answer for it when he's strong. Aster is still too young to judge, and by the time he takes the throne, the situation will have changed again."

"In brief, then, Antea's a colorful show with blood and thunder but no real threat," the king said.

"Exactly," Paerin said.

"You're wrong," Cithrin said. "All apologies, but that's wrong."

Komme scowled.

"You have a different analysis, that's fine. But Paerin's been my man in Antea for almost a decade. He knows the country. How it works."

"Has he had the Lord Regent between his legs? Because I

have. I've seen who he is when no one's looking, and *nothing* you've just said applies to that man."

King Tracian's eyebrows rose and Paerin Clark coughed in a way that didn't mean he had a tickle in his throat. Cithrin ignored him.

"You're treating Geder like he's political or religious. Like he's the kind of man who runs kingdoms. He's not that."

"Perhaps the magistra will enlighten me about the kind of man he is," the king said.

"He's ... he's sweet and he's lonesome and violent and he's monstrously thin-skinned." Cithrin paused, looking for the words that would explain what she'd seen in Geder Palliako. "He's a bad loan."

Komme Medean grunted as if struck by a sudden pain. Paerin looked somber.

"I don't understand," the king said, "Have you given him money?"

"No," Cithrin said. "And I wouldn't. There are things you see when you've made a mistake. You don't always, but often, and they mean that the money's gone. You have a man who takes his payment and then starts to spend like he's rich. He looks at the money and he sees the coins, not the payments he's making to have them. He spends as if it was his money and there would be more. That's Geder. He's one of those boys who needed a mother in order to grow up and didn't get one. Now he has power and no restraint. He'll spend coin. He'll spend lives. And there's no one to stop him. He's drawing from the biggest coffer outside of Far Syramys.

"And when things go wrong, a bad loan denies it. Everything is someone else's fault. Antea is already looking for who to blame when the starving starts. I've heard it in the taprooms. And it won't be Geder."

Cithrin sat back. She found she was out of breath. That was interesting.

"Komme?" the king said.

"It's a valid perspective," Komme Medean said. "But I'm not sure what we'd do with it."

A soft knock interrupted them, and a servant came in bearing silver cups of cold water. No one spoke until he left.

"Magistra," the king said. "If I were to agree to your reading of the text, what would you recommend?"

Cithrin considered. War wasn't something she knew about. It wasn't something she studied. And yet her opinion was asked, and after the line about lying down with Geder, it seemed late to be demure.

"I would recommend gathering forces together now. Don't act against him, but make your predictions about where he'll go and share them discreetly with allies. If the predictions start to come true, you'll seem like the one who knew what trades to make before the ships arrived, and everyone will want to know what you knew."

"I have friends in Sarakal," Komme said. "Not business, but friends and with connections. I could send letters discussing things. At least we could see what people are saying near that border."

"We could make closer relations with Antea," the king suggested. "Your delegation was informal. If I put together a party. If I went myself."

"Don't do that," Cithrin said. "If he feels betrayed, he'll bite you harder than if you were an enemy from the start."

"No offense," the king said. "That might put you in an uncomfortable position."

"That occurred to me," Cithrin said.

Around the table, they were all silent. The air of confidence and reassurance was gone as if it had never been.

Cithrin drank her cup of water, enjoying the cool of it, and the faint taste of lemon.

"Is there anything that can be done?" the king asked.

"Watch. Wait. Hope he overreaches himself early on and badly," Cithrin said. "The best you can say about Geder is he's the sort of man who makes good enemies."

Clara

Over the days that followed, Clara was slowly convinced that in a way—in many ways—she'd died with Dawson on that terrible floor in front of all their friends and relations. She couldn't watch the violence, but she'd heard it. The sounds of it might have been worse than the actual seeing. But perhaps not. Everything that happened afterward made more sense to her if she thought of herself as dead when it happened. Walking from the Kingspire, widow of only a few minutes with no one she knew speaking to her. None of the women she'd known all her life to say a kind word. The only one who had touched her, offered comfort, had been the thin, pale merchant girl whose name she'd forgotten as soon as it had been said.

She'd been in a daze, lost even to her own mind. Doing the things that her body felt needed to be done. Visiting old friends and enemies. Well, that was what a ghost did, wasn't it? It made perfect sense, seen in that light.

The pain that came after Vincen Coe's reappearance wasn't the pangs of death, then. Those were done. These were the pains of being reborn, and much like the first time, they were terrible. She woke in the middle of the night weeping until she couldn't breathe. If she called out for him, Vincen would come and sit at the foot of her bed, but she tried not to call. There was nothing for him to do there except lose sleep. And eventually the seizure faded and she slept her normal sleep.

She found herself expecting to see Dawson. Especially, she found herself trying to think how she would explain being there in her night clothes with the family huntsman sitting beside her in nothing but his hose. And then she would correct herself. She would never explain herself to Dawson because he was dead. And then she'd weep for a bit and move on with her day. It wasn't strength that kept her going on; it was a lack of options.

"You going out again today, ma'am," the house woman said. Her name was Abatha Coe as it turned out. One of apparently several dozen cousins that the Coe clan had spread throughout Antea. Before Abatha, Clara hadn't really considered whether Vincen had a family. He was a servant, and apparently she'd thought that servants sprang out of the walls when you wanted one and left again when they got pregnant. Looking back, she hoped she hadn't been too much the noble lady.

"Yes, I am."

"Back for lunch?"

"I doubt it. I'll be walking nearly to the Kingspire, and I don't think I can manage that without something fortifying while I'm there."

"Apples just come in," Abatha said. "Go all right with cheese."

It had taken Clara three days to realize that this was not only an offer, but the only offer that Abatha was likely to make. This time, she didn't say *That sounds lovely* or *Really don't bother about me*. If she had, the conversation would simply have ended, and her without apples or cheese.

"Thank you," she said. It was safe because it didn't require a response and it was good for her because her ghost-self still thought she should be polite.

She wore a grey mourning dress and her hair wrapped in a cloth, and she walked with the air of a woman who knew where she was going. Down the narrow, shit-stinking street to the broader but still nameless way that would eventually give way near the Prisoner's Span. In all the years she'd lived in Camnipol, she'd almost never crossed the Prisoner's Span, and she didn't care for it much now. The groaning and wailing from the cages hanging beneath it upset her, and once she was upset it could be difficult to stop. She'd been weak and wailing on a bridge once already. It was quite enough.

But it was the quickest path, and now that there were no carriages or litters or palanquins, the number of steps began to matter.

Vincen was about today too. Looking for work, he said. She felt oddly guilty about that. She was supposed to provide for him, not the other way around. He was her servant, only of course he wasn't. And she couldn't very well ask Jorey to give her money for his support. It would have felt too much like having her son support her lover, which was ridiculous because Coe had kissed her exactly once, and that was a lifetime ago. But even she had to admit that between his constant, gentle, dog-loyal presence, her own painful, slow remaking of herself, and the fact that he was an undeniably beautiful man, it was growing somewhat less ridiculous.

She reached the far side of the Prisoner's Span and looked back. It was much shorter looking at than actually crossing. She took one of the apples. It was red and ripe and she knew that she shouldn't eat it now, because she'd only be hungry on her way back and not have it. The first bite was tart and sweet and lovely. The second was too.

Her first stop was a baker's that made its trade at the point where another dozen steps would have made it too unfashionable to go to. It was literally the last place one of her old friends would look for her. Ogene Faskellan was a distant sort of cousin at best, but she was hopeless when it came to knitting and Clara had always been sure to change the activity when she was with the party so that she never had to. Small kindnesses, it turned out, paid large returns.

"Clara, you look wonderful," Ogene said, rising from the little table. "Please, let me get you something. A little to eat."

"No," Clara said. "You're doing far too much for me already. I don't want to feel any more a charity than I am."

"A bite of this?" Ogene asked, holding up a plate with soft white pastry and a red cream that smelled of strawberries.

"Just a bite," she said, "and tell me, have you heard from Elisia?"

The air in the bakery smelled of cinnamon and sugar, and Clara spent her last coin on a cup of lemon tea that tasted sharp and wonderful. For the better part of an hour, Clara took what news she could of her children. Jorey and Sabiha were fighting, which was to be expected given how hard the season had been. With luck they would get through it. It didn't help that Barriath had vanished one day for places unknown. Ogene had heard that a letter had come to a woman of his acquaintance in Estinport from him, and that the courier had spoken with the accents of Cabral. Elisia was still away with her husband and his family, waiting until the shame of ever having been a Kalliam faded. The good news was that Vicarian's position within the priesthood had been secured permanently. He was being sent to Kavinpol, which wasn't his first choice, but regardless, he would not suffer worse for being his father's son. It was a small victory, and she savored it more than the strawberry cream.

When, too soon, Ogene had to leave, Clara kissed her cheek and hugged her, mindful to do it in the bakery and not on the street where someone might see. Ogene's reputation had to be safeguarded as well. It was the world they lived in.

After that, it was north toward Lord Skestinin's little house, dodging carts whose wide wooden wheels tossed up the muck of the street and the dogs who would follow her for half a mile, sniffing at her in hopes that she would share her food with them. She'd remind them that they didn't like apples, then she'd try and the dog would look reproachful and hurt, and then think how funny it was and that she'd have to tell Dawson, and then she'd weep for a while and go on.

She worried how Jorey would do over the winter. He'd have to go to Estinport. He couldn't come to Osterling Fells. Poor Jorey, being saved by the girl he'd been saving. It all went back to Vanai, of course, and the guilt of having killed all those people at Palliako's request.

She slowed as she reached the better part of the city. The ones she knew. There was a temptation to make an extra stop, drop in on someone she used to know, if only to see how they received her. It might only have been her imagination or a reflection of her particular life and place that the high courts of Camnipol were looking more anxious than they had even during the war. There was a pinched look to people's faces, and more often, she was seeing the wire-haired priests in their brown robes walking among the black cloaks that Palliako appeared to have made into a permanent fashion. Sparrows and crows, Dawson had called them. Every now and then he had managed a truly memorable phrase.

"Mother," Jorey said when she came into the garden. His embrace was brief but fierce. She kissed his cheek.

"Clara," Sabiha said, coming to her. Her eyes were red-rimmed from crying. Much like Clara's own, she imagined.

Clara made a point to kiss her as well. There was so little she could do for the two of them and so much they needed.

"I've come for my allowance," Clara said with a smile she only half felt. "I hope the timing isn't bad."

"You're always welcome, Mother," Jorey said, biting at the words. It was eating him. She saw that.

"You're kind," she said. "It's your weakness. It's mine too. Sabiha dear, I was wondering if, now that I'm disgraced, I couldn't spend time with my grandson."

"Your..." Sabiha said, then flushed.

"I told you to forget him once," Clara said. "I was wrong to do that. We are not the family we had hoped to be, but we are the family we are. You are important to me, and so he should be as well. If I have your permission."

"My permission?" Sabiha said.

"Of course, dear," Clara said. "You're his mother."

"You have my permission," Sabiha said.

"No tears. None of that," Clara said.

They visited for slightly longer than usual, and Clara would have stayed longer if it weren't such a long walk home. She left when there would be enough light to make it the whole way. She didn't like the streets around her boarding house, but she liked them even less at night.

She was almost to the Prisoner's Span when five men with drawn knives stepped in front of her.

When they lifted the cowl from her head, she was in a wide, dark room. The light came from an iron chandelier overhead, but she wouldn't have been surprised by torches. Soldiers with bows at the ready were on either side, rising up impossibly high, a wall of men. And before her, a huge black bench topped by Lord Regent Geder Palliako. Clara felt the fear starting to shake her. Her ghost-self wailed and turned away in fear, and she went part way with it. The high priest stood behind her where she could not see him, though Geder could.

"Clara Kalliam," Geder said. "Forgive the intrusion, but I had some questions I felt I had to put to you. If you lie to me, I will know and you will suffer. Badly. Do you understand?"

Her mouth was dry. How had she come here? What had she done? It was like she'd fallen asleep and come to a nightmare she couldn't wake from. She felt caught at something, but she didn't know what.

"I understand you are no longer living at your son's house," Geder said. "Is that true?"

Her breath was so ragged, she was afraid she wouldn't be able to speak. Wouldn't silence count as a lie? She didn't want to think what he could do to her. What he would do.

"It is," she managed.

"Why is that?"

"My presence makes it difficult for Jorey and Sabiha to dissociate from the court's memories of Dawson."

"Have you been meeting with Ogene Faskellan?"

"Yes. We have had several visits."

"Have you been meeting with Ana Mecilli?"

"Yes. Twice, I think."

To her right, one of the soldiers shifted slightly, the sound sharp and dry. Her heart raced.

"Are you loyal to me?" Geder asked.

Clara shook her head, not *no*, but *I can't answer that.*

"Are you loyal to me?" he asked again, his voice growing harsher.

"I don't think about you one way or the other, my lord," she said.

The sound of cloth shifting came from behind her.

"Really?" Geder asked. He sounded genuinely confused.

"You are Lord Regent, and the man who killed my husband, and Jorey's friend from campaign. You're the man who helped me to expose Feldin Maas. But none of that particularly affects what I have to do in my day. I suppose it should on some level, but I certainly don't spend my time considering the question."

"You're meeting with all of these people. Are you organizing them against me?"

She laughed. She didn't mean to. If she'd thought about it, she wouldn't have, but there it was and the archer didn't kill her for it.

"No. God, no. The thought never occurred to me. I've been trying to hold my family together."

"Your family?"

"Yes. Barriath's gone with hardly a word to anyone. Jorey and Sabiha are having a terrible time of it, and not even married a full season yet. Vicarian is the only one who hasn't been seared by the whole terrible business. Well, and there's Elisia. She appears to be doing well, but I can't think she's happy. Not really."

"Oh," Geder said.

"And of course with Dawson gone, there's no one to hold it all together. There's not even the house, which when you think about it is a fairly weak way to hold a family together, but we had it once, and now we don't. And so there's all this walking."

Shut up, shut up, *shut up*, she thought, but her mouth kept tripping on ahead without her.

"And then there's the question of mourning. How long does one wait, because on the one hand there's a right and a wrong in court, but I'm not in court any longer, and so I don't know what rules apply. I have to go about making them up. It's terrible. It really is."

"But you haven't been conspiring against me or the throne?"

"No," she said.

There was a pause.

"All right, then. Thank you for your time. You can go."

Clara walked out into the open air. She was in the King-spire. Her head was spinning a bit, and she stopped at the street gate to catch her breath. She felt absurdly relieved. As if she'd been attacked and escaped only through luck. Perhaps that was true. She understood the pinched faces now. The feeling of fear and oppression that hung over everything like black crepe. She wondered how many people had been taken away without warning and made to play Geder's game of magistrate. More than only her, she was certain.

When she felt steady again, she made her way to the street. The Division was before her, and the Prisoner's Span looked terribly far away. The sun was low and red and swollen in the sky, turning all the buildings west of her to silhouettes like a painting for a burning city. And what was worse, somewhere in the confusion, she'd lost her apples and cheese.

The sun had set long before she got back to her boarding house. Her feet were shouting with each step. Her spine felt like a column of fire. The smell of Abatha's stew was actually attractive, which only gave an idea of how hungry she'd become. She made her way to the kitchen with the sole intention of paying her rent and buying a bowl of greasy stew, but Vincen was there, sitting by the oven. When he saw her, he leaped up, crossing the room in a stride, and lifted her in his arms.

"They told me you were gone," he said. "They said the Lord Regent's men took you."

"They did," Clara said and let herself fall into the embrace. Just a little. "You can put me down now if you like."

"Never, my lady."

"Very romantic," she said. "Put me down."

She sat by the oven, and Abatha gave her a bowl for free, so she bought a pipeful of tobacco instead. She told about her meetings with Ogene and Jorey and Sabiha, and then coming home only to be stopped by Geder's men and carried away with a cowl over her face. She finished the last of her stew as she got to the strange dark room with the soldiers and Geder Palliako towering before her, demanding that she answer questions. She felt herself growing calmer with the retelling, as if she were seeing for the first time what had happened. The distance was reassuring.

She lit her pipe from the stove. Abatha's stew might be salty and bland, but she did manage to find genuinely decent tobacco. Clara sat at the stove, puffing thoughtfully for a long moment before she realized Vincen and Abatha were waiting for her to go on.

"And then they let me go," she said, rather gamely.

"But what did they ask?" Abatha said. Her face looked really animated for the first time since Clara had met her.

"Oh, that. They asked if I'd been conspiring against Geder Palliako and the crown."

"What did you say?"

"That the thought hadn't occurred to me," she said.

"And?" Vincen said.

Clara raised an eyebrow.

"And now it has."

Entr'acte

Master Kit

Suddupal was at first a community of cities, their buildings and structures tall and solid, and then it was a dark
and monstrous hand reaching out toward them with piers
for fingers, and then it was gone, and they were alone on the
wide sea. Adasa Orsun could sail the little ship by herself,
moving from one line to another, lifting up the sails and
shifting the angle of the rudder until everything was exactly
as she wished it to be. Every now and then, she would tell
Marcus to help her with some task where three hands were
better than two. She never asked Kit, and honestly Kit didn't
mind.

It had been a very long time since he'd set out in a small
craft over large water. He had almost forgotten the way the
horizon-wide water and the open arch of sky conspired with
the smallness of the boat and left him feeling overwhelmed
and constrained at the same time. So much space all around
him in all directions, and yet two paces this way, three in
another, and a belowdecks so cramped that he couldn't
stand upright.

His life had become that as well. After his flight from the
temple and the goddess and the only life he'd known, the
world had unfolded before him, every new discovery egging
him on to the one after. He'd learned that many of the things
he'd been taught in the temple were true: the dragons were

gone from the world and their slave races had made it their own, people of all races deceived each other almost constantly, wherever there were people gathered together in large groups there would be violence and death and theft. But he'd also found just as many that were wrong: that truth guaranteed justice, that the thirteen races were doomed to hate each other, that people like Adasa Orsun—Timzinae— were a separate and lesser kind of humanity. Finding his way through the mixture of myths and lies had become not only a life's work but a joyful one.

He'd traveled widely and with men and women whose company he enjoyed. He'd listened to practical philosophers about the nature of the world. He had taken lovers and lost them. And in that wide, open sea of options and choice, his way had come down to this tiny boat on its way to a series of events both difficult and inevitable. In the face of the ocean, the tiny boat. In the face of freedom, only this: to save the world he'd discovered and come to love, or else die in the attempt.

It sounded heroic and romantic. The truth was sometimes something less.

"I ate a cockroach once," Marcus Wester said. He was sprawled on the deck, shirtless, an arm flung across his eyes.

"You didn't," Kit said.

"I ate a mouse once."

"You didn't."

There was a pause, and the world was only the soft wind and the lapping waves against the side of the boat.

"I ate a worm once."

"Why did you do that?" Kit asked.

Marcus grinned.

"Lost a bet," he said.

Adasa Orsun rose up from belowdecks, stretched her arms over her head, and yawned a wide, deep yawn.

"We've made good time," she said, and she believed it. So probably they were.

"How can you tell?" Marcus asked. "It's not like there's a road you can follow or landmarks to see."

"The water changes," she said. "We'll be to the islands in two, three more days. We have enough water and food until then."

"We probably will," Kit agreed.

"Was that in question?" Marcus asked. "I thought we'd intentionally packed enough to make it to the place we could get more. Did I misunderstand that?"

The Timzinae woman snorted derision.

"It's the sea," she said. "There's always a question."

What about questions?" Marcus asked three days later as they walked down the stony streets of the island waystation. Ahead of them, Adasa Orsun was haggling with a Southling.

"What about them?"

"Can you have a false question?" Marcus said. "For instance, if I said something like, *Isn't Sandr full of himself?* or *You can't do that, can you?* They both mean something, but it's not something that's true, exactly, is it?"

"You're forgetting. It isn't truth. It's *never* truth. It's certainty. A question is uncertain by its nature."

"But if I say, *I don't know...*"

"You can be certain that you're ignorant," Kit said.

The Southling held up two fingers, the Timzinae three.

"What about, *I think her name is Adasa.*"

"You're certain of that, yes."

"I think her name is Mycah."

"You aren't certain of that. In fact, I suspect you're certain that it isn't. Though I wouldn't know that based only on what you said."

"That's a strange line you walk," Marcus said as they came to a rough corner. Nothing in the waystation was straight. The roads twisted and turned, following the shape of the rock. It gave the place an inhuman feel that Kit recognized and respected. It felt like the temple from which he'd fled.

"I think we all walk it all the time. I may be a bit more aware of it. I believe this is the place we needed. Only let me tell our captain where we've gone."

He walked over to her. The spiders in his blood were excited, dancing and tugging at him. Being around so many people caught their attention after so long with only the same two. And there might only be five or six dozen people on the island, so small was it. To go from a long voyage into a real port was a deeply unpleasant experience. But that was a problem for another day.

"I can't go lower than this and make enough to buy food," the Southling man was lying.

Kit touched Adasa Orsun's shoulder.

"Forgive me. I'm thinking of taking Marcus to the geographer's shop over there. When you're done here, will you look for us there?"

"I can," she said.

"Thank you, and he can go lower and still buy food."

"You are a madman," the Southling called after him. "Madman!"

Inside the shack, an old Southling woman sat on a stool. Her wide black eyes took them in without seeming to see them. Or perhaps it was only that she passed no judgments.

"You've come for a map?" she asked.

"I hope we have," Kit said. "I'm looking for the reliquary of Assian Bey."

"You and everyone else," the woman said, amused.

"Do you have a copy of the Silas map?"

To the degree that a Southling's eyes could narrow, hers did.

"That map doesn't exist," she lied.

"It does, and I am the man who is to have it," he said. In his blood, his body, the tiny things began to stretch and flail. He felt their delight. "Listen to me. Listen to my voice. You need to show me that map."

"I don't..."

"I do," Kit said. "It's going to be all right."

The woman scowled, but then she held up a single finger.

"Wait here," she said. "I have to go look at something."

Another lie, but perhaps not too far from the truth. If she didn't have the map herself, she at least might know where it was.

"What's a Silas map?" Marcus asked.

"It's the one that the last people to try to reach the reliquary used," Kit said. "It seems like the best starting place."

Marcus put a hand on Kit's shoulder, turning him gently.

"Have you just told me that you don't know where this place is?"

"I do. It's on the north shore of Lyoneia," Kit said. "Probably."

Marcus closed his eyes.

"You don't know."

"I could be more precise, but I think I'd be less accurate," Kit said. "I believe there's a word for reliquaries that are easily found and commonly known."

"Is the word *empty*?"

"All words are empty, until a living will fills them," Kit said. "But yes. I'd been thinking more of *looted*."

"You could have told me before."

"Would it have made a difference?"

"Yes," Marcus said, and they both knew he was lying.

Dramatis Personae

Persons of interest and import in *The King's Blood*

IN IMPERIAL ANTEA

The Royal Family

King Simeon, Emperor of Antea
Aster, his son and heir

House Palliako

Lehrer Palliako, Viscount of Rivenhalm
Geder Palliako, his son. Also Baron of Ebbingbaugh
    and Protector of the Prince

House Kalliam

Dawson Kalliam, Baron of Osterling Fells
Clara Kalliam, his wife
Barriath
Vicarian, and
Jorey; their sons
also various servants and slaves, including
Andrash rol Estalan, door slave to House Kalliam
Vincen Coe, huntsman in the service of House Kalliam
Abatha Coe, his cousin

House Skestinin

Lord Skestinin, master of the Imperial Navy
Lady Skestinin, his wife
Sabiha, their somewhat disgraced daughter
her illegitimate son

House Annerin

Elisia Annerin (formerly Kalliam), daughter of Clara
and Dawson
Gorman Annerin, son and heir of Lord Annerin and
husband of Elisia
Corl, their son

House Daskellin

Canl Daskellin, Baron of Watermarch and Ambassador to Northcoast
Sanna, one of his daughters

Also, various lords and members of the court, including

Lord Ternigan, Lord Marshal to King Simeon
Sodai Carvenallin, his secretary
Sir Curtin Issandrian
Sir Alan Klin
Sir Gospey Allintot
Sir Lauren Essian
Sir Soluz Veren
Sir Sesil Veren
Fallon Broot, Baron of Suderling Heights
Daved Broot, his son

Lord Bannien of Estinford
Count Odderd Mastellin
Estin Cersillian, Earl of Masonhalm
Mirkus Shoat, Earl of Rivencourt
and also Houses Flor, Estinford, Faskellan, Emming,
Tilliakin, Mastellin, Mecilli, Caot, and Pyrellin,
among others

The Players

Kitap rol Keshmet, called Master Kit, apostate of the
spider goddess
Cary
Hornet
Smit
Charlit Soon
Mikel
Sandr

Basrahip, minister of the spider goddess and counselor
to Geder Palliako
also some dozen priests

IN BIRANCOUR

The Medean bank in Porte Oliva

Cithrin bel Sarcour, voice of the Medean bank in
Porte Oliva
Pyk Usterhall, her notary
Marcus Wester, her guard captain. Also the hero of
Gradis and Wodford
Yardem Hane, his second in command

The bank's guard, including:
  Barth
  Corisen Mout
  Ahariel Akkabrian
  Roach
  Hart
  Enen

Iderrigo Bellind Siden, Prime Governor of Porte Oliva

Qahuar Em, rival to the Medean bank and former
  lover of Cithrin
Arinn Costallin, his business acquaintance from Herez

Maestro Asanpur, a café owner

Capsen Gostermak, a poet and keeper of doves

Maceo Rinál, a pirate

Dar Cinlama, a hunter of ancient treasures and seeker
  of lost places

IN NORTHCOAST

King Tracian

The Medean bank in Carse

Komme Medean, head of the Medean bank
Lauro Medean, son of Komme
Chana Medean, daughter of Komme

Paerin Clark, husband of Chana

Magister Nison, voice of the Medean bank in Carse

IN ASTERILHOLD

King Lechan

Sir Darin Ashford, ambassador to Antea

IN SUDDAPAL

Epetchi, a cook

Adasa Orsun, a sea captain

THE DEAD

Feldin Maas, formerly Baron of Ebbingbaugh, killed
 for treason
Phelia Maas, his wife, dead at her husband's hand

Magister Imaniel, voice of the Medean bank in Vanai
 and protector of Cithrin
also Cam, a housekeeper, and
Besel, a man of convenience, burned in the razing of
 Vanai

Alys, wife of Marcus Wester
also Merian, their daughter, burned to death as a
 tactic of intrigue

Lord Springmere, the Mayfly King, killed in
vengeance

Morade, the last Dragon Emperor, said to have died
from wounds

Inys, clutch-mate of Morade whose manner of death
is not recorded

Asteril, clutch-mate of Morade, maker of the Timzinae, dead of poison

Drakkis Stormcrow, great human general of the last
war of the dragons, dead of age

An Introduction to the Taxonomy of Races

(From a manuscript attributed to Malasin Calvah, Taxonomist to Kleron Nuasti Cau, fifth of his name)

The ordering and arrangements of the thirteen races of humanity by blood, order of precedence, mating combination, or purpose is, by necessity, the study of a lifetime. It should occasion no concern that the finer points of the great and complex creation should seem sometimes confused and obscure. It is the intent of this essay to introduce the layman to the beautiful and fulfilling path which is taxonomy.

I shall begin with a brief guide to which the reader may refer.

Firstblood

The Firstblood are the feral, near-bestial form from which all humanity arose. Had there been no dragons to form the twelve crafted races from this base clay, humanity would have been exclusively of the Firstblood. Even now, they are the most populous of the races, showing the least difficulty in procreation, and spreading throughout the known world as a weed might spread through a rose garden. I intend no offense by the comparison, but truth knows no etiquette.

The Eastern Triad

The oldest of the crafted races form the Eastern Triad: Jasuru, Yemmu, and Tralgu.

The Jasuru are often assumed to be the first of the higher races. They share the rough size and shape of the Firstblood, but with the metallic scales of lesser dragons. Most likely, they were created as a rough warrior caste, overseers to control the Firstblood slaves.

The Yemmu are clearly a later improvement. Their great size and massive tusks could only have been designed to intimidate the lesser races, but as with other examples of crafted races, the increase in size and strength has come at a cost. Of all the races, the Yemmu have the shortest natural lifespan.

The Tralgu are almost certainly the most recent of the Eastern Triad. They are taller than the Firstblood and with the fierce teeth and keen hearing of a natural carnivore, and common wisdom holds that they were bred for hunting more than formal battle. In the ages since the fall of dragons, it is likely only their difficulty in whelping that has kept them from forcible racial conquest.

The Western Triad

As the Eastern Triad marks an age of war in which races were created as weapons of war, the western races delineate an age in which the dragons began to create more subtle tools. Cinnae, Dartinae, and Timzinae each show the marks of creation for specific uses.

The Cinnae, when compared to all other races, are thin and pale as sprouts growing under a bucket. However, they have a marked talent in the mental arts, though the truly deep insights have tended to escape them. As the Jasuru are a first attempt at a warrior caste, so the Cinnae may be considered as a rough outline of the races that follow them.

The Dartinae, while dating their creation from the same time, do not share in the Cinnae's slightly better than rudimentary intelligence. Rather, their race was clearly built as a labor force for mining efforts. Their luminescent eyes show a structure unlike any other race, or indeed any known beast of nature. Their ability to navigate in utterly lightless caves is unique, and they tend to have the lithe frames one can imagine squeezing through cramped caves deep underground. Persistent rumors of a hidden Dartinae fortress deep below the earth no doubt spring from this, as no such structure has ever been found, nor would it be likely to survive in the absence of sustainable farming.

The Timzinae are, in fact, the only race whose place in the order of creation is unequivocally known. The youngest of the races, they date from the final war of the dragons. Their dark, insectile scales provide little of the protection that the Jasuru enjoy, but they are capable of utterly encasing the living flesh, even to the point of sealing all bodily orifices including ears and eyes. Their precise function as a tool remains obscure, though some suggest it might have been beekeeping.

The Master Races

The master races, or High Triad, represent the finest work of the dragons before their inevitable fall into decadence. These are the Kurtadam, Raushadam, and Haunadam.

The Kurtadam, like myself, show the fusion of all the best ideas that came before. The cleverness first hinted at in the Cinnae and the warrior's instinct limned by the Eastern Triad came together in the Kurtadam. Also, alone among the races, the Kurtadam were given the gift of a full pelt of warming hair, and the arts of beading and adornments that clearly represent the highest in etiquette and personal beauty.

The Haunadam exist to the greatest extent in Far Syramys and its territories, and represent the refinement of the warrior impulse that created the Yemmu. While slightly smaller, the tireless Haunadam have a thick mineral layer in their skins which repels violence and a clear and brilliant intellect that has given them utter dominion over the western continent. Their aversion to travel by water restricts their role in the blue-water trade, and has likely prevented military conquest of other nations bounded by the seas.

The Raushadam, like the Haunadam, are primarily to be found in Far Syramys, and function almost as if the two races were designed to act as one with the other. The slightest of frame, Raushadam are the only race gifted by the dragons with flight.

The Decadent Races

After the arts of the dragons reached their height, there was a necessary and inevitable descent into the oversophisticated. The latter efforts of the dragons brought out the florid and bizarre races: Haaverkin, Southling, and Drowned.

The Haaverkin have spent the centuries since the fall of dragons clinging to the frozen ports of the north. Their foul and aggressive temper is not a sign that they were bred for war, but that an animal let loose without its master will revert to its bestial nature. While they are large as the Yemmu, this is due to the rolls of insulating fat that protect them from the cold north. The facial tattooing has been compared to the Kurtadam ritual beads by those who clearly understand neither.

The Southlings, known for their great black night-adapted eyes, are a study in perversion. Littering the reaches south of Lyoneia, they have built up a culture equal parts termite hill and nomadic tribe worship. While capable of sexual reproduction, these wide-eyed half-humans prefer to delegate such activity to a central queen figure, with her subjects acting as drones. Whether they were bred to people the living deserts of the south or migrated there after the fall of dragons because they were unable to compete with the greater races is a fit subject of debate.

The Drowned are the final evidence of the decadence of the dragons. While much like the Firstblood in size and shape, the Drowned live exclusively underwater in all human climes. Interaction with them is slow when it is possible, and their tendency to gather in shallow tidepools marks them as little better than human seaweed. Suggestions that they are tools created toward some great draconic project still in play under the waves is purest romance.

With this as a grounding, we can address the five philosophical practices that determine how an educated mind orders, ranks, and ultimately judges the races...

Acknowledgments

I would like to thank Ty Franck for his help in navigating the particularly difficult waters of this book. Also my agents Shawna McCarthy and Danny Baror, whose hard work and attention allow me the career that I love, and DongWon Song, Anne Clarke, Alex Lencicki, Jack Womack, and the whole team at Orbit who have been brilliant and supportive. But especially, I would like to thank my family for taking up the slack while I was conducting wars and intrigues in my own head.

Always, any errors and infelicities are entirely my own.

extras

orbit

meet the author

Kyle Zimmerman

DANIEL ABRAHAM is the author of the critically acclaimed Long Price Quartet. He has been nominated for the Hugo, Nebula, and World Fantasy awards, and won the International Horror Guild award. He also writes as MLN Hanover and (with Ty Franck) James S. A. Corey. He lives in New Mexico. Find out more about the author at www.danielabraham.com.

introducing

If you enjoyed
THE KING'S BLOOD,
look out for

THE POISONED SWORD

Book Three of The Dagger and the Coin

by Daniel Abraham

CITHRIN

Had Magistra Isadau and her niece been speaking of matters of family or politics, even questions of finance and the running of the bank, Cithrin would not, she told herself, have eavesdropped. But instead, she walked down the wide polished-granite hall bright with the light of morning and almost cold enough to see her own breath, heard the voices of the elder Timzinae woman and the young woman who followed her, and picked out the words *love* and *sex*. Her journey to the kitchens suddenly became less immediate. Curiosity sharpened her ears and softened her footsteps and she edged closer to the office chambers.

"That too," the magistra said. "But not *only* that."

"But if you really love him, doesn't that make it all right? Even if there is a baby from it?"

The girl's voice was strong, but not confrontational. This wasn't an argument but a deposition. A discovery of the facts. Magistra Isadau's laughter was low and rueful.

"I have loved many, many people," she said, "and I've never meant the same thing by the word twice. Love is wonderful, but it doesn't justify anything or make a bad choice wise. Everyone loves. Idiots love. Murderers love. Pick any atrocity you want, and someone will be able to justify it out of something they call love. Anything can wear love like a cloak."

There was a pause, and then the younger girl's voice again.

"I don't understand. What does that mean?" the girl said. Cithrin felt a warm glow of gratitude for the child and the question. She didn't understand it either.

"*Love* isn't a word that means one thing," the magistra said. Her voice was gentle. Almost coaxing. It was the voice of a woman trying to gentle an animal or call it out from under a table. "You love your father, but not the way you love this hypothetical boy. You love your brothers. You love that girl you spend all your nights with. Mian? You love Mian. Don't you?"

"I do," the girl said as if she were conceding a point to a magistrate.

"Someone may love their country or their gods. An idea or a vision of the world. Or because it can mean so many things, it's possible to call something love that's nothing to do with it. If the edict comes to march north into Sarakal, chances are it will say it is for the love of our brothers and cousins in the north. But it will really be fear. Fear that the war will come here otherwise. Does that make sense?"

"Yes."

"Love is noble," the magistra said. "And so we wrap it around all the things we think perhaps aren't so noble in hopes no one will see what they really are. Fear. Anger. Shame."

"I'm not ashamed," the girl said.

"You want this hypothetical boy. Don't. Lie to your mother about it if you'd like, but not to me. He opens your body in ways you can't control. He fills your mind in ways that disturb you and wash your best self away. You're drunk with him. And so you want it to be love, just the way the generals want their fear of Antea to be love."

"But..."

"I'm not telling you what decision you should make. God knows you have enough people to do that for you. But I am reminding you that you love a great many people you don't want to take your dress off for. Longing isn't love. Not any more than fear is."

A discreet scratch interrupted, and then the sound of the office door sliding open.

"Courier come for you, Magistra," Osin said.

"Bring the reports here, then."

"Can't, ma'am. Courier says he can't give 'em to anyone besides you or Miss Cithrin."

In an instant, Cithrin was powerfully aware that she was standing in the bright, chill corridor, bent like a child trying to overhear her parents. She turned back the way she'd come, took a half dozen near-silent steps, and then turned back, collecting herself as if she were only now beginning her interrupted errand.

The niece came into the corridor ahead of her. The black, insectile scales that covered her face and neck, her hands and arms, were darker than Cithrin remembered. Perhaps it was how Timzinae blushed. She didn't know.

Cithrin smiled, and the girl nodded back, but didn't speak. Cithrin strolled down the corridor, wondering what to do. On the one hand, she wanted to go back and see what the courier had brought, on the other doing so without it being mentioned to her might lead the magistra to suspect she'd been spying. With a sigh, she went on to the kitchens as if she didn't know anything that she wasn't expected to.

In truth, the magistra's niece wasn't much younger than Cithrin herself. She wondered what it would have been like to be first coming into herself with older women there to speak with. Her own mother was little more than a few fleeting impressions and entries in an old, yellowing ledger, but had she lived, she might have given Cithrin advice on questions of love and sex, men and hearts. In the kitchen, Cithrin exchanged banter with the cooking servants as they made her a bowl of stewed barley with butter and honey, but her mind was elsewhere. Even the rich sweetness of the first bite hardly registered.

Who did she love? Did she love anyone? Did anyone love her? Now that she asked the questions straight on, she realized she'd been thinking at the edges of the question for some time.

Since, in fact, the day she'd heard that Captain Wester had gone. Now *that* was interesting.

She considered whether she loved Wester the way she might have a proposal of business. Dispassionately, and from a careful distance. Yes, she thought, maybe she did. She didn't feel any particular desire toward him, but that was the point Magistra Isadau had been making. Desire and love weren't the same thing.

Cithrin sat at one of the low stone tables, looking south over the wide sprawl of Suddapal's third city. Where the land ended in a spray of small islands, she could just see the traffic of tiny boats, black against the throbbing morning blue. Desire wasn't the same as love. Love, she decided, was when something went away and left you emptier. By that definition, certainly—

"Magistra?"

Cithrin looked up. Yardem Hane towered in the doorway. He looked older than she imagined him, but perhaps it was only the light.

"Yes?"

"A report's come. Magistra Isadau wanted to consult with you on it."

"Something from Porte Oliva?"

"No," Yardem said. "I think it's about the war."

The pages themselves were fine linen, made without a watermark. The hand that had written them was neat and precise. Everything had been ciphered twice, once with the bank's usual trade cipher, and then again with a schema Cithrin didn't recognize. Forty pages of message transformed down into a ten-page document, and even that was in Magistra Isadau's relatively broad script.

"More information from the mysterious source?" Cithrin said.

"Or a forgery," Magistra Isadau said. The cheerfulness in her voice was as false as paint. "Komme wanted you to look it over. See whether you had any insights to add."

The information was clear and succinct. The first section was a rough accounting of the armies in the field. How many sword-and-bows, how many mounted knights. The supplies of food and fodder. Cithrin found a map of Sarakal and plotted each of the groups against the small nation on the desk before her. With each new mark, her belly grew heavier. Nus, the Iron City, had already capitulated, and all paths to the south and east were growing thick with soldiers.

"I thought Antea was losing," Cithrin said.

"They were. They should be," Magistra Isadau said. Her expression was unreadable. "They go into battle with fewer men and barely enough to supply them. And then they win. They reach a town that should be ready to hold back a siege for months, and it falls in weeks."

The older woman spread her hands.

"They can't come as far as Elassae, though," Cithrin said. "They don't have the men or food. And we're seeing the refugees from Inentai starting to come through."

"They don't have the men or food to take Sarakal either," the Timzinae woman said. "But they're doing it."

Cithrin turned back to the report. The unknown writer went on to list a half dozen other forces outside of the churn of war and violence in Sarakal. These were smaller groups with fewer than a dozen soldiers, but better supplied. The names of individual captains leading these smaller forces were listed with them. Emmun Siu and fifteen men, the report read, moving into the northern reaches of Borja. Dar Cinlama and twelve men traveling over water to Hallskar. Two groups answering to Corinn Steel bound for Lyoneia. Another group, the smallest with only seven people, two horses, and a cart, led by someone named Bulger Shoal requesting diplomatic passage into Herez.

"What are these?" Cithrin asked. "Scouting missions for new invasions?"

"We don't know," Magistra Isadau said. "I think Komme was hoping you might have some insight."

Cithrin cast her mind back through the long months into the darkness under Camnipol. Hallskar, Borja, Lyoneia, and Herez.

She tried to recall whether, in the long hours of darkness, the Lord Regent had said anything to connect those places. The office with its gentle arches and brilliant sunlight seemed to defy the memories of darkness and dust.

Magistra Isadau's nictitating membranes clicked closed and open, blinking without blinking. Cithrin felt the pressure of the older woman's attention, and frowned, willing herself to think of something—anything—that would justify it.

Nothing came.

"There's no hurry," Magistra Isadau said, folding the papers and putting them back into her private strongbox. "I don't need to send a reply for a day or two. If anything does come to you, I can add it."

"How old is the information?" Cithrin asked.

"A month, at least. Probably more. But Inentai isn't under siege yet. So perhaps it still counts for something."

The Timzinae woman shrugged and smiled. Cithrin thought that she saw unease in her dark eyes and the angle of her mouth. It was hard to be sure.

"Will the war come here, do you think?" Cithrin asked, and the physical memory of asking the same question assailed her. She'd said almost identical words once to a man now dead, in a city now ashes.

"You know better than I do," Magistra Isadau said. "All I have is the numbers and reports. You know the people."

"The person," Cithrin said.

"The person. So. Knowing what you do of Geder Palliako, will the war come here?"

Cithrin sat forward, her hands clasped. Memories of the Lord Regent of Antea rose before her mind like fumes from a fire. His laughter. The roundness that fear gave his eyes. The rage as he slaughtered the traitor from within his own court. The taste of his mouth and the feel of his body. A shudder passed through her. Magistra Isadau made a small clicking sound at the back of her throat and nodded as if Cithrin had answered.

Perhaps she had.

*   *   *

A thin fog rose just after nightfall. Wisps and patches littered the streets like a cloud had shattered and fallen to earth. Cithrin sat in the counting house, contracts and ledgers spread before her in the buttery light. The wide, carved timbers above her gathered the shadows in close, cradling them. The history of the Medean bank in Suddapal seemed less important now than its future.

The trade of Elassae relied on the traffic of metalwork from the north, textiles and cloth from the Free Cities, and spice and gold from Lyoneia. The mines and forges of Sarakal might fall under the control of the Severed Throne, but the trade would remain. Or she thought it would.

Or the armies of Antea might burn them all, as they had Vanai. Surely Magistra Isadau was selling letters of credit to the nervous and wealthy, transferring the gold and jewels of Elassae into paper that could go west, to the safer ports, farther from Antean blades. There would be a way to move that wealth away from Suaddapal before the end came. Before the armies. Before it burned.

She shook herself, turned back to her books, and found she'd lost the thread of them. Her fingers were on a payment entry, and she could no more say what deposit it came from than she could will the sun to dance on the seashore. She said something vulgar and closed the books. It was late, and the cold would soon change the fogs to frost. She could sit here, in her leather-slung chair, or go back to her rooms and stare sleepless at the walls. The knot in her belly didn't permit anything else.

She put the books back in their places and stacked the wax trays with her notes in a corner with a strip of red cloth that would tell the servants to leave them undisturbed. When she snuffed the lamp, the darkness fell on her.

Living in a compound peopled entirely by Timzinae made her more aware of their habits and customs. The sensual music of reed flute and sanded drum that made their hymns murmured even in the darkness of midnight. More than any other race she knew, the old men and women of the Timzinae turned away from sleep. The compound—indeed the five cities of Suddapal—only rested. They never slept. She found herself drawn toward the music and the promise of company and warmth, but it was an illusion. She didn't know the songs. The snapping of her pale, soft fingers wouldn't give the sharp percussion of Timzinae hands.

She wondered if Yardem was on guard duty. Or any of her little retinue from Porte Oliva. She wondered where Cary and Sandr and Hornet were tonight. She wondered what Captain Wester was doing.

In her own room, the servants had set a fire in the black iron stove and left a lamp burning low. Her window let in a spray of moonlight, the cool blue mixing with the gold of the flame. She changed into her night clothes and slipped her legs beneath the thin wool sheets, sitting with her back against the wall.

Sleep wouldn't come. She already knew it. She could lie in the darkness and stew in her own thoughts or turn up the lamp and read through the essays and histories Magistra Isadau had assigned her along with the books of the bank. Both options sounded equally unpleasant. For an hour, she only sat, listening to the fire mutter in its stove, the distant whisper of drums.

She rose sometime in the darkness after midnight, turning up the lamp's wick more for variety's sake than from any real desire. The floor chilled her feet. The papers waited on her bedside table, held down against the breeze by the old dragon's tooth. Cithrin lifted it now, running her finger idly along its serrated edge, as she considered the writing beneath without really caring what it said.

The war was coming. As much as she wished otherwise, she knew it would spill past Sarakal. Perhaps to Elassae. Or into Borja. Or turn west toward Northcoast and Birancour. It was like a fire. She might not know where the flames would jump, but wherever it landed it would burn.

But Herez? Hallskar? Lyoneia? None of them shares a border with Imperial Antea. Perhaps Geder and his counselors were looking farther ahead, to a wider, greater conquest. She tapped the tooth against her palm. The thought didn't sit comfortably. There was something else. Something about the dragon's roads and the places they didn't pass through.

Understanding came to her with an almost audible click. She stood up, her heart racing and a grin pressing her lips. The cold forgotten, she didn't even pause to throw a cloak over the night clothes. The dragon's tooth firmly in her hand, she strode out into corridors darker than mere night. Her footsteps didn't falter. She knew the path.

Magistra Isadau was in her office chamber, reclining on a divan with a book open on her knees. She looked up as Cithrin entered the room without a sense of surprise.

"May I see the new report again?" Cithrin asked.

The Timzinae woman marked her place and closed her book. Opening the strongbox was the work of a minute. Cithrin took up the pages, turning them silently until she found the passages she sought.

A small group to Borja, led by someone named Emmun Siu. Two groups to Lyoneia under Corinn Steel. And one to Hallskar, led by Dar Cinlama.

Dar Cinlama, the Dartinae adventurer who had once given her a dragon's tooth. Cithrin tapped the page.

"Something?" Magistra Isadau asked.

"These aren't scouting groups for the armies," Cithrin said. "They're looking for something..."